Prologue

Cadwallader Castle, Karadok

"You're not returning to court so soon?" asked Mason with a heavy frown. "Our father has not been buried for more than a sennight."

"He was buried three weeks ago today," Oswald corrected him.

Mason ignored him. "The King can surely spare you for another month."

"He surely can," agreed Oswald mildly. "But I have much work awaiting me on my return."

"You're not going straight to Vawdrey Keep then?" asked Mason with a heavy frown. "Much work awaits you there too, now you've inherited it."

Oswald gave a thin smile. "That can wait. After all, the old place hasn't fallen down yet."

Mason pursed his lips and fetched a pitcher of apple wine off a side table. He poured two goblets. "Not for want of trying," said Mason with a sigh, thinking of their late father's seat, which lay some fifty miles north of Cadwallader. "If you would wait for a month or so, then I could accompany you..."

"Nay, brother." Oswald shook his head. "You have responsibilities here. Your son is not yet nine months old. Linnet needs you here with her."

1

His brother did not argue, he noticed as he passed him a cup, but continued to frown moodily into space. "The old place will be halfway to rack and ruin," Mason said finally. "It has been much neglected. I fear that is partly my fault."

Oswald smiled at this and took a small sip of wine. "Why? Because Father practically moved in with you after his grandchildren were born?"

Mason grunted. "Who'd have thought the old bastard would have it in him?" He gave a grudging smile. "He fairly doted on both the girls."

"Archie's birth was his proudest moment," agreed Oswald. The smile dropped off his face. "You made him very happy, Mason," he said quietly. "I hope you know that."

"He wanted you just as happy," said Mason, surprising him. "It's true," said his brother gruffly. "He spoke to Linnet of it at the end."

"Did he?" Oswald was startled. "He never mentioned it to me. Just told me to look after his dogs and Meldon," he said dryly.

Meldon was the Vawdrey family retainer, and a curmudgeonly old sod who Oswald would rather pension off than keep in his employ.

Mason cleared his throat. "He didn't find that sort of talk easy."

He wasn't the only one, thought Oswald wryly as he took in his brother's discomfiture. Mason had always been useless at any

2

talk of feelings or emotions. Oswald rolled his eyes and took pity on him. "I'll speak to Linnet, shall I?"

"Aye," agreed Mason, looking relieved. "She was waiting for the right occasion to speak to you of it. We thought—hoped—you would stay on with us longer."

Oswald smiled. Come what may, he was always assured a welcome at Cadwallader.

The door opened and he heard his sister-in-law's light tread as she rounded the door. "Here you are," she said with a warm smile. She was carrying a chubby baby with a shock of red hair in her arms who was watching proceedings with great interest from his mother's arms.

Trailing her skirts were two black-haired little girls who immediately ran around her with a screech of "Papa!" to leap into Mason's arms.

He lifted them both effortlessly and kissed the tops of their heads. "Girls. Uncle Oswald is talking of leaving us," said Mason, immediately dropping him in it.

The smile fell from Linnet's face. She whirled around to face him. "So soon?" she cried. "But we hoped—"

"He has much work at court, Linnet," said Mason swiftly. "You know how the King relies on him. Then, when he has time, he also has to set Vawdrey Keep to rights."

Linnet bit her lip. "It will be a lot of work for you, Oswald, but perhaps with someone at your side…" She hesitated and looked at her husband expectantly.

3

Mason picked up on the unspoken hint and jiggled his twin daughters on his arm. "Shall we go and find Cuthbert, girls?" he asked, naming his squire and their great favorite. Oswald felt a fleeting pity for poor Cuthbert, who at fifteen was frequently irritated by the attentions of Lily and Margaret.

"Cuffbert!" they both caroled in glee.

"What a good idea!" Linnet beamed, whisking her skirts and scurrying over to kiss Mason on the cheek. He turned his head and caught her lips instead, making her laugh. Oswald acknowledged that Mason had absolutely no problem showing affection or emotion toward his wife and children. His transformation in that respect, since his marriage four years ago, had been quite remarkable.

"Sure you don't want me to stay?" Mason asked his wife hesitantly, and threw a troubled glance Oswald's way. For some reason, it put Oswald immediately on guard. *Why should Mason ask that?* He and his sister-in-law had always been on excellent terms. He turned in his chair to watch suspiciously as Linnet shook her head and held up baby Archie for his father to kiss. Mason pecked a chubby cheek dutifully.

"Kiss the baby," Linnet told both her daughters, who hurriedly complied. Like everyone else at Cadwallader, they adored the new heir, their brother. "Be good for Papa," she called after them as Mason left the room with his daughters in tow. "Oh dear," said Linnet distractedly as she sat in the chair opposite him. "Poor Cuthbert was hoping for some quiet time to practice his sword skills this afternoon. I fear the girls will soon put paid to that scheme!"

4

Oswald smiled as he watched her fussily arrange Archie on her lap. "No doubt," he agreed. He had a suspicion it was not Cuthbert she wanted to discuss with him.

"We will be very sorry to see you go," she sighed. "Mason always worries about you so."

"Worries about me?" echoed Oswald in surprise.

"Yes indeed. For he says if he does not, then no one else will."

Oswald considered this startling piece of information in silence a moment. "Mason need not worry," he said firmly.

"Oh, we know you're terribly successful at court," Linnet hurried to assure him. "And we're both awfully proud of your achievements in the King's council. Mason said you are Wymer's most trusted adviser these days, and, certainly everyone agrees, the most competent."

"Then why the concern?" asked Oswald with a directness that made Linnet's gaze skitter away.

"'Tis only that we worry you might be…rather lonely," she said gently.

"Lonely?" repeated Oswald blankly. "Linnet, I'm surrounded at any time by the King's court, some hundred or so people, not counting servants!"

She waved a hand dismissively. "All that counts for naught if you have no close friend or confidant among their number."

"As to that…" He shrugged. "I've always kept my own counsel, and never been much for sharing confidences."

Linnet's gaze was very steady, and suddenly he found he was the one avoiding her keen regard. For all her gentleness, his sister-in-law could be uncomfortably perceptive at times. He gave a short laugh. "My personality is very different to Mason's and my father's," he pointed out.

"I know," agreed Linnet softly. "But you are a good person, Oswald, and Mason loves you very much…" He shifted uncomfortably in his chair and cleared his throat.

Linnet gave a sudden laugh. "You are not as different from the other men in your family as you think, Oswald," she said, shaking her head. "Really, why are you getting so uncomfortable when I tell you how much your family cares for you?" She sighed and then tried again. "Mason says he never appreciated growing up, how much you always watched over him and cared about him. He thinks you are quite the cleverest person he has ever met."

She hesitated a moment. "Your father, too, came to see that he had never recognized your full worth. He was very proud of your career at court," she said quietly. "He said he always knew you were book-clever, but he never realized how you would be able to turn that learning into a position of power and influence in the kingdom."

It was news to Oswald that his bluff, blustering father had any pride in his quiet, oldest son and heir. If he had, it was the first he'd ever heard of it. He opened his mouth and then closed it again. After all, what was the point in being churlish over the fact he and his father had never seen eye to eye? "I can't see where this conversation is going, Linnet," he admitted.

"That must be a novel experience for you, with all your intrigues and politicking at court," his sister-in-law joked. Then her expression sobered. "You know your father asked for me at the end," she said softly.

"He had grown very fond of you," he answered automatically. Surprisingly, it was nothing less than the truth.

"Yes," she agreed, misty-eyed. "I was the daughter he'd never had."

Oswald thought briefly that if Baron Vawdrey had ever had a daughter, he would have made her life a misery, but he kept this to himself. "He did mellow a lot in recent years," he said instead diplomatically.

"Oh, yes. He was wonderful with the girls. They adored him." Astonishingly, this was also true. Despite the fact that Linnet had first presented him with two granddaughters instead of the longed-for grandson, he had swiftly recovered from the disappointment and come to see the baby girls as blessings and the twin apples of his eye.

Archie's arrival six months ago had sealed Linnet's position as his favorite female in the whole world. It wasn't really surprising that he had wanted her to be the one to hold his hand at the very end.

"His last words," she said gravely, "were of you."

Now that did surprise him. He blinked. "Me?"

"Yes, you. He had regrets, and you were one of them." She looked so serious, he sat up in his seat. Hell. This did not sound good. "He wanted very much for you to marry, to have what Mason has in his life."

Oswald gave a startled laugh. Linnet looked hurt. "Forgive me, Linnet, I know how well suited you and Mason are together. I flatter myself that I was one of the first to appreciate it." He paused, considering his words. "Even two brothers can be cut from different cloths. I do not think that sort of life would suit me. I am set in my bachelor ways now. My career…my position at court are what consume my days."

"And what of when you retire from active service to the King?" asked Linnet, tipping her head to one side. "Will you not be sorry to find yourself lacking a helpmeet, a companion in life?"

Oswald shrugged. "Meldon assures me there is a pack of dogs awaiting me at Vawdrey Keep," he said with a grimace. "I will not neglect restoring the estate. Indeed, I have plans drawn up to raze the old manor house to the ground and rebuild on a much grander scale."

Linnet's eyes widened. "I did not realize you intended as such."

"You are the first I've told of it."

She nodded. "You need a grander residence now you are an earl," she said slowly.

He smiled wryly at that. "I doubt Father would have thought so."

"You might be surprised," she answered with a soft smile. "He would have been pleased to see you making your own stamp on the place."

"Perhaps."

"He would have thought you needed your own countess though," she sighed. "At one time I did think my friend Enid Jauncey might suit you very well."

Oswald smiled. "Do you imagine you were discreet in that thought, Linnet?" he asked, making her laugh.

"I am not subtle, I know. Mason says he can see my every thought forming on my face."

"I can well believe it," he commented. "You would make a terrible spy."

The smile dropped from Linnet's face. She looked down at her sleeping baby. "Is it true you are the King's spymaster now, Oswald?"

"Linnet," he cautioned her. "Do you really want me to answer that?"
She paused, considering a moment, then shook her head. "Please stay safe," she urged. "You have made your fortune now and earned your new title. Can you not look to retire from such dangerous service to the Crown?"

"You must not worry about your bachelor brother-in-law," he told her lightly. "I am a very dull fellow and do all of my best work from behind a desk."

Linnet frowned faintly. "If you say so, brother."

"How is Enid?" he asked, changing the subject. "Still a merry widow?"

"She is currently being courted by two suitors," admitted Linnet. "But neither of them is as distinguished as you. Or an earl."

"We would not suit each other at all, you know," said Oswald. "Enid would be a demanding sort of wife. She would not appreciate a husband who left her in the country while he pursued his career at court."

"Is that what you would do with a wife?" asked Linnet.

"Undoubtedly."

Linnet nodded, considering this. "Enid's first marriage was a love match so doubtless she would not understand a marriage of convenience. But there are many eligible ladies who would understand that sort of arrangement only too well."

"Well, perhaps I'll reconsider if Vawdrey Keep's refurbishment becomes too much of a burden to me."

Linnet looked skeptical but was distracted by Archie letting out a yell at being ignored for so long.

Thurrold Manor House, Sitchmarsh

Fenella Thane dropped her embroidery into her lap and stared at her sister-in-law in disbelief.
"I'm sorry, Orla, I think I misheard you," she faltered.

Orla's rather long nose quivered with excitement. "You poor thing. It must be a lot to take in… Indeed, it's a hard day when a wife finds herself usurped from her husband's favor." She gave a mournful sigh that didn't quite conceal the gleam in her eye. "But indeed, it's true. Ambrose loves another. Even now he petitions the King at his winter court in Aphrany."

"Divorce?" choked out Fenella. "Ambrose means to divorce me?"

"Indeed 'tis so." Her sister-in-law held up her letter with a flourish. "Do you wish to see it in his own hand?" she asked. "I don't wish to be indelicate… Of course, my brother writes to tell me all. It was always so, ever since he was a babe. He has always confided in me and me alone," she gloated.

Fenella surprised her by holding out her hand for the missive. She had herself received a letter from Ambrose two weeks ago that had mentioned no word of it.

"Oh!" Orla stammered, clearly taken aback. "Very well…"

She handed it over grudgingly and Fenella pored over Ambrose's words. *These last few months have revealed my true feelings to me… Colleen is the love of my life. In truth, I never loved Fenella as a wife.* She reread the last sentence three times over. *I mean to divorce her on my return.*

The words swam on the page. He'd never loved her! In eight years of marriage! The words blurred before her eyes as she stared down at the piece of paper feeling numb. And yet it was unmistakably Ambrose's perfectly round neat script. Her husband of several years spoke of casting her off like an old, worn-out glove.

"You're crumpling my letter!" squawked Orla, snatching it from her hand. "Are you mad?" She clucked her tongue. "You know I always keep all of Ambrose's letters pressed in my ledger!"

Fenella stared at her as Orla fussily pressed out the creases from the page. Orla was jittery with excitement. Her sister-in-law was gleeful at the prospect of her brother casting off his wife, she realized, feeling faintly sickened. *Maybe,* a voice whispered in her head, *just maybe Orla thought she could rule the roost with a younger mistress at Thurrold.* A nasty taste in her mouth told her this was probably true. Bors, her old black Labrador, whined at her feet, and she bent down to stroke him.

"It's alright, Bors," she murmured reassuringly, although she almost choked on the words.

Orla sniffed. "I doubt it, as far as he's concerned. They won't let you keep a dog at the convent."

"Convent?"

"Of course. That is where you'll be placed as a cast-off wife. You can hardly hold a property unwed."

Fenella's face flamed. She straightened up abruptly. "My father left me two properties—"

"And they became Ambrose's when he married you," cut in Orla smugly. "You have nothing now. Not a penny to your name."

"But if he no longer wishes to be my husband, why should he keep what is mine? What was my father's?" asked Fenella in a voice that shook.

Orla shrugged. "'Tis the law of the land," she sniffed. "What can us weak women do?"

Fenella balled her hands into fists so hard her nails pressed into her palms as she gazed down steadfastly at her dog, unable to face her traitorous sister-in-law. The same sister-in-law she'd sewn, eaten, and gossiped beside for the last eight years. She felt betrayed. *Betrayed.*

Bors panted up at her in slavish devotion, a slight wheeze emanating from his graying muzzle. She thought suddenly of her father, who'd always maintained that the lowest act a man could commit was to cast off an old dog who'd been loyal in his service. She felt the burning conviction her father would feel the same contempt for the man who would cast off his own wife who had been loyal and true to him for almost a decade.

A wife who had brought him wealth and prestige and had always honored him as a spouse. She was a Bernard of Sitchmarsh Hall. Her black bear was quartered even now on her husband's standard. How dare he try to throw her in a convent and take some young bride to the bedroom she'd furnished!

She bit her lip so hard she tasted blood. "I'll not go to the convent," she said with resolve.

Orla gazed at her with a slack jaw. "What choice have you?"

"I don't know," Fenella admitted slowly. "But I'll not go quietly. Ambrose has made a huge mistake if he thinks I will." She gathered up her skirts to stand as her sister-in-law stared at her in alarm.

"Fenella…wait. You don't mean to go to court?" she gasped. "You know the King does not agree with unescorted women presenting at court."

That was true enough, thought Fenella despairingly. King Wymer was a traditionalist where women were concerned. She doubted he'd lift a finger to help her. Rumor had it he was currently flushed with success from his recent reconciliation campaign in the north. Those who had been useful in negotiations with the powerful northern barons were being lavishly rewarded.

Ambrose, as his diplomatic equerry in the north, would be in prime favor. She'd expected her husband to return home any day now from his two-year sojourn. An expectation she'd held in vain, she thought bitterly. Fenella felt her gall rise at the faithlessness of men.

"I won't stand for it!" she burst out, anguished, holding the back of her hand to her mouth. Suddenly, she felt nauseated. The floorboards beneath her felt like they were heaving. Thurrold had been her home now for many years. She'd come

14

to love the handsome timbered moated manor house with its abundant fields of barley and fruit trees.

She'd been happy here, making a home and a rich family life for her husband. And all this time… He'd never loved her. The vows he'd made. The promise he'd given her father to cherish her. *All lies.* She felt Orla's fingers close over her arm like a claw and realized her skinny sister-in-law was struggling to hold her up.

"You'll be fine," Orla panted, sounding panicked. "It's just the shock." Fenella gave a low moan, sinking to her knees as Bors keened and ambled to his feet around her, giving a series of low barks. "Fenella!" Orla pleaded. "What ails you? You've never fainted in your life."

No, she never had, she thought dully. She'd always been so sensible and down to earth. Ambrose had always maintained he despised showy, hysterical women who made displays of themselves. She'd prided herself on her levelheadedness. *Well, pride comes before the fall.*

"Fenella!" She realized Orla was chafing her hands now between her own. "Get a hold of yourself! If…if you don't want to go into a convent, well, we'll think of something else…" Orla gabbled.

"We will?" Fenella whispered, her eyes filling with tears. "Help me, Orla," she appealed directly. "If you ever valued me as a sister…"

Orla's expression wavered. She looked flattered. *Maybe I never did let her do enough around the place*, Fenella found herself thinking. *Maybe I was too managing as mistress of Thurrold*

15

and did not consider her feelings as daughter of the house?
Why am I thinking of this now? Why can't I focus on the crisis
at hand?

"Let me think," Orla prevaricated. "Let me think…" She darted
a wild look at her, as if expecting her to pass out or vomit at any
moment. "Wait! I have something…" she said, holding up a
finger.

"What is it?" asked Fenella, passing her arms around Bors's fat
neck and holding him still against her. His big warm body felt
solidly comforting.

"You could…counterpetition the King?" Orla suggested
weakly.

"Counterpetition?"

"Beg him to take your loyalty into account as both subject and
wife."

It sounded weak to Fenella, but then she remembered
something else, something her father had once told her—when
he'd had a few flagons of ale. A grievance over a broken
betrothal in her girlhood.

If I had more of a taste for battle, my girl, he'd said,
brandishing a roll of parchment, *I'd take this matter further. But
I just don't have it in me to take on the likes of Baron Vawdrey.*
Fenella had never blamed him. Baron Vawdrey was a fierce,
booming man with a great bushy beard, and she'd always rather
dreaded his visits.

It had broken her heart at the time, to lose his handsome son as a prospective bridegroom, but it had all seemed rather unreal, even when it was happening. But now, she wondered, could this same document be used as leverage in her favor? Even out here in Sitchmarsh, she'd heard tell of Oswald Vawdrey's startling rise to ascendency at court.

Word had it that he had the King's ear. She glanced down at Bors, who was looking up at her worshipfully, and felt a sudden recklessness take hold. *I can't let my beautiful boy go homeless*, she thought with a spark of spirit. *And I'm damned if I'll go quietly to a nunnery!*

"Very well." She nodded, suddenly decided. "I'll go to court and counterpetition the King myself."

Orla squawked as Fenella rose to her feet determinedly. "You'll what? Wait! Let us discuss this calmly… We need a man to present at court for you! You must write to your oaf of a brother, and…"

"No time, Orla," she replied grimly. "I will have to collect Gil on the way to Aphrany. Sitchmarsh Hall is not too far out of my way, and Ambrose could have his audience with the King even as we speak."

"True enough," agreed Orla grudgingly. "But what can you do to halt it?"

Fenella was brought up short by this, then her spirit flared. "I may have something, and Ambrose has left me with no choice. I must be bold," she announced dourly. "I'm riding to the royal palace at Aphrany."

"You've run mad!" her sister-in-law screeched, sounding scandalized. "What if your brother orders you home? What if—"

"He will do no such thing once I have explained. You can come with us if you like, but you'll need to fetch your cloak," Fenella told her grimly as she headed for her chest of papers. Surely her father's old paperwork was stored in there? Jeoffrey Bernard had not believed in throwing anything away. She was sure the old betrothal paperwork would be in there still.

"I think it would be better if I stayed here and held the fort," Orla called after her as Fenella started up the steps.

She wasn't surprised and simply cocked an eye at Bors, who lumbered up the staircase beside her. Orla was a poor horsewoman and would only slow them down, she thought, practical to the last. She and Gilbert could ride at a cracking pace if they went alone and cover the entire journey in a day and a half. She leaned over the balcony. "Orla?"

"Yes," called up her sister-in-law.

"Take care of my boy while I'm gone."

"You and that dog," tutted Orla. "Oh, very well!"

The King's Palace at Aphrany

Oswald Vawdrey dipped his pen in the ink pot and called, "Come in."

His eyes did not lift from the page as he dashed off another sentence and then blotted it. The midday bell had just rung, which meant he had only an hour left to finish his first draft of the peace treaty for the King. A slight frown appeared between his brows as his secretary came through the door. Bryce looked distinctly uneasy.

"I heard your step in the corridor," Oswald said in an attempt to put the younger man at his ease. Bryce looked a shade less unnerved and advanced across the room with a pile of paperwork. "Sit," said Oswald, when Bryce hovered uneasily in front of his desk. It crossed his mind again that Bryce might not last long in this role.

This would be inconvenient as he was punctual and scrupulous, and, Oswald suspected, incorruptible. Unfortunately, he was also scared of him, which was not something Oswald was sure he could remedy. Usually, his friendly veneer worked just fine.

Sadly, Bryce seemed to have caught a glimpse of what lay beneath the surface. And what he had seen had left him badly rattled. Oswald was not sure how he could make him unsee it. He lowered his pen and sat back in his seat. His secretary was staring at the pile of parchment in front of him. Oswald's eyebrows rose.

Bryce noticed it and stammered, "I thought you were working on the new peace treaty with the north counties this morning."

"I am."

"B-but when I left last night, all you had was my notes…"

"And very useful notes they were too," said Oswald briskly. "Thorough."

"You've written the whole thing," said Bryce faintly.

"You flatter me. This is only the first draft." His secretary continued to stare at him wide-eyed. "After you left, I summoned an army of imps using the dark arts and they wrote it for me," said Oswald dryly.

Bryce visibly started and color flooded his cheeks. "I don't listen to gossip, my lord," he said hastily.

Oswald smiled. He could tell from the color draining from Bryce's cheeks that it wasn't a particularly nice smile. He stopped smiling abruptly, and his secretary looked relieved. "Well," said Oswald briskly. "And what have you for me this morning?"
Bryce lifted the first letter from the pile. "Lady Portstanley wrote to her daughter in the Western Isles this week."

"And?"

Bryce cleared his throat. "There's a rather unflattering description of the King's character in it."

Oswald's eyebrows shot up. "Indeed? Treasonous?" he asked sharply.

"N-no, I don't think—"

"Bryce," said Oswald softly. "We are not concerned with unflattering descriptions. I need you to be able to pick up patterns, if anything sounds odd or unnatural—as though someone might be writing in code."

"And all letters to the northern barons," Bryce reminded him.

"That is merely a matter of routine," said Oswald with a shrug. Suddenly, he felt badly in need of some light relief. "Incidentally, what did Lady Portstanley say about the King?"

Bryce's color bloomed again. "Erm…" He held the letter up as he read aloud, "'Wymer is nothing but a buffoon with a crown, a disgrace to his standard. His golden lion is a lazy braggart. His lioness is ten times as fierce as he'll ever be.'"

Oswald tapped his pen against his desk surface. Bryce fidgeted in his seat. "It's sort of coded," he said miserably. "She equates King Wymer to a lion and therefore the lioness refers to Queen Armenal."

"True," conceded Oswald. "But she names Wymer, and the metaphor is an obvious one. The golden lion is the King's standard, as everyone knows. Post that one," he said curtly. "She's not telling her daughter anything she doesn't already know."

Bryce looked shocked, and Oswald realized, suppressing a sigh, that Bryce would have to go. Edwards, his predecessor, had

21

been so satisfactory until he had started blabbing state secrets to his mistress. Unfortunately, she had also been in the employ of a foreign minister. "How do you feel about women, Bryce?" he asked on impulse.

"They cannot be depended on, my lord," said Bryce, primly folding his hands in his lap. "Their souls have a lot less substance. Their judgment is untrustworthy. Their characters, weak."

"Indeed? I should like to hear you share your views with Lady Portstanley. I believe she would have plenty to say to you on the subject."

Bryce went pale. He loosened the neck of his tunic, which seemed suddenly to have grown rather tight. "Lady Portstanley is a lady of strong opinion," he said nervously.

Well, that was one way of putting it. "Anything else?" asked Oswald, pinching the bridge of his nose. He had sat up most of the night, and Bryce's company wasn't exactly stimulating.

"A letter here from your sister-in-law, the Duchess of Cadwallader."

"You opened it?" asked Oswald, fixing his eyes on him.

"O-of course not." Bryce looked shocked. "I merely recognized her husband's seal—the leopard. The Cadwallader leopard."

Oswald relaxed. He held his hand out for Linnet's missive and then dropped it unopened into his top drawer. He would read it later at his leisure. He already knew the contents. His brother's warm regards, a few charming stories about his nieces and nephew, and then some veiled hints about him settling down with a wife.

Ever since his father's death three months ago, Linnet had been like a dog with a bone. Probably because the old baron had died clutching her hand, and apparently spouting remorse about the fact his son and heir had never married. Linnet was sweet, and Oswald was fond of her, but he had no place in his life for a bride. He had absolutely nothing to offer to one.

"There was one other thing," said Bryce unhappily.

Oswald dragged himself away from thoughts of his family. He would not see Mason or Linnet for a good while now. "And that is?" he asked.

"Viscount Bardulf is waiting in the outer chamber to speak to you."

Oswald's eyebrows snapped together. What the devil did he want? He sighed, massaging his temples. "Send him in." Well, that was all he needed!

It was with a sour look on his handsome face that Oswald watched Viscount Bardulf saunter into the room in a ridiculous purple doublet with slashed sleeves revealing a pale lavender silk undershirt.

Bardulf looked every inch the frivolous courtier, but Oswald knew him better than that, unfortunately. He dragged a blank sheet of parchment across to cover his handwritten document, an action which Bardulf noticed with a smirk.

"My dear Vawdrey," he greeted him languidly and drifted over to the window to look out at the quadrangle. "What an industrious fellow you are. Even at this hour."

"As you see," murmured Oswald, sitting back in his chair. He knew from experience that it was pointless trying to rush the scented and curled Bardulf, who would only come to the point of his visit as, and when, it suited him.

"Smells of candle wax in here. Someone's been working long past the midnight hour," he said, fiddling with the braided curtain cord. "I hope the King appreciates your devotion to his cause."

Oswald didn't comment. The King had given him an earldom last month for his service, as well everyone knew. The fact was that Bardulf was the Queen's creature as well as her countryman. No doubt Queen Armenal was behind this little visit. He waited patiently as Bardulf approached and threw himself down in the chair Bryce had so recently vacated. "Is this a social visit?" asked Oswald. "Shall I ring for honey cakes?"

Bardulf smiled but did not answer. "Your new assistant looks harried," he said. "Probably realized what he's let himself in for, poor fellow."

Oswald was inclined to agree. He shrugged. "Junior positions often involve long hours," he said vaguely.

Bardulf tutted. "Such a pity about Edwards," he said lightly. "He seemed so well suited to the job."

Oswald's gaze narrowed. "Yes, a great pity," he agreed dryly. Edwards had been lucky to be dismissed with his head on his shoulders. As well Bardulf knew.

"A sad business," Bardulf sighed, inspecting his cuffs.

"Indeed."

"Loose tongues can be so troublesome at court." Bardulf let his gaze wander around the office, as he kept his tone casual. "Even a little harmless gossip can take on sinister undertones if it involves a significant person. And you, my dear Vawdrey, are most definitely a significant person." His eyes snapped back to Oswald with an unmistakable message in their depths.

"This is true," agreed Oswald smoothly. He spread his hands wide. "But I am hardly a subject for gossip, a dull, worthy fellow such as myself."

Bardulf smiled, but this time he looked genuinely amused. "The Queen has always found you most fascinating. And a little sinister," he added softly. "The Vawdrey wolf who creeps among the sheep. You are surprised at that? But you should never underestimate the Queen, my friend."

"I have always greatly admired Her Majesty's intelligence." Which was nothing less than the truth. Even if he was often on opposing sides to her at court. In all honesty, the King and Queen were frequently engaged in an unspoken power struggle. And he was the King's creature, as much as Bardulf was the Queen's.

Still, they sometimes found themselves on the same side, united against a common enemy. He wondered if this was one such

25

occasion. After all, why else would Bardulf be warning him? He waited patiently.

"Intelligence," mused Bardulf. "Is that not a word that spymasters use also?" He looked delighted with himself for making the connection. "But I keep you from your important work for the Crown," he said regretfully, motioning toward the document on Oswald's desk.

"Not at all," lied Oswald.

"You are too polite. I know your time is valuable, unlike mine," said Bardulf, gently shaking his head as he rose from the chair and sauntered over to the bookcase. "Allow me to extend my congratulations on your earldom," said Bardulf blandly. "What a shame Baron Vawdrey did not live to see your elevation."

Oswald shrugged. "He knew it was on the cards."

"One son a duke and the other an earl. What an illustrious family!" drawled Bardulf. "And resourceful too, as neither of you were born into those titles."

Oswald smiled, refusing to be drawn. "Perhaps the Queen can put in a word for you at some point," he suggested blandly.

Bardulf seemed to consider this as he ran his finger down the spines of several leather-bound tomes. "Alas, I fear the price she might demand would be higher than I'm prepared to pay."

"Indeed?" Oswald's eyebrows rose. Bardulf's tone surprised him. He sounded sincere for once. "I am sure you put in many hours of loyal service," he murmured automatically as his brain scrambled.

26

Bardulf cocked his head to one side. "Yes," he agreed. "But I am not willing to put my domestic life at the Queen's disposal."

"Domestic life?" repeated Oswald. "You spend your life in court quarters, as do I."

"Bachelor quarters," Bardulf agreed with him swiftly.

Oswald's frown became more pronounced as he began to get a deep feeling of unease. "You are considering matrimony?" he asked carefully.

"Good gods, no!" Bardulf gave an elaborate shudder and returned to the seat opposite him. Oswald regarded him steadily as Bardulf reached across the desk to pick up a paperweight of colored glass. "This I like," Bardulf said. "I could use one like this in my study."

"You don't have a study," Oswald pointed out mildly.

Bardulf smiled. "My office is the salons and ballrooms of the rich and mighty. That is why I am always so well informed." He pointed a long, elegant finger toward him. "You should take a leaf out of my book. Then you would not need all your spies hiding around corners and sifting through people's letters." His lip curled at the idea of such bad manners.

Oswald smiled at this. "People do not tend to discuss treasonous plots at balls."

"Of course they do, my dear Vawdrey!" Bardulf contradicted him roundly. "But I can see you are laughing at me. Your spies

27

are at the parties also, are they not, my friend?" He gave a sly smile.

Oswald waited patiently. He was sure more would be forthcoming if he bided his time.

"Which reminds me, were you present at the King's Winter Ball? I forget if I saw you there…" He held up a white hand. "No, I remember. You had to send your apologies. Again, as you were so hard at work on the King's foreign policy."

Oswald nearly rolled his eyes. Bardulf was aware as anyone that he very rarely attended such events. Still, he put a thoughtful look on his face and steepled his hands. "The Winter Ball, you say? I do not think I was able to tear myself away…"

"Such a shame," tutted Bardulf, settling back into his seat. "For you quite missed the dazzling court debut of the Cecil sisters." Bardulf inspected his immaculate nails and Oswald's eyebrows snapped together.

"Sir Phillip Cecil's daughters?" he hazarded.

"Nieces," Bardulf corrected him swiftly.

"And they were universally admired?" asked Oswald politely.

"The elder sister was held up as a paragon of virtue and accomplishment."

"And the younger?" asked Oswald.

Bardulf smiled. "Her virtue was not so immediately apparent," he admitted. "But the attention she garnered came from rather more exalted corners." Oswald shut his eyes briefly and then reopened them. "Quite so," said Bardulf gently. "She simply entranced the King with her twinkling laugh and fulsome…hair."

Oswald winced. "The Cecil family would never allow one of their number to become one of the King's mistresses," he said, suddenly tired of all the subterfuge.

Bardulf gave him a direct look. "Therein lies the problem, my friend."

Oswald guessed the Queen had sent Bardulf to him in a fit of pique at this latest bauble to catch the King's roving eye. "I don't see—"

"Do not mistake me, my friend," said Bardulf, guessing his line of thought. "The Queen did not send me."

Oswald sat up straighter in his chair. In his experience it was very rare that Bardulf ever came flat out with anything. "Then…?"

"Word has it the little innocent is not so naïve after all. She is pleading her reputation and demanding some recompense from the King if she is to deliver her prized virtue up to him."

"Such as?"

"A high-ranking marriage," said Bardulf gravely. Oswald sat very still.

"In short, my dear Vawdrey, you will need to step very carefully or you will find yourself ensnared in the parson's trap, and shackled to the King's latest paramour." Oswald leaned forward in his chair. "But perhaps you would not mind so very much," said Bardulf airily. "After all, everywhere I go, everyone whispers of your monk-like existence. Your devotion to the King's cause."

Oswald realized he was drumming his fingers against the desktop and snatched back his hand.

"After all," carried on Bardulf leisurely. "It may consolidate your position of power if the little who—your pardon, lady in question manages to hold his attention."
Oswald snorted. "She'd be the first one who did."

"Of course, you'd end up raising royal bastards to inherit your title and lands," added Bardulf wryly.

Oswald made an impatient gesture with his hand. "That's quite out of the question," he said, surprising himself with his vehemence.

"Your family does have a history of elevating bastards," pointed out Bardulf.

"Mason was my father's bastard—not another man's."

"Yes, there is that distinction," agreed Bardulf, still watching Oswald closely.

"I must thank you, Bardulf. For bringing this to my attention," said Oswald. "Forewarned is forearmed."

"I will await your next move with great interest," said Bardulf, looking amused. "But I think you may find this predicament beyond even your ingenuity, Vawdrey." He looked a little rueful. "I have not given you as much notice as I would like."

Oswald smiled wanly. "We shall see."

3

His Majesty King Wymer's Court at Aphrany

Oswald slid into his seat opposite the dais and tapped his assistant discreetly on his shoulder as the King listened to his latest petitioner. Bryce nearly jumped out of his skin, and then looked so relieved he might cry.

"My lord," he whispered. "I was so worried. You *never* miss an audience with the King, and His Majesty was quite put out to start without you."

"Who is this?" Oswald asked in a low voice. Bryce was right, he never missed one because someone had to keep an eye on the King. And that someone was usually him.

Bryce cleared his throat. "This is His Majesty's equerry to the north, Sir Ambrose Thane," he whispered back.

"Ah, Thane." Oswald looked down the list his assistant had provided for him. Thank gods he was the last on the list today for this morning's session. He had a stack of work to get back to. Oswald frowned as the King made a gracious speech of acquiescence which had Sir Ambrose breaking out in smiles all round.

An insipid-looking blonde on the sidelines squealed and ran forward to clutch Sir Ambrose's arm. "What exactly did he ask for?" he asked with slight misgiving. Wymer could get carried away sometimes in granting requests, and Oswald had to admit he had taken his eyes off proceedings for a moment there.

"A divorce," responded Bryce helpfully.

Oswald's eyebrows rose. "A divorce?" he echoed. "On what grounds?"

Bryce coughed. "Sir Ambrose did not go into the specifics."

Wonderful, thought Oswald grimly. Watching Sir Ambrose kiss the hand of the blonde, Oswald guessed he had a replacement lined up already. He cast a sour look Wymer's way. He just hoped the previous wife did not come from a powerful family or there could be hell to pay. "What was the name of the discarded wife?" he asked with a frown. He'd scarcely slept a wink the previous night. He could really do without any added complications this morning.

"Lady Fenella Thane," muttered Bryce helpfully.

"Her maiden name, Bryce," he clarified testily.

Bryce blushed faintly. "I'm afraid as to that, my lord, I could not say…"

"Never mind, the damage is done now," Oswald interrupted him. He would have to cross that bridge when he reached it. Giving himself a slight shake, he moved over to where the King was now signaling for the doors to be opened, the public royal audience having ended for another month. "A divorce?" he murmured reproachfully.

King Wymer shrugged. "I looked in your direction," he said defensively. "And you weren't there to give me any indication either way!" Oswald suppressed a sigh. "You think it will be a problem?" asked the King with a yawn. "It seemed like the quickest way to shut the prosy bore up."

33

"Very likely," agreed Oswald dryly. He pressed a finger and thumb to his eyes.

"You look tired, Vawdrey," grunted the King, clapping him on the shoulder. "You work too hard. Get a bit of shut-eye."

"I've got that treaty to finalize for tomorrow," Oswald reminded him.

"So, you have," agreed the King heartily. "Better get back to it. Don't want me to look a fool in front of all those visiting dignitaries, eh?" He punched Oswald in the shoulder and guffawed. "Thought you might like to join me for supper later," he added airily. "Lord Schaeffer is joining me."

His casual air instantly struck a false chord with Oswald. "You usually sup with Lord Schaeffer on a Tuesday night, Your Highness," he commented.

"Oh yes," the King agreed with a wave of his hand. "But I thought you might like to join us, you know."

Oswald shot a sidelong glance at the King, but he was emanating nothing but a cheery bonhomie. Immediately, this put Oswald on his guard. "There is something you wish to discuss with me?" he suggested.

The King hesitated. "Not here," he said, tapping a finger to his nose. "Somewhere with a bit of privacy, eh? Little idea I want to run by you." Oswald's brows snapped together. Wymer rarely had ideas of his own, but when he did, they usually meant trouble. "You're a good-looking devil, Vawdrey," said the King appraisingly. "How old are you? Seems long overdue you were leg shackled."

Oswald nearly choked on his own spit. Bardulf's warning had barely been in time. He eyed the King much as he would a snake pulled back to strike.

"Probably my fault, taking up all your time," said the King jocularly. "But it's not too late to put it to rights! Never fear!"

Oswald glanced around to see if their conversation was overheard. As usual, there were courtiers on every corner, eager to listen to any royal gossip. "It has not been a priority of mine," he murmured in an effort to quell the King's enthusiasm.

"And well do I know it!" sighed the King, shaking his head. "But it's not natural for a man in his prime like you are, Vawdrey!" He eyed Oswald. "What number you, in years? Thirty?"

"Thirty-three," Oswald corrected him automatically. His brain was scrambling. He really hadn't expected the King to go on the offensive so soon.

"And I've never yet heard of you playing the lover to any of our beauties at court," complained the King. "It's not right, begad!"

Beauties at court. Oswald felt the hairs on the back of his neck rise. In his peripheral vision he saw a shadowy figure by the window to his far left, only just in sight. It was Lord Phillip Cecil. Out of the corner of his eye, Oswald saw him exchange a charged look with the King.

35

Wymer cleared his throat and turned his back to Cecil in a clumsy attempt to distract Oswald's attention from it. *Ah*. It all clicked into place. So, it was true. Bardulf was right. Oswald felt cold anger course through his veins.

"If you'll excuse me, Your Highness," he said coolly. "I must return to that treaty immediately."

"Of course, of course," blustered the King. "Don't forget. Around nine o'clock in my private chambers."

"I'll see what I can do," Oswald responded with a brief bow, and strode from the room.

4

Anyone who had followed Lord Vawdrey that morning would have found he did not return to his study as avowed, but instead made his way to the Vawdrey family quarters in the coveted west wing of the palace. He was not followed, something he knew for sure as he discreetly glanced about him as he made his way unhurriedly down the warren of cloistered passages.

It would not do for Wymer's spymaster to be followed, and he did this mostly from habit despite his inner turmoil. No one would have guessed at this either, for his face was an impassive mask. But inwardly he was seething.

He had no sooner spotted the door to their rooms than a maid slid out the door carrying what looked like her own petticoat and stockings. She giggled and pulled her chemise up over one bare shoulder as Oswald averted his eyes, surmising his brother would be found within.

He was right. As he entered the room, he found Roland sat at the table, half-dressed and picking at some bread and cheese. He looked up as his brother came in, and made a noise with his mouth full of bread. Oswald guessed it was some form of greeting. "Who was that?" he asked as he crossed the room. "Not a member of the palace staff, I hope, at this advanced hour?"

Roland lolled back in his chair. "Relax. Tavern wench," he said. "I've learned my lesson. Maybe you should try it."

"Learning my lesson?" asked Oswald, taking a seat directly opposite him.

"Tavern wenches," his brother corrected him with an impertinent grin. "Might make you seem a bit more human."

Oswald considered the youngest Vawdrey as Roland continued devouring his plate of cheese and grapes. Roland had been a late bloomer, but in the last four years had turned into a heavily muscled copy of his father and older brother. "How's your arm?"

Roland snorted and rotated his shoulder. "It would take more than the strength of that simpleton de Bussell to stop me from competing tomorrow," he boasted, referring to the tournament being held the following day. "My lance arm is fine."

"That's good," murmured Oswald. "Who knows, there may be some new champions in that party lately returned from the north?"

Roland shrugged. "We can but hope. I've beaten everyone else round here."

"That's why you're the King's champion," pointed out Oswald with a smile at his brother's boastfulness.

"As to that, all that plaguey title's done is reduce my winning purse," complained Roland. "Who will bet against the King's champion? Wish he'd never bestowed it on me."
"Is that why you masqueraded as the black knight with no sigil at Cereny?" asked Oswald dryly.

Roland gave a visible start and then colored up. "You set your spies on me?" he asked belligerently.

"Of course not," scoffed Oswald. "I hardly need the aid of a spy to recognize my own brother."

Roland shrugged a brawny shoulder in annoyance. "Always forget how bloody observant you are," he muttered. "Why bring it up now? You never let on before!"

Oswald sighed. "I don't know. No reason."

"There's always a reason with you," said Roland darkly.

Oswald wondered with surprise if that was true. "I'm tired," he admitted, "and speaking without considering my words."

"Must be a first for you," retorted his brother. "Ever the damned politician." Roland pushed his plate away and contemplated his brother frowningly. "What is it? What's got you rattled?" he asked slowly.

"It's nothing," said Oswald aloud. "Just a trying morning, that's all." He smiled wanly. "So far there's been a divorce and a suspicious invitation to supper."

"Who got divorced?" asked Roland with a raised eyebrow. They very rarely discussed Oswald's business.

"Sir Ambrose Thane."

"Oh?" grunted Roland suspiciously. "Who's he?"

"Diplomatic equerry to the King in the north."

Roland pulled a disgusted face. "Oh, a damn ambassador! Court's overflowing with dullards these days! Who's the wife?"

"Which one?" Oswald answered wryly.

Roland choked on his cup of ale. "The devil you say! I've heard a lot of things about the north, but I didn't know they practiced polygamy!"

"He's not northern," said Oswald absently, reaching for the fruit bowl. He helped himself to a grape.

"How did he end up with two wives then?"

Oswald watched his brother as Roland pushed away his plate of half-eaten cheese. He was suddenly sick of Sir Ambrose Thane and his many wives. Instead, he realized this was the first conversation he'd had with his youngest brother in weeks. "Did you read the letter from Mason that came last week?" he asked in an abrupt change of subject.

Roland shrugged. "I glanced it over."

"It seems unlikely he and Linnet will come to court in the next few months." His brother grunted. "It can't be easy to travel with three children," Oswald said mildly. "Especially Archie," he added with a vague shudder, thinking of his godson.

"Why don't they leave them at Cadwallader then?" said Roland belligerently. "Especially that red-haired little demon spawn!" They both brooded a moment on the subject of Archie Vawdrey, their nephew.

"Don't let Mason hear you refer to his son and heir in those terms," warned Oswald. For some reason their brother and sister-in-law insisted on believing their son was some kind of angelic protégée, instead of the little villain he really was. "Maybe he's improved in the last two months since we last saw him?"

"He could hardly be any worse," retorted Roland.

"Still," said Oswald, "it would be good to have all the family together again." He hesitated. "Since Father died…"

"Save it," Roland growled.

Oswald sighed. It was strange to think their blustering, purple-faced sire had been the glue that held them together. "I know you were closest to him…"

Roland dragged his chair back abruptly. "Are we done here?" he gritted out.

Oswald shrugged. "Apparently."

Roland crossed the room and shut the door behind him with a loud bang. He was still touchy over their father's death. And by all accounts, burning the candle at both ends with wine, women, and the tournament circuit. Oswald just hoped his younger brother wasn't riding for a fall. They weren't close, and never had been. Was it too late to close the gap between them?

Of course, he had more pressing problems, with this threat to his marital state. Not that Roland could help in any way, even if they were closer. Oswald took no one into his confidences. He had always kept to himself. Linnet had been right. He had no close particular friends or confidants. His powerful role at court did not encourage such bonds.

His brother Mason was probably the closest person to him, and even he only knew the side of Oswald that he presented to him. The fact was that he was a very private person. And the idea of being pledged in marriage hit him in a raw place, as it was something his father had taken great liberties with when he was a young man.

Match after match had been drawn up and then cast aside as another more lucrative prospect came into view. It had been humiliating to be bartered like goods, and the only relief he found from the embarrassment was to remove himself emotionally and physically from the parade of young women who had been presented to him time after time as his future wife.

If Oswald had ever considered taking a wife, it had been purely in the most theoretical of terms. He had vaguely imagined some helpmeet who matched him in ambition and capability. Perhaps someone in the mold of Lady Anne Sumner, with her cool, quiet beauty and secretive, devious mind.

She made an excellent spy, that much Oswald knew. And what else would he require of a wife, other than being presentable, even-tempered, and willing to be put firmly on the sidelines while he furthered his career? The rub of it was that Lady Sumner had been married for years to colicky old Lord Sumner, who, despite his apoplectic appearance, seemed determined to live to a grand old age. So, Lady Anne was out of the picture, more's the pity, and could not factor in his solution to this current problem.

He rubbed the pad of his thumb over his bottom lip as he considered what impediment he could cite to the King when he suggested his marriage to the Cecil female. For that was what he was sure the King was about to do. He had no idea which of the Cecil girls had taken the King's fancy, but clearly, she had not fallen on her back when the King snapped his fingers.

No, this female was made of sterner stuff. She wanted a ring upon her finger before bestowing her favors. And as the King was already on his second marriage, then Wymer must have promised to find her some nobleman to act the cuckold while he made her his royal paramour. And Oswald was damned if he would be the sacrificial victim.

His lip curled. While it was true, he had no ambition to play the husband and father, he also had no intention of bestowing his title on one of the King's bastards or giving his name to a highborn whore. His fingers played at his black signet ring as he twisted it about his finger. His own father would have been appalled at such a notion, and it made him wryly smile to imagine the old baron's reaction.

For once, father and son would have been of the same accord, he thought with wintry amusement. Something that had only happened very rarely while Baron Vawdrey was alive. Returning to the problem at hand, he supposed he would have to go for good old consanguinity, which was a tried and tested impediment. No one wanted cousins marrying after all, even the King. He would have to get that rogue Carleton to draw him up another forged family tree. It wouldn't be the first time, though his own family wasn't usually one of the entangled branches.

Once he'd made up his mind, he felt better and reached for an apple from the fruit bowl across the table. He would scribble a missive to Carleton and get a few good hours in at his study to work on the treaty.

43

In fact, he thought as he took a bite into the apple, some fresh air might do him good. He was overtired after working through the night. And quite frankly, he was due some extended leave from court. It was high time he put some groundwork in at Vawdrey Keep. His father had died a full four months ago, and he had done nothing with the estate, despite the full set of plans in his desk drawer.

Yes, he vowed as he rose and exited his apartments, turning toward the south aspect of the palace. He would go down to Vawdrey Keep and scout out the lay of the land before he hired a workforce to raze the place to the ground and start the rebuild process. That would be all the rest he would need before returning reinvigorated to court. He gave a brief nod, satisfied with his decision. Then all would return to normal, and he could forget all about this ridiculous notion of Wymer's to see him married.

Slipping through a concealed door in the wainscoting, Oswald made his way through the labyrinthine dark passages that crisscrossed the castle. Somewhere along the way, he caught up a plain black cloak from a row of hooks and threw it about his shoulders, concealing his black velvet doublet with ornate silver buttons. He drew a plain hood over his curling black hair, concealing his face in shadow.

When he emerged some quarter of an hour later, it was from an unobtrusive doorway near the bustling palace kitchens. He strode straight across the courtyard and exited the west gate into the crowded street outside. He had always loved the anonymity of a crowd. Oswald let the surging crowd of hawkers and market traders sweep him along, dictating his walking pace until he reached the city's south quarter.

Here, at the market square, he broke from the throng and headed down a narrow side alley, and then another, and then another, until he was in a crooked little street with hardly any pedestrians or through-trade at all. These were more specialist establishments, only frequented by those who walked on the shady side of life. And Oswald Vawdrey had been known to walk that path when occasion demanded.

He swiftly ducked under the eaves of a cramped establishment with a carved quill feather hanging from a chain on the roof, announcing the trade of its occupant. Inside, he paused a moment, letting his eyes grow accustomed to the dark, cramped interior and the smell of musty old parchment before he heard a voice grudgingly say, "Oh, it's you, is it, Mr. Roberts? Thought I hadn't seen you in a while."

"Good morning, Mr. Carleton," Oswald greeted him smoothly. "Aye, 'tis indeed."

"Humph!" The old man adjusted himself precariously on the tall stool he was perched on. He returned to adding bloodred ink to a coat of arms he was drawing on a map. Oswald leaned across the counter and inspected the document with interest.

The old man growled at him. "This be for another client," he pointed out irritably. If it wasn't for the fact the ink was still wet, Oswald was sure he would have whisked it out of sight.

"And I commend your devotion to confidentiality," Oswald answered him smoothly. "However, if you want that to pass for the Chassington Phoenix then you need to remove the second fleuron from its crest."

The old man's jaw snapped shut angrily. "Their arms has a double fleuron," he objected. "I seen it right here." His finger jabbed at another document under the counter.

"I'm sure. However, you have dated this map twenty years old and they were only granted the use of the second fleuron a decade ago." Oswald smiled his blandest smile and the old man gnashed his teeth angrily and threw down his quill pen.

"That fool never mentioned it," he grumbled.

"I take it your client is the younger son," murmured Oswald. "Alas, not the sharpest blade in the knife box. I suspect his plan to bilk more lands from the legal heir will fail. Despite your best efforts." Oswald tutted his tongue. "Such a pity to squander your talents on so unworthy a cause, my good Carleton."

"Hah! And let me guess, you have a much worthier cause for me to work on."

Oswald bowed slightly. "As you say."

"Well, it will have to wait!" grouched the old man, hunching his shoulders. "I got several pieces of work waiting on me."

Oswald retrieved a purse from his doublet breast pocket and placed it unhurriedly on the counter. "I will, of course, recompense you for prioritizing my task."

The old man grunted and glanced at the purse. "Gold?"

"Carleton, you wound me," he said gently. "Would I even dream of paying you with inferior coin?"

The old man nodded. "You're good for payment, I'll give you that." Oswald smiled at him. "And what might this urgent task be that I needs must prioritize over my other work?" Carleton asked grudgingly. He eyed Oswald rather curiously. "I sometimes wonder…"

"About what, my friend?"

"What line of business you must be in that you so often require the services of a forger."

"Getting curious in your old age, Carleton? Alas, I think it better that you do not know me outside of this establishment."

"S'what I figured," sniffed the older man.

"I'm sure I'm not your only reticent client."

"Far from it," agreed Carleton with a dry cough.

"Then why the curiosity?"

Carleton frowned. "Dunno, especially." He hesitated. "Funny thing is, I sometimes think I wouldn't even *recognize* you outside of here."

"Nothing funny about that." Oswald shrugged. "I'm a very forgettable person."

"No you ain't, my lord. You'm just wearing a disguise."

"What did you call me?"

A slow smile spread across Carleton's face. "What? You think I don't know the Quality when I sees it, *Mr. Roberts*?"

"A word of caution, old friend," said Oswald, leaning across the counter. "Be a little less curious when it comes to me. Do we understand one another?" He hesitated. "I would be very sorry to have to cut my connections when your work has always been so satisfactory." He let his words sink in before adding, "I'll be in touch shortly about the commission." He left the gold where it sat and swiftly left the store.

5

"We're here to see Sir Oswald Vawdrey himself," repeated Fenella loudly to the third servant who had come their way and tried to hurry past them, avoiding eye contact. She was starting to think it was the mud-splattered cloaks and boots that were doing them a disservice.

He looked them up and down doubtfully. "Earl Vawdrey, you mean?" he asked.

Fenella drew in a sharp breath. "He's an earl now?" The servant blinked at her.

At her side, her brother, Gilbert, shuffled his feet. "*Fenella…*" he mumbled awkwardly.

Fenella cleared her throat. "Yes, of course. *Earl* Vawdrey," she corrected herself. "We're old neighbors of his. From Sitchmarsh."

The servant's glance flickered over her once again. Fenella felt a twinge of anxiety about her mustard-yellow wool dress. It was the best one she had. The servant's nostrils flared, and he gave a brief bow before retreating from view.

"Maybe we should just leave," grumbled her brother. "I don't believe these fellows are even passing along the message."

"Of course they are, Gilbert," Fenella assured him with a confidence she did not entirely feel. "Doubtless it will take a little time to locate him. This palace is so very large after all." She looked nervously over her shoulder at the vast stone corridor.

Large was not the word. The royal palace was *huge*. Much grander than she'd ever imagined it would be. She fixed a bright smile on her face as another set of footsteps drew near and then retreated without approaching them. "Oh dear," she muttered, her face falling.

"Fenella," her brother began, squaring his shoulders. "I'm beginning to think this a fool's errand. Perhaps we should ask instead for Ambrose's whereabouts…"

Fenella's stomach lurched. *Ambrose.* Her treacherous husband. When she tried to think of what she would say to his face, her imagination failed her. A quiet cough behind them had Fenella whirling around.

A plump young man, in what looked like a monk's robe, stood surveying them with vague disapproval through his pale blue eyes. Fenella's face fell. Even after eleven years, she knew this was not Oswald Vawdrey. "Yes?" she asked expectantly when he did not speak. "Have you brought some message to us from Lord Vawdrey?"

The young man looked slightly affronted by her eagerness. He pinched his lips and directed his gaze toward Gilbert. "Earl Vawdrey will see you privately in his study," he said in a clipped, concise voice.

Fenella's heart thudded in her chest and she gave a faint gasp. She glanced at Gilbert, who had turned rather red, and seemed rooted to the spot in horror. She widened her eyes at him and nodded her head.

"Ah yes, yes of course," stammered her brother. "Delighted to…er…lead the way." The young cleric seemed to give a faint shudder and then gestured for them to follow him with a sweep of his arm.

"I hope you've thought through what you're going to say to this man," said her brother in an urgent undertone. "You certainly haven't shared it with me! Damned awkward business!"

Fenella felt her stomach roll again. Her desperate stratagem had seemed worth a try back at Thurrold Manor, but here at the royal palace, her nerves were quaking.

"I shall appeal for his mercy of course, as an old family acquaintance," she croaked back as they swept along the cold flagstones. "Our fathers were friends after all."

Gilbert looked unconvinced. "Not for years and years!" he objected. "Why, Father had barely a good word to say about the old baron after your betrothal was broken off." He pulled on his blond beard self-consciously. "You don't suppose he'll be—" He hesitated. "Out of sorts about being bothered with this business?"

Fenella nearly lost her footing. "My abandonment you mean?" she asked a little shrilly.

Her brother winced. "Ambrose may have come to his senses by now," he whispered hoarsely. "Just because he brought some doxy back from the north with him doesn't mean he meant to marry the wench. How could it, when he's wed to you?"

"But Orla said…"

"Orla's a foolish old maid!" burst out her brother in frustration. "What the devil does she know about what goes on between a man and a woman?"

Fenella shook her head resolutely. "You didn't hear the letter Ambrose wrote to her," she insisted. "Besides, Ambrose is not the kind of man to be interested in...doxies."

Her brother made a rude noise.

Fenella noticed the contemptuous twist of the cleric's lips at their hushed conversation and realized their every word was overheard. She forbore to answer her brother's insensitive words, and instead tried desperately to think of a way to ingratiate herself with Lord Vawdrey.

Perhaps she would not need to break out the paperwork at all? She would rather she did not have to coerce him to act on her behalf. Perhaps the past association of their families would be enough to sway him to her cause? She devoutly hoped so!

After all, she had merely been the first in a long line of ladies who had been betrothed to Oswald Vawdrey over the years. She had certainly been the humblest and obscure in origin. Her father's estate, now Gil's, butted up against the borders of Vawdrey Keep.

The old baron had struck up their engagement as a means to execute a land grab and extend his boundaries. She had been a mere twelve years old at the time, and Oswald Vawdrey had been a young man of nineteen.

She remembered vividly how tongue-tied and awed she had been in his presence on the handful of occasions they had met.

She could scarcely believe that she was to wed such a godlike youth with his dark hair and green eyes. And she had been right not to believe it, for after three years, it had all come to naught.

True, he had been patient and kind to the tongue-tied child with puppy fat and mud-brown hair. Much kinder than her own brother, who had not appreciated her in those days and barely tolerated her presence.

She remembered well the Solstice Eve they had been promised. Oswald Vawdrey had spoken to her quietly when the rest of the high table was roaring with boisterous laughter and loud jests she did not understand. He had taken the care to draw out the nervous child and ask what gifts she had been given for the Winter Solstice, what games her family always played on Solstice Eve.

He had bowed his head to listen to her and smiled at her hesitant replies. When a toast was raised to their future marriage, he had raised his goblet and covered her hand with his, as if being engaged to an awkward, plain girl of twelve was not the supreme embarrassment their brothers seemed collectively to think.

When he had handed her up into her family's conveyance at the end of the evening and bade her good night, she did not think he could have failed to see the hero worship shining out of her own eyes. It had not dimmed for a good three years after that, if not longer. Even after her father had brusquely informed her the betrothal was at an end, her regard had limped on. It had been with each announcement of his subsequent engagements that her admiration had flickered and fizzled away.

Each successor had been higher born than the previous noblewoman. Each one had a larger dowry. And yet, still he did not marry. Ambition, overweaning ambition would lead to his downfall, her father had predicted. But he had been wrong. Oswald Vawdrey's fortunes had flourished. Even the periods of fighting in the north had not slowed his ascent. Injury, imprisonment, and being held to ransom had been mere steps in his journey to the top.

And here he was, at the very pinnacle of success. An earl, one of the King's most trusted advisers no less, and a powerful lord in his own right. He had outstripped his father's rank and forged his own way at the royal court. Indeed, no one could say he was not an outright triumph. Their home county spoke of him now with a sense of awe.

Fenella almost bumped into the back of the clerk, who had stopped abruptly in front of a studded wooden door flanked with suits of armor. The servant cast a censorious look over his shoulder at her and then knocked softly on the door.

The voice that commanded "Come in" did not sound familiar, but after all it had been years. She was ushered into a room which looked like a vast library with a ceiling painted like a celestial sky and great wooden bookcases that reached up as though scaling the heavens.

She did not have a chance to dwell on these for long as her eyes were drawn to a large desk placed in the center of the room before a tall arched window. Seated behind this desk, imposingly dressed all in black, was the man she had once thought she would marry. Oswald Vawdrey.

He smiled a wintry smile, and just like that, Fenella felt as gauche and foolish as she had at fifteen, when she'd last seen his handsome face. Her cheeks flooded with color and her feet came to a halt. Why, oh why, had she thought this wretched stratagem would be a way out of her current woe? How fervently she wished she'd never thought of it! He was even more beautiful than she remembered, and it almost hurt her eyes to look at him. Gilbert had come to stand beside her and stood as dumb as a block of wood, so she was forced to speak.

"My Lord Vawdrey," she said loudly, hoping to rouse her brother from his stupor. A sidelong look showed her Gilbert's eyes were glassy and he looked a little queasy. She tugged at the back of his tunic and sank into a curtsey she hoped was deep enough for an earl. Without ever meeting one before she was not really sure. Gilbert stumbled into a bow beside her, and at last Oswald Vawdrey stood up unhurriedly and gave a very slight bow. She had forgotten just how tall the Vawdrey males were.

"Bryce," he said, addressing the cleric behind them. "You will fetch us some refreshment."
The door closed with a discreet click and it dawned on Fenella that Oswald Vawdrey might not even remember her. There was no acknowledgment in his gaze, which was impassive and quite calm. He smiled an easy smile. "Please come and sit," he said, gesturing to the wide-cushioned seats that lined the room.

Fenella started at once to retrieve one for herself. She dragged it across the floorboards and plunked it down heavily next to the one Gilbert had lugged over from the opposite side. They both sat down and she looked up to see an irritated look cross Oswald's face. She had no sooner noticed it than he blinked, and it was gone.

55

She wondered if she'd fetched the wrong chair, but to her untrained eye they all looked identical with their clawed feet and tasseled cushions. Maybe she had imagined his displeasure? Without looking down, he opened his desk drawer and drew out a piece of paper that she did not recognize, held it aloft a moment, and then placed it on his desk, all without glancing at it.

"Lady Fenella," he said, looking straight at her. "Please accept my apologies for this morning's proceedings. It was highly irregular, and I'm afraid must have been very distressing for you."

Fenella sat up ramrod straight. "Lady Thane," she corrected him through dry lips.

He regarded her steadily, without saying one word. There was faint pity in the depths of his green eyes.

Oh gods, thought Fenella. *No, no. It can't have already happened. I can't surely be too late.* She gripped the arms of her chair. "Is it possible—" she faltered. "That my husband has already approached the King?" Her voice sounded high and thin and wholly unlike her own.

"He was one of the supplicants at this morning's audience with the King, yes," he answered steadily. "I have here the official record of the King's judgments," he said, glancing at the piece of paper he had retrieved. "Sir Thane's case included." Fenella stood up so fast her chair overturned.

"Fenella!" It was her brother, Gilbert, who spoke, but she turned her back to him and walked across the room to the

56

window. She had no idea of the view, for she stared sightlessly out of the glass pane a moment, desperately striving for the composure to turn back around. Trying to will the hot tears that welled up and spilled down her cheeks to disappear.

Instead, she brushed them from her face and took a deep breath. "If only I could have some private word with Ambrose," she said unsteadily. "Remind him of what we have been to one another. I feel sure that he would reconsider…"

Lord Vawdrey did not answer her, so she turned around to face him resolutely. "You are a very important man at court these days. Is that not so, my lord?" Her voice was husky with tears, but she knew it carried to where Oswald Vawdrey sat watching her with his uncanny stillness. He looked surprised by her change of tack.

Fenella ignored him and drew the thick roll of yellow parchment from her cloak. "Perhaps this might persuade you to intercede on my behalf, my lord," she said, once more approaching the desk. She placed the parchment on the shining wooden surface where it rolled slightly to the left and then sat looking innocuous a moment. Fenella held her breath and swayed slightly on her feet. She felt slightly horrified that she had been forced to produce her trump card at all.

"What is it?" asked Oswald Vawdrey after a moment's pause.

"Perhaps you should look at it," she said boldly, raising her chin.

"Perhaps you should sit down," he replied dryly. "Before you drop." He shot a look of disgust at Gilbert before advancing around the desk and setting her overturned chair to rights.

57

"Here," he said, and caught hold of her upper arm in a surprisingly firm grip before guiding her back to her seat. "Sit." Fenella dropped into the seat and promptly burst into tears.

"Fenella!" remonstrated Gilbert. "What the *hells* do you think you're—?" He broke off his words abruptly, though Fenella could not say why, as her hands were covering her face. She heard the door open discreetly behind them.

"Ah, here is Bryce now with our refreshment," said Oswald in an easy tone. "If you could just set it down on the desk here and pour a cup for Lady Fenella, who is overtired from her journey."

Fenella drew a shaky breath and lowered her hands to find Oswald Vawdrey holding an immaculately white linen handkerchief in her face. She took it and dabbed her cheeks. What she really wanted to do was heartily blow her nose, but she didn't dare on such fine linen. His disapproving assistant passed her a cup of something that smelled like spiced wine. She took it with a murmur of thanks and moistened her lips with it.

"My lord—" started Bryce.

"You can leave us now, Bryce," Oswald interrupted. "I will let you know when I need you."

"Yes, my lord." Bryce backed out of the room with surprising grace for a portly man and closed the door behind him.

Oswald sighed and made his way back around to his own side of the desk. "Help yourself," he said, addressing her brother. "I don't believe I caught your name." Gilbert looked dumbfounded.

"His name is Bernard, my lord," quavered Fenella, lowering the handkerchief. "It seems you do not remember us, but we were your neighbors growing up. The Bernards of Sitchmarsh Hall?"

Oswald Vawdrey's eyes flickered a moment and then narrowed. "Bernard? As in Sir Jeoffrey Bernard?"

"My father died five years ago," said Fenella quietly.

"We were sorry to hear of your own loss. A grand man, Baron Vawdrey," put in Gilbert, making an effort.

Oswald reached for the scroll without comment. Fenella watched his eyes dart to the seals and signatures at the bottom of the document as soon as he had unfurled it. His gaze snapped to meet hers a moment before returning to the top of the document.

Fenella took a hurried sip of the spiced wine, her color rising. She ignored Gilbert's quizzical look, for she had not told him of the document, and stared into the depths of her cup as the silence stretched out.

"You realize what this is, of course?" asked Oswald, his voice startling her. She wasn't sure how long he had pored over the document, but it had certainly been several moments since any of them had stirred.

"Betrothal papers," she answered automatically. "Drawn up between your father and mine and agreed one Solstice Eve fourteen years ago."

"Not quite," he answered, rising from his chair. Paper still in hand, he walked to the window. He stood still a moment, and then turned to face them both. "I don't think you realize what you have here, my lady."

Fenella cleared her throat. "My father always said he had grounds for considerable recompense, should he have chosen to pursue it…" Oswald gave a short laugh. "But that is *not* why I am here," she explained hastily. "I merely ask that you use your position to espouse my cause with my husband and—"

"Fenella," Oswald cut in, shocking her by addressing her so familiarly. "According to this document, I *am* your husband."

Gilbert made a strangled noise in his throat as Fenella stared at him, stunned.

"You must surely be mistaken, sir," she stammered, forgetting his title altogether.

"There can be no mistake," answered Oswald Vawdrey mildly.

"But—but that's *impossible*!"

"I assure you, it is legally binding," he said grimly and held the document up. "This is a marriage contract. Signed. Sealed. Dated."

Her brother turned to her. "Did you know about this?" he hissed in what he no doubt imagined to be an undertone.

"Don't be ridiculous, Gilbert! How could I? Why, I've been married to Ambrose for eight years!"

"I hate to contradict you, Fenella," put in Oswald mildly. "But your marriage to Thane was not legal." Fenella reeled, shrinking back into her chair with a gasp.

Gilbert sprang up in agitation. "You're telling me my sister is a bigamist?" he asked hoarsely.
Lord Vawdrey sat back down and poured himself a cup of wine to which he liberally added water. He looked at her quizzically and held the jug aloft.

"No, thank you," she answered in horrified fascination. He looked so calm, while her hands were shaking so badly, she was nearly spilling her cup, which was only half-filled.

Gilbert wheeled around. "What if we burned it?" he demanded wildly.

Lord Vawdrey's eyebrows rose. "Certainly not," he retorted. "That would be quite reprehensible. And as Sir Jeoffrey—your father—stated, you are due some recompense."

But what sort of recompense? wondered Fenella, breaking out into a cold sweat. *A jail sentence? A spell in the stocks? A heavy fine?*

"That's not what he meant at all," she objected weakly. "He thought—only that your family had not honored their promise...not that we were..." She broke off distractedly before rallying. "How *could* we be married, my lord? Your father wrote to mine, breaking off the agreement..."

"I was nineteen when this contract was signed," Lord Vawdrey cut in, tapping his tunic. She realized he had already secured the document inside it, and she hadn't even seen him do it. "Three years later, my father had no grounds to attempt to nullify the contract on my behalf. He had no legal right, as I had already reached my majority of twenty-one."

Fenella frowned at him. "Are you quite certain, my lord?" she asked, feeling sick with anxiety. There was something about his steely calm that disturbed her. Why wasn't he railing and disputing all this? Why wasn't he cursing their family to perdition? Her feet itched to get out of this imposing room with its unpredictable master. She had no idea what to make of this man her betrothed had grown into. She did not know him at all. But then, she reminded herself, she'd never really known the boy either.

He smiled, and Fenella almost shivered to see it, for it did not touch his eyes one bit. "I am quite certain," he answered gravely. "You have been my legal wedded wife these last fourteen years."

6

Oswald shut the door behind him and breathed out. It seemed almost too good to be true. Now he had no need of a trumped-up case of consanguinity to rebuff the King's absurd marriage plans. He had an impediment all of his own—an existing wife. A smile curled his lips, which he hastily concealed when he saw Bryce blinking at him from the other side of the corridor.

What a shame that Bryce was not the type to listen at doors. His predecessor, Edwards, would have had his ear glued to the keyhole the entire time, and within the hour the rumors would have started to circulate. Ah, how he missed dependable, treacherous Edwards.

"Ah, Bryce," he said, crooking his finger to summon him over. "I need you to make some discreet enquiries for me, to find out if Sir Ambrose Thane's remarriage has yet taken place."

Bryce's eyes goggled. "Yes, my lord. He applied to marry as soon as 'twas possible. The King granted this and the use of the Lady Chapel in the west wing." He hesitated. "Is there some lawful impediment that's come to light?" he asked hopefully.

"Nothing of that nature. I need to run a small errand myself, so if you could nip along to the Lady Chapel and see that the ceremony is completed, that would be most useful. You need do nothing, merely hang back until you have confirmation it is done and dusted." If Thane was safely remarried then it might help reconcile Fenella to their own wedded state, he reasoned.

Bryce looked alarmed. "Should I send word to the King, my lord?"

Oswald held up a hand. "Calm yourself, Bryce. I will be back presently. A stroll will do me good." He glanced back at the door. "And…er…take the Lady Fenella and her brother some repast. They have traveled many miles this day. Assure them I will be back in good time." He moved to the outer door, hesitated, and turned back. "Do not let her leave my office under any circumstances, Bryce," he added. "If needs be, summon a guard to reinforce this."

"I will, my lord!" agreed his assistant fervently. "Never fear!"

Things had sorted themselves out without him having to exert himself at all, Oswald congratulated himself as he made his way unhurriedly to the east wing of the castle. Fenella Bernard was a short, rather plump female of twenty-six years. She had a round face and brown eyes, which either looked wounded or startled, and she dressed rather like a merchant's wife. She would be extremely ill equipped for court life, which meant no one could blame him when he relegated her to Vawdrey Keep at the earliest opportunity.

Yes, it was all very satisfactory.

He had decided to walk past the chapel himself on the way. As he approached, he heard raised voices and saw a small straggling group emerge from the chapel entrance. He thought he recognized Sir Ambrose, though he could only see the back of a short male figure and hear a peevish voice as he waved away the gaggle of palace squires and pages who had gathered in the doorway.

"Get away, the lot of you!" the groom objected, fussily holding his arm out for his new bride.

"Oh, how they crowd one, Ambrose!" she complained. "It makes one feel quite faint!"

Oswald leaned against a convenient pillar on the edge of the crowd. "Who's the bridegroom?" he asked a passing group of young pages who were dispersing with disgruntled expressions.

"Some ambassador got wed," the nearest boy told him with an indifferent shrug.

"Sir Ambrose Thane?" asked Oswald, showing a silver coin between his fingers.

The boy next to him perked up. "Yes, my lord. That was him. Come back from up north."

"It's naught but a poor showing though," piped up the first boy. "No tokens or coins being distributed. Not even ribbons. Proper nipcheese, he is!"

"Well, that is a shame," said Oswald gravely. He held out a silver coin to the first, and then the second boy, in turn. They grinned at him. "Have you heard if he's to host a celebration feast?" asked Oswald.

"Not him," snorted the second page. "He's far too mean!"

Oswald looked thoughtful. "Indeed, that is too bad," he murmured before setting off once more in the direction of the castle kitchens. Once he was out of the castle's west gate, he briskly made his way back to the forger's doorstep.

The old man looked up in some surprise. "Knew you'd be back," he admitted. "But not this soon!"

Oswald withdrew the betrothal document from his tunic and unfurled it. "I no longer require a falsified family tree," he said without preamble. "But instead, have for you a far simpler task involving this contract." He looked up at Carleton and smiled. "You may keep the purse of gold, for I'm afraid I must wait for it to be completed now."

The old man tutted but approached to take the contract and scanned it with his keen eyes. "Fenella Bernard and Oswald Vawdrey," he read aloud without curiosity. "Dated over ten years ago. Seems fairly standard. Looking for a loophole, are you?" His rather reptilian gaze flickered over Oswald, who ignored the question.

"It's a remarkable thing, is it not?" Oswald ruminated aloud. "How very little material difference there is between a betrothal and a marriage contract."

Carleton's eyes narrowed. "Aye, true enough. Oftentimes, just a matter of the consummation," he agreed after a slight pause.

"Not in this case," Oswald said swiftly. He leaned over the counter. "The bride was of tender years," he explained, pointing to the birth date of Lady Fenella Bernard and then the date of the contract.

Carleton puffed out his cheeks. "You want him locked in tight," he said.

"No escape," agreed Oswald.

"Poor bugger," said Carleton. "What did this"—he glanced down—"Oswald Vawdrey ever do to you?"

Oswald considered this a moment. "He did not keep his word," he said softly.

Carleton peered down again at the paperwork. "Naught but a lad of nineteen," he objected.

"A promise is a promise. And besides, it's for his own good."

"In your opinion," interjected a skeptical Carleton.

"I imagine, on this subject, he is in complete agreement with me," replied Oswald airily.

Carleton pulled a face. "It's always easier to imagine that about other people, Mr. Roberts."

"Can you do it?"

"Of course I can do it," spluttered the older man indignantly. "Question is, should I? Could wreak havoc with other people's lives this could!" He shook his head.

Oswald sighed. "I can assure you, both parties involved will be somewhat better off for our intrusion. There will be no adverse repercussions, you have my word." When Carleton's expression did not waver, he added, "I left one purse of gold with you already this morning. Don't force me to take my custom elsewhere."

Carleton snorted. "You know there's none better than me, in all of Aphrany."

Oswald smiled. "Prove it. You have precisely a quarter of the hour to bind this youthful pair into a respectable married couple of some fourteen years."

"Quarter of an hour!" grumbled Carleton, but he snatched up the document as soon as Oswald wandered to the other end of the room, peering at a map. "The ink may still be wet, mind you!"

"It can dry on my way back home," he replied mildly.

*

"Bryce," said Oswald softly, some half hour later, startling his assistant nearly out of his skin. "The deed is done. Ambrose Thane is remarried."

Bryce pursed his lips. "Some would say with undue haste, my lord," he said distastefully.

"Some would," agreed Oswald. "However, here at court, we try not to judge His Majesty's decisions." He let this sink in until Bryce's cheeks turned pink, then added: "It seems the gentleman in question is somewhat hesitant to throw a celebratory feast."

"Perhaps he thought it might seem in poor taste, my lord?" answered Bryce, who was clearly made of sterner stuff than Oswald had previously imagined.

Oswald frowned at him a moment. "Of course, the newlyweds must have some form of celebration, or it would be much commented on at court."

Bryce looked bewildered. Oswald never usually showed the slightest interest in the social events. "Indeed?" he said lamely when his master continued to regard him in steady expectation of a response.

"I'm glad to see we are of the same mind on this, my good Bryce," he said cheerfully. "I want you to extend an offer to Sir Ambrose offering the use of the audience chamber below. It is rarely used, and he will bother no one, gathering his friends and family there."

Bryce looked startled. "But, my lord!" he protested, before lowering his voice to a loud whisper. "It would hardly seem decent with—with—his first wife in such close proximity!"

"I fail to see your point."

"What if she should wander into the antechamber? Why, it adjoins the gallery above—"

"I am aware of the fact."

"But what if she were to venture out?"

"Oh, she will venture, Bryce. And you're going to make sure of it."

"I am?"

"When I leave her alone presently, I want you to open the door leading out into the gallery. That should give her a very good view of the wedding party." Bryce's face froze. "You disapprove, Bryce?" sighed Oswald.

"It's not my place to approve or disapprove, my lord," said Bryce stiffly.

"My dear Bryce, you look the picture of outraged virtue. Do you think me unduly cruel?" Bryce folded his lips, his double chin giving a slight wobble. He made no reply. "To let her continue in false hope would be far crueler," pointed out Oswald gently. "I'm afraid Lady Fenella must realize her current position. Sir Ambrose Thane is lost to her. Forever."

"It's a wicked world, my lord," said Bryce.

Oswald looked pained. "You are not in the seminary now, Bryce," he pointed out. "You would do well to become a little more worldly." He paused heavily while Bryce chewed this over. "I want you to tell Thane's man that the use of the room is offered 'by a well-wisher at court' who wishes to remain anonymous until they are reacquainted. Do you think you can manage that?"

Bryce fidgeted in his seat. "Yes, my lord," he said unhappily.

"If not, I can send another, but I'd rather keep this between us." *Edwards would have leaped at the chance of a little intrigue*, thought Oswald bitterly. He really was going to have to do something about Bryce! "Off you go!"

"Now, my lord?" asked Bryce, glancing at the window.

"Yes, for it will take him time to arrange for the refreshment and entertainment," Oswald said with exasperation.

"Very well, my lord."

Oswald waited a moment until his assistant had reluctantly left the room and then, and only then, he reached into his tunic, extracted the paperwork, and unfurled it. Reaching across the desk, he took up Bryce's pen, dipped it in the ink, and added his own signature next to his father's. He blotted it and waited a moment for it to dry, and then refolded it, and slipped it back into his doublet. Then he rose with a satisfied nod and headed for his office.

7

Fen had never felt so wretchedly miserable in her entire life. She huddled in the chair by the fire, fighting back tears and listening to her brother complain about having to take her back into his household.

"I had thought to take a wife by the end of the year," he said in an injured voice. "Fat chance of that now, with a woman with her feet under my table already," he grouched. "Sarah Yondy wouldn't even touch me with a spinster sister nearing thirty years as a dependent."

"I'm twenty-six," she murmured tiredly, though in truth she felt eighty. All her bones were beginning to stiffen and ache from the ride and the rain. She felt both hot and cold at the same time. Mayhap she'd caught a chill.

A chill that would develop into a full-blown inflammation of the lungs and carry her off by morning in a high fever, she thought. *Then Ambrose would be a murderer and then he'd be sorry!* Looking down, she found the limp, damp rag she was twisting in her fingers was Lord Vawdrey's once-pristine handkerchief.

It looked as abused as she felt. Lifting it up, she gave her nose a good, hard blow. To her embarrassment, when she looked up, Lord Vawdrey was back in the room with his eyes on her. She wasn't even sure how long he'd been gone.

"You must forgive me, my lord," she said haltingly. "I can scarce believe that after eight years of marriage I am to be cast off in such a fashion…" She stifled a sob. "It's…it's too callous!" She looked up at him fiercely. "Could you do such a thing to a wife who has always been loyal and true?"

"I'm scarcely in a position to say," he replied shortly. "For almost half the years I've been married, my wife has been living with another man." She gasped and fell back at that. "Forgive me for my bluntness," he added smoothly. "It seems to me that, now we are aware of the legal status of our union, we should set about setting things to right immediately."

Her brother cleared his throat and made a noise of agreement. "He's right, Fen," he said, shaking his head. "Need to face up to it, girl. Ye've to face two divorces in as many days. Good thing our mother's not around to see these goings-on. But I suppose the fault's not really yours."

"Of course, I'll sign whatever paperwork you deem fit, my lord," she said dully.

"And—ah—perhaps you may see your way clear to—" Her brother coughed.

"Gilbert!" Fenella sat up in her chair in embarrassed horror. "You must not—!"

"He said himself we were due some reparation!" said her brother belligerently.

"There is no need for either of you to be concerned for Fenella's future," cut in Oswald.

"I suppose I'll take you back to Sitchmarsh Hall with me directly," grumbled her brother. "To keep house for me."

73

Fenella opened her mouth to reply, but again Oswald forestalled her. "That is quite out of the question, I'm afraid," he said firmly. Both of them turned to look at him in surprise. He looked Fenella square in the eye. "I will expect my wife to take her rightful place at my side."

Fen stared at this imposing stranger a moment and found words failed her. "My lord," she began in her most dignified voice. "You must realize that is *impossible*..."

"Why must I?" he asked, advancing into the room, and to her alarm, drawing a chair up next to hers.

"You mean, you actually want to take Fen to wife?" asked Gilbert incredulously.

He was ignored as Lord Vawdrey reached for her hand and took it in his. "Now, Fenella," he said in a calm, even voice. "There's really no need for you to lose your head over this."

"But—"

"You're getting yourself all tied up in knots over nothing," he said calmly, and placed a hand firmly on her knee, anchoring her to the seat when she would have jumped up. "This is an arrangement that will work to our mutual advantage," he carried on, and smiled at her.

It should have been a reassuring smile, she realized, quivering with alarm. But she didn't find it remotely reassuring. Here, in such close quarters, she could see Oswald Vawdrey up close and personal. Those cold, glittering eyes above the amiable smile. The hard muscle under his fitted doublet. Her every

74

nerve and instinct were screeching that he meant danger and was not to be trusted.

He stroked a thumb absently over her knee, and she almost shot off the chair in alarm. "Shh, I promise you won't regret our bargain," he continued in even tones which started to soothe her almost in spite of herself.

"Bargain?" she asked hoarsely. "I made no bargain. That was just our fathers, they—"

"No, no," he tutted. "The marriage bargain is between you and me, Fenella. You are my wife—" He broke off when she gave a murmur of distress. "Yes, that is settled now, you must resign yourself to the fact." He sounded, she thought, almost apologetic, but not quite. It was the oddest thing.

"But we needn't let the marriage inconvenience us in any way," he carried on matter-of-factly. "I have my position here at court to maintain, which takes a good deal of my time and energy. You have your—" He broke off for a moment, lost for words. "What is it you like to do?"

Fenella opened and closed her mouth. He waited patiently. For the life of her, she could think of nothing. Her mind had gone a perfect blank. When no answer was forthcoming, he carried on. "Your brother tells me you kept house for Thane very competently. Now you can do so for me. There will be little material change."

Little change? He must have seen the expression on her face, for he started up again at once. "You find that hard to believe? But it is true, I am very rarely to be found at Vawdrey Keep. It must be some…four or five years since I last went home."

75

Fenella stared at that. *Four or five years?*

He smiled wryly at her surprise. "You see? I will hardly be underfoot, disturbing your daily routine. You will only be a few miles from your childhood home. How many brides have that selfsame luxury? Your friends and neighbors will all remain the same. Your brother will be close at hand, and after all, Gilbert may marry one day," he said mildly. "With your own household, your position as head of it will be secure."

That was true enough. As an unmarried spinster dependent on her brother, her position was just as precarious as that of a divorced wife. She swallowed. Her head was reeling. Every word he uttered made sense. But how could she be contemplating such a thing? She fixed a look of pained intensity on her face. "But what about my things?"

"Things?"

She frowned. "My clothes. My…my books. My lute." She had come to a halt.

Oswald smiled at such a trivial concern. "It is my place to furnish your needs now," he pointed out.

"My father bought my lute."

"I am sure Gilbert can have it sent over to Vawdrey Keep waiting for you there," he said mildly.

She colored up at his tone. "Oh…of course. 'Tis only…"

"Yes?" He spoke a little sharper than he had heretofore, making her jump.

"I—I've considered Ambrose Thane to be my legally wedded husband for eight years, my lord," she started awkwardly. "It will take me some time—" Her face was turning crimson under his close regard. "To consider another man in that role…" Her words trailed off miserably. "To transfer my affections and loyalty so quickly…"

He gave a brief wave of his hand. "That will all happen in due course, I am sure."

"It will?" Her eyes fixed on him in pained regard.

He shrugged. "People remarry all the time, Fenella."

"Yes, but usually because they have been widowed. And your position is so much more elevated than Ambrose's was…" Her words tapered off desperately. "Will you not have many other requirements of your countess? Acting as hostess to all the dignitaries you need to entertain? I don't know the social etiquette around so many noble folk. I would not know where to even start!"

"Fenella," he said again, taking her hand in his. "You are my wife, and I will explain to the King that we are, in truth, married."

"I never intended for this to happen, my lord," she said wretchedly, staring down at their hands. "This must be a great inconvenience to you." She blinked rapidly in an effort to dissipate any gathering tears.

Oswald Vawdrey looked momentarily taken aback. "I see I shall have to be frank with you," he said, taking both her hands in his now. He pressed down lightly on her fingers. "It really isn't inconvenient, you know. In fact, quite the opposite. There are reasons why it will be expedient for me to be married at this point in time."

She held her breath, wondering what on earth could make it convenient for him to have a wife in existence. "It's complicated," he said, seeing the question in her eyes. "Court life is fraught with difficulties and political pitfalls."

"I see," she said when nothing else was forthcoming. Of course, she saw no such thing. Then a sudden thought struck her. "Are you engaged to another lady presently?" she blurted, then bit her lip.

"Certainly not," he answered shortly. "I haven't been engaged to anyone for years." *Well, that was something in any event.* Without even taking his eyes off her, he said in a louder, carrying voice, "I wonder if I could ask you to wait outside for us a moment, Gilbert. We will be with you shortly."

To her surprise she heard Gil's footfalls heading away from them and the sound of the door, but when she tried to turn her head to see, Oswald Vawdrey's hand flew to her jaw, keeping her face turned toward him.

"Are you persuaded, Fenella?" he asked quietly. "I assure you I will not be a demanding husband. You have nothing to fear from me on that score." Fenella sat immobile, surprised as much by his touch as the startling words. So, he was offering her a marriage in name only! She experienced a moment of light-headed relief and gulped, lowered her eyes, and nodded. "I'll need words to strike the bargain," he said gently.

"Aye, my lord," she said huskily, and could have sworn his green eyes gleamed.

"There's my good girl." He raised one of her hands and kissed it lightly on the backs of her fingers. And, for a moment, she could almost have imagined herself to be a foolish twelve-year-old again, for her head swam and she felt quite giddy.

The rest of the afternoon passed in a numbed blur of heartache and mortification. Lord Vawdrey and Gilbert had spent the best part of an hour poring over the marital document and discussing the terms and conditions that needed to be fulfilled.

Then the men had partaken of a meal of roast meats and ale. She'd not been able to eat more than a mouthful, though she'd made a great play with the napkin and sipping on her watered-down wine. The color in her cheeks ebbed and flowed as she thought of all the neighbors back home and what they'd say when Ambrose returned with a completely different wife in tow. And what would the servants think when she never returned?

Her throat ached, though whether with unshed tears or the beginning of a sore throat she could not say. At some point, she rose from her stupor to clutch Oswald's sleeve and tell him about her dog.

"My dear, that is no problem. We can simply have him sent to Vawdrey Keep. There's a whole pack of dogs there he can join," said Oswald easily.

"Send him to a strange house? Full of strangers?" she croaked. "No, no. I need him with me!" Her fingers tightened on his sleeve as she stared at him intently, trying to make him understand. For some reason, she felt like she was trying to run through fog. Her brain felt dull and stupid.

"No need to cry over a dog, Fen," said Gilbert, looking embarrassed. "Send him over to me at Sitchmarsh Hall if you don't trust Ambrose to look after the beast."

"I shall never trust Ambrose again," she said. "And I want my dog with me."

"There, there, poor thing's overwrought," said her brother with an uneasy laugh. "She's not usually so hysterical, my lord," he assured Lord Vawdrey.

Fen ignored him. "Bors can join me?" she asked. "Here?"

Lord Vawdrey gently removed her hand from his sleeve. "If those are your terms," he said. "Then, of course."

She sighed with relief and settled back into the chair. She felt so tired. Her eyelids felt like they were burning.

"She's about done in," remarked Gilbert.

"It's hardly surprising," replied Oswald Vawdrey. "I shall ring for Bryce to fetch her a blanket."

Fen must have dropped off, for the next thing she knew she felt a warm wool covering being draped around her shoulders. "Shh, go back to sleep," murmured Lord Vawdrey. She managed to focus her eyes on him for a second. *How strange,* she thought. *I really don't know what to make of this man.* And then she followed his advice and fell into a deep sleep.

8

Fenella woke with a start in the dark room. She gasped, clutching at the arms of the chair as she strove to remember just where she was. Then it all came flooding back to her. She blinked as her eyes accustomed themselves to the unfamiliar shadows of Lord Vawdrey's study crowding in on her. He'd forgotten her and left her alone. *Again.*

How ironic that the betrayal of her husband had sent her running into the company of the very first man who'd ever scorned her all those years ago! Her long-forgotten fiancé, Oswald Vawdrey. Just how much humiliation did the fates intend to heap on her this day? she wondered bitterly. And how cruel that Oswald Vawdrey was even more powerful and handsome at thirty-three than he'd ever been at nineteen. And she'd thought him the most glamorous and beautiful thing she'd ever seen in those days. She glanced around uneasily. Where was he? And where was Gilbert?

She slumped in her chair and rubbed her tired, gritty eyes. It had been a day and a half's ride to Aphrany. Now that the initial rush of anger and fear that had sent her thither had worn off, she felt exhausted. Her joints ached, but whether 'twas from the long ride or falling asleep in such an upright chair, she wasn't sure. Probably both. She wondered what her sister-in-law, Orla, was up to back at Thurrold, and if she was helping the alewife to soak the barley grain in the buttery, like *she* would be if she were home. Somehow, she doubted it. Langdon always said Orla was more of a hindrance than a help and made things twice as complicated as need be!

A burst of laughter and applause startled Fenella, making her turn in the chair to look back over her shoulder. A shaft of light was coming through the doorway at the far side of the room. Someone had left it open. She hesitated, wondering what she should do. She could hardly stay here, cringing in the dark, waiting for a man who had probably forgotten her very existence. Then again, she could hardly go prying and poking where she wasn't wanted. She sat frozen in indecision until she thought she heard a voice she recognized, making her turn her head sharply. Surely that was Ambrose!

She rose from her seat and crossed the floor seeking out the familiar voice among the general babble of conversation. When she reached the door, she peered around it nervously, but found the room empty. Then she realized her mistake. It wasn't a room at all, but a long gallery lined with paintings and lit sconces.

The sound of people was coming from the chamber below, which the gallery overlooked. Full of trepidation, she crept toward the balcony, holding her breath. Suddenly, there below her was a large reception room full of people. She blinked at all the rich colors and sounds of celebration, the vivid velvets, flashing jewels, and uproarious laughter. Like a nightmare, Fenella's feet felt rooted to the floor as she struggled to comprehend what she was seeing.

The merry gathering was drinking a toast with goblets upraised. They cheered and Fenella's gaze swept along the hubbub with a sense of impending dread until she found them. The subjects of the toast. The happy couple stood before the large stone fireplace with beaming faces and arms entwined. Fenella's eyes widened so far she thought they might pop out.

There was her husband, Ambrose, who she hadn't seen for two years, gazing fondly into the pretty face of her replacement. He didn't look much different, for all his affections had changed! Still a neat, tidy figure of middling height, his brown moustache tidily trimmed. He wore a feather-trimmed cap she'd never seen before and a burgundy tunic studded with pearls. The Ambrose she remembered had been frugal with his money and had certainly not worn adornments such as pearls on his clothing.

Still, today was his wedding day, she reminded herself with faint horror as she backed away from the parapet with shaky steps until she bumped her back against the gallery wall. Then she sank down until she was sat on her heels, clasping her knees. Tears streaked down her face. Ambrose was remarried. And so, to all intents and purposes, was she.

9

"Let's get you up, shall we?" murmured a voice close to Fenella's ear. She flinched and realized a candle was being set down on a refectory table, casting a soft golden light down around her. "Have you been here the whole time?"

It was Lord Vawdrey come back, she realized numbly. She glanced toward the door, but she was almost certain he did not come in that way. He had appeared like a specter. What did it matter now? She wiped her wet cheeks with the back of her hand. How long had she been crouched here? Her gaze flew to the balcony but there were no sounds of revelry coming from below now. Everyone had retired for the night long ago. Including Ambrose and his new wife.

She turned her swollen face away from him as he slid an arm around her waist and levered her up off the floor. "Ow!" she grimaced. He tightened his grip as she sagged against him, her feet numb with pins and needles.

"Are my floorboards not comfortable?" he asked so pleasantly she almost missed the mocking tone. "You have some objection to chairs?"

Fenella struggled to right herself, but he did not let up his grip on her one bit. If she wasn't so wrung out, she'd be mortified. "I need to go home," she sobbed softly. Even she knew this was nonsense. She had none now.

He squeezed her side. "And so, you shall," he said soothingly. "Presently."

Of course, he was just trying to comfort her with empty words. She had not meant Vawdrey Keep, a forbidding old stone fortress she had not visited since she was fifteen. "What will my poor Bors think," she wept nonsensically.

Lord Vawdrey had no answer to this, instead he picked up the candlestick and led her toward a tapestry covered in an intricate pattern of vines. He lifted the corner of this and rubbed his thumb along a piece of paneling. There was a light click and then a segment of the dark wood swung inward.

To her surprise, Fenella found herself being ushered into a small, dark cupboard. Was this what Lord Vawdrey did with unwanted wives? Bundled them into cupboards? But no, she was mistaken, for he was still with her, one arm wrapped around her, clamping her to his side. Fenella had no sooner noted that it was draughty in the cupboard than she realized she was being swept along a dusty confined passageway.

After a while, she gave up trying to even comprehend what was happening. Her eyes drifted shut and she allowed herself to be propelled along by the strong, tall man at her side. He seemed to have no problem pushing and pulling her this way and that, and she was so exhausted, both physically and mentally by this point, that she could barely think of a reason why he shouldn't.

Finally, they came to a halt, and he extracted a key from around his neck. Unlocking the door, he turned back to her and placed a finger to his lips in a gesture of silence. Fenella found herself nodding and then he took her hand, locked the door behind them, and led her into a bedchamber where he set down the candle.

"Come, let's take this off you," he said, pulling her toward him and deftly unlacing her dress. Fenella sucked in a breath to object, but he forestalled her. "It's too late to summon a maid now," he said reasonably. "And you're dead on your feet. Come now, we will leave you in your shift, so all is decent."

Fenella's mind reeled. *Decent?* Her conscience tried to tell her this was extremely indecent, but her brain was too sleep-deprived to comprehend it. She opened her mouth to try to vocalize this sentiment, but he forestalled her.

"All will be well," he said reassuringly. "Things will look very different in the morn. Come now. Arms up." He yanked her dress up and over her head, and Fenella blinked up at him in sleepy confusion, swaying on her feet. He cleared his throat. "Into the bed."

Fenella glanced over her shoulder at the huge bed. This was a very large bedchamber, she thought as she tottered toward it. Who on earth could have a guest room this big? Then she remembered vaguely that it was a royal palace after all. She heard a light curse behind her as she fumbled for the sheets.

Suddenly they were stripped back, and she was scooped up and unceremoniously dumped onto the mattress. She blinked up at him as he tucked her in and murmured something under his breath. She tried to catch it, but her thought processes were shutting down and she had no chance.

Some of his dark hair fell forward across his face, distracting her. It made him suddenly look like that handsome boy he had been. She smiled sadly at the memory which could still sting, and then rolled onto her side, her burning eyes squeezed shut as the oblivion of sleep claimed her. She was so tired that she didn't even wake a few moments later when the bed dipped, and he joined her under the covers.

10

Fenella woke with a gasp. Her dreams had been disturbing, but it was a shock to be wakened from them by the sound of shattering pottery. She peered into the morning light to see a servant hovering by the door with a scandalized look on his face.

"Meldon, for the lord's sake," groaned a voice by her ear, startling her anew. She whipped her face round to find a head beside hers on the pillow. It was Lord Vawdrey's, she realized with horror. And the entire length of his body was pressed intimately against her back. And he was naked.

She froze as she felt the press of his flesh against her backside. If she didn't know any better, she would think he was aroused. Very aroused. She opened her mouth to scream, but then remembered he was her wedded husband. How on earth had this happened to her? Mercifully, her shift was still intact, assuring her that nothing untoward had happened, but still, she was mortified.

"Milord!" said the servant reproachfully as he stooped down to retrieve the shards of the water basin. "I never expected this from the likes of you!"

"Watch your tongue, Meldon," Oswald responded groggily. He rolled gingerly onto his back and Fenella breathed a sigh of relief. "This is your mistress," he said thickly. "Not some doxy."
Both Fenella and Meldon gasped at this pronouncement.

"Mistress?" echoed Meldon, screwing up his eyes.

"Doxy?" cried Fenella in dismay.

Oswald's eyes flickered open again. "You're focusing on the wrong thing, Fenella," he said with a trace of humor in his voice. Was he laughing at her? Fenella caught the sheets up to her chin, staring at him in bewilderment.

"Ye mean to say you're legally wed to this lass?" demanded the servant suspiciously.

"I do," he answered. "Now leave the water and go."

"Humph! A likely tale!" The servant stalked out of the room belligerently and slammed the door after him.

"You must excuse Meldon," said Oswald, his eyes still shut. "He's been with the family since his infancy, many moons ago. It gives him the right to be abominably rude." Fenella stared at him.

His eyes flickered open again and roamed over her face. "Fenella?"

"I—what—?" Fenella broke off helplessly.

"I did say things would look differently in the morn." *Differently from the viewpoint of his bed?* wondered Fenella incredulously. Oswald propped himself up on one elbow. She wished his hair wouldn't fall forward like that. "You're shocked." He sighed. "But after all, you are my wife," he reminded her. Fenella inched slowly away from him. He reached out and grabbed the bedsheet, halting her progress. Fenella's eyes grew wide. "Where are you going?" he asked politely.

"I—I hardly know." She gulped. "Wh-where is your smock?"

"Smock?" He looked flummoxed. "Er, they're all being washed," he said after a moment's hesitation. Fenella had a horrible suspicion he was lying. Ambrose had *always* worn a smock to bed. And a nightcap without fail. She tried hard not to feel scandalized and failed.

"Let me get you some water," he said, sliding out from the other side of the bed. Fenella averted her astonished eyes from his naked body. To her surprise, he had a very nasty scar running from one shoulder blade to his middle back. It was deep and wicked looking and had left the recovered skin purpled and churned up along its curved route.

Despite the evil scarring, his tall body was a thing of beauty with strong, lean, well-muscled limbs. Somehow Ambrose had never looked that naked. Maybe because he was so much shorter. And less muscular. She shied away from any other comparisons. Mostly because they'd be vastly indelicate.

Fenella slumped back against the pillows and squeezed her eyes shut. A rustle of fabric on the other side of the bed led her to hope he was getting dressed.

"Here." The voice by her side made her jump. He was disturbingly light on his feet for such a large male. She opened her eyes and found him resplendent in a scarlet satin dressing robe. The sleeves were decorated in a dazzling gold pattern. It must have taken the embroiderer hours and cost a fortune.

It was somehow even more startling to see Oswald Vawdrey in red satin than naked. In her memories, he had only ever dressed in conservative black. And then there was the fact she knew he was naked beneath it. She took the glass of water he offered and gulped it down, her throat feeling dry and raspy.

To her horror, he sat down on the bed next to her. It took every ounce of self-control for her not to cringe away from him or cower under the covers. Instead, she handed the empty glass back to him like an obedient child, and he placed it on a carved wooden chest next to the bed.

"Fenella, I want you to know I'm a reasonable man," he said with a charming smile that somehow chilled her to the bone. "I understand you are not entirely to blame for the fact you have been living bigamously with another man for the past eight years, and I'm willing to overlook this lapse of judgment."

Fenella drew in a shaky breath and stared up at him. "Lapse of—?"
He held up one hand, halting her. "Let us not waste time with recriminations," he said easily. "Instead, let us forge together a union that will be mutually beneficial and provide for our future."

Fenella could not think of a single word to say to him. Not one word. Instead she clutched the bedsheets even tighter. To her consternation, her silence didn't seem to bother him one whit.

"I'm aware that the last twenty-four hours must have been somewhat *wearing* for you, but I have every confidence that you will rise to the occasion and prove yourself an admirable ally," he continued smoothly.

Ally? Fenella shook her head to try to dispel the fog that surrounded her. "Wh-what kind of union?" she managed to croak. He looked surprised for the first time that morning. "You said we should forge a union?" she continued, feeling foolish beyond belief.

"I was speaking of our marriage," he explained calmly.

Once again Fenella was plunged into terrified confusion. "But—but…"

He sighed. "Fenella. We are married. You need to adjust. Sadly, there is no time for you to do this, so I must ask you to place your faith in me, and trust that I will see you right."

Trust and faith. Fenella's eyes filled with tears of despair. "I'm afraid I have very few reserves left of either of those traits, my lord," she said in a wobbly voice. "You see…"

"I'm well aware of your circumstances," he cut in. "However, I am not Ambrose Thane."
Fenella jerked as if she had been slapped. There was a moment's silence, and then she felt his hand cover hers on the blanket. She blushed violently, feeling his warm skin on hers for the second time that morning.

"Forgive me, Fenella, that was uncalled for," he muttered in a low voice. "It seems I am not entirely reasonable after all." He sounded rueful, and when she raised her eyes to meet his, he gave her a reassuring smile. "I am not really so bad as I appear to you right now. You will not find me an exacting husband, I assure you. I will expect us to lead our own lives, yet to always show every consideration for the other. I will make no unreasonable demands on your time. I can provide for you every comfort to which you have been accustomed and more."

93

Lord Vawdrey's voice ebbed and flowed as he outlined his extensive properties, his wealth, and his titles, all of which—astonishingly—it seemed he intended to share with her. Gradually, however fantastical a notion it seemed, it dawned on Fenella that he truly did consider their future paths to be intertwined.

She reached up periodically to wipe her wet cheeks dry as his voice carried on in a measured tone. To her confused mind, it seemed he deftly rewrote their history together and obliterated Ambrose Thane from its pages altogether. According to him, they had been married for the last fourteen years. She was a countess, *his* countess, and her place was at his side. It was so bizarre that she started to feel quite feverish.

"Fenella," he said suddenly after a few moments. "Have you heard one word I have said?"

"I'm barren," she said heavily, surprising them both. It was a dark thought, one she had never before spoken aloud. But the fact remained that in eight years, she had not produced one child.

He did not even miss a beat. "My brother has issue. I have a godson and nephew. It is enough for me." He paused again. "What else?"

What else? Fenella swallowed and tried to focus on the important things. "I want my dog," she said, raising her chin.

This did seem to give him pause. "Ah, yes. You mentioned this yesterday. Where is it?"

"He's at Thurrold."

"Thane's seat?" he asked. She nodded. "Description?"

Fenella thought a moment. Something told her that words like *endearing* and *like an adorable bear* would not impress Oswald Vawdrey, who was now looking very intent and business-like, despite his astonishing attire. "Black. Large. Old. Answers to Bors."

He nodded. "He will be here by daybreak tomorrow."

Daybreak? "But what if…"

"Daybreak tomorrow," he repeated with a faint smile.

"Thank you."

He looked wryly amused. "You're welcome," he said, his glance wandering down from her face to flicker over her. Fenella cleared her throat and dragged the sheets around her a little tighter. Surely he couldn't see anything? "I'm prepared to be patient, Fenella," he said rather huskily. "You have no need to be afraid of me. I'm your husband. It's my duty to take care of you from this point. Anything you need, you come to me. Am I understood?"

She nodded, at a loss for words. "Good," he said. "Now get dressed. I need to take you with me to meet the King with all haste."

"The King?" she repeated in some dismay.

"Yes. King Wymer needs to be informed immediately. His inner circle is not permitted to marry without his consent."

95

Fenella's eyes widened. "Will he be angry?" she blurted in some alarm.

Oswald tipped his head to one side. "He will not be pleased, but as our marriage took place years before I was a member of court, I do not think he can realistically hold it against us." He reached for the chest of drawers next to his bed and opened the top drawer. "These papers are the proof of our marriage contract. I think it would be better if I told the King you brought them with you to court as leverage." He dropped them on the bed next to her.

Fenella looked down at the sealing wax and spotted her family bear and the Vawdrey panther. She glanced up at his face, but his expression was inscrutable. "Should I bring them with me?" she asked in surprise.

"Wymer may ask to see them," admitted Oswald, and she felt another twinge of alarm at the royal reaction to their marriage. He stood up. "I'll send in fresh water for you to wash and dress."

She swallowed and nodded. "Yes, my lord."

"Fenella," he said softly. "I'm sure I don't need to explain to you the significance of you spending last night in our marital bed." Her gaze darted to meet his, stunned. "If the King should ask, I know I can trust to your discretion."

Fenella watched him as he left the room, her startled brain wondering what on earth he meant by that! The grumpy manservant knocked loudly on the door moments later and then brought her fresh water. He murmured something that sounded

96

like "milady" as he set down the basin of warm water, so he must have accepted the truth of his master's claims at any rate.

She washed and dressed quickly, lamenting that all she had was her mustard dress, which looked all the worse for being traveled in yesterday. In truth, it had never been a handsome garment. Now it looked positively frightful. She speedily braided her thick dark hair into a single braid and tossed it over her shoulder as she mourned the fact she had no head veil with her.

In her haste yesterday, her cloak hood had sufficed. Today was an altogether different matter. It was unlikely that Lord Vawdrey would have such a thing lying around, she thought sadly, and resisted the urge to peek in one of his large chests.

She wondered if half of it might be taken up with midnight black and the other half with surprisingly colorful dressing robes. Oswald Vawdrey was a man of secrets and surprises. Squaring her shoulders, she marched out of the bedroom and into the wood-paneled adjoining room, which seemed to be a communal area with a fireplace, large window, and dining table.

Oswald was seated in his scarlet robe in the window seat, slicing a pear with a small fruit knife. "Meldon will be in with breakfast presently," he said, looking up briefly. She hesitated a moment, and then sat down at the table where she found a jug of ale and a jug of water.

Helping herself to a cup of water, she tried not to stare at Oswald Vawdrey, who looked almost extraordinarily exotic to her. It boggled her mind to think that she could be expected to get used to such a display of masculine beauty every morning.

"Um, where is Gilbert?" she asked after taking a sip. "I don't really remember him leaving yester'een..."

"You fell asleep and he left after dinner," said Oswald. "His reasoning was he could be home by midday tomorrow with very little bother."

The door slammed and in stumped Meldon carrying a tray of pickled herring, smoked anchovies, a round white loaf, and a dish of butter. "Those palace kitchens will be the death of me," he complained as he rattled the dishes down on the table. "That bloody manservant of Lord Bardulf's insisting his master has the best pandemain for his morning 'sop in wine.' I ask you!" He looked from Lord Vawdrey, who made no response, to Fenella and stuck his chin out aggressively.

She cleared her throat. "It certainly sounds foolish to use the finest bread if all you intend to do with it is soak it in wine," she conceded.

"Exactly what I says to him! And do you know how he answered?" Fenella shook her head. "Says his master is *accustomed to the best*, if it please you!"

"I expect he probably is," said Lord Vawdrey. Meldon clicked his tongue in annoyance.

"It must be a very strange setup if all the personal servants apply to the palace kitchens for their master's meals," puzzled Fenella. "How do the palace kitchen staff cope with such demand?"

"The majority of courtiers will eat in the main hall," responded Lord Vawdrey, taking the seat next to hers.

"I see," she said, feeling foolish. Of course. The Vawdreys were important enough to dine in their own chambers. She wondered briefly about her own kitchens at Thurrold. This week she had planned to order the pear trees stripped in the orchard and taken to the kitchens to be preserved in honey. Then, she remembered with a pang that this was no longer her concern. Thurrold had a new mistress now.

The rattle of a plate set down before her brought her out of her reverie. Lord Vawdrey had sliced her some of the bread himself. "Will you take some fish?" he asked her politely. "You will need your strength," he reminded her with a glimmer of a smile. "To face our monarch."

Any inclination to smile withered on her lips at the mention of King Wymer. "I haven't got a head covering," she worried aloud as Meldon carried in her ankle boots, which looked a lot cleaner than when she'd last seen them. "Oh, thank you. They look much better."

"I'll need to take a dry brush to your hem and all," he said disapprovingly. "It's looking in as much of a state as your boots were!"

"Meldon," said Lord Vawdrey mildly.
"I'm afraid he's quite right," said Fenella, biting her lip. "This dress really isn't fit to be seen in. Especially not by the King."

"Eat your breakfast," Lord Vawdrey told her, tucking into his own.

Fenella sighed and did as she was told. Her head was still swimming and ached, but if it was the onset of a cold, then you were supposed to feed a cold after all. She couldn't afford to get ill. Not now she had to fend for herself in a strange place. She couldn't really taste the food, but she managed to eat a slice of bread and butter.

The only indication Lord Vawdrey gave that he'd paid any attention to her was just before they left his rooms. Meldon was sat kneeling at her feet scrubbing her hem with a dry brush when Oswald stepped back in the room holding a rectangle of white linen. "Will this do?" he asked, passing it to her.

"Oh yes, thank you." She shook it out and then wrapped it around her head. Without any pins or brooches, the most she could do was a few very simplistic passes before securing it with a knot behind her braid. She then looped her thick braid so it tucked neatly under the linen instead of hanging down to her waist. "How does that look?" she asked, feeling slightly self-conscious under the scrutiny of both Lord Vawdrey and his manservant.

"Very wifely," said Lord Vawdrey with an encouraging smile. He held his hand out to her, and she rose wondering if that was a nice way of saying matronly or frumpy. Unbidden, an image in her head rose of Ambrose's new bride.

She hadn't had the best view of her the night before, but she'd been young and slim. Her blond hair had been caught up in a horned headdress that was no doubt the height of fashion. A comparison between them right now would be laughable, she thought. The cast-off dumpy wife and the young, pretty bride in all her finery. She hoped no one would be cruel enough to remark on it. Her emotions felt raw and bruised.

It was perhaps not surprising that Fenella was a quaking bag of nerves by the time she was swept along the royal corridor to the outer chamber of the King's state bedroom. Her new—*or was it old*—husband saw her seated by the fire, and then left her there with a bunch of strangers while he breezed on into the inner sanctum.

The guards fell back at once to admit him, reminding Fenella uneasily that Oswald Vawdrey was a very important person indeed in royal circles. She stared down at the hem of her woolen dress and tried not to fret about the darker patches from where Meldon had brushed away yesterday's dried mud. She felt acutely aware of the fact she wore no adornment, and yet every other person in the room was decked out in jewels, velvets, and furs and hats dripping with feathers.

She smiled glassily in the direction of the curious onlookers and tried not to worry about the fact that no one would actually meet her gaze. They didn't even know who she was yet, she told herself, trying to check her own rising panic. Maybe it was because everyone else waiting for an audience was male, she thought, staring at her ankle boots. Meldon had polished the scuffs from them without even a grumble, although he had kept a beady side-eye on her the whole time.

She wondered why there were no other women waiting to see the King. The truth was, she was ill prepared to be presented at court. This had been a crazy idea, and she had been out of her mind to have even thought of it. She certainly had not a clue how it would turn out. Which was just as well, or she never would have dared to set one foot outside of Thurrold Manor. No one could have anticipated that she would end up married to a completely different man before daybreak!

She shivered in spite of the proximity of the fire. Perhaps this was all just a bad dream, and she would wake up any moment now in her four-poster bed at Thurrold with Bors lying at her feet and a piece of half-eaten cheese on the nightstand.

The door opened and a guard from inside stepped out. "The King requests the presence of Lady Fenella Vawdrey," his voice rang out.

A low murmur started through the room as Fenella forced herself to stand, instead of sinking down in the chair in mortification. The ten or so steps across the room were some of the most torturous Fenella had ever taken as she forced herself not to trip or run and look like a fool.

The guard stood aside to make room for her, and she slipped into the vast room, her gaze darting about until she saw the tall figure in black that she recognized. Lord Vawdrey was stood over by a window with a stocky man of medium height with tow-colored hair who was dressed in a royal blue robe and had a look of peevish indignation on his face. "Approach, approach," he said testily. "Let's have a look at this troublesome female who dares to overset my plans!"

Fenella felt her face flush and looked to Lord Vawdrey for guidance.

"Come, Fenella, and meet your King," said Oswald, holding out a hand to her. She scuttled to his side, her face turning a dull red of embarrassment.

"Aye, you may well blush," scolded the King as she sank into a hasty curtsey. "I've heard of your ill-advised deeds of yesterday!"

Fenella gulped and forced herself not to glance at Oswald as he took her hand in a reassuring grip. "Your Majesty," he murmured in slight reproach. "As I explained, the documentation is beyond doubt…"

"Pshaw!" burst out the King in high dudgeon. "If you weren't such a stickler for decorum Vawdrey, we'd have faced this out between us! But now, you've let this woman work her wiles on you and you're well and truly leg-shackled!"

Fenella stood frozen to the spot, not knowing what to say. The King was clearly in an ill temper.
"What did you do, get him drunk?" The King squinted at her balefully. "He'd never have fallen for such a ruse if he'd been in possession of his faculties."

Fenella's mouth fell open, but before she could even speak the King had turned back to Oswald. "It's well known you've no head for alcohol, Vawdrey," he tutted. "And it's not natural to live like a monk for as long as you have. Only told you the other day. It's a sure way to fall prey to unscrupulous females! I knew something was wrong when you didn't turn up to supper. I wish now I'd sent an armed guard to escort you!"

Fenella did not dare to turn her head to look at Lord Vawdrey as he muttered some noncommittal reply.

"One of your household no doubt gave her admittance to your bedchamber," carried on the King grouchily. "You should beat your manservants soundly. Teach 'em all a lesson."

Fenella didn't even hear the reply Oswald made to this. She had just noticed there were a few other shadowy figures in the room

103

who were witness to the entire humiliating spectacle. Strangely enough, one of them was an old woman with a face like a sheep and a fussy headdress. Fen wondered if this was the foreign queen everyone spoke of.

"Well, you're a more forgiving man than me!" harrumphed the King. "That's all I can say, Vawdrey!" He turned back to Fenella and inspected her from head to toe. "Humph!" he snorted in disgust. "I daresay you're vastly proud of yourself, madam! But you'll find there's more to being a countess than bedding an earl!"

Fenella just about managed to bite back her gasp of dismay. Her face flamed as the King made a dismissive gesture with his hand. "Get her out of my sight," he said. "Damn dismal start to the morn!"

"Of course, sire," said Oswald Vawdrey, and she felt his hand at her waist, guiding her tottering steps from the room. When they reached the outer chamber, she held her head high and faced straight ahead. Even then, she could hear the excited whispers around her.

The cool rush of air as they exited the King's apartments back into the corridor told her it was safe to draw a shaky breath. Her head was spinning. The King seemed to think she had seduced her way back into Lord Vawdrey's life! There could be no other explanation of his words. When she stumbled on an uneven flagstone, Oswald Vawdrey's grip on her righted her at once.

"Well, that went most satisfactorily," he murmured. Fenella's feet stopped walking, though he carried her a few steps on his own momentum. "Fenella?" He turned back to her.

"Satisfactorily?" she echoed. She took a deep breath. "My lord, the King did not seem *at all* pleased!"

"He'll be fine presently," he assured her with a slight smile. "You'll soon become familiar with his ways."

Fenella thought she would be hard-pressed to think of anything she would like less. "I find that difficult to believe," she responded stiffly. "He seemed to take a strong disliking of me. He called me an 'unscrupulous female,'" she pointed out indignantly.

"Fenella, if he had taken a strong disliking, you would be in the dungeons right now," he answered dryly. "He'll soon recover his spirits, when he's found a new sacrificial lamb."

Fenella stared a moment, and then allowed him to pull her forward into a measured step by his side. "I scarcely ever know what you're referring to, my lord," she admitted hopelessly. "Do you mean to take me into your confidences?"

"Good lord no," he said lightly. "I don't think that will be at all necessary."

Fenella swallowed hard. It was most disconcerting, but sometimes his words felt like a slap to the face. "I...I find myself quite at a loss around you," she confessed. "I don't know how to act or even what to say."

"You will soon become accustomed to me, Fenella," he assured her. "I am sure we will deal admirably together."

Fenella was not so sure. "There were other people in the King's chamber just now," she said awkwardly after a moment's pause.

"Yes," agreed Oswald. "After all, the King is very rarely alone."

"They must have overheard every word!" fretted Fenella. "I do hope no one will speak of it."

Lord Vawdrey's eyebrows rose at this. "You have not been much at court, have you, Fenella?" he asked with a twist of his lips.

"Only once when I was presented," she agreed. "But I did not see the King in close quarters then. He seemed taller. And a good deal more benevolent."

"We all have good days and bad days," said Oswald Vawdrey enigmatically. For a moment, she almost thought he would laugh at her.

She could not read him at all, she thought despairingly, and gave up even trying. "Who was that lady in the headdress?" she asked instead. "Was that the Queen?"

"The Queen?" he repeated with a short laugh. "Dear me, no. The King would never admit Armenal until noon. That was his old nurse, Bathilde."

"His nurse?"

"She is the only person permitted to wake him every morn."

Fenella digested this astonishing piece of information, and then asked in a small voice, "What will happen now?"

"Now?"

"Will you take me to Vawdrey Keep?" she asked hopefully, thinking of the old Vawdrey seat, which bordered her own late father's estate. It was deep in the countryside, and she could hide herself there and try to recover her wits.

"In good time," he said airily. "We must establish you here at court first."

Fenella felt a tremor of misgiving. Just what did that entail? "But not while I am in disgrace with the King, surely?"

"It would be better to get your social debut over with at once, don't you agree?"

Fenella eyed him doubtfully. "What if the King calls me shameless again?"

"Did he call you shameless?"

"He implied I got you drunk," she pointed out with as much dignity as her tattered pride had left. *And you did not contradict him*, she thought but did not quite have the nerve to say aloud.

"Is it really the King you're nervous of meeting again socially?" Oswald asked her abruptly. "Or someone else?"

Fenella felt her color rising. Lord Vawdrey was both silent and still, but somehow radiated displeasure. "I confess I do not like unpleasantness," she answered, avoiding his gaze. "Is that so wrong? After all, there is only so much humiliation a person can take in one week."

"So, it is Sir Ambrose Thane and his new bride who you do not wish to see abroad?" Again, his words were mostly toneless, but she could still pick up on the fact he was not pleased by her avoidance.

"After all, my lord, I was married to him for eight years and…"

"This documentation says otherwise," he said, sounding bored and tapping the wad of paperwork against his thigh. Fenella stared at the rolled-up parchment. She had been holding that in the King's room. She hadn't even noticed that he had taken it back off her!

"If you were a *sensible* woman," he said, "you would seize this opportunity to save face." Fenella felt the barb sink into her tender flesh, and it stung. Regardless, he continued in his measured, even voice. "Few wives so publicly cast off are given means and opportunity to restore their stock in one fell swoop."

Fenella's lip trembled. He had been kind to her all those years ago, perhaps a little indifferent, but certainly not cruel. But on this gray, drizzly October morn, she realized he did not have one whit of genuine empathy for her predicament. "Perhaps you're right," he said, capturing her dipping chin and tilting her face to the window so he could watch the tear tracking down her cheek. "And it is too soon." He clicked his tongue. "A pity."

Fenella flinched, but his tight grip on her didn't allow her to back up from him. He leaned down so his mouth was by her ear. "Unless you want everyone here to think you are in utter disgrace with me, you will need to walk now beside me with some modicum of calm."

Fenella's eyes darted left and right and took in the figures lurking around the corners. The servants darted out in the pursuit of their errands, their gazes fixed on her. The courtier in the navy doublet, who materialized from behind a curtain in a window seat, gave a dry cough before continuing on his way. She hadn't even realized they were there.

"Now walk," murmured Lord Vawdrey. His breath tickled her neck, making her shiver. "I'll escort you back to our rooms where you can wallow in as much misery as you like, *in private.*"
Fen tried, she really did, not to let the tears spill over, but alas, during the walk back to the west wing, they fell from her eyes in a continuous, humiliating stream.

Her head ached. Her throat ached. *Her heart ached.* She managed to put one foot in front of the other and to keep her head held up, but that effort exhausted her, and by the time Oswald threw back the door and propelled her inside, she was fit to sink to the floor.

Oswald closed the door shut behind them and called for his servant. "Light the fire for Lady Vawdrey," he said when Meldon stumped in, drying his hands on a piece of linen. "She wishes to spend the day barricaded up in here. In seclusion."

Fenella dropped into a seat, feeling drained of all energy. Lord Vawdrey's displeasure with her was clear to see. Indeed, it must have been evident to everyone who saw him marching her through the palace. Unfortunately, she had been only too aware of the staring courtiers and the whispering behind hands. Her face was as red as a beet by the time they reached his rooms.

"Is that right?" grunted Meldon. "I got other errands to run, you know! Can't be expected to hang around here all day, waiting hand and foot on this one!"

"Well, it is unfortunate you feel that way, Meldon, as that is precisely what I expect you to do," answered Oswald crisply. "You are to admit no visitors."

"Where you going to be?" demanded his manservant, belligerent as ever.

Oswald turned to him with a frown. "I will be in my study in the main wing, as usual."
The door shut carefully behind him. Somehow, Fen had the oddest notion that he would rather have slammed it.

"Well, that didn't last long," sniffed Meldon. "The rosy glow worn off already?"
Fenella burst into noisy tears. "Now, now," rasped Meldon hastily. "None of that, my girl!"

Fenella rose shakily from her chair. "Do not trouble to light the fire in here," she said, mustering her dignity with effort. "I'm feeling unwell and will return to bed for an hour or so."

"Humph!"

She heard him mutter under his breath, along with something about "fine ladies lying abed all hours." Ignoring this, she dragged her heavy body back into Lord Vawdrey's bedchamber, and after struggling a moment with her lacings, gave up and crawled under the covers fully clothed. She felt so cold that the idea of stripping down to her shift was abhorrent anyway.

She felt like she'd never get warm again. Wrapping her arms about herself, she lay shivering under the bedclothes and prayed for the oblivion of sleep where nothing hurt, including words, and her poor overtaxed emotions could have some respite.

11

Oswald scored through another line of script before casting his pen down in frustration. He could not concentrate. Every time he tried to get down to work, he kept remembering Fenella Bernard with tears silently rolling down her face. He had no idea why it was bothering him so much; except he didn't usually let his own manners slip like that.

Normally they were firmly in place, disguising every emotion to the onlooker. Oswald knew full well that he was often callous, unsympathetic, even ruthless when occasion demanded. But he scrupulously said the appropriate thing out loud and wore the corresponding expression.

He was, first and foremost, a politician. Wearing a mask was second nature to him. Why then, had he just marched his day-old bride through the palace and thrown her into his rooms like they were a dungeon cell? He groaned and massaged his eyelids with his finger and thumb. He had acted like a complete ogre of a husband. And he really had no idea why! It just wasn't like him to react like that.

His scheme had been going so well. Wymer had been well and truly thwarted. The King had conceded he was defeated by Oswald's trump card, Fenella. He had even accepted the intimation that, in a moment of weakness, the marriage had been consummated! And then…what?

He frowned, trying to remember exactly where it had all gone awry. Fenella had balked at the idea of being paraded before the court, and more specifically, her recently wedded husband, Thane, and his replacement bride. *And why wouldn't she?* he asked himself uneasily. It was too soon.

He had rushed her into wearing his colors when he should have been insinuating himself into her life by degrees as a person who could be trusted and relied on. He had acted like—what? *Hardly a jealous husband.* He shied away from such a ridiculous idea. He could barely remember the little Bernard girl his father had betrothed him to all those years ago.

Unbidden, a fully-fledged vision of his past assailed him, called up from some dark recess in his mind. A vision of Lady Fenella Thane. Nay, not Thane then, but Bernard. Lady Fenella Bernard. She was much younger and wearing a dark green velvet dress with a small necklet of pearls.

He held her unwavering attention as he made polite conversation over a meal. Not just any meal, but a feast; the Winter Solstice. And finally, he remembered clearly his very first betrothed. *He had all but forgotten.* After all, he had only been nineteen and slightly embarrassed to have such a young betrothed on his arm.

He had long become immune to his father's jibes and insults, knowing full well that he was his least favorite son. In truth, at nineteen he wore this as a badge of honor. He considered his father to be a boorish lout. Still, appearing in front of a packed great hall, with a child for his future wife, had not been something he had been looking forward to.

She had been a plain, solemn little thing, afraid of his father and shy. But she had taken her place by his side, and when Baron Vawdrey had asked, mockingly in his great booming voice, if she did not count herself fortunate to have such a "fine peacock of a boy" for her future husband, she had answered him with a loud, unflinching "Yes, very" that had rung from the rafters.

113

The guests had guffawed, and his father had roared with laughter. But under the table, a little hand had slipped into his, and Oswald had realized that Fenella Bernard was his indomitable ally. He swore now, as the years rolled back, and he became aware of how badly he had failed her.

"Bryce!" he shouted and heard a chair scrape back against the floorboards in the next room. He waited as he heard his assistant's feet pad across the floor and then the door creak open.

"My lord?"

"I've just realized that I may have neglected to inform you of my marriage."

Bryce blinked. "My lord?"

"Fenella Thane that was, is now Fenella, Countess Vawdrey."

Bryce rocked back on his heels. "But when?"

"Fourteen years ago," said Oswald briefly. "Her marriage to Thane was not legal." Bryce's jaw dropped. "So, now you are caught up," he said breezily. "I need you to engage my tailor. Have him attend Lady Vawdrey at his earliest convenience."

Bryce gulped. "I do not believe signor Pezzini usually attends to ladies."

"He will, if the purse is fat enough," replied Oswald. "She needs a full array of clothes. I also need you to make enquiries about new shoes and"—he waved a hand—"trinkets?" He looked questioningly at Bryce.

"Err…female adornments?" Bryce suggested, watching Oswald's rotating hand. "Erm…hair pins, belts, cauls, gloves and the like?"

Oswald nodded, looking relieved. "Yes, yes, all of the attendant paraphernalia… What else?"

Bryce tapped his chin. "A harp?" he guessed desperately.

Oswald looked undecided. "I believe she said she plays a lute."

"A horse?" suggested Bryce. "Perhaps a hawk?"

"She has a hound already," said Oswald dismissively. "And a horse. Her brother left it stabled here."
"Needles and silken threads?"

"I seem to recall—perhaps tapestry?" hazarded Oswald. "Or, at any rate, as a girl she was fond of it, I believe." The memory was hazy, but there. Twelve-year-old Fenella had spoken of tapestry, and her eyes had shone. It was strange how vivid the flashes of memory were when they returned to him. His memory did not usually play hide-and-seek with him.

"Books?" hazarded Bryce. "Devotional books, prayer books?"

"Poetry is more fashionable for ladies at court, Bryce," Oswald corrected him. Bryce looked disapproving and folded his lips.

Oswald's eyebrows rose. "Moralizing again, Bryce? You forget the Queen is fond of poetry. Order Fenella a few volumes of whatever is popular at present."

"Yes, my lord," muttered Bryce.

"Bryce, you are forgetting jewelry."

"You wish to see a jeweler, my lord?"

"I do not," said Oswald firmly. "Just get her two of everything."

"Everything?" asked Bryce, looking out of his depth.

"Brooches, rings, necklaces, you know the sort of thing."

Bryce floundered a moment. "Not really, my lord," he admitted.

"Confound it, Bryce," said Oswald without heat. "Have the jeweler attend Lady Vawdrey with some samples of his wares."

"You have a particular jeweler in mind?"

Oswald shrugged. "Aphrany's best."

"Very well, my lord."

"Have we forgotten anything?"

"Undoubtedly, sir."

"I'm inclined to agree with you," admitted Oswald. "No matter, at least we've made a start. We can remedy any oversights later."

"My lord?" asked Bryce in bewilderment as Oswald locked his drawer and stood up from his chair. "Are you attending the King this afternoon?"

Oswald shook his head. "I'm going back to my quarters," he said. "I have a new wife to pacify."

It was a pity, Oswald thought on his way back, that he had no clear vision of how he would actually achieve this. The problem was that he had rushed her. He had not wanted to bother with wooing or any of the other rituals people went through when selecting a spouse. He still didn't, but he would have to make some concessions.

It wouldn't kill him to take her to a few of the palace entertainments and introduce her around. Also, he admitted to himself with unease, letting the King think she had coerced him into accepting the veracity of their marriage had not been chivalrous of him. He was not sure how he could set about righting that wrong. After all, he had only instigated their marriage as a means to an end, but that did not mean he should be inconsiderate of her feelings.

The King, no doubt, would be vocal with his displeasure and others would pick up the tale, which could be humiliating for Fenella. He frowned over this a moment, before deciding the best way to counter the court gossip would simply be for them to show themselves abroad as an amicable wedded couple. After all, reflected Oswald, how hard could that be? People married all the time. Many stupider men than he managed to maintain functioning marriages.

117

Thane was an insignificant, mediocre little man. The fact he had inspired such strong feelings in Fenella was a good thing, he told himself. It was a sign that she was worth cultivating. In time, with encouragement, she would transfer her loyalty to him and then all would be well. He just had to ease her over this rough patch while she adjusted to the changes in her life.

His steps felt lighter once he'd decided on his course of action and he entered his rooms feeling positive. It was an unwelcome surprise to find the fire unlit and the living quarters empty despite his earlier orders. Meldon was nowhere to be seen, and neither was Fenella. He walked straight through to his bedchamber and was surprised to find his wife a huddled lump in the bed.

"Fenella?" He walked around to her side of the bed and flipped back the blanket to find her hot and shivering and fully clothed beneath the covers. "Fenella?" He pressed the back of his hand to her cheek and found her hot and feverish. She whimpered at his touch and tried to turn away. "What was that?" he asked, catching a hoarse whisper.

"Cold," she repeated, pulling the covers tighter around her.

"Nay, you're burning with fever," he corrected her. "We need to get you undressed."

"No, please," she wept.

"Fenella," he said reasonably as he stripped back the blankets, rolled her onto her side, and started unlacing her dress. "You've no doubt caught a chill on that long ride yesterday and then sitting on draughty floorboards last night. It's hardly to be wondered at."

Her eyelids kept drifting shut as he maneuvered her around until he could pull the wool dress up over her head, leaving her in her thin shift. "I'm so cold," she mumbled. Her eyes had a dull, glazed look. He wasn't entirely sure she recognized him.

"I'll get the fire lit in here for you," he said, laying her back down on the mattress.

She caught his hand and held it tight. "Please don't leave me," she said, looking right at him.

Oswald paused. Her hand clutched his convulsively. "Very well," he said. "I won't." Gently withdrawing his hand, he dumped the yellow wool dress onto the floor and then, after a moment's hesitation, dragged a chair from against the wall next to the bed. "I'll just fetch some wood for the fire," he told her, disappearing into the adjoining room where he raided the larger fireplace, which was stacked up with chopped wood.

He cursed Meldon under his breath as he lay and lit the fire in the bedchamber. Clearly the old rogue had gone off on his errands after all, despite his express orders to stay in attendance of his mistress. Once the fire was burning merrily, he returned to her side and poured her a fresh cup of water from the jug. "Fenella, you should drink this."

Her eyes snapped open to look at him. Suddenly, she lurched forward, trying to scramble out of the bed. "I'm going to be unwell," she gasped.

Catching her meaning, he reached behind him for the basin off the dresser and held it in front of her as she retched and clutched at the bowl until she vomited.

119

Oswald held the basin steady with one hand and stroked her back with the other. "Shh, all will be well. You'll feel better presently," he murmured as she shivered and apologized. "Is that the last of it, do you think?"

"I think so," she rasped. "I'm so sorry."

"Drink the water." She took a hurried sip. "Rinse your mouth out and spit." She followed his orders, seeming lucid for the first time since he'd returned. "Now get back in the bed," he told her as he carried the bowl to the door.

"Are you leaving?" she asked, sounding panicked.

"No, I'll return presently." He was surprised to catch a look of relief in her eyes at his response.

Meldon was just coming through the door as he emerged from the bedroom. "Ah, here you are, at last. I have something for you here." He placed the basin of vomit on the table. "You can fetch more firewood and fresh water for your mistress."

"Who's been a-sick?" asked Meldon in surprise. Oswald directed a withering glance at him and disappeared back into the bedroom.

Fenella was peering over the edge of the bedsheets with anxious eyes. "I do apologize—" she started but he cut her off.

"No need for an apology, Fenella. You're unwell." He approached the bed and laid a hand across her forehead. "You're still overwarm. How do you feel?"

"A lot better actually, now I've been sick," she said. "But my head aches and my throat is sore."

"Lie back in the bed," he said, taking a seat in the chair.

Her eyes widened. "You're really going to stay?" Her gaze skittered away from his as she bit her lip. "It wasn't reasonable of me to ask."

"Wasn't it?" he asked wryly. "I think I was the unreasonable one this morning. Will you allow me to apologize?" he asked quietly.

Her fingers twisted in the bedsheets. "You've been nothing but kind, my lord," she said in a choked voice.

"I wish that were true," he said gravely. "But I'm afraid I was not kind outside the King's chamber."

Her eyes filled with tears, but she blinked them away. "There was much truth to your words, my lord," she whispered, then closed her lids. "I hope I will not let you down."

"Sleep now, Fenella," he said, and watched as she shifted onto her side and settled into sleep. He watched for a long time, even after she had drifted off into fitful sleep, her cheeks bright red and her brow furrowed with discomfort.

When she woke two hours later and vomited again, he was on hand to attend her and force her to drink a full cup of water. This time her temperature did not rocket back up and she slept sounder.

Meldon poked his head around the door at one point with a clean linen shift for Fenella. "Master Roland's asking for you. What am I to tell him?"

"Tell him I'm newly wed and otherwise occupied," said Oswald, who now had his stockinged feet up on the bed and his doublet unbuttoned. "I'll see him at supper."

"Oh aye," muttered Meldon sourly as he scooped up the wool dress and shut the door behind him.

Oswald picked up a sheaf of papers he had retrieved from the chest of drawers and started reading through them, glancing over periodically at the sleeping occupant of his bed. When he was three-quarters through, he glanced up and found Fenella silently watching him from the bed. "How are you feeling?" he asked, glancing at the candles on the dresser. They were nine-hour candles and around three-quarter burned through.

"Much better," she answered him in a slightly scratchy voice. "Have I slept the entire day through?"

"Yes. Can I get you anything?"

"I feel sweaty and horrible," she admitted. "Would it be possible for me to wash?"

"Of course." He rose from the chair. "I'll send for hot water."

"My lord?"

"Yes?"

"Thank you for staying with me." She held his gaze.

He paused. "I'm your ally, Fenella. I want you to know that. I'm on your side. Your problems are my problems. We're in this together."

She swallowed and nodded as he lightly touched her head. After two palace maids carried the buckets of hot water into the bedchamber, he left her to wash and change into the clean linen shift. When he reentered, the maids had changed the bedsheets, so everything was fresh, and Fenella was sat combing out her wet hair in front of the fire.

Oswald crossed to the chest where he kept his surcoats and tunics and extracted a dressing robe for her. "We don't want you catching cold," he said, passing it to her. "Put it on and fasten it up to your chin."

"Such beautiful silk," she marveled, stroking the peacock-blue fabric. "And so finely embroidered around the sleeves." Her fingers traced the golden thread. "Are all your dressing robes so…colorful?"

Oswald, who was in the act of removing his doublet, paused at her curious tone. "I only have three," he prevaricated.

"I've seen the scarlet one and now the peacock blue. What color is the third?"

He looked back over his shoulder at her. "You disapprove?"

"Not at all!" she assured him hurriedly. "They're beautiful." Instead of answering her, he walked back to the dark wooden chest and extracted a jade green silk robe. "Oh, that's lovely."

"I'm glad you like them," he said, shrugging it on over his shirt, "as the same tailor will be addressing the matter of your wardrobe shortly."

"Mine? But surely I can send for my clothes from Thurrold."

"You will need court clothes, Fenella," he pointed out. "Not country clothes." He sat on the edge of the bed and removed his ring and a discreet chain from round his neck with several objects suspended on it.

"Even if I will be sent to Vawdrey Keep shortly?" she asked in puzzlement.

"You can maintain two wardrobes. One here at court and one in the country." The extravagance of such a notion appeared to shock her. "When you were presented at court formerly," he persisted, "you would have had a formal court gown."

"Oh yes," she agreed. "My father had it commissioned. But that was years ago."

Oswald nodded. "Before or after our marriage?" he asked, swinging fully onto the large bed. He piled some pillows behind him and patted the wide mattress. "Come and join me, Fenella."

She looked nervous as she approached the bed from the opposite side, still fastening the long row of round silver buttons down the front of the dressing robe. It was far too long for her, and she almost tripped on the hem before clambering onto the bed and arranging her own pile of cushions to recline on. He saw she held her breath when he reached across to touch her face with the back of his hand.

"You don't feel feverish," he commented, withdrawing. He heard her in-drawn shaky breath as he rolled back to his own side of the bed. Really, the bed was so wide that they could both sleep in it without ever touching. Doubtless, she was remembering that very morning when she had woken to his hard cock pressed against her buttocks. His lips twisted. No one had been more surprised than he to wake up to soft female body in his arms.

Reaching behind his head, he grabbed a large pillow and then dropped it lengthways between them. "I'm afraid I do expect you to sleep in the same bed as me while we are at court. But we could use a bolster between us if it makes you more comfortable about my intentions."

"Thank you," she said with such clear relief it almost made him smile. He watched her relax back onto the pillows and rearrange his robe around her.

"Are you hungry? I've told Meldon to serve our meal in here. Otherwise I'll have to perform introductions to my brother Roland that I'm sure you're not prepared for."

"I remember Roland," she said, surprising him. "He spent our entire betrothal feast pulling faces at me."

Oswald grimaced. "Yes, that does sound like him," he agreed. "I'd like to tell you he has improved with age, but that would be a lie."

She looked a bit taken aback. "Well, you met my brother, Gilbert," she said lamely. "He—he does have some good qualities," she added painstakingly.

125

Oswald was tempted to ask what they were but didn't want to make her freeze back up again. He had seen no discernible virtue in her brother. Certainly not in the way he had abruptly abandoned her to his own tender mercies. "You did not answer my question," he said instead.

"Question?"

"About your court dress."

She cleared her throat. "I was aged fifteen years when I was presented at the summer court at Caer Lyonnes. I suppose we were married at that time," she said weakly. "Though, of course, we neither of us knew of it." She cast a quick, appraising look at him. "You were in battle at the time in the north. We heard tell you were captured briefly at Adarva." She tucked her feet up behind her and rolled onto her side to look at him.

Aiming to keep their conversation flowing, although not a subject he was keen to discuss, Oswald nodded in agreement. "Yes," he answered, "for four months."

Her eyes were wide. "You were a prisoner?"

"You must not imagine I was in some dank prison cell. Nothing so terrible, I assure you. Instead my status wavered between guest and hostage, depending on the fickle loyalties of my host, Sir Arnold Pryke. It was a trying time, mostly due to a healing battle wound and my frustration at being cooped up against my will."

She digested this a moment. "It must have been hard at twenty-one. How did you escape?"

126

He smiled again. "I didn't. You must not expect heroics from me, Fenella. My father finally paid the ransom, and I was free to join the King's army again."

"What happened to Sir Arnold Pryke?" she asked, fixing her gaze on him expectantly.

He was silent a moment. "I forget now." He yawned. "He came to some inglorious end, I'm sure. It's never wise to provoke a savage beast." He turned his head to look at her. "Wymer's sigil is the golden lion. He is very warlike in battle. My other brother is his chief general. Do you remember Mason at all?"

"Yes..." she replied. "He was closer to you in age and very stern, even at eighteen."

"Stern?" Oswald considered this. "Perhaps. His upbringing was not particularly joyful as my father's bastard."

"But he is distinguished now?" she ventured. "Is he not?"

"Very," he agreed. "I believe you will like my sister-in-law, Linnet. Mason dotes on her."

She looked surprised by this piece of information. "Do they come much to court?"

"Infrequently of late. They have three children and the youngest is still not a year old."

A knock on the door startled them both, but it was only Meldon scowling over a dinner tray. He set it down with a rattle on a side table. "Anything else?"

Oswald surveyed the trencher with a selection of roast meats, cheeses, and apples. "I thought, after feeling unwell, you would not want a heavy meal this evening," he said to Fenella, shooting her a look of enquiry. "But if you are feeling up to more courses, then we can send Meldon down to the kitchen for more."

"No, no, this will certainly suffice," she hurriedly assured him, sending a quick smile Meldon's way.

"I believe that will be all for this evening," said Oswald to his manservant. He wanted the relaxed mood between the two of them to continue. "I have instructed for some tradesmen to attend you over the next few days. It would please me greatly if you would engage their services." He passed her a goblet of wine which she took.

"Yes, you said." She nodded. "A tailor." She took a sip of wine.

"And a few others," he added casually. Fenella lowered her cup, looking confused. "A shoemaker, glove maker," said Oswald, waving a hand. "That sort of thing."

"Oh."

He lifted two chairs from against the wall and drew them up to the small table with the food tray. "Come and sit," he said, glancing over to where she was watching him from the bed. "I'm afraid this is very informal but in the light of our long-standing legal status…" He watched her covertly as she slid off the bed and crossed the room to join him, her bare feet peeking out from under the blue silk hem as she walked. He cleared his throat. "Of course, there is the matter of some betrothal token betwixt us…"

Fenella's color rose into her face as he pulled out a seat for her. "Is that really necessary? Only it seems a little late in the day for that."

"I notice you wear no ring for Thane?" he said, setting some meat on her plate.

She looked at him blankly a moment. "Ambrose did give me a brooch when we were promised," she said. "But I left it in my jewelry box at home. I did not want to lose it, and the pin was loose."

"At Thurrold," he corrected her. "Thane's home."

Her eyes flew to his. "Yes, that's what I meant—" she stammered. "Forgive me, my lord. It will take me a little time to accustom myself."

"Of course," he said smoothly as he sliced the loaf. "It is not to be wondered at." He could hear her rapid breathing and the fact she was quietly panicking but was not sure how to reassure her. Instead, he buttered her bread and placed it on her plate. "Eat, you need to build up your strength."

"Yes, my lord," she mumbled and took a bite.

"I don't remember if there *was* a token between us previously," mused Oswald with a slight frown. He looked at her questioningly as she froze, bread in hand. "I'm inclined to think not. My father was not good with the niceties of social

129

occasions. I doubt I would have known much about engagement traditions at nineteen."

Fenella dropped her bread onto her plate. She gave an awkward laugh. "I am heartily glad to hear you say so, my lord," she said and took a hearty sip of cider wine. "I'm afraid I sent you some very juvenile examples of my tapestry work." She winced. "I am much encouraged that you do not remember them."

Oswald frowned. "I thought I remembered something about you weaving or the like."

Her shoulders relaxed down. "I wonder what happened to them," she said. "Hopefully your father threw them out."

"Very likely," agreed Oswald dryly. "Or his pack of dogs slept on them. My father was no connoisseur of the arts."

Fenella laughed. "That would be all they were fit for. And if that was their fate, they would have fallen apart long ago."

He noticed she looked quite cheerful about the fact. Fenella's tapestry must be very bad, he thought and hoped Bryce had not added a loom to the list of things to purchase on her behalf. "And I gave you nothing in return," he mused. "You must see why I must be allowed to make amends now."

She paused in the act of lifting a slice of apple to her mouth. Forcing a smile, she nodded her head. "If it would please you, my lord."

"It would please me. I was clearly very remiss."

"We were just children after all," she murmured. "I don't suppose you have heard from my brother today?" she said, changing the subject.

"Not yet. Indeed, he made no promise to send immediate word on reaching Sitchmarsh. Is that his usual practice?"

She shook her head. "Gilbert is not much of a letter-writer. I only thought, because of the unusual circumstances…" Her words trailed off.

"Perhaps I should have sent word," he said smoothly, filling the awkward gap. "But I did not wish to worry him by telling him you were unwell," he lied calmly.

"Oh, of course. That was thoughtful." She looked uncertain, but that could be if her brother would much care. He had not struck Oswald as the caring type.

"I think it would be better if you kept to these rooms for the next few days while you recuperate, and we ready you for court," he carried on casually. "After all, first impressions are important, and we don't wish to give rise to more gossip and speculation than is strictly necessary."

Fenella swallowed her mouthful of food. "Of course, my lord. I am sure you know what is best and will be led by you."

Yes, he thought, looking at her as she wiped her mouth with a napkin. *She would be a sensible sort of wife, the sort that caused very little bother*. He remembered the solemn child he had once been betrothed to. She had listened to every word he had uttered, with a surprising intensity.

131

She still did that, he realized with a faint smile. She would do very well for his purposes. He would just have to remember to be considerate toward her. Doubtless she did not anticipate much consideration, if her boorish brother was anything to go by. And at the end of the day, that would be far more practical to him than even an ambitious, clever, or beautiful wife. He had done well.

12

Fenella woke several times during the night, mostly with her sore throat and stuffy nose. The first time, she was surprised to find Lord Vawdrey reading by candlelight on his side of the bed. "Did the light wake you?" he asked quietly.

"No, no," she said, taking a hurried sip of water. "It is just my scratchy throat. I will fall asleep again presently." She lay back down and rolled onto her side away from him, closing her eyes. Luckily sleep soon came, and the next time she woke, the room was all in darkness.

She could hear his steady breathing from close by and lay awake awhile listening to it. It seemed so odd to think this was her husband now. This stranger lying on the mattress beside her. She reached out tentatively and felt the bolster solidly between them. Her eyes could make out no shape in the dark, but she lay awhile anyway, trying to make out his profile in the shadows.

She must have dropped off to sleep, for the next thing she knew, she was waking to gray morning light and the heavy, warm feeling of a big male body pressed against her back, one large hand resting on her hip. Fen blinked into her pillow. Not again! Where was the bolster? She lifted her head to twist her body and peer over her shoulder, but the hand tightened its grip on her hip holding her in place.

"Keep still," a disgruntled male voice, thick with sleep, growled at her. Fen was so surprised, she did just that. Oswald Vawdrey's face pressed into the back of her neck and breathed out. He shifted closer to her, his hand sliding round from her hip, over the swell of her stomach and settling at her waist before pulling her firmly back into his sleeping body.

Fen gave a gasp of surprise, but his breathing had evened back out, and she realized after a few moments that he was sound asleep again. She lowered her head back onto the pillow and squeezed her eyes shut. After all, it would be pointless remonstrating with a sleeping man.

To her own astonishment, she did manage to drift off to sleep again, for the next thing she knew she heard the door opening and Meldon's shuffling footsteps and the sloshing of the water ewer. However, when she tried to move, she realized her legs were firmly entangled with two much longer, stronger, and more muscular than her own. She lifted her head and held her breath as she felt him startled out of sleep behind her.

"What the—?"

"Meldon's here," she said hurriedly. He cursed and disentangled himself, rolling onto his back. Fen made haste to pull her shift down, which had ridden up high on her legs.

Meldon regarded them both askance. "Washing water," he said. "And a clean shift for the mistress." He threw it over a chair back before stomping back out.

"I suppose I should really procure you a lady's maid," mumbled Oswald, rubbing a hand over his face. He yawned. Fen surreptitiously glanced over the bed but could see no sign of the bolster.
"Will you wash first, or will I?" he asked, turning to her.

She pondered this a moment. From what she could see, Lord Vawdrey once again was not wearing a stitch of clothing under the sheets. "I will, if that is agreeable to you," she said hurriedly and averted her eyes from his lolling figure. She didn't know if she could go through that spectacle again.

"Of course," he said.

Fen clambered from the bed with as much dignity as possible, but it was so high that she had to slide down the side with a thud. Hoping he had not received an unimpeded view of her bare backside, she scrambled to pull her shift back down around her plump knees.

Lord Vawdrey coughed. "How's your throat this morn?" Fenella turned back to look at him and promptly went sprawling onto the floor as she tripped over some unseen object on the floor. "Fenella?"

Fen sprang up, red-faced, and once again had to straighten her wretched shift. If he hadn't seen her generous behind before, he certainly had now, she thought, dying of mortification. She looked down and saw the bolster lying innocuously on the floor. So, there it was!

"I'm fine," she panted, flinging her braid over her shoulder and trying not to look flustered. "It—it feels practically recovered today," she assured him, not daring to look at his face. She approached the pitcher of hot water and sloshed some into the basin. Snatching up a cloth, she dunked it and starting to wash furiously at her face and neck.

"Don't scrub so hard your face rubs off," said a voice closer than she'd expected. "I happen to like the way you look." She

135

whipped round to find Lord Vawdrey picking the bolster up off the floor and tossing it onto the bed.

He was still naked. Fen dropped the washcloth through nerveless fingers. It landed in the bowl with a loud splash and soaked all down the front of her thin shift. She squealed. What the hells was wrong with her this morning?

"What is it? Did you scald yourself?" He was right behind her now.

"No, no," she hurried to assure him and nearly jumped out of her skin when his hands came to rest on her upper arms.

"Did you hurt yourself?"

Fen took a shaky breath. "No, my lord."

"Good." He dropped his hands and picked up the peacock-blue robe of his that she had worn the evening before. To her surprise, he put it on. She glimpsed the scar on his back as he swung the robe on. But what was she supposed to wear?

She looked around for the clean shift Meldon had brought her. That wouldn't be warm enough. Did he expect her to remain abed again today? But if so, Meldon had not lit the fire in the bedroom. When she realized his eyes were back on her, she returned to her ablutions with renewed vigor, anxious to avoid his gaze.

Lord Vawdrey retreated to the other side of the room. When he returned, he had his red satin dressing robe over his arm. He placed it on the bed for her next to the clean shift. "When you're dressed come into the adjoining chamber," he said.

136

"We'll have breakfast in there." He paused. "If you need any help—"

"No, no," Fenella hastened to assure him as she tried to obscure the fact her already transparent shift was soaked and plastered to her chest. "I'm sure I can manage, thank you."

He stood a moment and then abruptly turned on his heel and strode from the room. Fen breathed out a relieved sigh and immediately dragged the wet shift over her head. She hopped over to the bed and pulled the clean one on. The only consolation she could draw was that there was precious little else she could do to humiliate herself in this man's presence!

So far, he had seen her cry, vomit, and lie in his bed in a state of sweaty delirium. Giving him an unsolicited glimpse of her chubby body was probably the least of the awful things he had been exposed to! She turned her attentions to donning the scarlet dressing robe with its heavily decorated sleeves.

It really was beautiful, and she was surprised that he had given her this one to wear. They had done a swap from the previous evening. She hurried over the gold toggle-type fastenings down the front of the robe until her shift was concealed. Then she set about tidying her long brown hair into another braid.

It was the best she could do without any of her hair ornaments from home. Shrugging off her less than conventional appearance, she headed for the door and into the adjoining room where she could hear male voices speaking in low tones. To her surprise, she had no sooner opened it than a black muscular form hurtled toward her.

"Bors!" she exclaimed joyfully as her old dog made a valiant effort to act puppyish, weaving around her legs and panting happily. "I'm so pleased to see you, boy," she murmured into his shiny black coat as she dropped to her knees to embrace him. His tail thumped heavily against the floor. Looking up, she found two strange men bowing to her.

"Thank you so much for bringing him to me," she said, smiling brightly at them, guessing they must be Lord Vawdrey's men, although they wore no badge or sigil to that effect.

"They brought some of your other personal effects also," said Lord Vawdrey, gesturing to the table where Fenella was surprised to see her leather writing case and a chest of her papers and documents.

"Oh, that is most kind!" she exclaimed. "And didn't even occur to me," she confessed. "I don't suppose my clothes—?"

"Unfortunately not," Lord Vawdrey interrupted her. "These gentlemen were running some other errands in the area and simply dropped by Thurrold en route."

Fen turned curious eyes back on the two men who were of middling height and dressed in plain brown. There was nothing distinguishable about them; they could have been merchants, menservants, or anything at all.

Fen doubted she would even recognize them if she saw them again. "Oh, I see," she murmured. "Tell me, did my sister-in-law, Orla, send any message to me?" she asked, looking from one to the other. To her surprise, they both looked to Lord Vawdrey rather than answer her.

"It was more of a fleeting visit to Sitchmarsh," he said after a small pause. "I'm afraid they did not meet any of your former household."

Fen blinked in surprise. "Was the house quite empty?" she asked in astonishment. "Where was everyone?" Again, both men steadfastly avoided her gaze and turned to their employer.

"They met only one servant, who was paid to deliver your belongings speedily into their hands," Lord Vawdrey said with an air of finality and turned back to dismiss them both. They handed him a small bundle of documents and with another small bow, left the room altogether.

Fen was still crouched on the floor open-mouthed when Meldon entered with a tray of breakfast foods. He did a double take on seeing Bors and muttered something under his breath which sounded suspiciously like, "Another mouth to feed."

"Come and be seated, Fenella," said her husband, pushing her belongings to the other side of the table. He pulled out the chair next to his and she joined him. Bors settled comfortably under her chair. He seemed none the worse for wear for his journey, and she guessed they must have placed him in some sort of cart-like conveyance for there was no way that he would have been able to walk such a distance these days.

She reached down to pat his head discreetly as Meldon rattled down the dishes of fish, bread, butter, and eggs. Fenella avoided the ale jug and instead tried the one next to it, which proved to be the juices of some fruit—she guessed plums.

Lord Vawdrey was just placing some smoked fish on her plate when the door on the far end of the room opened and another

139

tall, dark male entered the room, yawning loudly. He was clearly a Vawdrey, and Fenella lowered her cup, realizing this must be Roland, the younger brother. He was heavier set with muscles than Oswald, but the resemblance with the height and the dark hair and eyes was striking. He checked a moment on the threshold at the sight of them seated at the table. "Very domesticated," he drawled.

"Fenella, this is your new brother, Roland," said Lord Vawdrey. "Roland, this is my wife, Fenella Vawdrey."

Fenella started to stand but found Roland had thrown himself into a seat opposite them and wasn't looking at her anyway. His tunic was unfastened to his waist and he needed a shave.

"A pretty state of affairs," said Roland jeeringly, looking straight at his brother. "I hope you realize the whole court's talking of it."

Fenella sat back in her seat with a bump. Lord Vawdrey placed the bread and butter on her plate, ignoring his brother. "Will you have eggs?" he asked, turning to her.

"Thank you, no," she answered, finding she had sadly lost her appetite.

He frowned. "You have a lot ahead of you today," he reminded her. "Have some, to please me."

Fenella opened and closed her mouth. "Very well, my lord," she said meekly. He gave a brief smile of approval and dished some onto her plate. She wondered if he would always feed her like this at meals. Ambrose certainly hadn't. When she looked up, she found Roland staring at them.

140

"Is she wearing your robe?" he asked with a derisive snort.

Oswald looked up from his plate. "Fasten your tunic," he said. "No one wants to see that when they're trying to eat."

Roland looked down in surprise at his own muscular torso. Fenella wondered if he had been sotted the night before. He had the confused air men wore on the morning after a heavy night's imbibing. He fumbled a moment with his lacings, scowling the whole time.

"Suppose I've got this to look forward to every morning now," he complained before seizing a serving spoon and ladling food onto his plate. He attacked it aggressively. Roland had even worse manners than she remembered.

As if reading her thoughts, Lord Vawdrey said: "This must be reminding you of old times, at least, Fenella. Roland putting you off a perfectly good meal." Fenella almost choked on her mouthful of fish.

"When the devil did I do that?" Roland demanded, lowering his knife.

"Our betrothal feast," answered Oswald succinctly.

Roland looked aggrieved. "I was just a child," he pointed out with dignity.

"A repulsive child," his brother responded. Fenella took a hurried sip of plum juice. The whole meal was starting to seem rather unreal to her, like a peculiar dream.

"So, it is you then," said Roland abruptly. He was looking right at her.

"Yes, it is me," she responded, unsure what else to say.

"Got what you wanted in the end, in any event," he said caustically.

There was really no response she could make to that. Fen lowered her cup, seeing Oswald about to intercede. "I'm not sure I would have recognized you, Sir Roland," she said hurriedly. "But you were only ten or eleven at the time."

"You weren't much older," he pointed out dismissively and looked away at the clutter of her things at the end of the table. "What's all this?"

"Fenella's belongings," answered Lord Vawdrey.

"That all she brings with her? Not much of a dowry, is it," said Roland scornfully.

Oswald straightened up in his seat and a look passed between the brothers. Roland lapsed into silence and started shoveling his food again. Fen took a shaky breath. She was not sure she was equipped for life as a Vawdrey *at all*!

*

After breakfast, Oswald informed her that his assistant, Bryce, would be attending her that morning while the tradesmen called. Fen glanced down at the scarlet robe fastened down the front with golden buttons. It was the single most exquisite garment she had ever worn, but the fact remained it was not an

142

outfit intended for receiving visitors in. "But surely——" she started.

"You are entirely covered from neck to foot," Lord Vawdrey forestalled her. "Come," he said, drawing out a chair by the fire. "Sit here. Keep your charming toes tucked under and there will be no impropriety, I assure you."

Fen found herself blushing faintly as she sat down. He was so much taller than she that the scarlet robe puddled into a train at her feet, entirely concealing the fact she was barefoot. Almost, she wished she could take another look at her toes. No one had ever thought to compliment them before.

Once he had washed and dressed, he disappeared to his office in the main palace. Roland retreated to his bedchamber, she suspected to sleep off a bad head. Bryce turned out to be the rather reserved, plump young man in a cleric's robe she had met previously. He sat at the table with a piece of paper and pen and snubbed every effort she made to engage him in conversation.

She was relieved when the first of the visitors arrived, which was the shoemaker. He measured her foot and showed her various samples of shoes, which seemed to be either long and narrow with a pointed toe or extremely round at the end like a horseshoe. The one thing that they all had in common was that they were made of two colors.

The outer leather was one color with lots of cutouts in either diamond or teardrop shapes, revealing the second color of leather underneath. Fenella was charmed, and after careful consideration ordered one pair of round-toed black shoes with cut-out shapes showing green leather underneath. The

143

shoemaker commended her choice and then looked at her expectantly.

"I already have a pair of boots," she told him.

His eyes flitted to Bryce, who cleared his throat. "Lord Vawdrey said you were to have at least two of everything, my lady."

"Two?" repeated Fenella. "Oh, I see! Perhaps—er—" She pointed mutely to a model of a narrow red leather shoe with black diamond contrast shapes and narrow red laces on either side.

"A popular choice, my lady," murmured the shoemaker.

"Oh good," Fen seized on this eagerly. She breathed a sigh of relief and reached down to touch Bors as if he were her talisman in an uncertain world. He nosed her fingers reassuringly.

After the shoemaker came the glover, who brought in some beautiful samples of gloves in knitted and embroidered linen and silk. Fenella gasped over the beautiful quality and ordered one pair of short gloves in dark red knitted silk which were decorated at the cuffs in golden rosettes.

They felt warm and would be ideal for walking out on cold days, but the longer gloves, which went to the elbow, confused her as to their functionality. When she glanced at Bryce for guidance, he blushed so vividly that she hurriedly ordered one pair of the long silk gauntlets in a cream and gold and left it at that.

A pouch maker followed with a selection of purses on strings to hang from your girdle belt. Fen selected a deerskin purse with a pretty braiding detail for use by day, and one made of black silk brocade with a velvet trim for evening wear. She noticed Bryce was keeping a list of things ordered and felt comforted that he would tell her when she reached the end of her budget.

A leather worker came next with a selection of belts to choose from. Mindful that she already had a good belt at home, Fen selected a woven braid belt made of blue wool with brass buckles. The seller let her have this straightaway, which pleased her, but Bryce interrupted them to say that Lord Vawdrey would certainly expect her to order a leather belt as well.

These looked very costly and were finely tooled with riveted silver mounts. When she finally chose a red leather belt with pretty silver trefoil discs, the craftsman looked pleased with her choice. Then he told her he would have to return to his workshop to stamp the correct heraldic device onto the silver casings before it would be ready. Fen thanked him and then wondered how much of Oswald's coin she had spent that morning already.

"Is that the last of them?" she asked Bryce, who glanced at his list and shook his head.

"We've barely started, my lady."

"Barely started?" she echoed with dismay. "Oh dear." She hesitated. "Have you made a note of the costings involved?" she asked, gesturing toward his list.

Bryce looked highly affronted. "I thought it might be advisable to make a record of your purchases," he said stiffly.

"That is a very good notion," she said, not wishing to cause him any offence. "And I heartily approve. I only meant I wish to remain within the boundaries Lord Vawdrey has set for spending."

"Lord Vawdrey did not set any boundaries," said Bryce.

Fen sat back in her seat. "Oh." She considered this a moment in stunned silence. In her past life, she was used to keeping an exact list of household and personal expenses. Indeed, even while Ambrose had been away for the last two years, he had expected her to send him a monthly record of her spending at Thurrold. Quite often he sent back demands for justification on some purchase he thought was too exorbitant or to upbraid her if she had not been thrifty enough. It seemed her new husband was to be very different in this respect.

Next was the tailor, a fussy man called signor Pezzini, who measured her from head to foot and muttered under his breath the whole time, scribbling down notes onto a bit of paper. When he deigned to speak to her at all, she could hardly understand him, as he had such a heavy accent.

"Whatever you think, signor," she found herself saying over and over. "I am sure you know what is best." She darted anxious glances at Bryce every now and again, but he just nodded sagely as if all was going as it should. She really had no idea what had been ordered by the time he presented her with a very elegant bow and swept out of the room, but she felt badly in need of sustenance.

"Meldon, could you please bring us some light repast when you have a moment?" she asked as he straightened up from adding a log to the fire. He rolled his eyes, but duly stumped off to the kitchens. Fen wondered if she should raise the idea of a lady's maid with Bryce as Lord Vawdrey *had* mentioned it only that morning. She couldn't quite bring herself to though after all the purchases she'd just made. He would no doubt think her an extreme spendthrift.

Instead, she tried to squint at Bryce's paper without seeming too obvious and then to recall mentally a list of all the purchases she'd made. Whilst she was counting them on her fingers, Meldon reappeared with a selection of cured meats, hard biscuits, cheese, and fruit.
He'd even brought a meat bone for Bors, which made Fen exclaim with pleasure. Bors lay under her chair and worried the meat bone with every appearance of satisfaction. Just as she was pouring some wine, the door opened, and Lord Vawdrey appeared.

13

"My lord!" exclaimed Bryce. "I did not expect you. You said—"

"I changed my mind, my good Bryce," Oswald said, directing a slight frown toward his assistant. Bryce jumped up out of his chair next to Fenella, and Oswald rounded the table and sat next to her. "How goes it?" he asked, picking up her hand and casually kissing her wrist. He watched the blush rise up her neck and spread to her cheeks.

"Well, I think, my lord," she said weakly, "I have bought many, many things." She looked a little nervous about the fact.

"Good," he said with a shrug. "That was the general idea."

"To be honest, my lord, I do not have the faintest notion what gowns I commissioned from signor Pezzini. He forms his words so fast, and the harder I try to catch their meaning the more lost I become. Bryce had the forethought to keep a list," she said, gesturing.

"Did he?" Oswald drew the piece of paper across the tabletop toward him and read it with raised brows. "Two pairs of shoes, two pairs of gloves, two purses, and two belts." He lowered the paper. "Bryce, it seems you took my suggestion of two of everything far too literally!"
His assistant looked uncomfortable.

"It's not Bryce's fault," said Fenella hurriedly. "And I am sure we ordered more than two dresses from signor Pezzini."

"I sincerely hope so," said Oswald heavily and glanced back down at the paper. It seemed Fenella was not the only one who had struggled with Pezzini's accent. Bryce had merely written "full court wardrobe" next to the tailor's name.

Oswald could only hope that the tailor had more of an idea of what was required than his wife and assistant, who both looked at him with matching expressions of uncertainty. "Perhaps I ought to stay for the rest of the afternoon," suggested Oswald dryly. "Or you'll end up with two lutes, two hawks, and two hats to add to your collection."

Bryce looked heartily relieved. "I can return to the office, my lord?" he asked hopefully.

"Yes, Bryce, I think that would be for the best." Oswald's sarcastic tone seemed lost on him.
"Thank you, my lord." He hesitated and bowed toward Fenella. "My lady," he said stiffly and beat a hasty retreat through the door.

Fenella frowned as she poured a liberal amount of water into her wine cup. "Bryce does not seem…altogether comfortable in the company of women," she said carefully.

"No," agreed Oswald. "I don't believe he is."

"Why is that?" asked Fenella, looking up.

Oswald was taken aback. "I haven't the faintest idea," he admitted. "Is it relevant?"

She stared at him, almost as if he was speaking in a foreign language. "I meant, perhaps he has no sisters, or his mother was sadly absent from his upbringing?"

Oswald cudgeled his brains. "I believe his background was religious before he came here as a clerk. He hoped to join the brotherhood, but for some reason it was not meant to be."

Fenella looked intrigued. "I wonder what happened?" she mused aloud as she set the dishes from the tray onto the table. "I could imagine he would be suited to life as a religious cleric. In fact"—she assumed a confiding air—"when I first met him, his robe was so plain and dark that I quite took him for a monk." She looked expectantly at Oswald.

"Did you?" he asked dutifully. He had no idea why he was watching her so closely, but for some reason he found he couldn't tear his eyes away from her. Maybe because he had never had a woman preside over his table before. But no, it was more than that. He tried to put his finger on it while she piled up a plate with cheese and grapes and slid it toward him.

"Yes," she said solemnly, interrupting his thoughts. "Of course, I was a little overwrought at the time." She pulled a face. "But I think I can see why I mistook him for one. He looks so very…" She cast around for a word. "Earnest," she settled on. She poured him a cup of water and set it before him. It seemed she remembered he rarely imbibed.

"Indeed," he agreed. Other than ascertaining the necessary facts when he employed Bryce, he had taken no interest in his assistant's motivations or family background. He did not want to admit this to Fenella though. It was apparent she thought one should take a lively interest in your servants. "What say you of

150

Meldon?" he asked, curious what she would make of that old, misogynistic stick-in-the-mud.

"A very capable and resourceful man to have around," she said after a moment's consideration.
Oswald nearly choked on his sip of water. "Isn't that right, Bors?" she asked, looking over the arm of her chair. Her dog's tail beat a steady thump against the floorboards. She turned back to Oswald. "Meldon found Bors a meat bone, so will now be considered a great favorite," she said and dimpled at him. *Dimpled.*

Oswald lowered his cup and cleared his throat. She reached across and touched his sleeve fleetingly. "I'm so glad you're remaining here with me this afternoon," she said quietly. "I'm sure I will adjust," she added hastily. "But at the moment, I don't really feel like I've found my feet. It's comforting knowing I have an ally so close at hand," she said shyly.

Ally? Her choice of words displeased him, until he realized she was echoing his own words back at him. *Who the hells called their spouse an ally anyway?* What had he been thinking? He had to school his features to hide his own reaction. It was odd, he realized as he watched her select and eat a piece of cheese.

If she had said the same thing to him only two days ago, he would have been encouraged. But for some reason…not today. He had slept in a bed twice with her since then. He had felt how soft and warm she was against his body, and he had seen her naked. Or as good as.

Catching the direction of his thoughts, Oswald cleared his throat. He was surprised, quite frankly. Licentiousness had never been one of his vices, but there was something very lush and bountiful about Fenella, he reflected. He gave his head a slight shake.

Lush and bountiful? When was the last time he'd lain with a woman? It had obviously been too long if he was now panting after this woman, who, a mere two days ago, he'd decided was dumpy and plain and wearing the ugliest wool gown he had ever seen.

"Would you like some more bread, my lord?" she asked, nudging the trencher toward him.

"Thank you, no," he replied. It was partly her voice, he thought, that affected him so strongly. One instant it was breathy and husky and the next it was full-bodied and brimming with emotion. It gave him strange random desires, such as hearing her say his name. *Naked.*

It was damned inconvenient! Why the hells this drab little female had such a siren's voice was beyond him. It didn't match the rest of her in the slightest! He took a good look at the short, full figure, the indeterminate brown hair in a thick braid hanging over one shoulder. The wholly unremarkable brown eyes. There was absolutely nothing for him to be getting hot under the tunic about. Let alone eyeing her like a delectable morsel he wanted to wolf down in one bite!

He needed to remember her circumstances and respect them. The poor thing had been in the grip of strong emotion ever since he had met her. She had been buffeted from pillory to whipping post. And quite frankly, if Thane was the pillar, then he was the post.

He had selfishly used her for his own ends too. And he needed to remember that she wasn't some sophisticated courtesan. She was not trying to toy with him, or seduce him with those flashes of pale, smooth flesh or rounded limbs she kept affording him. *For god's sake*, he reminded himself irritably, she had even been quite ill!

He watched her covertly now as she nibbled on a thin, fried biscuit with a cautious expression. Seeing her wearing his robe pleased him for some reason he didn't want to examine too closely. Mind you, anything was an improvement on that muddy gown she'd shown up in, he thought with a twist of his lips.

Suddenly, he wanted to see her in a dress that actually became her. Perhaps like a jewel in an ugly setting, she would shine when set more becomingly?

She looked up, no doubt noticing he had fallen silent. "Why don't you try one of these, my lord?" she asked, gesturing to the biscuits. "Their texture is surprisingly pleasant. I think the flavor is anise," she added thoughtfully.

Oswald took one and bit into the crispy round cracker. "Who are we expecting next?" he asked.

"I hardly know," she admitted, selecting a grape. "Is it on Bryce's list?"

Oswald turned the paper over and found she was right. "The hat maker, followed by the jeweler," he read out. Bryce had been methodically crossing them off as they arrived. He frowned. "Did Bryce not ask you about any of your pastimes?"

153

"Oh yes," Fenella assured him. "He offered to order me a new tapestry loom but they take up so much room and I already have one at Thurrold. I will write to Orla to send it to Vawdrey Keep. Orla does not enjoy needlework so I know she will not wish to keep it."

"But mayhap the new Lady Thane will?" he pointed out as gently as possible.

She blinked at this, but then rallied. "Oh—well if that is the case, I am sure I have an old one at my brother's house. It is large and a bit antiquated, but should still be fit for purpose," she told him brightly. "Though it may need a few repairs."

"I see." Mostly what he could see was that Fenella was extremely frugal. On reflection, it probably wasn't Bryce's fault that she had not loosened his purse strings that morn. He smiled thinly to himself, mentally making a note to have Bryce order her a new tapestry loom. It was certainly not her brother's place to supply her needs, now she bore his name.

She would need careful handling, he thought, to get through the jeweler's visit. "I'm afraid there are no Vawdrey family jewels to pass on," he started as she was stacking the empty plates and leftovers back onto Meldon's tray. "My father was not the kind of man to buy any of his wives baubles." He could see from the expression on her face that she had no difficulty believing that of the old baron. "However, as the wife of an earl you will be expected to dress to a certain station."

Her mouth formed an unspoken "Oh" of understanding. Meldon appeared beside her and seized the tray with an indignant look which clearly said *That's my job*. Fenella sat back in her seat. "Perhaps if you made a list of the bare minimum required by

154

the rank of countess it might be helpful?" she suggested uncertainly.

"The jeweler will be able to advise us on that," said Oswald easily. "He is used by many at the palace."

"I see," she said, biting her lip. "But perhaps if you were to set a sum now—?"

"I do, of course, have a sum in mind," he assured her smoothly.

She waited expectantly, but he refused to be drawn. Looking disappointed, she turned back to finishing her cup of watered wine. Bors barked from under her chair, making her jump, and almost simultaneously a knock sounded at the door.

"Come in," shouted Oswald. The door opened and in came a middle-aged couple carrying a woven basket between them. They set it down and straightened up, bobbing politely. "Greetings," said Oswald briskly. "You must be representing Watkyns Quality Hat Makers?" he said, glancing at the paper again.

"Aye, my lord, I'm Arnold Watkyns and this here is my wife."

"Thank you for coming," said Fenella.

"You are presenting your wares to my wife, the Countess Vawdrey," said Oswald, gesturing to Fenella.

Mr. Watkyns bowed again and then whisked the lid off the basket. "Does my lady have a clear preference on what head covering she generally wears?" asked Mrs. Watkyns as her husband started lifting examples out and draping them across the back of a chair.

"Generally, I wear just a veil and wimple at home," answered Fenella obligingly. "In general, I prefer to wear a woolen veil in winter as 'tis much warmer and I tend to wear a practical color such as blue or gray rather than white."

A stunned silence greeted this pronouncement, and Mr. Watkyns nearly dropped his armful of finest linens and silks. Belatedly, Fenella seemed to realize that they had brought along only the purest whites to show her. "Of course, it is quite different at court," she said weakly.

"How right you are," agreed Oswald smoothly. "Perhaps if you could show Lady Vawdrey your finest examples?"

The Watkyns were instantly all smiles. "If your ladyship would permit me," murmured Mr. Watkyns, approaching with a delicate white veil, which he held up for Fenella's inspection. She took it from him gingerly. "I am sure you can see the quality of this piece of linen for yourself."

Fenella looked it over. "Linen?" she asked with surprise. "Why, it's so delicate I would almost have thought it silk…"

Mr. Watkyns bowed with a small smile. "It is of the very best material, my lady."

Fenella turned it over in her hands. "It has no seam!" she exclaimed, looking at Mr. Watkyns in wonderment.

"You are in the right of it," he answered. "It is made in one piece."

156

"One piece?" she echoed. "Remarkable…"

Oswald cleared his throat and nodded meaningfully at Mr. Watkyns, who caught his meaning at once and laid one aside with all haste.

"Mayhap her ladyship would care to try wearing her veil with a torque or a templar instead of the wimple?" suggested Mistress Watkyns. "Or perhaps a padded headband? You will find they are very fashionable at court these days and you wear your veil suspended from it." Fenella looked back at her blankly.

"Perhaps you could demonstrate this headwear for us," suggested Oswald, resigning himself to a good hour of the Watkynses' company.

"Of course, we'd be only too glad to." Mrs. Watkyns beamed. Oswald steeled himself for the ordeal, but it wasn't as bad as he'd anticipated, mostly because he spent the time watching his wife.

She had pretty manners. A little old-fashioned perhaps, but in general he liked the way she conducted herself. It's true, she was a little more animated than fashion dictated, he conceded, his eyes wandering over her heart-shaped face. Certainly, she was not conventionally or fashionably beautiful, but he *did* find her appealing.

By the time they had left, Fenella was the owner of no less than four veils. In addition to the seamless one, she now owned a stiffened and frilled veil, one edged in gold thread and pearls and one barely there silk gauze veil, which Fenella looked vaguely scandalized by. To wear along with these, she had a

157

gold netted caul, a black and gold damask coif that tied under the chin, and a pretty fillet band decorated with semiprecious stones. She also had a velvet and brocade padded headband, which she wore now as Mrs. Watkyns had helped her put it on and then pin the veil from the back.

"At court you must dress as if every day is a feast day," marveled Fenella as the Watkynses departed. "I shall hardly recognize myself in so much finery." She touched her headdress self-consciously.

"You will soon become accustomed to it," Oswald told her. "It looks well."

She smiled. "Perhaps a little strange paired with your dressing robe?" she said, looking down at herself.

Oswald let his eyes flicker over her again. "I can see nothing amiss," he said lightly and cleared his throat.

A rap at the door told them the final craftsman of the day had arrived. Meldon scuttled across the room like a spider and admitted them. "The Antonys of Aphrany," he announced flatly and waved them in. It was an old man and a young boy with him carrying two large wooden cases and a ledger.

"Welcome, Mr. Antony," he said, hailing the jeweler. "And this must be your apprentice?"

"And grandson," the old man said with a bow.

His grandson bowed likewise and then nodded toward the table. "Do you permit, my lord?" he asked in a clear, childish voice.

"Please," said Oswald with a quick gesture. The boy set the cases down carefully on the table.

"I believe my assistant will have outlined our requirements," said Oswald. "My wife requires some betrothal and wedding jewelry."

Fenella shifted in her chair. "Perhaps a brooch?" she suggested brightly.

Mr. Antony Sr.'s eyes flew to her and then back to Oswald. "We will need several pieces," he corrected her. "Starting, I think, with a betrothal ring."

Mr. Antony's tanned face wrinkled into an approximation of a smile. Not for one moment did he betray even a flicker of surprise at a man buying his wife a betrothal ring. "But of course," he said. "We are sure to have the very thing." He looked to his grandson, who sprang forward and opened the case to the left. He looked up expectantly at his grandfather. "Perhaps"—the old man hesitated and looked back at Fenella— "the second tray."

The boy extracted a tray from the case and then walked toward Fenella with it extended.

"What is in the first tray?" asked Oswald, dropping his voice as Fenella started chatting with the boy.

"Examples of commissioned pieces," answered Mr. Antony in a matching tone.

"Perhaps you would bring them along to my office afterward?" suggested Oswald after a pause.

159

The older man's eyes lit up. "Of course, my lord." He bowed.

"These are pretty," said Fenella, cautiously bending over the velvet-lined wooden tray. She looked every inch the thrifty housewife, and Oswald could see she longed to ask how much they cost.

"Ah, the posy rings." Mr. Antony nodded. "They are often used as betrothal tokens. They are gold and finely engraved with leaves and flowers."

"Lovers get them inscribed," piped up his grandson, "on the inside. With a personal message. Like 'promised forever,'" he elaborated.

There was an awkward silence. "I see," said Fenella. "Our circumstances are a little unusual in that we are already married, so a message seems a little after the fact."

"Not as unusual as you may think," said old Mr. Antony smoothly. "Sometimes the groom, he could not afford much more than a piece of string when they were promised, but later on"—he wagged a finger aloft—"then he can afford the real gesture."

"Perhaps our combined initials?" suggested Oswald.

"That would be most appropriate," agreed Mr. Antony, reaching for his pen and paper.

Oswald thought the grandson looked a bit underwhelmed. The boy shrugged. "Would my lady care to try one on?" he asked.

Fenella frowned, then reached into the tray and slipped one on her finger. She turned her hand to show it to Oswald.

"Do you like it?" he asked. She nodded and he glanced at the tray. "Choose one with a stone," he said, "to wear while that one is inscribed." Fenella's eyes went wide, and she opened her mouth, no doubt to protest, but Oswald forestalled her by turning back to Mr. Antony.

"We need some foundation pieces, for a family collection," he said. "Perhaps a necklace and a coronet? Things that can be worn to royal banquets." He did not look at Fenella. Mr. Antony opened the second case and angled it toward Oswald.

"How about a girdle belt fit for a queen?" he asked, drawing out a long belt of gold medallions set with blazing diamonds and punctuated with large double pearls. Oswald heard Fenella gasp in the background.

"That looks just the thing," he said, holding out his hands for a closer look. He could tell it was exquisite before he even felt the weight. "I've never seen one like it."

"No one has," boasted Mr. Antony. "And with the diamonds, this belt could be worn with any color gown."

Oswald nodded. "We'll take it. What else?"

"How about this one?" he heard the boy ask Fenella, who was clearly distracted from her task of selecting a ring. "It's a sapphire."

Mr. Antony cast a shrewd look his way, before returning to his case. Wordlessly he passed Oswald a heavy necklace of gold

161

filigrees connected with pearls. Each filigree had a round ruby glowing in the middle and the centerpiece was an even larger gold filigree with an enormous glittering emerald from which a white teardrop pearl elegantly dangled. "This is as fine a necklace as any you will see here at the royal court," he said with quiet confidence.

Oswald could believe it. He gave a decisive nod, and Mr. Antony beamed and snapped the case shut.

"You have the perfect judgment, my lord." He rolled the *R* so that the word stretched out. "I hope you will remember our establishment when you look to expand your jewel collection."

Oswald glanced at Fenella, who looked a little glassy-eyed and pale. "Did you pick a ring?" he asked.

"I—yes. This one," she said hoarsely.

Oswald glanced at it, a gold ring with green enamel leaves and a small turquoise set in a central rectangular mount. He might have known she would not pick the sapphire. "Does it need resizing, or can you wear it now?"

She slid it wordlessly onto her third finger where it sat looking perfectly at home.

"Excellent," he said. Then he remembered something. "Did you still want a brooch?"

"No, no," she said quickly, sitting up in her chair and coloring hotly. "This is more than enough, thank you."

"Come and try the diamond girdle," he said picking up the belt. When she reluctantly approached, he circled it around her hips and fastened the clasp, so the front length hung down to her knees.

"It's heavy," she murmured.

"Take a look in the glass," said Oswald. He watched her walk to the glass and turn before it to catch the glittering light on the diamonds. He turned to the jeweler, who had a look of quiet satisfaction on his face. "Come with me to my study and I will give you payment and speak to you of that other matter."

"My lord," replied the jeweler with a bow.

"Will you not take the belt with you for safekeeping?" asked Fen in alarm when he headed for the door.

Oswald turned back to her. "Fenella, you are at court. The very reason you have jewels is to show them off to others." He waved toward the table. "Try on the necklace. I will be back presently for supper." He disappeared along with the bowing Antonys and she watched the door shut behind him with dismay.

14

"I got a goddaughter," said Meldon confrontationally as Fenella sat kneeling on the floor in the bedroom. She had found space in the cupboard next to her side of the bed to keep her new headwear and was folding her new veils and tidying them away. He stuck out his jaw as if expecting her to argue.

She paused, casting about for a suitable reply. "You have?" she settled on warily.

"Aye. I'm not saying she's anything special," he said, shaking his head.

Fenella blinked. "I'm sure you're fond of her," she said uncertainly. He snorted. "Was it her mother or her father you are close to?"

He bridled. "Neither!" he snapped. "They'm both dead!"

"I see," said Fenella, who did not see remotely why he was telling her this. Instead she turned back to her task and started filling up the bottom shelf. She could tell he had not moved away and was still stood watching her. Still, she took her time arranging things to her satisfaction before turning back to him.

He was stood watching her critically. "You shouldn't be grubbing about on your knees. She could do that for you." Light dawned. Meldon wanted to secure a lady's maid position for his goddaughter. She hoped the girl's attitude was better than his, but in truth, it could scarcely be any worse. "Shall I bring her by then?" he asked impatiently.

Fenella rose from her knees to shut the cupboard door and then turned to face him. "Very well," she said coolly. "But you should be aware, Meldon, that I have run my own household for eight years. I have standards I will expect. Has she acted as lady's maid before?"

He looked taken aback. "She's been all sorts. Aphrany born and bred," he prevaricated. "But she's been working in a cooper's shop since she took up with that useless lump of a husband of hers." By the curl of his lip, she could tell he did not approve of the fact.

"Well, the fact she's a city girl could be useful to me," she conceded. "What is her name?"

"Trudy."

"Her age?"

"Thirty-five or thereabouts," said Meldon reluctantly. He scratched his chin.

Hardly a girl then, thought Fenella. "Has she any children?"

"Aye, but they'm apprenticed out now and not suckling babes."

"By all means, bring her by," Fenella agreed with a nod. "I would be happy to meet her."
Meldon shut his mouth tightly and nodded. "And could you possibly find me some writing ink and parchment?" she asked. "I would like to write a letter to my sister-in-law."

He stalked off and Fen placed the heavy ruby and emerald necklace and the diamond belt on the bed neatly. She had

165

glanced around but could see no strong box in the bedroom. Perhaps Lord Vawdrey kept it under the bed or under a loose floorboard.

She hardly felt she had the right to go poking around his room in search of it, so instead she placed both the necklace and the belt into an empty drawer and went back to the outer room, taking a seat at the table next to the fire where Bors was dozing.

How on earth was one supposed to fill one's time as a courtier anyway? She couldn't even walk her dog when she had no decent clothes to wear! And she had not even been to check on her horse since she had left her in the palace stables. Hopefully poor Rowena was being adequately cared for.

With a frown, she wondered if she should try to venture out. Her cloak would cover the scarlet robe. But where was her cloak? With a start, she realized she had not seen it since that disastrous meeting in Oswald Vawdrey's study. It was probably being cleaned along with her dress, she surmised hopefully. They had been quite muddy from the road after all. Her thoughts were interrupted as a tray was set down in front of her with a rattle. On it lay a metal pen with two different nibs, a sheaf of parchment, and a bottle of black ink.

"Thank you, Meldon," she said, picking up the pen at once and inspecting the state of the nibs. To her relief, they were in good order and she would not have to scratch over the page, blotting ink as she went. Immediately she set about composing a missive to Orla, which proved most difficult to write and took her the best part of an hour.

She scratched her temple and scrunched her nose as she tried to find a delicate way to tell her sister of eight years that far from halting her divorce, she had instead found that she was legally wed to a completely different man! Orla would be scandalized, and who could blame her? thought Fen dolefully. She then apologized for any worry her sister-in-law might have experienced on Bors's disappearance and assured her he was safely with his mistress at court.

Then she wrote out a paragraph with instructions to forward her personal possessions and clothes to her brother's house, finishing with a postscript hoping that Turvey, the household steward, was well and Langdon the cook.

Their relationships with Orla were strained to say the least, and Fen wondered how long things would continue amicably there, without her to smooth any ruffled feathers. She thought longingly of Thurrold where everything was familiar and ordered. In truth, she had always loved it far more than Sitchmarsh Hall, her girlhood home. All she could remember of Vawdrey Keep was a tall stone fortress with a draughty great hall and a booming-voiced master.

He was gone now of course, and from everything her new husband had told her, she would be free to make it her home without any involvement from him. It was five years since he had even been there by all accounts. *What a strange setup*, she reflected as she heard a door open and Roland Vawdrey stomp through wearing a chain mail shirt and hood over his head.

He spared her a scornful glance before wrenching open the main door, exiting through it, and then slamming it behind him. She sighed, drew another piece of paper across the table, and started a letter to her brother, Gil, this time assuring him that she was fine and asking him to take care of any of her things that Orla would be sending his way.

She didn't like to have them sent straight to Vawdrey Keep as it seemed presumptuous somehow. Besides, they would be neighbors soon and it would be easy enough to have her possessions fetched over in a cart.

Lord Vawdrey was carrying something when he arrived back at their rooms. "We are attending a banquet tonight," he announced and dropped a parcel onto one of the chairs.

"But I have nothing to wear," blurted Fen in alarm.

He gestured toward the parcel. "You can wear this," he said.

"You had my dress cleaned already?" said Fen with relief as she made for it. "Is my cloak in there too?" It was a very big parcel.

"No," admitted Oswald after a pause. "An acquaintance sent this for you to borrow."

Fen lowered the parcel with surprise. "But how do they know what will fit me?"

Oswald shrugged. "It will probably need some alteration," he said. "She is sending along her maid presently to attend you."

His acquaintance was a woman, she thought with a jolt, but he had walked straight past her and was pouring himself some water. "Roland has gone out, dressed in armor," she told him.

"Has he?" He could not have sounded less interested if he had tried. There was a knock on the door and Oswald walked to it. He opened it and admitted an efficient-looking young woman with hair so blond it was almost white. It was braided and

168

pinned very neatly around her head. She bobbed a curtsey and headed straight for Fenella.

"You got it then?" she said, nodding at the parcel. "Shall we take a look how it fits?"

Fen surmised this was the maid of the acquaintance and nodded. "By all means. Follow me," she said and headed for the bedroom with the maid following closely behind her. "It is very kind of you to come and aid me. What is your name?" asked Fen as she started undoing her buttons.

"Jenny," the other tossed over her shoulder as she attacked the string securing the parcel. "I'm Lady Sumner's personal maid."

"Lady Sumner," repeated Fenella. She did not know the name. "I believe she is an acquaintance of my husband's."

Jenny nodded. "You'll meet my lady tonight," she said, unbundling an undergown of cream and gold brocade. "She can't wait to clap eyes on *you*," she added, turning and shaking out a silken underdress. "Though she pretended to yawn when she told me, like it was the greatest bore." Jenny snorted. "But you can't fool a maid you've had for ten years," she sniffed. "Be she ever so clever."

"Is she very clever then, your mistress?" asked Fenella.

"That's her reputation, milady." Jenny compressed her lips. "But it's all book learning!" she scoffed. "She's never turned a distaff, nor a meat spit her entire life. Not with them white hands!"

169

"I see," said Fen, stepping out of the red robe. She shivered in her shift. Jenny cast an appraising eye over her. "Well, you've much more flesh on you than my mistress, I can see that for nothing. I shall have to let out the seams."

Fen blinked. *Well that was plain speaking!* "I hope it will not mar the gown," she said. "Could I help?"

Jenny shook her head. "It'll be quicker if I work alone," she said, crossing to sit on one of the high back chairs. "Why don't you unpack the rest of it," she said around a mouthful of pins. "I'll get started right away."

Fen crossed to the bed and picked up a luxurious overdress of rich brown velvet. The low neckline was studded with pearls and colored stones. "It's very beautiful," she gasped. "This must be your mistress's best gown."

Jenny snorted. "Not her," she scoffed. "She's got about ten of those, and rest assured, she gave you the one that becomes her the least. She's never even worn that one," added Jenny. "Probably planned to wear it when she's in mourning for his lordship."

Fen was startled. "She is anticipating a bereavement?" *Poor woman.*

"She's been anticipating it since she married him," said Jenny pertly. "My Lord Sumner is eighty-five years of age."

"Oh, I see," said Fen, who saw nothing of the kind. She badly wanted to ask how old Lady Sumner was but knew she should not encourage the maid so kindly sent to help her to gossip about her own mistress.

170

"She's thirty-five," said Jenny, giving her a sideways glance. "In case you're wondering."

"A fifty-year age gap!" exclaimed Fen before she could stop herself.

Jenny smirked. "Indeed. And it suits my lady greatly to be left to her own devices." Her needle flashed as it went in and out of the shimmering fabric.

"I see," murmured Fen as she shook out the folds from the heavy fabric. "Have they been married for many years?"

"Ten years." Jenny shrugged.

"Only ten?" Fen had thought that perhaps Lady Sumner had been married to him as a very young bride when he was in his late fifties or early sixties perhaps.

The fabric rustled as Jenny turned it over to expose another seam and then snipped at it with a small pair of silver scissors from her belt. "Let us have a look and see if this will suffice," she said, standing up.

Fen crossed the room and held out her arms as the maid the slipped the brocade dress over her head and then yanked it firmly over her shoulders and chest where it was already a tight fit despite not yet being laced to close.

"I don't think this will fit," said Fen doubtfully as Jenny pulled and pushed at her shift out of sight and then manipulated the stiff fabric to slide down her body.

"Nonsense," huffed Jenny. "We just need to—if you'll pardon me, my lady." She shoved Fen's breasts upward where they strained against the low neckline. "There!" she said triumphantly. "Now, let me fasten the side lacings whilst we can. If you'll just support your bosoms while I move around to the side, milady."

"Er…like this?" Fen said, making a shelf out of her arm. She looked down at the two scoops of her milky-white flesh and blanched. "I don't think—" Jenny cut off her words with a tight pull of the side laces. "That's a little tight!" she exclaimed in alarm.

Jenny patted her reassuringly. "I knows what I'm about, milady," she said. "Never fear!" She stepped to the other side and started on the fastenings there too.

"Don't forget I have to be able to sit down in comfort and even eat a morsel or two," said Fen uneasily.

Jenny yanked on the lacings. "None of them fine ladies are ever sitting comfortably," she said wisely. "You just has to relax your face like you are. Then the men believe it, fools that they are." She nodded then straightened up and spanned her hands around Fen's admittedly much smaller waist. "You see?"

"Yes…" admitted Fenella. She kept catching sight of her elevated bosom. It was distracting. She could only hope that the overdress would somehow make her look more decent. She bit her lip.

As if reading her thoughts, Jenny crossed to the bed to pick up the brown velvet. She returned and slipped it over Fen's head

172

and tugged it down over the cream and gold gown. Then she moved to the back and started lacing that too.

Glancing down, any hope that Fenella had for concealment was dashed. The overgown was tight fitted to the waist. Its jewel-encrusted neckline was even lower than that of the scanty undergown. It seemed to start from her armpits and its placement was just about level to her nipples. A strip of the cream and gold brocade could be seen just above it, skimming the tops of her swelling breasts.

The most substantial part of the ensemble was the voluminous sleeves, which were fitted to the elbow and then extended down almost to the floor so the sleeves of the shimmering undergown could be seen. Jenny stood back and surveyed her a moment, before kneeling at her feet and taking more pins from her mouth to start artfully arranging and pinning the overdress so that it revealed the brocade gown underneath. Fen had to admit that the maid knew what she was doing. She had no idea that glass-beaded pins could be put to such use. It hardly seemed respectable!

She wondered fleetingly if Lady Sumner could be some kind of courtesan, but then reminded herself she was a respectably married lady. Jenny took her time over the arrangements of her skirts. She straightened up several times to survey the results of her labors, even crossing the room to check on Fenella's appearance from a greater distance. Finally, with a nod, she seemed to be happy with the results. She gestured toward the looking glass. "Very nice," she pronounced. "Take a look for yourself."

Fen crossed the room and barely recognized the sophisticated and alluring woman before her in the mirror. She gulped. "But what about—?" She glanced down at her straining bosom. "I can't be expected to go out in public like this, surely?"

Jenny looked back at her in shock. "Of course not, milady. Your chests are quite naked."

Fenella's shoulders slumped in relief. "So, what do we use to cover them?"

"Your jewels, of course," said Jenny simply.

Fen blinked. "My jewels," she repeated dazedly.

"You do have some, I take it? You being a countess by rights," retorted Jenny with a frown.

Fen tottered toward the chest of drawers and withdrew her long diamond girdle belt and the ruby and emerald gold necklace. She turned back to Jenny, who gasped with delight.

"I should say you do," she said admiringly as she took the belt in her hands and wrapped it about Fenella's waist, fastening it so the front hung down. "I've never seen one so fine," she marveled.

"It was a wedding present from—my—from Lord Vawdrey," said Fen. She blushed faintly. It seemed so wrong to refer to Oswald Vawdrey by any term of familiarity.

"Well, he must hold you in a very high regard, and no mistake," the maid replied. She turned back for the necklace and then fastened it about Fen's neck. Fenella flinched at the contact of her soft skin with the cold metal and jewels. Jenny twitched the central emerald so that it was placed directly in the center of her décolletage. The dangling teardrop pearl hung down in the valley between her breasts. If anything, the jewelry seemed to accentuate her near-naked top half.

"Perfect," said Jenny, who clearly had no such reservations. "Now, what are we doing with my lady's hair?" she asked.

Jenny redressed Fenella's hair and arranged it so her thick, dark braids looped around her velvet hair band before being caught up at the back in her new gold hairnet. The result looked vastly sophisticated to Fenella, who had blinked at her reflection feeling quite dazzled. She had never looked so well, she thought dazedly. Not even in her first flush of youth, nor on her wedding day. She turned her head again to look at the elaborate arrangement of glossy brown hair.

"Very nice," pronounced Jenny again and plunked her hands on her hips. She gave a crack of laughter. "She'll regret sending you this outfit," she said, ushering Fen out of the bedroom. "You see if she don't!"

Lord Vawdrey was rising from his chair, no doubt to go and change his own clothes. On spotting her, he paused and straightened up. His eyes narrowed and he stood very still, just looking at her. Fen stood hopefully and clasped her hands. Would he think she finally looked like a sophisticated countess?

She felt breathless, waiting for his verdict. Although, to be fair, that could just have been the tight lacing. Roland gave a low whistle and she turned her head, not having realized her brother-in-law was now sat at the table. "Not wholly contemptible," he said with a shrug, and they all turned to look at him with annoyance.

175

Jenny giggled. "I'll see myself out," she said, skipping toward the door.

"Thank you, Jenny," Fen called after her. When she turned back, the bedroom door was slamming shut behind Lord Vawdrey. Fen felt her shoulders droop in disappointment. Perhaps her transformation was not worthy of comment after all.

"If you're hoping to set Oswald ablaze with ardor, you're wasting your efforts," said Roland dryly. Fen felt herself blush at his indelicacy. He gave a smirk. "I see you don't deny it."

"Why should I?" Fen asked coolly. She could see Roland Vawdrey was baiting her. After all, she had not been raised with a brother of her own for nothing. She crossed the room to the window seat and carefully sat herself down. A quick glance down reassured her that nothing had slipped out of its confines.

Roland had leaned back in his chair. "He's got ice water in his veins instead of red blood," he elaborated. "Women just aren't his passion."

"I see," said Fen politely. "That, doubtless, is his work."

"You know *nothing* about him," he carried on contemptuously. "You're still that little girl trailing after him, pretending to wear his ring."

Fen gave a start of surprise at this. She *had* once pretended that the old ring her father gave her was her betrothal ring. "I was only twelve," she pointed out. "And I seem to remember *you* were pretending to be a giant devouring the bones of villagers.

176

You kept making squeaky voices, begging for their lives as you ate your meat."

Roland looked annoyed. "I was an ogre," he said indignantly. "Devouring the bones of the innocent."

"Still, I'm impressed you even remember," said Fen. "It was so long ago."

"My memory is actually pretty good, despite the fact I'm considered the family blockhead," he said sourly.

"Are you the family blockhead?" Fen tipped her head and considered him awhile. "Why would anyone think so?"

Roland tsked under his breath with annoyance. He held up three fingers. "Mason married money and a title," he said, lowering one. "Oswald is a slithering snake at court." He lowered a second. "And I have a strong sword arm," he said flatly.

"'Slithering snake'?" repeated Fen, feeling confused.

"Gods, you're stupid," said Roland crossly. "Think about it. All the strange, anonymous men that appear to do his bidding, the ones that all look interchangeable?" He looked at her expectantly.

Fen thought of the two men who had brought Bors to her. Her dog, she noticed, instead of defending her honor, was currently sat under Roland's chair getting his ear scratched with a look of bliss on his face.

"Do you even know what Oswald does at court?" Roland asked impatiently. He switched to Bors's other ear.

Fen flushed. "He is the King's chief adviser," she said uncertainly.

"Among other things," snorted Roland. "Gods, you're as bad as Mason. Both of you are completely blind where Oswald's concerned, taking everything he says at face value."

"Well," said Fen, suddenly feeling fed up with Roland's insults. "Cheer up. If I'm so stupid, maybe I will replace you as family blockhead."

Roland's head snapped up, but before he had a chance to respond, the bedroom door opened, and Lord Vawdrey strode out.

15

Fenella stole a nervous glance up at Lord Vawdrey, but his handsome profile did not invite conversation. He seemed a little cold toward her, she thought in dismay. His strides were long, and she was starting to puff as she hurried to keep up with him as they made their way along the high-ceiling corridors. She clung to his arm and hoped her exposed bosom wasn't turning to gooseflesh. At least her hot face was getting a chance to cool down from the icy draughts blasting along the stone flagstone floors.

"My lord," she faltered, at last forced to admit she was getting a stitch in her side. "Could we slacken the pace a little? It is hard to catch my breath in this dress and I am having to take five steps to your every one."

He slowed at once and looked down at her with a frown. "Let us hope the dresses signor Pezzini makes will not be so tight," he said, and Fen felt mortified.

She gulped. "I expect they will fit better. Jenny said I am a lot more corpulent than Lady Sumner," she said and felt her eyes sting.

"*Corpulent* is not the word I would use," he said in a clipped voice. "Did you not look in the glass? Or do you want me to pay you a compliment?" Fen's lip wobbled and he seemed to catch himself. "Fenella…"

"No, no, it's nothing," she said hastily. "I did not expect—that is—I know I am not—"

Voices and footsteps were approaching, and she heard Oswald curse under his breath. He drew her backward into a stone alcove where they were hidden in shadow. Fen sucked in a surprised breath and stifled a gasp as he pushed up against her until the footsteps had passed. Fen did not recognize the voices, but then that was not surprising. She barely knew a soul at court. Her heart raced and she held her breath.

Oswald Vawdrey did not speak for a moment, and when he did, his voice was low and gravelly. "Fenella, under no circumstances are you to let yourself be alone with any other men when I am not in the vicinity. I don't care if you have to pretend to fall in a fainting fit, do not allow yourself to be sequestered by any other males—even the King. Do you understand?"

She blinked up at him. She could imagine nothing less likely. The King had even ordered her out of his presence in disgust the day before. But even in the shadows, she could make out the tight look on his face, so she nodded. "Very well, my lord."

He breathed out a ragged breath, then stepped sharply back, pulling her with him.

"My Lord Vawdrey!" exclaimed a surprised, yet cultured voice.

Fenella watched a look of annoyance pass briefly over her husband's face before it smoothed out into a perfect expression of urbanity. "My Lady Sumner," he said coolly and bowed before turning to her companion. "Lord Bardulf." He bowed again, but this time not so deeply.

The other man looked highly amused. "But who is this?" he said, turning deliberately to Fenella and letting his lazy gaze

180

travel over her. "Charming creature, and why were you…?" He turned back to look at the alcove from which they had emerged.

"Really, Bardulf," murmured Lady Sumner disapprovingly. She was very respectable looking and nothing like Fen had anticipated. She placed an elegant hand on her very white throat and averted her eyes as if confronted with something indecent.

To her surprise, Fen felt Oswald's hand slide about her waist and draw her closer to his side. "This is my wife, the Countess Vawdrey," he said in measured tones. Fen felt the gazes of the other two snap to her in surprise. Lady Sumner's mouth fell open. Bardulf collected himself first and gave her a deep bow. "Fenella," Oswald continued. "This is Viscount Bardulf and Lady Anne Sumner."

Lady Sumner dipped into an elegant curtsey. "I am very pleased to meet you," she murmured, giving Fen a swift, appraising look from head to foot. Fen saw the exact moment when she recognized the dress she had lent her.

"I, too, am very happy to make your acquaintance," said Fen and curtseyed in reply.

Bardulf appeared to be silently laughing as he straightened up. "Only you, Vawdrey, could arrange things so neatly," he said, shaking his head. "Even with my very great respect for you, I had underestimated your mastery of any situation. A wife, waiting in the wings," he said, turning to Fenella thoughtfully. "Really, no one could have anticipated such a thing."

"You must excuse the viscount, Lady Vawdrey," said Lady Anne, addressing her directly. Her voice was faintly

181

patronizing. "He is a droll creature and delights in saying outrageous things."

Fen opened her mouth to respond, but Lord Vawdrey cut across her.

"If you will excuse us," he said. "I have a great many people to introduce my wife to this evening." He squeezed her waist, propelling Fen to join him as they walked the last few steps toward the Great Hall.

"Are they friends of yours?" asked Fen.

Lord Vawdrey shrugged. "I do not have friends, Fenella," he said. "Let us say they move in the same circles as I."

They crossed the threshold into the Great Hall, and Fen blinked at the blazing torches and the press of nobles clustered in groups about the banqueting hall.

"The Earl and Countess Vawdrey!" announced a herald in a loud, booming voice. Fen heard the swell of conversation grow around them alarmingly. Lord Vawdrey had taken her arm now and was steering her firmly through the crowds. She could not see above the glittering company, but after the first few steps, she realized they were heading in the direction of a raised dais at the far end of the room and her heart sank.

She was not looking forward to another royal encounter. Raising her chin, she attempted to conceal the fact by not allowing her gaze to land on any of the curious faces turned her way. People put up their hands to muffle the words they were hurriedly speaking to one another, but she could distinctly make out *Thane* and *divorce*.

She swallowed and hoped she could blame her heightened color on the huge roaring fireplaces on either end of the hall, though in truth, it was draughty enough thanks to the high vaulted ceilings, which made it as cold as a cathedral. She felt Lord Vawdrey at her side nod to various people, though he did not pause to introduce her to any of them.

When they reached the dais, Lord Vawdrey paused a moment. The King was situated to the right and the Queen to the left. There was enough room between for them to be surrounded by two completely different crowds of people.

"Vawdrey," hailed the King, but almost simultaneously the Queen leaned forward in her seat.

"Lord Vawdrey, will you approach and introduce your wife to me?" she asked. The King harrumphed and waved his arm, indicating his assent, and Oswald approached the Queen with Fenella.

"Your Majesty, may I present my wife, Countess Vawdrey? Fenella, this is Queen Armenal."

Fenella swept down into a deep curtsey and rose up to find the dark-eyed Queen surveying her with great curiosity. Queen Armenal was vastly elegant in a rich green gown with deep borders stitched with gold leaves. She wore a heavy gold collar inlaid with colored enamel and precious stones. Her dark hair was dressed high off her face with a veil cascading down from a golden crown. Fenella had never seen a lady so tall and graceful.

"You may go and speak with the King, my Lord Vawdrey," said the Queen dismissively to Oswald. "I am keen to have some speech with your new wife."

His eyebrows rose, but he bowed again, and sending Fenella a reassuring look, he drifted over to the King.

"Now, Lady Vawdrey," said the Queen, "you must accept a cup of mead and come closer to me, unless you wish for our words to be overheard by the masses."

Fenella took a cup from a lady-in-waiting who had appeared at her elbow and then approached the Queen cautiously. She was dismayed to see there were no other chairs on the dais. She would have to hover like a moth around the Queen's flame.

"I am very pleased to finally clap eyes on this mysterious bride of Lord Vawdrey's," said Queen Armenal. "Who on finding herself scorned by her first husband, rides up so brazenly to the royal palace and demands an earl in recompense!"

Fen spilt a little of the honeyed wine down her sleeve and tried to ignore the cold trickle down her wrist as one of the ladies-in-waiting giggled. "But you are not as bold-faced as I was led to believe," said the Queen plaintively. She looked Fen critically up and down. "In truth, you are quite sweet-faced." She sounded disappointed. "And more comely than seductive."

Fen goggled at her. In all of her days, she would never imagine being told by a Queen that she was sweet-faced and comely! "Th-thank you, Your Majesty," she blurted. The ladies-in-waiting tittered again and Armenal looked irritated.

"If you are waiting on me, then take the step back!" she ordered. Several maidens shuffled backward with disappointed expressions. The Queen frowned. "The King insists on foisting these girls on me," she said in exasperation. "He would not be so happy if I chose his cabinet members by the shapeliness of their calves. We married women have much to bear, as I am sure you are more aware than most."

"Yes, Your Majesty," agreed Fen. She glanced to the side to check Oswald had not gone off and left her alone with this alarming woman. He was still stood close by the King now, engaged in conversation, but something about his stance told her he knew exactly where she was. She returned her eyes to Queen Armenal, who was watching her with a disturbingly hawklike gaze.

"And what do you make of this new husband of yours, Lady Vawdrey?" she asked in a quiet voice, tipping her head to one side.

Strangely enough, Fen suddenly remembered being asked a similar thing by old Baron Vawdrey once. "He is very fine," she answered foolishly and blushed.

The Queen's eyes flickered with surprise. "I hardly credited it at the time, but I did hear a rumor that you were childhood sweethearts. Can there possibly be a grain of truth to that tale?"

Fen cleared her throat. "I—er—I was very young, Your Majesty, when we first met," she said miserably and hung her head. This was disastrous. Instead of coming across as a woman of the world, she had a horrible feeling she looked every bit the overawed bumpkin. She breathed in and out and tried to collect herself.

185

"Dear me!" said Armenal. "You are not at all what I was led to expect." She gave a sad sigh. "It is so often the way. These court scandals are all fury and no substance."

Fen clutched her fingers together in tongue-tied misery. She had disappointed the Queen now as well as the King. "I should so like to have seen Lord Vawdrey led about by the nose for once," said the Queen sadly. "But I can see you are not the woman to do this."

"No, Your Majesty," she whispered. For one horrible moment, she thought her eyes would fill with tears, but she blinked them very fast and it passed.

"Well," said the Queen dismissively. "I doubt I shall see you much at court, Lady Vawdrey," she said with a yawn. "I expect your husband will tuck you away in darkest Vawdreyshire before the month is out."

"Sitchmarsh," Fen corrected her automatically.

The Queen sat up in her seat, and for a moment Fen thought she would get scolded for impertinence, but then she realized the Queen was staring past her. "Ah, how providential!" exclaimed Queen Armenal, clapping her hands together. "Who do you suppose I have just spotted across the room?" she asked Fenella in barely concealed excitement.

"I hardly know, Your Highness," Fen murmured, wondering if she could fall back from the royal presence anytime soon.

"Ah, but it is none other than your former husband," said the Queen with delight. "And the woman who supplanted you!" She clapped her hands imperiously and an attendant darted

186

forward. Fen froze. "Tell me," said the Queen, turning back to her as the attendant sped away into the crowd. "Have you seen him since his return from the north?"

Fen looked at the Queen's gleeful face with ill-disguised horror. "N-no, Your Majesty, that is…" Her voice trailed away, and she turned to see the crowds parting and Ambrose approaching the dais with his new bride, Lady Colleen. She swayed and suddenly felt a hard body had come up behind her, propping her up and placing a possessive hand at her side. She breathed out, recognizing Lord Vawdrey's presence, and leaned back into him in relief.

Oswald Vawdrey's thumb stroked against her side. He leaned down to murmur in her ear. "Don't be afraid. It is probably for the best to get this awkward encounter out of the way at once." She nodded obediently, though in truth this seemed the very worst way of doing it, in front of an avid audience of courtiers.

Through glassy eyes, she focused on Ambrose's approach. Far from seeming discomfited, he had a puffed look about him as he bustled forward, nose stuck in the air. He was wearing the pearl-studded tunic from his wedding feast, she noticed. He paused to help Lady Colleen mount the steps to the dais. Strangely enough, he seemed a lot shorter than she remembered. Could he have shrunk in the last two years?

"Sir Arthur," the Queen greeted him. Fen watched a spasm cross his face as the Queen got his name wrong, but he bowed very low and presented his leg to her. He was wearing burgundy tights, and Fen remembered Armenal's words earlier about calves. *Doubtless Ambrose would not have been selected on the strength of his legs*, she thought distractedly.

187

Ambrose straightened up, but his eyes scrupulously avoided Fenella and instead fixed on the Queen. His wife hovered at his side, her gaze darting from Queen Armenal to the watching courtiers as if she could not decide who she would rather look at. She curtseyed so low that her forehead nearly grazed the floor.

"Sir Arthur, Lady Thane," said the Queen. "May I present to you Earl and Countess Vawdrey, who I believe you will have something in common with." The Queen paused as their audience drew in a collective bated breath. "Being so recently newly wed," she added slyly, and a shiver of mirth ran through the crowd.

"How do you do," said Lord Vawdrey, sounding politely bored.

Fen fixed a smile on her face and dropped into a shallow curtsey. She couldn't go any deeper as Oswald's hand clamped on her side prevented it.

"I hope there is no awkwardness in this encounter," said the Queen archly. "Is this the first time that all of you have met since your divorce and subsequent remarriages?" she enquired.

"Yes, Your Majesty," said Ambrose, dropping into another bow. His wife bobbed again beside him.

Fen noticed how studiously he avoided looking at her. *Coward*, she thought with surprise. Had he thought to cast her off and never be troubled by seeing her again? She had not thought so ill of him. Her face was starting to hurt from the forced smiling, and the encounter was starting to take on the properties of a nightmare.

She placed a hand on Oswald Vawdrey's at her waist, as if to draw strength from his show of solidarity. Just as she thought it couldn't get any worse, she noticed the discreet string of pearls around Lady Colleen's throat. *Surely not*, she thought, her breath coming in very short, painful pants. The last time she had seen those they had been safely stored in her own jewelry box at Thurrold. She must be mistaken, she thought in anguish. Her replacement could not be flaunting her own mother's pearls.

She knew them so well, the small necklet with the red enamel clasp. Every seventh stone was not a pearl at all, but a gold-colored glass bead. Her straining eyes could see the very same details on the small necklace around Ambrose's bride's neck. Swallowing the painful lump in her throat, she realized there could be no mistake.

Ambrose had gifted *her* pearls to his new wife. And he had no right, she thought, her hand trembling as she placed it absently to her own throat. He had no right to give her own dear mother's pearls to that woman! She felt sick. Almost, she fancied she could see a gloating look on Colleen Thane's face, but that must be in her own mind, she told herself. Ambrose probably had not even told his new wife that he had not bought her them himself.

Unable to help herself, she looked across again and found Lady Thane was looking right at her now as she very slowly raised a hand to touch the necklace. It would look like a casual movement to any onlooker but herself. Fen gasped sharply. A smirk passed over the new Lady Thane's face, which almost knocked Fen off her feet. *She did know.* She knew she was wearing Fen's necklace, and she was triumphant of the fact! Fen's heart started thudding in her chest and she tightened her grip on her Oswald's fingers so hard that her fingers turned white.

"My dear," drawled Lord Vawdrey. "Perhaps you could loosen your grip before I lose all sensation in my hand."

She glanced up at him, and found they had been excused from the royal presence. The Thanes were descending the steps from the dais, and Oswald Vawdrey was ushering her to follow.

"I'm sorry, my lord," she said quickly and followed his lead. Everyone was drifting toward the long tables now as rows of servants brought out the first course. To her surprise, she found that Lord Vawdrey led her to the nearest table, whereas the Thanes were now disappearing down the hall. Then she comprehended those present would all be seated according to rank. And Earl Vawdrey ranked considerably higher than Sir Ambrose Thane.

A chair was drawn out for her, and she was seated as trays of glazed meats were circulated by squires and pages. Behind the top table was a dazzling array of velvet-draped steps covered in golden plates laden with food. In the center of their table was a large jelly in the shape of a swan, fully decorated with feathers and a golden beak. Fen had to stop herself from staring at all the sights.

She was introduced to Lord and Lady Schaeffer, who they were sat next to. Lord Schaeffer was gray and bearded and dressed in conservative navy blue with an air of affluence. His wife was a very handsome woman in her fifties with a regal bearing. Both were polite and welcoming, and Fen tried to smile and say the right thing although she felt dazed and miserable after her run-in with Ambrose.

The first course, a sturgeon served in parsley and vinegar, was served, and Fenella forced down a few bites, listening while Lord Schaeffer talked about the privy council with Oswald. She could not follow what they were discussing, though it sounded like the possible replacement of a member. Her goblet was filled with mead, and a troop of musicians dressed in red and green filtered into the hall and started to play. Fenella found she could not help but glance toward where the Thanes sat further down the hall.

Colleen was whispering with a stuck-up looking older woman, who was gazing around them in disapproval. Fen noticed they had not yet been served with any food or drink, which might be the source of her displeasure. Her own first course had been whisked away in the meantime and another plate set before her. She found herself speculating if the older woman was Colleen's mother and wondered how Ambrose would like having a mother-in-law. Her own mother had died years before their wedding.

"Fenella, do you think you could tear your gaze away from the Thanes long enough to eat a bite?" asked Oswald smoothly.

Fenella looked down in embarrassment at her untouched goose in garlic and grape sauce. She blushed. "I—that is—" She closed her eyes briefly, trying to rein in her misery. "I'm sorry."

"Are you feeling unwell?" he asked coolly.

"No, not unwell—"

"Then kindly pull yourself together, Fenella. You're making a spectacle of yourself and of me." She looked up quickly at him,

191

but there was something very disquieting about the fact that he could look so urbane, and yet speak so cuttingly at the same time. Blinking back her tears, she took a swig of honey mead. It was stronger than the one they made back home.

She managed to force a smile to her lips and forced her attention to the musicians at the other end of the hall. She could just about hear them over the babble of conversation and tapped her foot in time to the song, which had a tune she recognized, though the words were quite different to the ones she had learned in her youth.

She sipped steadily at the mead while they waited for the next course and was surprised when she reached the bottom of the cup. She glanced at Oswald, who was still engaged in conversation with Lord Schaeffer. She had disappointed him, she thought sadly.

Made bold by the mead, she leaned into him and angled her head up to whisper in his ear. "I'm sorry, my lord." He inclined his head slightly but other than that gave her no reaction. She felt horrible and churned up inside. He had bought her so many beautiful things and she had repaid him by looking like a cast-off wife who was pining for her former spouse. For that is what everyone would think, she thought wretchedly.

Slipping her arm through his, she tried again. "It's not what you think," she said in a low voice. This time he gave her no discernible reaction at all, did not even look at her. Instead he struck up a conversation with another courtier sat on the opposite side of the table. To make it worse, Lady Schaeffer sent a sympathetic look her way, which spoke volumes. Everyone thought her a pitiable thing.

192

"What a lovely necklace, Lady Vawdrey," the older woman said heartily. "The stones seem to glow with an inner fire. Are they genuine rubies?"

"Yes, indeed," rallied Fen, withdrawing her arm from her husband and touching the chain. "I am fortunate to have such a generous husband." In truth, it was probably worth five times what her pearl necklace was.

"Indeed. Mine refuses to buy me any more jewels," sighed Lady Schaeffer. She cast a sly look at her husband, who was too caught up in his conversation to respond to the jibe. "Still, we have been married thirty-two years," she acknowledged with a shrug.

"You forget, Lady Schaeffer," piped up a lady sat two seats down from Fenella in an arch, carrying voice. "That Lord and Lady Vawdrey have been married for some *fourteen years*." She turned wide, incredulous eyes toward Fen. "Is that not so, Lady Vawdrey?" Opposite her, another lady giggled. Fenella did not have the faintest idea who they were, but their spiteful expressions reminded her of a girl she had grown up with who was always there with a nasty jibe if you exposed any kind of vulnerability. Doubtless, they were of the same ilk as Nan Crosby with her cruel tongue.

"I'm afraid we haven't been introduced," answered Fen coolly. Then she deliberately turned her back to them and addressed Lady Schaeffer. "I wonder if you enjoy partaking of a walk in the mornings, Lady Schaeffer? My husband has kindly had my dog fetched to Aphrany, but I do not yet know of any good walks here in the castle grounds."

Lady Schaeffer's eyes gleamed a moment in appreciation. "But I would love to show you around the grounds, Lady Vawdrey," she answered swiftly. "And I myself have a hound who dearly needs the exercise."

"Then we must certainly do so," said Fen with a smile. "I would appreciate the help in navigating some of the more thorny and treacherous paths." They shared a look and Lady Schaeffer raised her goblet to toast her silently.

Suddenly Fen felt a whole lot more optimistic about the possibility of making friends at court. She glanced toward Oswald to see if he had noticed their exchange, but he was still looking remote, and her heart sank a little further.

Resolutely, she managed to avoid looking anywhere in the vicinity of the Thanes for the next two hours while the remaining four courses were served. Not just for her husband's sake, she thought, but for her own. She wouldn't give Lady Colleen the satisfaction of thinking her defeated. She needed to remember that her behavior reflected on her marriage. She had to behave in a fitting way for an earl's wife. It was the least she could do for her new husband after everything he had done for her.

On the way back to their rooms afterward she tried to speak to Oswald about the Schaeffers, but he wouldn't be drawn into conversation with her and answered only briefly and dismissively. As soon as he had escorted her inside, he made for their bedroom, and feeling uneasy, Fen followed him. He was moving around the room picking up various objects including a change of clothing.

"Where are you going?" she asked in alarm. "Are you leaving for somewhere?" He didn't answer her but turned back to the large chest where he kept his tunics. Fen hurried around the bed and laid her hand on his forearm. "Please, my lord," she said. "I can explain why I was so distracted."

"I'm not interested, Fenella." His words were entirely devoid of tone, and he looked pointedly down at her hand, waiting for her to remove it.

Instead of loosening her grip on his arm, she tightened it. "She was wearing my necklace," she blurted and could not help the tears which sprang to her eyes. "Which was why I was staring. They were my mother's pearls. Ambrose must have given them to her." She couldn't keep the emotion from her voice or the tears which trickled down her cheeks as quickly as she brushed them away.

Oswald's gaze snapped to hers. "*What* did you say?" he said softly.

"My mother's pearls," she repeated earnestly. "I could see quite plainly that's what she was wearing. And—and—" she broke off, taking a deep breath.

"And?" he repeated sharply.

"And she *knew*, I could tell—and—she didn't care, or rather, she was *glad* of the fact," Fen broke off with a sob.

Oswald stood very still for a moment and then suddenly dropped his pile of clothes with a sharp exclamation and made for the bedroom door. Fen watched him with an open mouth as he disappeared out of it. "Wait," she called weakly. "Where are

195

you going?" She ran after him to find him exiting the main door to their apartments. "My lord?" The door slammed shut after him and Fen stood dazedly at it a moment. Where had he gone?

She retraced her steps slowly back to their bedroom and picked up his discarded clothes, returning them neatly to his clothing chest. The fire had already been made up in the bedroom and a pitcher of still warm water was on the side awaiting their return. Loath to waste it, she poured half of it in the bowl, stripped down to her shift, and had a good wash.

She put away her jewelry into the drawer, took the pins out of her hair, rebraided it, and climbed into the bed. She was just debating blowing out the candles on her side when she heard the outer door swing open and footsteps heading toward her. Sitting up, Fen watched Oswald stride through the door carrying something in his hands.

He walked right round to her side of the bed, opened the lid of a wooden box, and emptied the contents onto the bedclothes in front of her. It was her jewelry. Fen stared at it. The pearl necklace sat at the top of the heap. Then she looked up at Oswald and moistened her lips. "How did you—?"

He held up a finger, halting her words. "I want you to go through this pile and separate what is yours, from *before* your travesty of a marriage with Thane. Then I want you to make a pile of what he bought for you, which we will be returning to his legally wedded wife. Is that clear?"
Fen nodded. "Now, Fenella," he added. "I want you to do it now." His words could cut glass.

She immediately scooped up her pearls, a tiny golden key, a pewter pilgrim's token she had bought once on a trip to

Hawkesbridge, and a bone ring carved in the shape of a bear's head that her father had given her on her tenth birthday. In the second pile she put a round silver brooch pin, a brass circlet to wear over your head veil and a leather belt with brass castings at the end. The second pile she pushed toward Oswald.

"These were from Ambrose," she said.

Oswald held up the wooden box. "And this?" he asked.

"That was his mother's," she said.

Oswald swept the three items back into the box. "I'll return these now," he said grimly.

Fen nodded and watched as he exited the room in long, purposeful strides. Then she opened her hand to look thoughtfully at her returned things. *Your travesty of a marriage with Thane*, he had said, rather bitingly. And perhaps he had a point.

After all, no husband who had ever respected her, let alone ever cared for her, would have sat idly by while she was slighted like that. Oswald Vawdrey had not sat by, she reflected, drawing in a shaky breath. He had restored her belongings to her.

She slid from the bed and added the four items to the drawer with her new adornments. She felt strangely calm now and determined to do better, to do right by her new husband. There would be no more tears for her old one, she vowed. She was Countess Vawdrey. And she needed to start acting like it so Oswald could be proud of her.

When he returned mere moments later, she was back under the covers awaiting his return. She waited silently as he stripped to the waist and washed and then slid into the other side of the bed. There was perfect silence between them for a moment. Then Fenella rolled onto her side facing him.

"I don't want to talk about it," he warned her.

"Very well, husband."

That seemed to silence him a moment. Fen blushed in the darkness, knowing full well she had never addressed him as that before.

"Next time," he said tightly, "I want you to simply tell me from the outset whatever is troubling you. I don't like misjudging you."

Fen thought about this a moment, weighing up his words. "Even if it's beneath your notice?" she asked in a small voice.

"If it's regarding you, then it isn't beneath my notice," he answered shortly.

Fen turned this over a moment too. It scared her a little, how much she liked his reply. "Very well, my lord," she agreed in little more than a whisper.

He sat up and blew out the candles on his bedside and then settled back onto the bed. Fen continued to stare at the spot she imagined his face would be. "Go to sleep, Fenella," he said in a throaty voice.

"I'm not tired now," she told him boldly. She reached out to lightly touch the bolster between them.

"You've had two cups of mead," he told her sternly. "You only think you're wide awake."

Fen was surprised he'd noticed how many cups of mead she'd had; he'd been so steadfastly ignoring her. But perhaps he had still been keeping a watch on her after all. The thought made her feel a little warmer inside. "Yes, husband," she said and could have sworn she heard him take a ragged indrawn breath and mutter something under his breath. "Good night."

She lay awake awhile, pondering on the different natures of her past and present husband. The funny thing was, Ambrose always fretted and worried about other people's true feelings or intentions, but usually only in relation to himself.

You could describe an event in minute detail to him, and he'd make all the right noises, and then at the end pat you on the head and declare it was all in your own head and you were making too much of it. A day or so later and he would have forgotten that you'd even told him.

Before now, she'd simply imagined that Ambrose's life was so much broader than her own that he simply did not have the space to consider her emotions overmuch. It seemed to her now that this was the absolute opposite with her new husband.

Lord Vawdrey did not make any sympathetic tuttings or murmurings in the right place of the story. He made no attempt to soothe hurt feelings. He fired a few short *uncomfortable* questions and then took swift and terrible action.

199

She could scarcely believe he had returned her pearls to her like that. She had thought at first that he was angry with her for being so trivial as to bring up something so far beneath his notice. The fact he had exposed himself to gossip and speculation simply to retrieve her property astonished her. When she finally dropped off to sleep, she was still marveling over it.

16

Fenella woke to the familiar warmth of Oswald Vawdrey's physical presence and lay a moment letting the happenings of the previous evening wash over her. She felt somehow comforted by the press of his firm, strong body as she recalled Ambrose's rude behavior, his refusal to meet her gaze, or even address her directly. That made her wince, but it was not the pain of betrayal she had felt a mere three days ago. She felt ashamed of him.

The man she had thought she had married would not have done something so callous as to make a gift to another woman of her pearls. Even Gil would be shocked by that. She resolved to tell her brother of it in her next letter, although she did not know the whole story of how exactly Colleen had got her pearls in her clutches, or how Lord Vawdrey had taken them back.

She had wanted to ask him last night, but he had been angry then, and she did not quite dare. She had slighted her new husband by acting miserably at the feast and that mortified her. She needed to make amends for that. He had done nothing but try to make things easy for her at court. And he had spent so much money on a full bridal trousseau for her.

She jumped, feeling his hand land on her thigh. But a sleepy murmur near her ear reassured her he was still fast asleep. She lay very still, and he huffed out a breath and shifted against her back. She examined the state of her own heart while she had a quiet moment. Her feelings still smarted and felt a little raw, but more like a bandage had been removed from a wound leaving it tender and sore rather than fresh and oozing.

She felt a flicker of optimism. Perhaps all *would* turn out well in the end? After all, was it not better to find out now if her husband was an unreliable philanderer who could not be trusted? While she was young enough to remarry? And despite all the odds, she had remarried well. According to Roland, ambition was Oswald's passion, not women. Therefore, was it not unlikely that he would visit similar disgrace on her in the future?

He seemed to feel strongly about according her the respect due to a wife. He had even been indignant on her behalf. Certainly, last night he had been angry. But at least part of that had been directed toward her, she reminded herself. For sitting in such misery when all at court were eager for a glimpse of his new wife. She would have to rectify that as soon as she got the chance, she vowed to herself.

The hand on her thigh gave her a light squeeze, and she turned her head to peer over her shoulder. Oswald Vawdrey's eyes were still shut, but he stirred against the pillows and frowned. She glanced toward the window to where gray light streamed through and wondered at the time. She fancied if she listened, she could hear Meldon going about his business in the rooms beyond theirs. No doubt he would soon be through with their washing water.

She wondered what she would be expected to do with herself today, when she still had no apparel to her name. It was most frustrating as she would have liked to have taken that walk with Lady Schaeffer. The latch clanked and the door swung open. Meldon crossed the threshold carrying a steaming jug of water.

She felt Oswald Vawdrey's head lift off the pillow behind her, then drop back down. He didn't hurry to move his hand from her leg, she noticed. The door had no sooner shut behind Meldon than it reopened, and he came in carrying a large leather pack, which he dropped down at the foot of the bed.

"What is that?" asked Oswald, though he did not move a muscle from where he lay.

"Come for the missus," said Meldon before correcting himself. "Her ladyship."

"For me?" Fenella struggled to disentangle herself and sit up. Oswald Vawdrey made a disgruntled noise, which she ignored.

"There be a letter too," said Meldon, throwing an opened letter onto the bed.

Fenella turned it over to see it addressed to Lady F. Thane. The seal, which was Ambrose's stag, had been broken. She frowned and then opened the letter which she realized at once was from Orla.

"'Tis from my sister-in-law," she said slowly.

"No, it isn't," said Oswald, finally rising from the bed and straightening up to walk toward the hot water pitcher. Fen kept her eyes riveted on the vellum sheet. She would never get used to his casual nudity. "That is not the Cadwallader crest."

"Cadwallader crest?" she repeated in confusion and then broke off. "Oh." He was referring to the fact her sister-in-law was now the Duchess of Cadwallader. "I meant, it is from my friend, Orla Thane," she corrected herself swiftly. "She writes that she has packed up my clothes, jewelry, and personal effects for their own safety, as she noticed that my document chest and

203

dog had both disappeared off the premises. Oh dear," she said, lowering the missive. "I did wonder if Orla might worry when she noticed Bors had gone. I asked her to take particular care of him, you see."

Oswald shook the water out of his eyes and reached for one of his dressing robes—the peacock-blue one this time. "Well, now we know how your pearls ended up around the wrong throat," he commented dryly. At her confused look, he gestured to the letter. "The package must have been delivered by mistake to the current Lady Thane."

Fen dropped her letter with an exclamation. "And she rifled through my things!" she said indignantly. "And took out what she wanted for herself! Well!" She jumped down from the bed and ran to the pack of clothes, which she started unfastening. "At least I will have something to wear at any rate," she said cheerfully. Oswald sauntered closer and grimaced as she pulled an old gray gown from the pack. "I use this one when tending to my herb garden," she said quickly.

"You cannot wear any of these at court, Fenella," he said firmly.

"Oh, but—!"

"They are strictly to be worn within the confines of these rooms, though I must confess, I would rather you did not." He eyed a shabby green woolen underdress with disfavor. In truth, it had seen better days but was still serviceable and warm.

"I was hoping to take Bors for a walk today with Lady Schaeffer," she said hurriedly. "It has been days since I've had any fresh air. Bors needs walking, and I have not been able to check on my horse."

"Roland has been walking Bors. And the royal stables will be adequately providing for your steed." Fen's face fell. Oswald came over and crouched down beside her, taking her hands in his. "Fenella, if you went abroad in these garments everyone would assume you were Lady Schaeffer's maid. What you fail to understand is that ladies at court are forever parading their wealth and standing."

"But surely Lady Schaeffer would not judge me so? She seemed a sensible lady of mature years."

"Lady Schaeffer would meet you in furs," he told her. "She would be most shocked indeed if you showed up in a threadbare gown and a patched cloak."

Fen's face flamed. "Sir Ambrose had been away from home these two years past," she said stiltedly. "I have not felt at liberty to refurbish my garments while I was running the estate."

Oswald Vawdrey's fingers tightened over hers. "You are my wife, Fenella. It is my right to provide for you." He released her hands and glanced disparagingly at the pile of clothes. "If I had my way, these things would be burned."

"Burned?" blurted Fen in alarm. "That would be most wasteful," she added. "There is still plenty of wear to be had from them. Perhaps I could give them to Meldon's goddaughter?"

"Who?" Oswald looked completely bewildered for the first time since she'd met him. He straightened up and held his hand out to her to pull her to her feet.

"Meldon has recommended his goddaughter for my maid," she explained as she took his hand. He pulled her upright. "She is married to a cooper and lives in Aphrany."

Oswald shook his head slightly. "Someone actually chose Meldon to watch over their child's well-being?" he said. "It almost beggars belief."

"Apparently she is thirty or thereabouts and a good, capable girl who has held several positions through her life," rattled off Fenella efficiently. "Shall I look to engage her?" She paused before adding reasonably, "The fact is, if we tried to introduce another maid to your household, Meldon would be sure to take umbrage."

"You may have something there," agreed Oswald with a grimace. "We can only hope she is not related to him by blood."

Fen tried to imagine a female version of Meldon and failed. She shook herself. "I said I would give her a trial, so I will tell Meldon you are in agreement."

"For your sake, I hope she is satisfactory," he said, then paused. "Was there anything else? In the letter?"

Fen looked down at the page of handwriting she still held in her hand. "Orla says she has not yet heard from her brother but expects to daily. She hopes I am well and is sure the servants are slacking off as she does not know the plan for preserving the autumn fruits."

She looked back to Oswald. "Orla does not take much interest in the running of Thurrold," she explained. "She and Cook do not get along either." Instantly, she felt foolish for confiding as such in Lord Vawdrey. Doubtless, he would have little interest in anything so trivial.

"I see," he said, not looking unduly disgusted, nor overly interested either. "I expect Miss Thane will receive the letter you wrote her any day now, which will explain the change in your circumstances."

Fen's expression brightened. "That is true," she agreed.

"I will see if I can procure you a cloak," said Oswald. "Perhaps, if it is sufficiently grand, you could get away with wearing that dress"—he pointed at her very best blue houppelande gown— "underneath it for your walk. I make no promises however."

Fen clasped her hands together. "That would be wonderful," she breathed. He was heading toward the bedroom door, no doubt to break his fast. For some reason, the sight of him walking away emboldened her to add: "Will you ask Lady Sumner for the loan of a cloak?"

He paused and looked back over his shoulder with a faint frown. "Is there any reason I should not?"

"No," she admitted, twisting her hands. She wasn't even sure why she'd asked. Suddenly it had seemed imperative to know. "It is just, to inconvenience her twice in as many days…" Her words trailed off.

207

"I'm sure she has a chest stuffed full of cloaks," replied Oswald.

"You must be very good friends," she added lamely.

"I thought I told you last night that she was an acquaintance at best."

"Oh yes, so you did," she said brightly.

"Put on a robe, Fenella, and join me next door for breakfast," Oswald said firmly and left the room.

17

Oswald arrived in his study, some half hour later, feeling decidedly out of sorts. He dashed off a request to Lady Anne Sumner for the loan of a cloak and sent Bryce to deliver it. His assistant gave him a very old-fashioned look when he saw the name on the note. "Yes, Bryce, you have some comment to make?" asked Oswald testily.

Bryce sucked in his cheeks. "It's not my place to say, sir."

"Bryce, you are aware, are you not, that Lady Anne Sumner is in my employ."

Bryce bridled. "I am aware of it, my lord," he conceded.

Oswald laid down his pen. "Yet you seem to act as though the fact I am now a married man means I can no longer have a correspondence with my employee?"

Bryce sniffed and Oswald regarded him with exasperation. "Just deliver the note, Bryce."
And consider yourself fortunate I do not have the time presently to devote to finding you a replacement! he thought grimly. He could almost forgive Edwards, Bryce's predecessor, for his act of near treason, but he would never forgive him for saddling him with Bryce in his stead!

Bryce shut the door behind him, and Oswald sat in thought a moment before making a sudden decision. Pulling out the chain from his tunic that he wore around his neck, he selected a key and unlocked one of the drawers in his desk, retrieving a bundle of letters, which had been laboriously copied from Fenella's correspondence during the journey his two agents had taken back from Sitchmarsh. Swiftly untying the string they were bound up with, he smoothed out the pages. Then he picked up the one on the top dated two years ago, settled back in his seat, and began to read.

It was about an hour later that a knock at the door interrupted him, and Lady Anne Sumner slipped through it carrying a burgundy cloak over her arm trimmed with gray fur. She held it up by way of welcome and then draped it over the back of one of his seats.

"You are very kind," said Oswald. "But I did not intend for you to bring it in person."

"It was no trouble," said Lady Anne, approaching his desk. "Besides, I did not want to give Jenny another opportunity to gossip. That girl is becoming quite incorrigible." She gave him a sidelong look, and Oswald wondered if she suspected that Jenny was also in his employ these days. After all, spies were needed in the servants' quarters as well as the banqueting halls.

"Quite," he answered. "Though sometimes I wish Bryce would take the trouble to indulge in a little gossip. He would be so much more useful to me then."

"I think you will find that Bryce is not the gossiping type," said Lady Anne. "But then, that is why you employed him after all."

"True enough," agreed Oswald, wondering when she was going to get to the point of her visit. Lady Anne was flitting about his bookshelves now. Clearly, she had something she wished to share, but Oswald found himself itching to get back to Fenella's letters.

He had reached a crucial part where Ambrose was devoting page after page to a slight cold he had contracted and was bemoaning the inhospitable northern weather for prolonging his suffering. He found there was a sort of horrible fascination to reading Ambrose Thane's private letters to his wife. They were as dry and dusty as if he were writing to his housekeeper.

The main body was taken up with complaints about his position as a junior ambassador and the lack of respect with which he felt he was being treated. He perceived slights in the most innocuous of utterings and took umbrage at the drop of a hat. It seemed he expected his wife to enter into his petty feuds, as he spent several paragraphs berating her for suggesting various people meant no insult or harm.

His second favorite topic was haranguing her over the accounts she sent him of the household spending. He suspected she was not using the cheapest candles available merely because she did not like the smell of them, and he did not think the fact they made her eyes water when she tried to read at night to be a valid argument.

With the master away, he saw no need for the household to indulge in roasted meats or pastries. He thought the cook should manage without a full kitchen staff and the same went for the buttery. In fact, he pulled her up with some criticism of almost every line of her inventory.

From scanning the dates, it seemed poor Fenella was expected to write to him every month with a full account of the household monies. And she had done this for no less than two years.

In fact, Oswald was deriving considerable satisfaction from finding that Ambrose Thane was the most tiresome sort of husband possible. He was a whiner and a tight-fisted domestic tyrant. Only a strong sense of duty could induce a wife to love such a man. And he had sent her no scrap of affection, no word of written praise or encouragement in the whole time he had been away that Oswald could see. Of course, he only had sight of one side of the correspondence, but it was hard to imagine such letters could inspire much by way of spousal devotion.

"Someone brings you glad tidings," said Lady Anne, interrupting his thoughts. She had rounded his desk and was peering archly at the bundle of letters.

Oswald swept them into his top drawer. "There is something I can help you with, Lady Sumner?" he asked politely.

She sat in the seat opposite him with a charming smile. "It is rather something that I can do for you, my dear Lord Vawdrey," she replied.

He looked at her expectantly. "You are planning a trip, perhaps?" he prompted. "You mentioned the possibility of travel to your husband's northern estates?"
She waved a hand airily. "Oh, I have no immediate plans for that," she said dismissively. "No, it is here at court that I thought to be of service."

Oswald's eyebrows rose. "Go on."

"With your wife, the Countess Vawdrey. You are doubtless far too busy to introduce her around and about. See that she cultivates the right friendships, that sort of thing. But I, on the other hand, can devote the time to make sure she meets the right sort of people. Take her under my wing, so to speak."

Oswald felt himself stiffen. "You are too kind," he said. "But I will not be too busy to introduce my countess to the company she needs to keep."

Lady Anne hesitated and traced a finger across the desktop. "She seems a very sweet, wholesome sort of girl. Wholly unspoiled."

"She is twenty-six years of age," said Oswald dryly. He could tell that Lady Sumner was trying to say Fenella was hopelessly unsophisticated. And while she might have a point, it irritated him that she was making it.

"The poor dear must have been simply crushed after last night," began Lady Anne again. "She will need the comfort of friends to cushion her from the consequences of such a social misstep."

"She has her husband to comfort her," said Oswald brusquely. "And I trust I perform that function adequately. As for friends, I do not doubt that Fenella is equipped to make her own, without an employee of mine fulfilling that function."

Lady Anne's face tightened. "You misunderstand, my lord. I did not offer in the role of employee."

Oswald looked up at her steadily. "But you have no other role to me, Lady Sumner."

She gasped faintly at his bluntness and rose from her seat. "I see I am decidedly in the way this morning. I will take my leave of you now, Lord Vawdrey," she said. "I hope your wife will find

213

the cloak warm." With only the shallowest of curtseys, she whirled around to make her exit.

Oswald stared at the door as it shut behind her. In truth, he was not quite sure why he had been so abrupt with Lady Sumner. She was a very useful person to him at court, and it seemed unlikely he had been rude to her simply because he felt an implied insult toward his wife!

He rubbed the side of his jaw and considered this a moment. Up until now, he had imagined that Lady Anne Sumner was the epitome of the perfect polished female courtier. She was discreet, sharply observant, had the knack of being in the right place at the right time, and was an extremely efficient spy.

Why then had it rubbed him the wrong way when she had suggested she was the ideally placed person to guide Fenella in her court debut? Something told him he did not wish to look too closely at the answer, so instead he reopened the drawer and extracted Thane's letters to find out if that gentleman ever did get rid of his putrid sore throat, or if Fenella was ever allowed a decent candle to read by.

A knock at the door interrupted him just as he was finishing Thane's final letter, dated just over a month ago. He dropped it with a frown onto his desk and aloud said, "Yes?" Bryce appeared around the door with a tray of refreshment. "Ah, Bryce," he said. "Take a seat a moment. I have some tasks for you to add to your list."

Bryce set down the tray and whipped out some parchment and a pen and sat in the seat Lady Sumner had vacated an hour before. Oswald also reached for pen and paper. He dipped his pen and started writing, as he simultaneously gave Bryce his instructions.

"I want you to have this letter hand-delivered to the steward at Vawdrey Keep. I believe his name is Knowles. On receipt of this letter he will hand over his accounts to be brought straight back and delivered to my wife for her perusal." Bryce made a note, then looked up expectantly.

Oswald was still writing with a steady hand. "There is a cloak, lying over the chair next to the door. You will deliver it to Lady Vawdrey for her use. You will convey her message to Lady Schaeffer regarding a walk in the palace grounds this afternoon. You will then send word to Harris to have him follow at a discreet distance behind them."

Bryce nearly dropped his pen. "You will have them placed under surveillance, my lord?" he asked in horror.

"My wife does not have an attendant maid or page to accompany her at present, Bryce. Unless you are volunteering for the task?"

Bryce coughed. "I am not fond of the outdoor pursuits, my lord," he said with dignity.

"Besides," said Oswald as if he had not spoken. "It is for her safety. No other reason."

"Very well, my lord."

"And I wish you to send a message to Pezzini, explaining that Fenella's new wardrobe is a matter of the utmost urgency. I want him to send each dress as it is completed rather than waiting for it to be finished in entirety."

"Yes, my lord," said Bryce doubtfully.

"If you need to use an interpreter, speak to Lady Claremont's manservant, Charters. He is a master of languages and can translate for you."

Bryce perked up at this. "Yes, my lord."

"You will need to tip him generously." Oswald reached into another drawer and drew out a gold coin, which he tossed toward Bryce, who made no attempt to catch it, and simply watched as it rolled under a bookcase.

"Can you retrieve that, Bryce, or do you need another coin?" asked Oswald in exasperation.
Bryce eased himself off his chair to grope around on the floor for the coin. "Tell me, Bryce, did you have no brothers to play catch with as a boy?"

"No, my lord," answered Bryce as he reached underneath the bookcase.

Oswald thought of Fenella's words. "Nor sisters either?" he asked.

"I was an only child, my lord," said Bryce, clambering to his knees. He opened his palm to show the coin and then tucked it away in a pouch at his belt.

"Who brought you up then?" asked Oswald, suddenly curious.

"I was raised by my paternal grandfather," replied Bryce. "He was a legal clerk," he added when Oswald continued to regard him thoughtfully. Maybe Fenella was onto something after all, thought Oswald. "I see," he said aloud. "Very good, Bryce." His assistant bowed and exited the room with an air of injured dignity.

Oswald leaned back in his chair, his thoughts returning to the last letter from Ambrose Thane. There had been absolutely no change in tone in that letter. Nothing to indicate that her husband's feelings had undergone some dramatic change or that he'd become alienated from his wife.

True, if Oswald had read that letter and none of the others, he would have thought their marriage dead in the water. But the fact was that every single one of his letters was dull as ditchwater. Thane had mentioned a local family of influence who he dined with on several occasions, and if pressed, Oswald would have hazarded a guess that the Lady Colleen was one of the daughters of that house.

It did not really make any difference to him, but he realized that Fenella might well want some answers. He tapped one finger on the desktop as he pondered this point. He did not want her dwelling on the past, but he also did not want it to build up and become some great mystery in her life, rather than the brief rather dull chapter it was.

He drew another piece of paper across his desktop and addressed it to J. Francis, another of his agents. Briefly, he outlined a series of points that he wanted clarified in the courtship of Sir Ambrose Thane and his second wife. Then he sealed the envelope with hot wax and, selecting his Vawdrey seal, the passant panther, pressed its impression firmly into molten red wax.

Throughout the afternoon he had visits from various agents reporting their findings over the last week. They knocked on the door in various patterns, and two of them even arrived by his secret passage rather than using the outer door. Oswald punctuated their narratives with a few sharp questions but made few notes. Bryce came in during the second half of the afternoon and sat quietly in the corner observing.

"What do you think, Bryce? Anything of interest?" Oswald asked him as the door shut on the last visitor.

Bryce looked thoughtful. "I could not understand the significance of the message Jeffries intercepted to the ambassador to the Western Isles," he said slowly.

"You picked up on that," Oswald replied. "Good, I begin to have hopes for you, Bryce. Something seemed amiss, did it not?"

"Yes…" agreed Bryce hesitantly. "But I'm not sure what? The letter was so short. And you did not keep Jeffries overlong for interrogation."

"There would be very little point. He knew nothing, only that it did not arrive with the regular messenger and that the ambassador attempted to burn it."

"But why?" asked Bryce. "The body of the letter seemed very innocuous. It had no sinister intent that I could discern."

Oswald closed his eyes briefly. "Bryce," he tutted. "Think about it analytically. Barely any of it made sense. The weather last Tuesday week was not fine, it is highly unlikely that anyone would spot a sedge goose this far south, they are northern birds, and we know that Ambassador Hybridge does not hunt." Oswald drummed his fingers on the table. "So, what conclusion can be drawn from this?"

"It is in code?" suggested Bryce with a frown.

"Indeed," said Oswald. "Which is why I have asked Jeffries to make copies of any letters to the ambassador in the last six months and bring them to me. We will need to wade through them and see if we can decode it. Hybridge has been in post for some nineteen months," he ruminated. "His connections are respectable but there was a branch of his family that supported the Blechmarsh claim to the throne."

He grimaced thinking of the last of that troublesome line. Princess Una was shut up in a fortress under house arrest and had been for the last seventeen months. It didn't stop others from constantly plotting in her name. The sedge goose was a northern bird famed for its stubbornness and lack of common sense. Much like the House of Blechmarsh.

Bryce coughed. "But then, most families have similar stories in their not too distant past," he pointed out.

"Quite so, my dear Bryce. My own great-grandfather believed the Argents to be a bunch of upstarts with only the most tenuous link to royalty." Bryce tried to hide his shock but failed. "Come now, Bryce," said Oswald. "We must be realists. We have no proof that the ambassador is plotting against our monarchy, but even so, we must be vigilant."

219

"Yes, my lord."

"I want you to read through the correspondence Jeffries brings as soon as it arrives, and I want you to make notes around any birds, weather, or hunting references. See if you can spot a pattern."

"Yes, my lord."

"This afternoon I shall be meeting in the main chamber with the privy council. After that I will devote a few hours to the new trade agreements with the south."

Bryce nodded solemnly. "Very well, my lord."

"Have you anything for me?" asked Oswald.

Bryce shuffled his papers. "Signor Pezzini wished you to know he is an artist and cannot be hurried, however said he will send over two gowns this afternoon. That is the best he can do. The rest will arrive as it is completed." Oswald nodded. "Packages have arrived from the shoemaker and the glover; I have had them sent along to your rooms."

"Good."

"You have received an invitation from the Dowager Duchess of Lessing to attend a feast tonight in the lower chamber. She invites you and your new bride," said Bryce.

Oswald looked pained. "Ah, the good dowager does so dearly love to know all the gossip," he sighed.

"Shall I decline?"

"On the contrary, we will be pleased to accept. Especially now Fenella will have a choice of gowns," said Oswald wryly. "A married man cannot shirk social engagements like a bachelor. At least, not until his marriage is established fact."

If Bryce thought this a strange thing to say, he did not let it show. Instead he inclined his head. "It shall be done, my lord."

The strange thing was, Oswald found it difficult to keep his mind on the tasks at hand that afternoon. Even in the council meeting with his peers, his thoughts kept wandering back to his wife. It irritated him that under the cloak, she would be wearing that shabby gown bought for her by another man.
He wondered for the first time if the month-long induction to court life he had previously envisioned would be long enough before he shipped her off to Vawdrey Keep? And if it was to be longer, then Lady Sumner had a point. She would need a mentor.

He tapped his pen against the desktop and debated the point. The ideal person for the task would be his sister-in-law, Linnet. He did need to write to her and Mason informing them of his marriage. Should he ask them to make a protracted stay at court on his behalf? It could lead to awkward questions from Mason about his hasty marriage, which he did not look forward to answering. One of his fellow privy members nudged him, and Oswald frowned at him abstractedly.

"It is your turn to debate this article, my lord," the other prompted him.

"I abstain," said Oswald swiftly.

221

"But it was you who proposed this amendment last month," pointed out Lord Sutton, looking shocked.

Oswald glanced down at the document. "Did I? Many things have changed since last month."
There was a murmur at this, which Oswald barely noticed. He had not had an attractive wife to drive him to distraction last month. "There may be some new trouble brewing we should be aware of," he started reluctantly before the meeting came to its conclusion. "There were *discrepancies* with some diplomatic correspondence this last week." He paused heavily. "It may be there was some reference to a certain lady in the north."

A few indrawn breaths greeted this. "Have you told the King?" asked Lord Caterby, leaning forward in his seat.

"Not yet," admitted Oswald. "But it will have to be done."

Lord Schaeffer tsked. "That most unfortunate female will be drawn into dark intrigue all over again."

"That most unfortunate female will be lucky to keep a head on her shoulders if there's another plot to supplant the King," put in Lord Sutton dryly.

Oswald winced. This was unfortunately true if he did not think of a more lasting solution.

"I suppose," said Caterby hesitantly. "There's no question of her direct involvement…?"

"None whatsoever," answered Oswald swiftly, crushing their hopes of justified retribution. He would not have them

222

absolving themselves of any guilt if they pronounced a death sentence on the poor woman. "Una Blechmarsh is quite innocent."

The other privy council members shifted uncomfortably in their seats. Frankly, her innocence was nothing but a damned inconvenience to them, one and all.

"Is all well with you, Vawdrey?" asked Lord Schaeffer at the close of the meeting. His bushy eyebrows wagged. "You work too hard, my boy. Overtaxing that famous brain of yours."

Oswald glanced at him. "How long have you been married, Schaeffer?" he asked suddenly.

Lord Schaeffer peered at him closely. "Some thirty years or thereabouts," he answered vaguely. "Why do you ask?"

"No particular reason," Oswald fobbed him off. Schaeffer bored on for a while longer about approaching the King with some petition. Oswald nodded and made murmuring noises in the pauses and then, at the earliest opportunity, excused himself to return to some urgent work.

He could feel Schaeffer's eyes on his back as he left the room but was soon reabsorbed in this issue with his wife before he'd even reached the end of the long gallery. It boiled down to this: if Fenella was to be around any longer than a month, then he would need to address his own growing attraction to her, which could well be a problem, considering the fact she was still traumatized from her abandonment by her previous husband.

He had no proof, but he suspected it was him who kept throwing out the bolster between them as they slept. He seemed to gravitate toward her in his sleep, when his iron self-control also slumbered. He'd suffered a shock seeing her in that court dress the night before. Truth to tell, he didn't think he'd entirely recovered from it the whole evening. It had made him churlish and surly toward her when he should have been conciliatory.

Of course, he hadn't known that bitch Colleen Thane had stolen her necklace at the time, but even so. He was starting to find it a strain to always be around her when there were so many limits in place regarding their intimacy. In that dress, he had been confronted with the fact that his wife's looks were likely to be pleasing to more than just himself. In truth, he did not feel as secure of her as he would like before exposing her to all and sundry.

Had he made a mistake in his strategy, by giving her time to adjust to him as a husband? He had reached his office by this time and let himself in before sitting at his desk and unlocking his drawer. He placed the draft trade agreement on the desk before him and stared down at the title page as he debated the corner he had backed himself into regarding his marriage.

The thought niggled away in a corner of his mind, telling him he'd erred somewhere along the line. But he was damned if he could see where! He dropped back in his seat and groaned. Maybe, just maybe, he was overcomplicating things? After all, Fenella was a straightforward country girl. Her father and brother were nothing more than country squires. Buying her ruby necklaces and taking her to royal banquets was bound to unnerve her. Perhaps he should just take her to Vawdrey Keep and dump her there and be done with it?

Without her lying in his bed beside him each night, he could return to some semblance of normality in his day-to-day life.

While it was curious that she had wrought this effect on him, it was perhaps not unexpected considering how hard he had been working lately and how little time he had spent in the company of women.

He had been under a great deal of pressure. While the war in the north had ceased some four years ago, the unrest in the kingdom had rumbled on, and the peace had been maintained with the northern barons only with intense mediation and work behind the scenes. A lot of this work had been his responsibility, and he had pursued it ceaselessly ever since.

Indeed, his meteoric rise to prominence at court had been based on this work. His family, even the King, had often urged him to take a break from the heavy workload, but he had been like a man possessed. Even after the King had honored him with his earldom, he had refused to take a break from court life. He frowned.

Clearly it had taken a toll on his self-control. He could not remember the last time he had entertained a woman. Certainly, it was before he had joined the King's privy council. Since then he had lived like a monk. And before that…even as a soldier he had been particular in his tastes. Not for him a roll in the hay with a willing country wench, or the dubious charms of some camp follower.

He was simply more fastidious than most men. He even prided himself on the fact. And yet, here he was…coveting the leavings of an obscure nobody like Ambrose Thane. It was inconceivable. Doubtless it was overwork, he told himself sensibly. Once Fenella had fallen into line as his wife, all would fall back into its rightful place. The problem was…he just wasn't sure where a wife's rightful place was.

*

Oswald was late returning to their rooms to supper that evening. He sat distractedly while Fenella chattered away about her walk with Lady Schaeffer and that good lady's advice to her about how a respectable woman spends her time at the royal court.

"Lady Schaeffer explained she is the patroness of many artists," Fenella explained with a faint air of puzzlement. "She encourages them in their endeavors, and they often dedicate their works to her."

Oswald nodded as he pushed a pie crust around his plate. "That is quite usual practice," he agreed. "You could easily espouse some artist, if you so wished."

Fenella's eyes widened. "I would hardly know how," she confessed.

Oswald's mouth twisted. "As a highborn lady, it usually involves throwing the odd purse of money their way." As soon as he'd said it, he wished he hadn't. Why was he always showing his cynical side to the very person he should hide it from the most? With any other female he would trot out some flattering phrase, without even a second thought. He put down his knife. "Forgive me, that was ill considered and rude," he said. "I am sure Lady Schaeffer takes her duties as a patron of the arts very seriously."

Fen was looking at him in some concern. Hesitantly, she reached across to touch his hand. To his embarrassment, he jumped at her touch. "You're tired, my lord," she said softly. "You must have had a very busy day, I think?" He stared at her

226

abstractedly. "Please do not think you need to stand on ceremony around me, husband," she said, sweetly serious. "You should be able to speak your thoughts, without having to censor or filter them first for my consumption."

Her warm voice affected him oddly in the strangest of places. Gods, she was pretty, he thought, in the flickering candlelight. What the hells had he been thinking, considering her plain? His eyes searched her face. "Do you mean that?" he asked. Even to his own ears his voice sounded unnaturally husky. He took a hurried swig of water.

"Of course. After all, I am your wife," she answered with only a trace of self-consciousness.
Then he remembered Ambrose Thane's whining, self-pitying letters. *Of course, Fenella was used to crotchety, unreasonable husbands.*

"What is it, my lord?" she asked in alarm, and Oswald realized he was glowering.

He passed a hand over his face. "'Tis nothing, nothing," he replied gruffly.

"I hope you are not coming down with aught," she said worriedly. "Only your voice does sound a little hoarse this evening." She bit her lip and fiddled with her napkin. "I hope you would not think me sadly fussing if I suggested an early night?" she ventured.

Oswald sat silently a moment. "Fenella—" he started but found he could not continue any further.

She cocked her head to one side. "Perhaps I should ask Meldon for a posset? With honey, sage, and thyme for a sore throat?"

Oswald didn't have the heart to tell her that nothing afflicted him, except her. "How did the meeting go with Meldon's goddaughter?" he asked instead, ruthlessly shoving down his ignoble impulses.

Fenella cleared her throat. "I told her she could start on the morrow," she confessed. "Her husband has lately lost his business, through no fault of his own," she added hurriedly. "And poor Trudy needs the extra income for their family."

Oswald eyed her wearily. "Did she seem capable at least?"

Fenella avoided his eyes. "I am sure she will soon pick up the skills needed."

"So she has no experience," he deduced.

Fen fidgeted in her seat. "She's a very lively, bright sort of person, and given the opportunity, I am sure she will do well."

She was wearing the velvet headband again with the veil suspended down her middle back. The only jewelry she wore was the small turquoise ring. She had on the shabby blue dress she had said was her best from her previous life. Even that couldn't detract from her heart-shaped face and clear, creamy skin. He shifted in his seat. With a hand that trembled slightly he reached for the pitcher and poured himself a cup of water. "Did you receive any packages today?" he asked with a frown.

"Yes, I meant to thank you. Some books of poetry," she said with enthusiasm. "They are bound in red leather and have such

228

pretty clasps. I am very much looking forward to reading them." She glowed. Such a small thing. His wife went pale at the sight of jewels, but a present of books gave her a pretty blush.

He had forgotten he'd even ordered them. "What about clothes?" The neckline on the blue gown she wore was unfashionably high, and at this precise moment he had never been so glad of anything in his life. Current court fashion dictated the necklines were worn very low and Fenella's abundant figure would be spilling out of her dress.

He wasn't sure he could cope with such a sight in such close confinement. It had been bad enough at the feast the previous night. He tugged at his collar as he strove to banish such an image from his rioting mind's eye. What the hells was wrong with him? As if suddenly catching on to his inner turmoil, Lady Fenella straightened up and blushed.

"Oh—I almost forgot. How ungrateful of me. Yes, two very lovely gowns arrived from signor Pezzini." A sudden thought occurred to her which had her practically jumping out of her seat. Oswald spilt a trickle of water down his sleeve. If only the dratted woman would keep still and let him get control of himself!

"Shall I fetch them so you can see?"

"That won't be necessary," he assured her.

She settled back into her seat and peered at him again, leaning in closer. "Indeed, you do look tired, my lord," she told him softly. "Can I not persuade you to an early night's sleep?"

Her eyes were bright with concern. He had been quite wrong about their color, he noticed distractedly. Up close you could see they were more of a deep amber color than brown. Her mouth, he chose not to dwell on for it was wide and pink, the bottom lip disturbingly plump. Oswald's nostrils flared as he imagined her sat on his lap clad in nothing but a transparent shift.

He stood up jerkily from the table. "I find I am tired. No," he said as she came to her feet. "You do not have to rush to join me."

"Oh, 'tis no bother," she assured him. "If I come with you now, I can show you the gowns."

"Fenella," he said, squeezing his eyes shut a moment. The poor woman was clearly worried he was overworking, while he was sat imagining her underneath him! It wasn't like him. He wasn't usually such a pig.

"What is it?" She sounded alarmed.

"Pour me a cup of wine," he gritted out.

"But you do not drink," she pointed out, even as she reached dutifully for the wine jug.

"There are occasions when I do," he corrected her. An expression of curiosity flickered across her face, but some instinct held her back from asking what occasions. Instead she poured his wine and handed it to him. He tossed it down and handed it straight back to her. "Another," he said.

Fenella's eyes widened, but she refilled his cup. He took it and carried it with him toward the bedroom. He heard her footsteps following him, as trusting as a lamb, and prayed for strength. He had promised her that he would be considerate and give her time. His hard, yearning body did not care one whit for this. It was aching and ready to cleave to her and none other.

She shut the bedroom door behind them, and he set the wine down by his bedside and unbuttoned the top of his tunic. The wine was already flowing through his veins, making him flushed, though it had not taken the edge yet off his need. He could hear rustling behind him and guessed she was retrieving her new gowns to show to him.

Gowns he had absolutely no interest in seeing. He shut his eyes briefly and steeled himself to ignore the steady pulse in his groin. Abstinence had been a way of life for him for so long, that desire was almost a stranger to him. He had honestly thought he could sleep beside a wife and it not mess with his equanimity in the slightest. He had been a bloody fool.

"This one is very lovely, is it not?" she said happily, holding an expanse of green-gold brocade up for him to admire.

He gazed past the gown to focus on her and the blue gown she wore. "Very lovely," he said. "Take off that gown," he said testily. "I don't want to see you wearing it again."

She looked startled, maybe even a little crestfallen. But she did not argue. Of course not, he told himself savagely. She was used to peevish, unreasonable husbands. Instead she draped her new gown over a chair and to his alarm made her way round to his side of the bed.

She turned her body so that her back was toward him. "Do you mind?" she asked. Dimly he realized she was angling her lacings toward him to unfasten. "'Twill be the last time, for Trudy will start on the morrow and—"

He put his hands to her waist and yanked her almost roughly toward him. As his fingers worked on the strings, his mind raced. He wanted her. And why the hells shouldn't he have her? She was his. He had the documents to prove it.

"Is all well?" she asked timidly as he prized the lacings apart. He spun her round and clamped his hands to her waist again.

"You call me husband now," he said abruptly.

Her gaze wavered a moment uncertainly. "Yes." She nodded.

"Does that mean you have accepted me as such?" He had to work to keep his voice calm and even. He sounded confrontational, though it was not his intention.

She seemed to consider this for a heartbeat. "Yes," she answered in a quiet voice.

The pause annoyed him. He knew it was irrational and didn't give a damn. "Am I your husband, Fenella?" he asked in a hard voice.

"Yes," she answered, her eyes flying to his, and he had the oddest feeling she was trying to comprehend his gaze rather than his words. That probably wasn't something he should encourage. When had she started doing that?

"I want to bed you," he said harshly. "Tell me now if it's too soon."

She looked, quite frankly, astonished. "Oh," she said. Then seemed to struggle for words. "Of course, if that's what you want, husband—"

"That is what I want," he interrupted her rudely. "I want it now." Inwardly, somewhere, Oswald Vawdrey the courtier was wincing at his lack of finesse. Unfortunately for Fenella, his crude Vawdrey blood was up. Thank gods she wasn't a virgin, though the thought that the worm Ambrose Thane had touched what was his made his blood boil even hotter. He remained rooted to the spot, his eyes trained on her as if she was his prey.

"V-very well," she stammered, then looked away, her cheeks bright red. "Shall I undress and—"

"Yes, for starters," he said and started ripping off his own clothes. She began unpinning her veil and took a few steps toward her side of the bed. He reached out with a sharp "No" to prevent this, and she halted, turning back to face him in surprise. He had removed his tunic and shirt now and was unfastening his chauses. "Put your clothing on that chair," he said with a sharp nod toward it.

Fen opened her mouth as if to argue but then thought better of it. She laid her veil over the cushioned seat and then started unfastening her velvet headdress. He stripped his chauses off his legs and removed his tented braies in a trice. Once he was naked, he advanced on Fenella and started yanking down her bodice. Once he'd divested her of the gown, he flung it on the chair and put his hands to the hem of her thin shift.

"May I please keep the shift on?" she asked in a strangled tone.

He frowned. The shift was practically transparent and hid nothing. His instinct was to refuse her request; he wanted nothing between them. He forced this impulse down and released the hem, instead putting his hands to her waist, walking her backward toward the bed. Her breathing was shallow, but she didn't protest and he followed her down onto the mattress, his eyes not leaving hers. Her gaze skittered away and then returned before flickering round the room.

"Will you not snuff the candles out?" she whispered.

"No," he replied tersely.

"Can we get under the covers?"

"Are you cold?" he asked. He doubted it. His far bigger body was covering hers entirely and he could feel how much heat he was throwing out. He felt like his body was ablaze for her. He guessed that dolt Thane had only taken her under the covers with no light. *Wearing a smock.*

"No," she admitted with a frown. "I'm not cold, but you're shivering." She placed a hand on his upper arm and he almost had to bite back an exclamation.

"Not with the cold," he admitted through gritted teeth.

"What then?" she asked faintly.

"Need," he answered in a low voice.

"Need?" Her eyes flew wide.

234

"My need to join with you."

Her mouth formed a silent "Oh" and he felt her tremble slightly beneath him. She slid her hand down his upper arm in what she might have imagined was a comforting gesture, but he was far too overstimulated for her touch.

"Fenella," he breathed and then his mouth was on hers, insistent and demanding her participation. She whimpered when his kiss turned open-mouthed and carnal, her fingers tightening again on his arms, but she did not try to pull away. He ravished her sweet, tender mouth and rocked his hips against her in simulation of what his body craved so badly from hers.

She struggled slightly against him, and he pulled back, only to realize she had understood his unspoken demand and was sweetly parting her legs beneath him. He groaned, sliding his hand under her shift, and cupping her intimately, his thumb sliding through the dark brown curls.

She sucked in a shocked breath as he petted her there, her gaze seeking his for reassurance. After a moment she relaxed against his touch, so he hoped his scorching gaze managed to give her what she needed, before he pushed a finger into her tight, slick heat. Her eyes flew wide again at his groan, and he felt his brow start to bead with sweat at the idea of holding out much longer.

She felt small though, and he didn't want to hurt her. He remembered Thane had been absent for two years and forced himself to breathe steadily and take her mouth in a gentler kiss as he kept up his ministrations until he felt her start to pant and move against him. "Are you ready for me, love?" he asked. Though in truth, he knew he was still rushing her.

235

"Yes," she answered, and he aligned himself and started to push inside her. She made some small noise of discomfort, which he could well believe, as she was struggling to take him.

"Tell me if it's too much," he forced himself to say. "And I will stop." But her only reply was to grip his arms tighter, so he continued to bury his length into her until he was deep, with their groins tightly flush against one another. He was actually shaking now from the effort of holding back. He kissed her again and felt her take a deep breath.

"Thank you for being patient," she whispered. "You're very big and for a moment there…" Words seemed to fail her.

"You've taken me," he said gruffly. If she compared him now to Thane, he wasn't sure how he would react.

"Yes," she breathed and gave a small wriggle, which made him groan. "Are you alright?" she asked uncertainly.

"No," he answered tersely. "I need to move."

"Oh, of course." Tentatively, she slid her hands up from his biceps to his shoulders.

The words had barely left her mouth and he was surging forward, pressing her back into the pillows and thrusting into her tight heat. Time stood still. He caught his breath and felt his heart reverberate through his entire being. He closed his eyes and did it again.

She was softer than mink, sleeker than silk. Her breath on his neck felt exquisite; her flesh against his made him want to pass out from sheer pleasure. He drew back and thrust again,

236

luxuriating in the feeling with a low roar which came from deep in his chest. Her body under his was a revelation. So, this was where his wife belonged.

"Oswald?" Her voice was breathy. The fact she had spoken his given name made him gasp. He had to steel himself against the impulse to prematurely spill his seed as he throbbed deep within her. He gritted his teeth. Speech was beyond him, even if his life depended on it. The pleasure had struck him dumb. All he could do was move his body against hers in sensuous worship and beg her with his eyes not to ask him to stop. Looking into the depths of her own was dangerous. He could lose himself there. To distract himself, he brushed kisses against her brow, her jaw, and finally her delicious mouth.

She bumped against him, falling out of sync every so often with his steady rhythm. Every collision of their flesh was a delight. Unable to resist, he ran a palm down her full, bouncing bosom, and she shuddered and whimpered and rubbed against him, as if seeking his touch. The look on her face was one of astonishment mingled with shy delight. It drove him crazy to see it there.

"Say my name again." He barely recognized his own voice it was so gravelly.

"Oswald," she marveled. "Husband."

His own body's response took him aback. If anything, his ardor climbed higher. All finesse was going out the window. His desire was riding him hard, like he was Fenella. Reaching down, he hooked her leg over his forearm, opening her up to take his thrusts as he needed her to. He needed her to take it all.

237

For the life of him, he could not stop groaning as he pummeled into her. He set his jaw to stave off the overwhelming pleasure. He needed this. So badly. He forced himself to slacken off the punishing pace. "Fenella?" Her hand slid up his back as she gave a soft sob that had him pulling back to look at her face. "Am I hurting you?" It was an effort to form words. His body was given over purely to sensation. He broke out now in a light sweat as he resisted the impulse to pound into her to oblivion as he craved to.

"No," she assured him shakily. "It's just—" Her face twisted. "I hardly know. I feel so strange." Her hips shifted against him and she gave a soft *"Oh!"* and collapsed back against the mattress, gripping the sheets.

His pained expression cleared. Her own body was plainly seeking the same release as his. "There?" he asked with relief, following her lead. He moved his own hips experimentally in a similar motion, and felt a deep shudder run through her whole body. She gave a strangled gasp and struggled to sit up.

"No—please," she sobbed. "You must—stop that at once. Or I hardly know what will happen!"
A sudden suspicion had his mind reeling. Surely, *surely*, that bastard Thane could not be so inept that she knew not the pleasures of the marriage bed? He rolled onto his side, taking her with him so his weight was no longer pinning her to the pillows. "You're not in discomfort?" he clarified, carefully dropping his hand to cup her bottom.

"N-no," she sobbed. Her whole body was trembling, she was strung so taut. Being inside her was almost unbearable. Her body's embrace was so hot and tight he felt like he might lose his mind if she did not give him full reign over it.

238

"Do you trust me, Fenella?" he asked, stroking a thumb where the crease of her buttock met the top of her leg. She nodded her head, though she buried her warm face in his shoulder. He heard a muffled "Yes." "Then trust me now, my love," he said and swiftly rolled her onto her back, covering her body with his full weight and plunging back into her with the full driving length of his cock.

Her mouth opened in a silent scream, and he felt her convulse around him as her body climaxed and she went up in flames for him. His chest constricted and then expanded as she experienced the rapture he gave her. Her fingers dug into him, her back arched, and tears sprang from her eyes as she pulsed and throbbed on his dick. Baser instincts took over as he drove repeatedly into the grip of her blissful body.

He thrust and thrust again, keeping a ruthless check on his own release as she yelled and sobbed her surprise and pleasure. Her heels dug into the mattress, her legs shook, her eyes flew wide, and her body writhed against him in unspeakable pleasure. Disjointed words which made no sense burst from her lips. Her tight sex gripped his staff so hard he had to close his eyes to withstand it.

And finally, with a sigh, she went as limp as a rag and he risked taking her mouth again as his burning throat ached to. Her mouth was cool and delicious. He was still hard as iron, burning for her. Flexing his hips, he let her feel his still hungry cock in her and Fen moaned, tearing her mouth from his, her eyes flying open.

"Wha—?" She panted in dismay, her chest heaving, and her face streaked with tears. She looked utterly shocked and

239

bewildered. "You're still—?" He thought she looked a little frightened.

"Do you want me to pull out?" he forced himself to ask.

She swallowed. "You're not satisfied?" she whispered disbelievingly. "Why? What did I do wrong?"

"Nothing," he answered, his voice thick and gravelly. He dropped his forehead to touch against hers. "It's been a long time since I was with a woman." He swallowed, avoiding her eyes. "Well over a decade." Fen gazed up at him, her lips parted, her breath coming in rapid pants.
"Do you want me to stop?" His voice was raw. She tugged at her arms where he held them and he released them at once, steeling himself for her words.

"No, I want you to…find release too," she said, putting her hands lightly to his face.

His gaze snapped to hers. "Say it again?" he gritted out.

She looked nervous but repeated "I want you to find release in me" with a slight lift of her chin.

Holy hells. He didn't have it in him to debate with her any further. With a muffled groan he surged forward into her, bracing his arms against the mattress to try to keep himself from squashing her flat into the mattress. She gave a faint yelp but offered no resistance as he hammered into her with renewed vigor. "Fenella," he said hoarsely. For no fathomable reason he wanted her eyes on him, her mouth on him, her hands on him.

240

The poor girl had no idea. He was so greedy for her, it actually scared him a little. How did you tell your wife you wanted her hands squeezing your ass tight? Her mouth framing your name? Oswald shook his head. It had never entered his head to ask such a thing of any bedpartner. It beggared belief that he would want it now from his wedded wife.

"What is it?" she asked unevenly.

He could feel her soft breasts bouncing at his every thrust. He wanted to taste them. "I want to put my mouth to you," he confessed shakily. His words conjured another image. His mouth between her thighs, but he knew that was out of the question. Just the thought of it made him groan aloud. Fenella raised her head and kissed him chastely on the mouth. It surprised him so much, her taking the initiative, that his cock throbbed, and he started to spend inside her.

With a muttered curse, he reached down and grabbed the backs of her knees, spreading her soft, plump thighs even wider, so he could sink deeper still. Fen gasped as he pressed deep, and he groaned loudly at the glorious sensation. "Oh gods, yes. *Fenella*," he cried raspily as the bed creaked and the frame bumped against the wall.

He closed his eyes, the muscles of his neck strained as Fen's arms slipped around his back, the gesture of acceptance proving his undoing as, with a shout, he released inside her completely. She held him tightly in her arms, until he collapsed entirely against her, fully sated.

241

18

Oswald Vawdrey, thought Fen dazedly, was a rampaging beast between the bedsheets. She shifted her legs tentatively and winced. Her thigh muscles ached. Her lady parts burned. There was stickiness and slickness in embarrassing places, and she had no idea how she was going to get out of the bed to either wash herself or get a stitch of clothing on.

She clutched the bedsheets to her front and tried not to worry about the hard body pressed against her back. She wasn't quite sure what she'd unleashed in her heretofore restrained husband the previous evening, but he had been like a man possessed. A man possessed with lust.

She shivered. She wouldn't feel so bad if she hadn't behaved like an abandoned creature herself, she thought, closing her eyes with mortification. What in heavens had come over her? And what would her husband think of her this morning? She gave a soft groan and felt him stir against her. In more place than one. Fen gulped.

A big hand slipped possessively over her hip and gripped her there. She felt his warm breath on her neck and felt strangely quivery. *Oh, my gods*, thought Fen weakly. He couldn't want *that* again this morning, surely? She peered nervously over her shoulder.

His eyes opened and he smiled at her. She blinked at the sight and her chest squeezed tight. He was the most beautiful man she had ever laid eyes on. He shifted closer and pressed his face into her neck, his arms tightening around her to pull her in against him. She felt his hardness press into her buttocks and suppressed a faint whine. Surely he would not expect her to tryst with him again this morn?

"Good morning, wife," he said huskily and kissed her neck lingeringly.

"Good morning," she said croakily.

"Husband," he prompted her. She could hear the frown in his voice.

"Husband," she added hastily.

"That's better," he whispered and rolled her underneath him.

"Meldon," she blurted in a yelped warning.

He drew his head back to glance at the bedroom door, then returned his gaze to her. "Nay, he is not arrived," he murmured.

"Indeed, we must be expecting him any moment," babbled Fen. She waited breathlessly for him to remove his weight from her, but he did not.

"I have a key for that lock," he said distractedly, and ran a hand down her breast. "Somewhere." She gave a strangled groan as he lightly squeezed, and his gaze snapped to hers. "Are you sore, wife?" he asked in a throaty, low voice. His eyes were dark, and even if she could not feel his erect manhood pressing insistently against her belly, she could be in no doubt that he was keen to repeat last night's performance. The knowledge made her face burn.

"Yes," she confessed in a whisper.

"Should you like to take a bath, love?"

His words made her breath catch in her throat. "Together?" she asked in a scandalized squeak. Though in truth it was his use of the word *love* that really shocked her. She felt all of a flutter. He had used it last night once or twice. But even a naïve country girl such as herself knew you should not believe a word a man said when he was between your legs.

His elusive smile appeared again. It was so unexpected that she stared. He looked relaxed, she thought with surprise. That was the difference. His dark hair fell forward in his face, and the expression in his eyes matched his words for once. "I would very much like to bathe you," he admitted without a trace of shame. "But alas, I have to meet with the King this morning and cannot tarry."

Her face flamed. He'd like to bathe her. For a moment she thought she'd misheard him, but his face wore a quizzical expression. She tried to school her own features, so she looked less shocked. "Is that something that is done by a husband for his wife?" she asked weakly.

He shrugged. "Why not?" His hand had slipped beneath her now and he was stroking her backside with such familiarity that she kept forgetting to breathe.

Suddenly she remembered that Meldon's goddaughter was expected to start with them today. "The new lady's maid," she reminded him unevenly. *What was her name?*

"Hmm?" Oswald's eyes were on her mouth, but he didn't seem to be taking in her words.

"Trudy," she remembered suddenly, but his mouth was already on hers, warm and lascivious. His tongue slid along hers so teasingly that Fen felt it in her very loins, her whole body quivering.

He groaned into the kiss, and her hands flew to grasp his upper arms for strength as she strained against him. She clutched the flexing muscle and moaned herself when his hard thigh pushed between her own and rubbed against the tender spot there. He tore his mouth away at the sound of the latch and rolled onto his side, drawing the blanket firmly up around her.

"Her ladyship requires a bath," he told Meldon as the servant stomped over to the washstand. Fenella marveled at his steady voice. "Have one sent up from the kitchens."

"Aye," muttered Meldon.

"And I require the key for this bedroom door."

"The key?"

"That's what I said. The key."

Fenella closed her eyes and kept them shut as Meldon set down the water jug and then stomped back out again. "He won't be happy about having to fetch a bath," she commented.

Oswald shrugged. He was already rising from the bed. "He will reconcile himself. As you say, his goddaughter starts with you today so his duties will be lighter."

Fenella heard him pour the water from the ewer into the basin and snuck a peek at him as he started to wash. He did not trouble to draw on his robe this morning, no doubt thinking she was beyond being shocked by this point. Sadly, proving him wrong, she felt a blush spread over her neck and face as she hurriedly averted her gaze. He was clearly aroused, which was not something you could miss with a man as well-endowed as he.

"What will you do today?" he asked casually. "Have you made any plans?"

Fenella considered this as she listened to the sound of the water sloshing around. "Hester Schaeffer said she could introduce me to a gathering of ladies who meet twice a month to discuss the arts," she said without much enthusiasm.

The ewer chinked against the basin, and she guessed he was adding more hot water. "That could be instructive," he said, and she heard him shake out a cloth.

"They will all be very learned and cultured noble ladies," she said, plucking at the bedsheets. *Unlike myself*, she added silently.

"You will be fine," Oswald assured her in a slightly muffled voice. He must be wiping his face. "If you should feel out of your depth, simply offer to sponsor someone. There's always a surfeit of poets, playwrights, and painters loitering around court."

"But how will I know if they are any good?" she asked. "Sadly, I could not rely on my own judgment in this area." She heard droplets and thought he must be wringing out his washcloth.

246

"In such cases it is probably best to be led by those who are considered good judges," Oswald told her. "Lady Eden Montmayne is generally held to have excellent taste and a lively appreciation of the arts."

"Eden Montmayne," repeated Fenella, committing the name to memory. "Have I met her already?"

Oswald paused, considering this. "I do not think so. She is one of the Queen's favorite ladies-in-waiting. Lady Schaeffer can perform your introductions."

"Will Lord Schaeffer be at your meeting this morning?" she asked, attempting a wifely interest.

"No," he answered briefly.

"Is it a full meeting of the privy council or just yourself and the King?"

"Fenella," he said, and she heard the frown in his voice and looked up with surprise. He was rubbing a drying cloth across his chest. Luckily it hung down and obscured his groin area from her view. "I would prefer that your interest in my line of work was less lively," he said forthrightly.

Fen found herself tongue-tied. *Oh.* "I apologize," she managed to splutter at last. She remembered Roland's words when he was taunting her. Clearly her husband meant to make no clear explanation of his role at Wymer's court.

Ambrose had always liked a sounding board and would talk at great length about his duties as an equerry and his struggles and tribulations in the execution of those duties. It seemed Oswald had no such similar use for his helpmeet. For some reason, it felt rather like he had slammed a door in her face.

She lapsed into awkward silence as she cast about for some subject he would find less unwelcome. Unfortunately, her mind chose this moment precisely to turn blank. She heard one of the trunk lids fall and realized he was dressing now anyway and turned onto her side away from him to give him some privacy.

"Will you join me to break your fast?" he asked a few moments later. "You don't need to dress," he added, holding up the scarlet robe as she looked back over her shoulder at him.

"If you want me to," she answered, and he moved swiftly around to her side of the bed, shaking out the folds of the satin robe and holding it out for her to place her arms in the sleeves. Fen clambered out of the bed, tugging on the shift to make sure she had adequate coverage.

He folded her into the robe from behind, and then stood a moment with his arms wrapped firmly around her. "I do want you to," he said in a low voice which Fen felt in the region of her stomach. They stood a moment, motionless until the door creaked open again and Meldon peered around it.

"Is all decent within?" he asked caustically. "Only I've two men here with the bath."

"Have them bring it in," said Oswald coolly as he detached himself. A large wooden tub was rolled into the room. "It will take them several journeys to fill it," he said. "So, you can eat with me in the meantime."

Fen followed him into the adjoining room and sat at the table while he ate salted fish and white bread. She did not have much appetite and sat crumbling her bread feeling strangely skittish and shy. "How is your head?" she asked curiously as he took a swig of water.

"My head?"

"You drank two cups of wine last night," she reminded him.

He seemed to consider this a moment. "It is a little heavy and I can tell I have imbibed." He shrugged. "Other than that, I can feel no ill effects."

"Good," she murmured. Then on impulse, she asked: "Does the scar on your back never pain you?" He paused, a piece of bread to his lips. Then he put it in his mouth and chewed without answering her. "Did you get it during the war?" she plunged on recklessly.

"I don't speak of it," he said blankly. "It was a long time ago."

So, no questions about his work or his past soldiering. She lapsed into silence. Under such circumstances it was hard not to deduce there was only one kind of intimacy Lord Vawdrey wished with her. The thought was strangely depressing.

At the end of the meal he reached across and covered her hand with his. "I will see you this evening," he said easily. "We had a supper invitation from the Dowager Duchess of Lessing, which I accepted." He paused. "It will be an opportunity to wear one of your new dresses."

249

Fen nodded and was relieved when Roland's door opened, and her brother-in-law emerged along with her dog, Bors. He checked on the threshold and Oswald withdrew his hand and stood. "Enjoy your bath," he said and left the room.

Bors danced up to her and she gave him a few pats on his head. "Did Bors sleep in your room last night?" she asked Roland in an effort to distract herself.

He visibly bristled. "How should I know?" he said. "Woke up this morning and there he was."
Fenella looked at him askance. Once again, her brother-in-law looked a little worse for wear. Perhaps Bors had snuck in with him after he returned from his night's carousing?

Bors threw a sheepish glance her way and then went and flung himself under Roland's chair.
"Well! He certainly seems to have taken to you," remarked Fen.

"Dogs are known to be good judges of character," Roland boasted.

A series of servants had been trooping into the bedroom with steaming pails of water. The steady stream seemed to have now come to a halt. Anxious not to let the water go cold, Fen came to her feet. "Excuse me," she murmured to Roland, who was piling food onto his plate. He grunted something as she made her way back to the bedroom and closed the door after her.

"Oh!" she exclaimed on finding Trudy, her new maid, already employed in sprinkling herbs into the water. "Good morning. I did not see you come in, Trudy."

"Your pardon, milady," she said, dropping into a curtsey. "But you was breakfasting so I didn't want to intrude."

"That is quite alright," Fen replied as she pinned her braids on top of her head out of the way. "Though I would have taken the opportunity to introduce you to my husband."

Trudy's eyes widened. "I wouldn't want to interrupt him and get on the bad side of the master so soon," she said and anxiously crossed her fingers to superstitiously ward off bad luck.

Fenella, who was unbuttoning her robe, looked up in surprise. Meldon never acted in the least scared of Oswald so she was startled by his goddaughter's words. "Lord Vawdrey is not so easily put out of temper," she said as she shrugged out of the scarlet robe.

Trudy hurried over to take it off her. "Begging your pardon, but that's not what I've been hearing, milady," she said enigmatically.

Fen paused in the act of peeling off her shift. "Really?" she asked. "From Meldon?"

"Lord no!" Trudy's eyes went wide with alarm. "Please don't think that Uncle would ever gossip out of turn about the Vawdrey family. He didn't tell me nothing, except to mind my betters and not put him to shame!"

"I see," said Fen, who had approached the steaming tub and was now climbing in. She sighed as she sank down into the hot water. The steam was fragrant from the sweet green herbs. It was a luxury indeed to be fully immersed and the water still hot.

Trudy hurried over and passed her a sponge. "For your feet, milady." Fen took it gratefully. Trudy was running a line of string across the room which she secured by tying to a hook by the ceiling. Then she flung a white sheet over it and drew the sheet back along the line to suspend over the bath where it trapped the steam and provided a shelter over the tub. "Next time, I'll secure some rose petals for your bath, milady," she told her. "The oils is most beneficial for the skin."

"Thank you," said Fenella gratefully. "I don't think I've ever had so nice a bath."

Trudy looked gratified and started folding the scarlet satin robe before tidying it away into a chest. She approached again and hung a washcloth over the side of the bath and passed a ball of Castile soap to Fen. "If you turn about, I can wash your back for you, milady," she offered.

"Thank you." Fen rotated in the water and Trudy commenced scrubbing her neck. "How was your journey to the castle this morning?" she asked.

"Fine, milady, I made good time. It only took me a half hour. I ate my first meal with the castle staff in the kitchens. Hold out your left arm, milady."

"And how was that?" asked Fen, extending her arm.

"Oh, very good, milady," she said happily. "They filled me in on all the gossip regarding yourself and his lordship."

Fen blinked. "Gossip?" she repeated with some trepidation. "Oh dear!"

"Oh no, milady, it was very instructive," Trudy hastened to assure her. "It's better to know how things lie from the outset. Servants is always best for that," she said smugly.

"Really?" asked Fen doubtfully. "Only I do not think the castle servants can know…"

"Other arm," Trudy interrupted, and Fen lowered one and raised the other. "Oh yes, milady. They knows *all* about it."

"They do?"

"Oh yes!" Trudy nodded. "I even heard all about how Lord Vawdrey got your jewels back from the Thanes."

Fenella, who had been steeling herself to deliver a lofty speech about not paying gossip any heed, almost lost her footing on her sponge. "You did?" she squeaked and nearly swallowed a mouthful of bathwater.

"Yes, milady," said Trudy firmly. "Foot."

Fenella lifted one foot out of the water and rested it on the bath ledge. She stared at her maid in deep thought. "I have not heard myself how he retrieved them," she admitted finally.

Trudy looked a little smug at this information. "Would you like to hear the tale, milady?" she asked as she rubbed a soaped brush over Fenella's toes. "Only I should not wish to offend by passing on servant's tattle but…" She shrugged. "If milady would find it interesting, I could impart what I have learned this morn."

Fen considered this a moment. She really should not encourage her maid to pay attention to gossip, let alone circulate it. As if aware of her inner struggle, her maid held her tongue a moment. "Other foot," she prompted.

Fen switched feet and sighed. "I would like to hear it, Trudy," she admitted. "But…"

"As your personal maid, it is quite fitting that I should tell you," Trudy rambled on. Fen could feel her resolve waver. She did want to know after all. "And of course, other than you, I won't repeat it to no one," said Trudy virtuously. "'Cept for Jeb."

"Jeb?"

"My husband, milady. He loves to hear a tale or two of what the nobility get up to." She gently shook her head. "How it do amuse him!"

Fen chose to ignore this. "Very well, then," she said, relenting. Trudy released her foot and Fen drifted to the edge of the bath, resting her elbows on the ledge as her maid drew up a footstool.

"Well," said Trudy, making herself comfortable. "As you know, that woman what calls herself Lady Thane now was flaunting your jewels at the royal feast…"

"My mother's pearls," corrected Fen.

"Was they?" Trudy did not seem a bit interested in that detail. "And then afterward, you sent your new husband to fetch them back for you…"

"Well…not quite, but never mind. Do continue."

254

"Well, the Thane's manservant, Poulson, was attending his master when Earl Vawdrey reached their rooms. He said they heard Lord Vawdrey hammering on Thane's door so loud that Lady Thane's mother was afeared they would surely all be murdered in their beds! Sir Ambrose, he roared at Poulson to answer before the door caved in, though he cowered behind his own blanket like the veriest cur!"

Fen winced, but Trudy barely seemed to notice. "Poulson said he opened the door and found a cold-eyed devil stood there waiting for him, and he made the sign of protection when he heard how smooth he talked, all the while his eyes was blazing blue murder."

Fen sat up. She had herself noticed how Oswald's eyes so often gave away a completely different mood to the one set by his vocal tone. "Then what happened?" she prompted her maid.

"Poulson said he had no choice but to fetch his master out forthwith. Lord Vawdrey told him he will drag him from his bed himself if he did not come. And Poulson said he believed him, milady! And Sir Ambrose came, though he grumbled and moaned, and Poulson said he was right ashamed of him!

"A poor, bandy-legged sight he looked, milady, by all accounts. 'You have something that belongs to my wife,' says Lord Vawdrey. And Sir Ambrose, he started to protest, but the earl, he reached across and knocked his nightcap right off his head. 'Next time,' says he, 'It'll be your head from your shoulders, you faithless piece of—'" Trudy broke off with a cough. "Your pardon, milady," she said hastily.

Fen's eyes were almost out of her head. "Go on," she gasped.

"Well," said Trudy, seeing she had given no offense. "Sir Ambrose, he runs off and fetches the jewelry box, and Poulson said as he heard Lady Thane set up a caterwauling in the bedroom. 'Shut your mouth, woman!' he yells at her, and brings it out, muttering that it's all a misunderstanding. Poulson said he surely lied, for his face was as red as a beet."

Fen grasped the arms of her chair. "And what did Lord Vawdrey—?"

"Poulson said he looked at him so cold, he was surprised his master didn't contract frostbite on the spot. He snatched the box and leaned in close—like this." Trudy's face hovered close to Fen's. "'If you ever show your hand again, where my wife is concerned,' says he, 'then you will regret it. You and yours.'" Trudy nodded in satisfaction. "And Poulson, he said as he believed him about that too!"

Fen collapsed back into the water. She was trembling. "Of course," she said, pulling herself together. "Gossip always exaggerates a tale…"

"Oh no, milady," Trudy interrupted her. "I had that straight from Poulson himself."

That was a blow to her theory, but after a moment Fen rallied. "Y-yes, but mayhap, in the retelling it has grown a little more *dramatic* each time?" She looked at Trudy hopefully, but the maid looked unconvinced.

She sniffed. "If you say so, milady." She passed the washcloth and soap to Fen. "Do you want to finish up? You're all turning to gooseflesh."

256

Fen hurriedly washed under her arms and between her legs. Trudy had gone to fetch a much larger white cloth for drying and she held this open now as Fen climbed dripping out of the tub.

"Which dress will you be a-wearing of today, milady?" she asked.

Fen thought of the parcel which had arrived from signor Pezzini the previous day. The green and gold gown she had so admired would do very well for the supper Oswald was taking her to that evening. The other was a cream dress with a black and gold pattern.

She forced herself to try to focus on getting dressed, instead of the extraordinary scene that Trudy had just described to her, between her past and present husband. Walking over to a trunk, she flung it open and nearly lost the sheet she was wrapped in.

Trudy hurried over to help her. "This one?" she asked.

"Yes, that's the one." Fen wondered if it was too fine to wear to a gathering of ladies, but truth be told, she had nothing else now that Oswald had as good as forbidden her to wear her old dresses. And he had been right in his previous advice.

On their walk the day before, Lady Schaeffer had been wearing a gorgeous particolored kirtle of red and blue with a fur-lined mantle. Fen had been glad of the borrowed finery of Lady Sumner's cloak or she would have suffered by comparison indeed. It was certainly a lot easier getting ready with Trudy assisting her and she was in her shift and gown in next to no time.

257

"It looks very well, milady," Trudy told her admiringly. "Though you need a belt…"

"I had a new one delivered yestere'en," she said. "'Tis in the second drawer down. The red leather belt."

Trudy flew across the room. "This one with the silver badges?" she asked, lifting it out.

"That is the one."

"What manner of creatures be these?" Trudy squinted, looking at the heraldic devices that had been added by the smith as she walked back across.

"They are bears for me and panthers for my husband," explained Fen as her maid fastened the belt low to sit on the flare of her hips.

Trudy nodded. "And what will we do with your hair?" she asked.

Fen turned to look over her shoulder at the dizzying array of headwear she had purchased from the Watkynses.

"There's a black and gold damask coif that would match," suggested Trudy.

"Perfect," said Fenella thankfully. "You've been really helpful, Trudy. Are you sure you have not been a lady's maid before?"

"Well, milady, I did once serve a rich merchant's wife for six months before she was fetched off with a fever. And Uncle's been coaching me, so I don't disgrace myself."

Fenella digested this as Trudy brushed and dressed her hair. She deftly braided her thick brown hair and then twisted and pinned the tresses into place before adding the coif last of all, so it sat very high on her head. Fen turned her head to the looking glass. Her reflection was a surprise to her every time these days. "Thank you, Trudy, it looks very well." She had never worn a coif before, but to her own eyes she looked very sophisticated indeed.

Trudy turned back to the drawers with a satisfied smile on her face and selected dark green hose and yellow garters for her mistress. "Which shoes, milady?" she asked.

"The round-toed ones, I think, with the green leather."

"And jewels?" Fen paused, reaching for her turquoise ring. "Might I make a suggestion, milady?" asked Trudy. Fen looked up. "I think…the pearls, don't you?"

Fen gave a startled laugh. "Yes," she said, thinking it over a moment. "I believe you are right. The pearls." The two women smiled at each other.

19

"How well you look!" exclaimed Hester Schaeffer when they met in the long gallery. "Is that a new gown? How I admire the matching coif!"

"It is," said Fen gratefully. She touched her headwear lightly, checking it was secure. "I have a new maid that dressed my hair."

"How wonderful," enthused her new friend, looping arms with her as they carried on their way. "You must hold on to her. It is so hard to find anyone decent these days. I pay mine a small fortune, but you see I had to double what Lady Reed paid her to entice her away." She sighed. "Andrew would say it served me right for poaching her from another's service. Husbands can be so tiresome, can they not?"

Fenella smiled. "I suppose they can."

"We're going down the next two staircases to the lower salon," Hester instructed as they descended a flight of steps.

"Will there be many ladies attending this morning?"

"About fifteen or thereabouts," Hester replied airily.

"And will I meet Lady Eden Montmayne?"

"Of a surety, my dear. Of a surety. She will in all likelihood be deputizing for the Queen, who usually only attends when there is a special performance."

Fen was glad to hear it. She was in no hurry to see Queen Armenal again anytime soon. They soon reached the lower salon, where small groups of ladies were standing around in conversation although there seemed no discernible organization.

Hester tutted. "We are early, what a bore!" She drew Fen over to a quiet corner where they could chat without interruption. "There is no one senior here to take charge," she said with irritation as her eyes swept the inhabitants of the room.

"What about you, Hester?" asked Fen, as her friend was surely senior.

"Lord no!"

"Are you not one of the Queen's ladies-in-waiting?"

Hester grimaced. "Dear me, no! I'm far too frivolous. Armenal only wants women who are useful to her, and I refuse to be useful to anyone. Sadly, for her, she has still to shed a good number of ninnies the King engaged for her before their marriage."

"Yes, she did mention something of that." Fen remembered the Queen's words from their meeting.

"Did she really?" said Hester with surprise. She eyed Fenella oddly. "That sounds ominous."

"How so?"

"Like she might have intentions of asking you to join their ranks."

"Oh no, she was very disappointed in me. She said so."

"That's even worse," said Hester dryly. "It meant she felt she could be frank with you. The Queen only feels that way with people she likes."

Fen eyed her friend doubtfully. "I'm sure I made a very bad impression. I was tongue-tied and miserable."

Hester perked up. "Not the best combination for endearing yourself to others," she admitted cheerfully. "Let us hope you're right, and you got away with it."

"Is it so very bad to be an attendant of the Queen?" asked Fenella in surprise. "I thought it was meant to be a position of honor."

"That's what they tell you," said Hester darkly. "But I am not so easily fooled!" She cast another eye around the room. "There is no one here yet who is of any import, so I shall not trouble myself to introduce you to any of their number."

Nearby a throat cleared and both ladies turned. Stood before them was a stout matron and two blond-haired women, doubtless sisters from their strong similarity of feature, although one was far prettier than the other.

"My dear Lady Schaeffer," said the older woman. "Well met. May I introduce to you Jane and Helen Cecil who are the nieces of Sir Phillip Cecil and making their debut at court." Both girls curtseyed.

"Oh, it's you, Lady Morpington," said Lady Schaeffer, smothering a yawn. "How is that son of yours? Still giving you gray hairs?"

The other lady's face tightened. "Indeed, poor Rodrey is still suffering from a severe malady of the chest and recovering at our country estate at present."

"It is so dull here at court without him," mourned one of the blonde ladies sorrowfully. "How I miss dear Rodrey." Lady Morpington looked gratified.

"Indeed?" said Hester sharply. "I understood this was your first visit to court?" she quizzed the young woman, who colored hotly.

"You must excuse my sister," interjected the other, prettier blonde smoothly. "We all grew up together and imagined we would be escorted to our court debut by our friend, who is sorely missed."

Hester snorted. "You're quite the diplomat," she commented. "Which one are you?"

"Helen," she replied composedly, dipping into another curtsey.

"Well, I predict quite the career at court for you, Miss Cecil," said Hester. Somehow, the way she said it did not sound like a compliment, Fen noticed.

"Will you not introduce us to your friend, Lady Schaeffer?" asked Helen Cecil boldly.

Hester's eyebrows rose before she turned to Fen. "This is the Countess Vawdrey," she said. "Fenella, these are Helen and Ethel Cecil."

"Jane," corrected the first blonde, looking pained.

"And the Dowager Viscountess of Morpington." There were curtseys all round.

"I am glad to make your acquaintance," said Fen, noticing the Cecil girls were staring at her rather hard.

"Forgive my curiosity, Lady Vawdrey," simpered Jane Cecil. "But are those the famous Vawdrey pearls you are wearing?"

"Famous?" echoed Fen. She was sure no one had ever described her modest string of pearls as such before. "I'm afraid not, these were my mother's." She touched them almost as if for luck.

"You misunderstand," said Helen in a rather patronizing tone. "My sister meant—"

"How can they be Vawdrey pearls?" interrupted Hester Schaeffer loudly. "When my friend has just explained they belonged to her mother?" There was an awkward pause.

"Apologies if my young friends offended," said Lady Morpington with a stiff bow of her head.

"Not at all," answered Hester swiftly. "Though you may need more vigilance in curbing unruly tongues, my dear Lady Morpington."

Lady Morpington turned an unbecoming puce, curtseyed, and turned away. The Cecil girls followed after her, though they looked reluctant to leave and threw glances over their shoulders as they left.

"Impudence," tutted Hester.

"You do not like Lady Morpington?" ventured Fen.

"Her son Rodrey, Viscount Morpington, is a profligate, though she insists on talking of him as though he were a child," said Hester scathingly. "And those girls are not much better." She lowered her voice. "There is talk that the younger will become the King's next mistress."

Fen gasped. "Oh." Helen Cecil had indeed been very beautiful, but to her eye, the Queen was far more striking.

"Lady Vawdrey," said a cool voice, bringing her out of her thoughts.

Fenella turned and found Lady Anne Sumner stood behind her. "Lady Sumner," she greeted her with a curtsey. "I am glad to come across you here."

The other woman looked cautiously surprised. "Indeed?"

"Yes, for I wanted very much to thank you for your most generous loan of your gown and cloak. I'm afraid I completely neglected to do so at the feast the other night. Indeed, you must have thought it most remiss of me…"

Lady Sumner brushed these words aside with a wave of a white hand. "Not at all," she demurred. "I'm aware you have been very busy."

"My maid will pack them up to return them forthwith," Fen hurried to assure her, but Lady Sumner pursed her lips.

"Nonsense, I hope you will accept the gown at least as a gift. I certainly could never wear it now without suffering by comparison."

"Oh, but I couldn't! It is very fine indeed, and the alterations we made were not irreversible," Fen protested.

"It would only languish in the bottom of a trunk," Lady Sumner told her flatly. "No, I insist. You must accept it as a wedding present."

Fen paused, unsure how to proceed. Lady Sumner was not exactly bursting with friendliness and yet she insisted on giving her a most costly gift. "You are most kind, Lady Sumner, I hardly know what to say…"

"Pray do not trouble yourself to speak another word of it," said Lady Sumner with a barely there smile. She curtseyed to Lady Schaeffer and then swept past them to join some ladies on the far side of the room. Fen looked after her with a puzzled look on her face.

"Someone's put her nose out of joint," boomed a jolly voice, making Fen jump. A woman with high coloring joined them. She wore a rusty-red gown, which clashed unfortunately with her ruddy coloring and curly brown hair. Fen found herself unable to gauge her age.

"It is most curious indeed," agreed Hester Schaeffer, who had stood by silently during the exchange. "I wonder what has ruffled her feathers. She is not usually put so easily out of countenance."

The newcomer puffed out her cheeks. "Probably the fact her ancient husband's still breathing," she guessed. Fen's jaw dropped. She directed a startled look at her friend.

"Allow me to introduce the two of you," said Hester smoothly. "Fenella, Countess Vawdrey, please meet Lady Bess Hartleby."

Lady Bess gave a rather masculine curtsey that strangely looked more like a bow. Fenella bobbed a curtsey in return. "So, you're the resourceful countess?" asked Bess with great interest. "I must say, you don't look particularly forceful."

She cast a critical look over Fenella. "But I daresay you probably used your feminine wiles on Vawdrey. I hear men are most susceptible to them." Fen's smile froze in place. "Not that I'd know one if I saw one," rattled on Bess with a hearty laugh. "What d'ye know about playwrights hey? I've a fancy to sponsor one."

"Er…absolutely nothing, I'm afraid," admitted Fen, trying to recover herself. She had never met any woman quite like her before.

"Then you must get one too," said Bess firmly. "It's the only way to mask your ignorance."

"W-well, I don't know," started Fen doubtfully.

"But of course, you must, Fenella," Hester interrupted her. "You said yourself that Lord Vawdrey voiced no objection to the notion."

"Oh, but I've spent so much of his money already this week," she objected with a guilty look.

"Have you?" asked Lady Bess with interest. "He can probably stand it. After all, he is fabulously wealthy, is he not?" When the other two made no immediate reply, Bess continued. "Stands to reason, he must be. Otherwise, he could not afford to build his own palace."

"Palace?" echoed Fen faintly. It was the first she'd heard of it.

"Yes," murmured Hester, wrinkling her brow. "I did hear Andrew mention it a few times last year. He was rather envious of Vawdrey being able to draw up his own plans. But then he is so very clever, is he not?"

"Not clever enough to elude the parson's trap, eh, Lady Vawdrey?" joked Bess, nudging Fen in the ribs.

Fen gave a weak-sounding laugh. "I suppose not." She felt winded, and not just from Bess's elbow. Once again it was being brought home to her just how little she knew about her new husband. It never failed to give her a deep feeling of unease.

"Ah, here comes Eden now," said Hester approvingly as a young woman marched into the room, followed by a trail of miserable-looking supplicants clutching papers and hats.

"Why do artists always look so oppressed?" wondered Lady Bess. "Miserable-looking bunch."

"It can't be easy to come along with the begging bowl," said Hester sympathetically.

"The first one to crack a smile is mine," said Bess decisively.

Fen was studying Lady Eden Montmayne with interest. She had black hair and dark eyes and wore a black dress with only one brooch to alleviate the head-to-toe black. Certainly, it was an unusual look for one so young.

She somehow projected the fact she had a forceful personality into the air around her, which seemed to ripple with her energy. She was casting a quick, appraising look around the room and focused on their little group at once. She turned back to her gaggle of artists and made a few brief gestures with her hands. Three stepped forward as she bore down on them determinedly.

"Oh Lord," said Lady Bess. "She's going to organize us first."

"Such a redoubtable girl," said Hester in a murmured aside to Fen.

"She certainly exudes a great deal of confidence," agreed Fenella. Eden's face formed a quick business-like smile as she sunk into a graceful curtsey. They all bobbed back. This time Fen was convinced that Bess bowed.

"My dear Lady Schaeffer," Eden greeted her friend. "I am so pleased to see you here this morning. It has been a few weeks since you last attended."

269

"Allow me to introduce my new friend, Lady Fenella, Countess Vawdrey." Fen bobbed again and was pleasantly surprised to find Eden Montmayne had no comment to make about her marital status.

"How do you do?" she asked gravely instead. "I am very pleased to meet you."

"And I, you."

"And I am sure," continued Hester. "That you must be already acquainted with Lady Bess Hartleby."

"By sight only," answered Eden. "I am glad you have brought along new members to our society, for we have need of new blood."

"And new pockets, I'll be bound!" joked Lady Bess with a loud guffaw at her own joke.

Lady Eden squared her shoulders but inclined her head agreeably enough. "Indeed, Lady Bess. You speak the truth," she acknowledged. "Have you a mind to become a patron, may I ask?"

"You may," agreed Lady Bess. "And I do. But I want none of these milk and water artists," she boomed. "Give me a fellow of conviction. Not some poultry rhymer, reed-voiced singer or mere dabbler of paints."

Fen became aware that around them was the sound of inward breaths being drawn. Their little group was undoubtedly the center of attention.

270

"Of course not," Eden Montmayne answered, not looking remotely embarrassed by the fact they clearly had an audience. "I would never do you such a disservice." She looked back over her shoulder and signaled to a rough-hewn-looking man with bushy eyebrows and a shock of curly brown hair. "Signor Arnotti is a great painter who studied at the Ottoline school in Holbrahns," she said grandly.

Lady Bess gazed at him, looking unimpressed as he shambled forward. "D'ye paint dogs, sir?" she asked at length.

The artist's eyebrows waggled furiously. "Dogs?" he asked suspiciously.

"Hounds," she clarified. "I've a fancy to see mine on canvas, you see."

"How many do you own, Lady Bess?" asked Fen with interest.

"Six of the devils," answered Bess promptly.

Signor Arnotti slipped his thumbs in his pockets. "I will paint these dogs," he said, nodding his head. "But only at the feet of their mistress."

"Me?" boomed Bess. "Not likely!"

"That is my condition," he answered firmly.

"Is that so? Sure of yourself, aren't you?" Fen fancied she could hear a grudging respect in Bess's tone. Signor Arnotti nodded sagely. Bess gave an amused snort. "Very well," she conceded. "As you wish. But I wish you joy of turning this physog into a

271

work of art!" She pointed at her face. Someone nearby tittered, but they all ignored it.

"Excellent," enthused Eden. "We will leave you to arrange the details." She turned determinedly to Hester. "And now you, my dear Lady Schaeffer," she said brightly. "I seem to remember you were in need of a poet to add to your collection of artists?"

"Was I?" asked Hester, looking diverted. "Well, if you say I do, then it must be so, my dear."

"Superb." Eden clapped her hands. "Mr. Leadbetter," summoned Eden. "Approach, please."

Fenella listened as Eden ran through Mr. Leadbetter's body of work, sharing excerpts from his most recent sonnet. Hester professed herself charmed and agreed to be his patroness without much pressing from her young friend.

"Your cousin Lenora does not join us this morning?" said Hester. "A great pity. It would put those Cecil girls in their place to see the reigning court beauty shine."

"No," replied Eden, her lips pursing. "I had hoped she would, but…" Her words trailed off.

"She had a more enticing offer?" Hester ventured.

"Lord Loughridge asked her to join him hawking this morning," admitted Eden with disapproval.

"Young Loughridge?" repeated Hester. "Has he joined the ranks of her beaux now?"

"So it seems," said Eden. "She did say she would try to join us later, but she is a little disillusioned with artists of late. Her last three portraits have scarcely done her justice."

Fen could tell she really did not want to discuss her cousin's conquests. "I wonder," she said, clearing her throat. "That is, my husband did say…"

Eden looked up keenly. "Yes? You are interested in sponsoring an artist, Lady Vawdrey?"

"I thought, maybe a poet?" said Fenella uncertainly. "I mean, I don't really know anything about poetry but…"

"Do you have a favorite kind?" asked Eden.

"I prefer it when they tell a story." Fen shrugged. "Like a ballad maybe?"

"A story," repeated Eden thoughtfully. "How about a playwright? I have one that might suit you admirably. A Mr. John Entner." She took a step closer to Fenella and lowered her voice. "I'm afraid the unfortunate man is in rather straitened circumstances of late. He used to write in his spare time and maintain his family of five children by working as a clerk, but sadly his clerking position was lost. He is finding his muse elusive, with creditors hammering on the door."

"Oh, the poor man! No wonder his inspiration has abandoned him."

"But perhaps a new patron will bolster him?" suggested Eden hopefully.

Fen turned to look at the crowd of artists. "Tell me, which one is Mr. Entner?" she asked, already knowing deep down that it would be the thin, soulful-looking fellow who stood on the edge of the crowd clutching the brim of his hat and looking deeply sorrowful.

Eden gave a swift smile that lit up her face. "Allow me to fetch him, Lady Vawdrey." With a rustle of black fabric, she took off across the room with her light, quick steps and Fen found that becoming a patron of the arts was not so difficult after all.

20

"I might have known you would be taken in by a sob story," tutted Hester as they walked back to their rooms together arm in arm.

"Oh, but indeed, Mr. Entner has fallen on some very hard times," insisted Fenella. "And Oswald himself told me that I might trust Eden Montmayne's judgment of art."

"Oswald?" interrupted Hester, arching an eyebrow at her. "Why, I do believe that is the first time I have heard you refer to your husband in such informal terms, Fenella."

Fen felt herself turning bright red. "Is it?" she faltered.

Hester Schaeffer laughed. "I will not tease you," she promised. "But you must both come to dine with Andrew and myself one evening this week."

"Of course," said Fen, pressing her friend's arm. "Are you going to—" Her mind went blank. "Oh dear, some banquet this evening. The Dowager something or other—?"

"The Dowager Duchess of Lessing," Hester supplied. "We've had an invite, but Andrew is so stuffy, poor dear, and I really can't put him through more than one social event per week. He finds it very *wearing*. Especially after one of the council meetings. They can be quite involved."

Fen pressed her lips together, remembering Oswald's displeasure at her inquisitiveness that morning. Clearly Lord Schaeffer told his wife more than her own husband did.

"But there, you are not interested in such dry stuff," said Hester when she made no reply. "And I can't say I blame you. At your age I had no interest either." Fen nodded, reluctant to explain that she had been warned off having any such interest. "And here we are, your rooms," exclaimed the older woman. "Do you think you would be able to find your way back down again, my dear? This place is such a rabbit warren."

"I think so," said Fen hesitantly. "Although I might take a wrong turn or two as so many of the corridors look the same."

"You're doing very well," her friend assured her. "You should get Lord Vawdrey to give you a full tour of the palace at some point."

"Yes, I have really only seen parts of it," Fen admitted. "And I don't really have a clear idea in my head how it is laid out at all."

"I can certainly show you some more walking routes around the parks and walkways," Hester offered. "How about tomorrow morn?"

"Bors and I would like that very much," replied Fen warmly. "I'll take my leave of you then, my dear." Hester kissed her cheek and left Fen outside her door. "Have a nice time this evening and I will call for you on the morrow," she called as she disappeared around a corner.

"Goodbye." Fen paused a moment before entering into the Vawdrey apartment. It occurred to her that she would miss Hester Schaeffer when she went to Vawdrey Keep, but perhaps they could keep up a written correspondence?

Masculine voices brought her out of her musings, and she looked up to see Roland sat playing cards at the table, with two other young men dressed partly in chain mail. They both sprang to their feet though Roland remained lolling in his chair. "Oh! Roland, your pardon, I did not mean to interrupt—" she began, but her brother-in-law forestalled her.

"This is Bevan and Attley," he said, nodding to his friends.

"Lady Vawdrey," said the first, executing a creditable bow. "Your servant. Sir Edward Bevan."

"Sir James Attley," added the other hastily.

Fenella curtseyed. "I am happy to meet you both," she said brightly. They did not seem hostile at any rate, though they both goggled at her as though she were some sort of rare bird before dropping back into their seats. Both were well-built young men, and from their apparel, she guessed they had been practicing with arms and were part of the competitive tournament faction.

"See you got your pearls back at any rate, eh?" joked Sir Edward feebly. He pointed at his own neck to illustrate his point.

Fenella blushed and darted a look at Roland, who rolled his eyes. "Oh—er, yes," she agreed.

"Did you show them to Lady Thane?" asked Sir Edward with a chortle. His friend, Sir James, elbowed him in the ribs.

"Ignore Bev," Roland advised, not looking up from his cards. "We all do."

"You know, it would serve Thane right if Lord Vawdrey were to challenge him to a duel," carried on Sir Edward cheerfully.

Roland snorted. "Oswald would never challenge the likes of Thane in combat."

"Why not?" asked his friend. "Vawdrey was in the King's army, wasn't he? Could handle himself in a fight."

Roland turned a look of utter scorn on his friend. "Exactly, you fool." He looked at Fen and then back at his friend. "Gods, you all think you know him, but you haven't the first notion."

Sir Edward looked uncomfortable. "Steady on, Roly. There's a lady present."

"I tell you, you don't know him!" insisted Roland. "You only think you do." He was looking directly at Fen now, the challenge plain in his expression.

"You've said that before," said Fen. "But perhaps I am not such a stranger to his character as you suppose."

"Think so, do you?" sneered Roland, throwing down his hand of cards. "You've only been wed a week! If you truly knew him, you would run for the hills."

"I think not," said Fen, and for some reason, she suddenly thought of the scarring at Oswald's back. She may not know him as well as some did, but she knew some of his secrets alright. Even if he did not mean to let her into the heart of them. She lifted her chin.

"Tell you about his work, did he?" mocked Roland.

"No, would you recommend I asked him?" asked Fen mildly. She was determined not to let her brother-in-law get the upper hand.

"I thought not." He smirked. Bors peeked out from under his chair and yawned. Roland reached down and patted his head.

Fen approached the table to pour herself a cup of ale from their pitcher. She took a few sips and then sat down next to Sir Edward and opposite Roland. She saw a look of surprise flit over his face and was pleased. Did he really imagine she would go and hide in the bedroom? She was made of sterner stuff than that! "What are you playing?"

"Huntsman Bold," answered Sir Edward.

"You wouldn't know it," said Roland shortly. "It's not a ladies' game."

"I played cards with my brother, Gil, many a day," protested Fen.

"For money?" asked Roland.

Fen looked at the table. "I see no coin," she pointed out.

Sir James laughed. "She has you there."

Fen peered at the cards, which depicted various beasts of the hunt. They were a beautifully painted deck.

"What games did you play with your brother?" asked Sir Edward with interest.

279

"Let me see," said Fen, tapping her chin. "There was Find the Acorn…"

"A child's game," dismissed Roland.

"Heap of Fish."

"My dribbling nephew could play that."

"A Fine Red Apple…"

"Nursery fare."

"I made that one up," said Fen, leaning back in her chair. "You really are too predictable, Roland. I'll wager you're a terrible card player."

He smirked. "Now you're trying to bait me into letting you play. But you're not as clever as you think you are, sister."

"Or you're not as stupid," she replied before catching herself. Her eyes widened as his friends snickered. "Your pardon," she stammered.

Roland frowned. "Why are you apologizing?"

"Because I addressed you then as if you were truly my brother," she admitted.

He held her gaze a moment. Then he swept up the cards. "Attley, do you have your deck?" he asked.

His friend reached into his breast pocket and withdrew a well-worn set of cards. Roland took them and spread them across the tabletop. "Are you familiar with these?" he asked, quirking a brow.

Fen looked. "No," she said. These were crudely drawn, yellowing cards that curled at the corners. "What are they— professions? Guilds?" she guessed, spying what looked like a blacksmith with his anvil, and a miller with his grindstone.

"It's called Livelihood," said Sir James. "It's what all the hawkers and stable hands play."

"What's interesting is that the lowest suit wins out," enthused Sir Edward. "So, a fishmonger trumps a baron, and a beggar trumps a king. D'you see?"

"I do," said Fen. "So, it's like the Lord of Misrule. When everything is upside down?"

"Exactly," said Roland, who was now dealing the cards. To her gratification, he was dealing her a hand.

Sir James poured them all more ale, and Fen settled back into her seat and examined her cards. "What trumps a cleric?" she asked with interest. The other three sat still a moment.

"Errrr…" said Sir James, turning red.

Roland turned a card to show her a bare-breasted woman. He cleared his throat. "A nursing mother," he said shortly. Sir Edward had a coughing fit.

"I see," said Fen. Though she couldn't see why they were acting so skittish about it.

21

A gust of laughter surprised Oswald as he paused on the threshold before shutting the door behind him. Roland had better not have brought some tavern wench back to their rooms, he thought grimly as he made out female laughter above the male.

"Serves you right, Attley!" He recognized his brother's voice. Then, with a start, his wife's.

"And you thought I would be a hindrance," she said smugly. "But we have won the last three hands since we partnered up, have we not?"

Oswald walked through and found a card game in full swing. "Vawdrey!" He was hailed enthusiastically by Sir Edward Bevan.

"Pull up a chair!" encouraged Sir James Attley. Fenella beamed at him, while Roland looked defiant. Which was nothing new.

"What have we here?" he asked casually while unbuttoning his cuffs.

Meldon was piling logs on a roaring fire, and Bors was lying on his back on the hearth rug, snoring.

"We're playing cards, my lord," said Fenella. "Have you ever played Livelihood?"

He paused. "Livelihood. Not for a long time."

"Not since you were a soldier?" asked Roland provokingly.

"A soldier trumps a knight," said Fen, holding up a finger and looking pleased with herself.

"And a *nursing mother* trumps a cleric," stressed Sir Edward hastily.

Oswald gave him a hard look and the younger man flushed. "How long have you been playing?" he asked, noticing the amount of empty flagons lying around the table.

"All afternoon they been at it," said Meldon waspishly as he rose to his feet from before the fire, dusting his knees.

"I shall tell my friend Lady Schaeffer about this game," said Fen. "It far exceeds both A Heap of Fish and Find the Acorn."

"I wouldn't do that, Lady Vawdrey," said Sir James, looking dismayed. "It—er—is not really a ladies' game at all, you know."

"You mean because it reverses the social order?" asked Fen in puzzlement.

"You could teach your brother though," said Sir Edward. "That'd be alright. No harm in that, eh?"

"I'd have to get him a deck though," she pointed out. "Is it a local Aphrany game?"

"I expect so," said Sir James, nodding. "Leastways, I never heard of it before I came here."

Oswald rounded the table and held his hand out to Fen. She took it and he pulled her to her feet. Then he sat in her chair.

She stared down at him in consternation. "There are plenty of other chairs," she pointed out.

He patted his knee. "But I wanted to share yours," he said in his most reasonable tone.

Her brow cleared. "Oh!" she said and obligingly perched herself on his knee. He wondered idly how many cups of ale she'd had that afternoon. When he passed an arm around her, she sighed and settled against him. *A fair few*, he guessed.

"We'll share a hand," he told Roland, who was looking at him askance. His brother shrugged and started shuffling the cards.

Fen sighed and slid an arm around his shoulders. "This is nice," she murmured. Her breathy words went straight to his groin, and he had to take a deep breath to steady himself. He wondered how many rounds of cards he'd have to sit through before he could in all decency hustle her into their bedroom and get her on her back.

"I had a good day today," she told him quietly as he whisked up their cards. He liked the way her attention was focused now on him alone. Liked it too much. Around them, his brother and his friends laughed and joked.

"Did you? I'm glad," he responded automatically as he discarded and picked up a card. He fanned them, so she could see their hand, but her gaze was on his face.

"How was yours?" She sounded, he thought, a little wistful.

285

"Frustrating," he admitted.

"Oh no, why?" She bent her arm at the elbow and lightly touched his hair. He liked that too. *Damn it.*

"It didn't start the way I wanted." *Between her thighs.*

"Maybe it'll end that way?" she suggested encouragingly.

"I certainly hope so."

"I hope so too," she whispered.

She had definitely had too much ale, thought Oswald, flinging down another card.

"Laborer trumps lord," Bevan crowed, snatching up his card.

"You're bad at this game," his wife murmured fondly as her fingers lightly scratched at his neck.

"So it seems." His mouth twisted wryly.

"Want us to clear out after this hand?" asked his brother casually as Bevan and Attley argued if the fishmonger was carrying a carp or a cod.

"Yes," he answered as Fen simultaneously said, "No."

22

"I like Roland's friends," said Fen on a yawn as she pushed away a plate of flour biscuits and cheese. "I'm not really hungry."

"You should eat some more," said Oswald with a frown as slid a bowl of grapes toward her.

"Aren't we dining with someone or other tonight?" she asked in surprise.

"Change of plans."

"Oh." A thought occurred to her. "Then I'll need to tell Trudy, she'll be staying on to dress me—"

"I've already sent her home. Have you finished?"

She nodded. "You think of everything," she marveled as he rose from his chair. She took his arm when he offered it and let him lead her into the bedroom. "But if we aren't eating out, why did you order a bath?" she wondered aloud as they entered their bedroom.

It was already set up in the far corner of the room and tented around with white sheets. Oswald took the key from his pocket that Meldon had supplied him with and secured the door. He placed it on top of the chest. "We can take a bath after," he told her, maneuvering her toward the bed.

"After?" Her voice hitched.

"After," he agreed, spinning her round to find the lacings at her back. Her belt slid to the floor, and he lifted her gown up and over her head. He hesitated. "Do you want to keep your shift on?" he asked.

"Yes," she said over her shoulder.

"Don't fall asleep," he cautioned as she bent at the waist to rest her upper body against the mattress.

"Hmm, I won't," she assured him sleepily as she rested her cheek against the soft bedspread.

He fell to his knees behind her and slid off her shoes and stockings. Unable to resist, he ran his hands up the backs of her legs until he cupped her backside under her shift. "You have a beautiful backside, Lady Vawdrey," he said thickly.

He heard her sharply indrawn breath. "Really?" She sounded doubtful.

"You don't believe me?"

"Your compliments are rather unusual," she pointed out. "You said my toes were charming the other day."

"Ah, but I also told you I'm not in the habit of saying things unless I mean them," he pointed out as he stepped away and stripped off his clothes, never taking his eyes off her. She didn't move but remained bent over the bed.

An inclination entered his head which had him breathing hard, nostrils flaring. He stepped back up, flush behind her, pressing his erect manhood against her, letting her feel his hard length.

"Open your legs," he said. He drew up her shift. "Shall I turn you over?" he murmured. "Or enter you like this?"

She lifted her head off the mattress. "From behind me?" she asked, sounding shocked.

"Yes."

"How would that—?" She broke off her words, perhaps realizing exactly how it would work.

"We could try it this way?" he suggested, rolling his hips to give her a precursory taste.
She exclaimed as his fingers found their way to her slippery core and started spreading her moisture around her folds.

"Shall I mount you from behind, Fenella?" he teased. "Should you like that, my love?"

She sucked in a breath. "Like the beasts do?" she asked uncertainly. That surprised a laugh out of him. But then, she was a country girl after all.

"Shall we try it?" He was already poised at her entrance now and pushing into her wet warmth.

"*Yes*," she exhaled with a shudder.

He didn't need any more of an invitation but instead started the hot, deep slide until he was fully sheathed in her tight, welcoming body. *Finally*. He folded forward to cover her body with his and let out a deep breath between her shoulder blades.

"Oswald?"

"Just hold still a moment and give me this," he groaned. "I need it. I needed it this morning. I've waited to be here all the damned day long."

"Oh." She was silent a moment and all he could hear was her breathing. "So, when you said the day did not start right...?"

He gave a shallow dip of his hips, and she broke off her words with a breathy moan. He felt himself break out in a sweat at how good she felt. At this rate he wasn't going to last long. He lifted off her, bracing his hands against the mattress at her hips, and planted his feet square on the floor. "This is going to lack finesse," he said regretfully as he surged forward into her with a hard thrust.

Fenella exclaimed, and he saw her grip the sheets. He did it again, and her plump body bounced beneath him in a way that made him grit his teeth. From this vantage point, her shapely backside was on full view, along with her pale shoulders, and the sacral dimples at the base of her spine. And he liked it all.

Grasping one hip firmly, he ran the other hand up and down her back as he thrust into her. His heated gaze took in the way she undulated beneath his palm, as though she liked his touch. It made his throat burn. He clenched his muscles and seized both her hips hard as he thrust again and again. All these years of abstinence had probably been a mistake, he thought. A mistake Fenella was going to pay dearly for.

The pleasures of the flesh had never been a weakness of his, but you wouldn't know it from the way he was going at her. He reached around between her legs to find her bud and stroked it.

Fen gave a shocked cry and then a wail and he felt her body squeeze tight around him as she exploded in rapture.

He pushed into her with his full driving length and stayed planted deep while she shook and trembled around him in the aftershocks, sobbing into the mattress. Only when she was finally still did he roll her over onto her back.

"Stiff?" he asked, rubbing her arms and then her legs, as she winced and inched up the bed. Her eyes were drawn to his still inflamed manhood where it bobbed against his thigh, demanding attention.

"Not as stiff as you." She gulped.

He would have laughed if he still didn't have an edge of desperation about him. She held out her arms and he rolled atop of her. "Fen," he said urgently.

"All is well," she assured him, and wrapped her legs around his hips.

He aligned their bodies and then drove back inside her with a deep groan, which he breathed into her neck. He felt her hands settle tentatively against his back. The pace he set was brisk, but he managed to stave off frantic. For now. The bed rocked with his exertions; Fenella's breath hitched. Her hands slid up and down his back and the sensation of her touch made his pleasure climb even higher, until it was almost unbearable.

He ducked his head and kissed first one, and then her other full breast. It was only at this point he realized he had not kissed her lips yet that evening. He set that to rights at once. She returned his kiss with enthusiasm and the feel of her tongue in his mouth

291

triggered his release. He pinned her to the mattress and rocked his hips against hers until the blaze in his chest was quenched and his ardor was spent. He slumped over her, his breathing labored.

"You set me ablaze," he told her in a low voice, touching his forehead to hers. Then he rolled off her to give the poor thing room to breathe. "I don't know how you do it. Until now, I've always considered myself a prim, uptight sort."

"Prim?" she repeated in a choked voice. "Hardly." She fell silent a moment, then jumped when she felt him touch her hair. It was tousled and coming down her back, having lost half its pins. She rolled onto her side toward him. "It did look nice this morning," she said, patting a hand to her disordered locks.

"I rather like the way it looks now," he said. "Well tumbled. Like you." She was just about the most delectable sight he had ever seen.

She laughed. "You, Oswald Vawdrey, are about as far from prim as can be." He grinned at that pronouncement. "And where's my shift?" she asked, rolling to peer over the side of the bed. At some point, he'd divested her of it.

"You don't need it."

"What?"

"The bath, remember?"

"I'm too tired to take a bath."

"It's fine, I'll do all the work," he promised and rolled onto his side. To his surprise, he found he hadn't removed his signet ring or chain in his haste to bed his wife.

"What's that?" Her voice cracked as he removed the chain from round his neck.

He looked up in surprise. "This? Just my old seal ring." He showed her the gold ring that was suspended on the chain. It was an orange carnelian stone carved with the Vawdrey panther. "This one I wear," he said, turning his hand to show a large ruby seal ring, which was engraved with a crowned panther, denoting his status as earl. He supposed it was sentimentality that made him keep his father's old ring around his neck. "I normally take it off when I undress, but on this occasion, I was overkeen." He gave a rueful smile.

"Not the ring. The thing next to it. It looks like some kind of pendant?" she said in strangled tones.

He frowned slightly and looked down at the two items on his chain. "This?" He held up a small gold padlock shape. "I suppose. I've had it for as long as I can remember. It was my mother's, I think. I don't have the key."

"Oh."

Something in her tone was off, but when he looked up sharply, she dropped her gaze.
"Is it inscribed?" she asked.

He turned it over in his fingers. "Yes," he said and waited, but she did not ask him with what. "*Not Forgot*," he read out anyway. "Which is ironic, as I don't remember her." Fenella

293

had turned strangely silent. "What's wrong?" he asked, dropping the chain, and reaching for her.

"Naught," she assured him, and reached up to lightly touch his face.

He scooped her off the mattress and headed toward the tub. "I hope the water's still warm." He held her suspended over the tub. "Do you want to test it before I drop you in?" he said, quirking a brow at her.

She dipped her fingers into the fragrant water. "It's fine—" she said, and he released her with a loud splash.

He was over the side and in the tub with her before she had emerged, coughing and spluttering.

"I didn't think you'd actually drop me!" she said indignantly. His arms had already closed around her, hauling her up against his chest. "Or actually get in the tub with me," she admitted breathlessly.

"I seldom say something unless I mean it," he reminded her, enjoying the feeling of her body pressed against his.

"I expect the floor is quite covered in water."

He glanced over the edge. "A few puddles, maybe." She was staring at him. "What is it?"

She blushed. "You look so boyish when your hair is forward on your face like that," she said, tucking her wet hair behind her ears. "Like I remember you," she admitted in a rush. "From those years we were promised."

294

That gave him pause for thought. "I am generally considered to have a good memory," he admitted. "But that period of time is, I confess, a little foggy in my brain."

She screwed her face up. "Is that your tactful way of saying you do not remember me, my lord?" she asked.

He could tell she was joking, but for some reason he felt the oddest tugging in his chest. He put a hand over hers and placed it there. "I remember you, here," he said. "Where it counts."

Fen swallowed. "Oh," she said and seemed to struggle for words. They both looked at each other a moment.

"I remember that Solstice feast," he said slowly. "When you held my hand, under the table."

She drew in a breath. "You remember that, yet—" Her words broke off distractedly.

"Yet what?"

She recovered herself. "Yet you do not remember the gift I gave you, of my dreadful tapestries," she elaborated with a mock grimace. "Thank heavens for small mercies."

He reached behind him for some leaves of soap and a washing cloth. "Yes, but that wasn't what you were going to say," he objected and squeezed the cloth between her breasts, watching the droplets of water trickle down the generous globes of her breasts.

295

Fen dropped down beneath the water, crossing her arms. "I can wash myself," she protested.

"But I promised I would do it," he tutted. "As you're so worn out from my husbandly attentions."

She gave a gurgle of laughter. "I never said that."

"Well, then you can stand a few more, if that is the case," he said, maneuvering her round so that her back faced his front. "Let me wash your hair."

She sighed as he ran some soap leaves through the length of her wet hair. "Oh, very well, if 'twill give you pleasure."

"It sounds like it gives you pleasure," he teased as she tipped her head back and closed her eyes.

"It does feel nice," she admitted so artlessly, it made him ache for her again.

"Fen," he started. Then found he had no notion of how to continue.

Her eyes opened, and she blinked up at him. "Yes?"

"I plan to apply to have your marriage to Thane legally declared null and void." Where had that come from? In some dark recess of his brain, he had been turning that over. But he had not intended to raise it at such a time. Sometimes he astonished even himself.

"Oh?" Her gaze was wary.

"You're not divorced," he persisted, soaping up her hair. "Because you were never married to him in the first place." She frowned over this a moment in intense thought. "You were married to me. Understand?" he asked testily.

"Yes."

He breathed out a breath he wasn't even aware he was holding. "All along. You were mine. Say it."

"All along?" said Fen uncertainly.

He nodded and gathered her soapy hair in one hand like a pony's tail. Then he wagged her head. "Say the rest."

"I was yours?"

"You were," he said with conviction. "So, tell me."

"All along I was yours."

He nodded. "That's better."

Fen stared at him, her amber eyes wide. He felt it again, the strange tug in his chest. It propelled him to turn her to face him and then place a very gentle kiss on her lips. When he drew back, he knew the vulnerable look on her face was reflected on his own. What was he doing? "I'm going to wash out the soap now," he told her. "And then we're going back to bed."

*

Afterward, they lay propped up against the pillows with Fen at his side, curled into him. He felt strangely content and rested as he closed his eyes to savor the sensation. Almost, he imagined he could drift right off to sleep. Then he felt her palm gently rest on his chest.

He flicked his eyes open, but she hadn't moved her head from his shoulder where it rested. His eyelids were just drifting down again when he heard her draw in a breath as if to speak, and then dispel it again with a frustrated puff of air. "What is it?" he asked. Even to his own ear, his voice sounded sleepy.

"Nothing," she hurriedly assured him. "I just…"

Oswald's eyes sprang open. "Every time you assure me there is naught to worry about, I get tense," he said dryly.

She pulled back her head from his shoulder to peer at him in surprise. "Why?" Her damp hair was curling round her face.

He felt irritated that she was shifting her cushiony softness away from him. Removing a hand from behind his head, he hauled her back flush against him, then rested his hand at the dip of her waist. "Because," he said, "usually it means something is bothering you. Which means, it is going to bother me."

She looked bewildered, and he sighed. "Tell me what's amiss." He steeled himself in preparation for a barrage of reasons why she did not want her marriage to Thane annulled. If he kept his words calm and sounding reasonable, he could deceive her into believing it was a perfectly sensible thing to do.

It would be good practice for when he approached the King with it. Of course, he knew exactly how to get round Wymer. He would simply indicate he was after her original dowry.

When going over the documents with her dolt brother, he had been reminded of the betrothal terms. His father had wanted several acres from their estate, which bordered on Vawdrey Keep. He would just keep the terms vague, and let the King think it would still be desirable to him to have that land.

After all, Wymer knew all about his plans to build a grand estate on the old family seat. It would make perfect sense to him. How he would convince Fenella was a *little* less clear to him, but he was sure he would think of something.

"I just thought it might be nice to have some conversation and share our day," she said lamely and laid her head back against his shoulder. "It is of no import if you would rather sleep."

Share their day? Oswald lay a moment turning this over. Hadn't he already told her that his day had been an exercise in frustration? *Most of it sexual*. And she had already set that to rights for him, most satisfactorily.

Then he remembered Thane's letters. That bastard liked to tell her his every waking grievance and complaint. He frowned, stroking a thumb over her hip. "It's only that it is a little difficult," he said. "Much of my work is of a sensitive and confidential nature…" he began.

"Oh," she said, lifting her head again, but thankfully keeping her glorious body pressed against him. "But you need not tell me any of that." Her eyes shone with enthusiasm. "For instance, you could tell me how Bryce was today?"

"Bryce?" He had no idea why she would want news of his gloomy assistant. It threw him for a moment. When she continued to watch him expectantly, he cast his mind back to

299

Bryce. "He—er—seemed well," he ventured. "Or as well as he ever does." Fenella nodded in the expectation of more to come. He found he did not want to disappoint her. "I am not sure that Bryce will ever fill the large boots left by his predecessor, Edwards," he admitted.

Her cheeks flushed, and she looked pleased. She nodded at him encouragingly. "Who was Edwards?" she asked and shifted to settle so that she was draped further across him and could look directly into his eyes. He didn't mind that at all. He cast about for some information that might please her. "Edwards was my previous assistant. A very ingenious and resourceful young man with a bright future."

"A protégé of yours?" she suggested. "And did he? Move on to bigger and brighter things, I mean."

Oswald winced. "Sadly no. A woman was his undoing. He could not hold his tongue, and she was in the employ of a foreign ambassador." For the first time, Oswald felt a pang of sympathy for Edwards. At this precise moment, he could well understand why Edwards had told a pretty woman anything she wanted to know.

"Oh dear!" Fen nibbled on her bottom lip. "Was he—?" She broke off. "Actually, I don't want to know."

"He was banished," he told her. "Not executed."

"Well, that's something. And his ladylove?"

His mouth twisted at her choice of words. It seemed Fenella was a romantic. "She disappeared," he said heavily. "The ambassador was very apologetic about it, and insisted they had

300

no notion of what became of her," he said, skepticism dripping from every word.

"And yet," she pointed out, "you speak of him having large boots. As though you do not think Bryce stands up in comparison to a man who was dismissed in disgrace?"

"True," he admitted fairly. "Before his fall from grace, Edwards was my idea of the perfect assistant."

Fenella pondered this. "Perhaps your idea of the perfect assistant needs modifying?" she suggested gently. Oswald regarded her in surprise. "Bryce has many excellent qualities which you need to appreciate. Such as trustworthiness and a strong moral compass."

He made a noncommittal noise, not knowing how else to respond. He guessed that this was how Fenella imagined a good wife operated. She tried to think of constructive ways to help her spouse. It was unfortunate it made him remember Thane's letters. He almost wished he hadn't read the damn things.

"He likely knows that you contrast him with his predecessor," she mused. "And that would make him overly anxious and lacking in confidence."

"I know how he feels," he muttered darkly.

"Pardon?"

"Why don't you tell me about your day?" he suggested instead, hoping for safer ground.

Her expression cleared. "Trudy did very well on her first day. Indeed, I am persuaded she will be quite an asset to the household. She *has* been a maid before, and I can only think Meldon did not mention it because her employer was a merchant."

"Meldon is quite the snob in his own way," Oswald acknowledged mildly.

"And your wife is now a patron of the arts," she said grandly. Then ruined it by looking almost instantly uneasy. "Mr. Entner is writing a play about a donkey and its labors. He says it is a metaphor of man's struggle to raise his stock in the world."

Oswald considered this a moment. "The subject matter appealed to you?" he asked doubtfully.

"No," she admitted. "But poor Mr. Entner has five children and no regular employ."
"I see. You do realize that we will probably have to sit through a performance of this play at some point?"

Fen looked guilty. "I thought, if it is very bad, I might ask Lady Eden Montmayne to accompany me instead of you."

"To spare my feelings?" he teased. "Or because you would prefer Eden Montmayne's company?"

She smiled at his words. "I would not wish you to sit through it if it is very bad," she explained. "Whereas Lady Eden must share some of the responsibility in his selection, for she short-listed the candidates."

"That does seem fair," he conceded.

"Lady Eden is very sophisticated for one so young, is she not?" asked Fen wistfully. "She is so very graceful and knowledgeable. It is small wonder she is a lady-in-waiting to the Queen."

"That is certainly her reputation." Her reputation was also for being a managing perfectionist, exacting and extremely uptight, but he did not mention this.

"Speaking of accomplished women," said Fen. "I saw Lady Sumner also at the gathering."

"Oh?"

"I thought she seemed a little cool with me, but then she is quite reserved, is she not?"

"I've never really thought about it," he admitted. This conversation was turning out to require a lot more input than he had anticipated. He shifted uneasily, which, of course, made Fen shift about also until they were both resettled. He wondered how much longer they would need to *verbally share* their day.

"It was not just me that thought it," she hastened to assure him. "Both Hester and Lady Bess Hartleby thought her manner was decidedly off-kilter."

"Bess Hartleby?" repeated Oswald.

"Yes, for Hester introduced me. By the way, she wants you and I to dine with her and Lord Schaeffer one night this week."

Oswald frowned. Everyone was asking them to dinner these days! Couldn't a man get a moment's peace with his own wife!

"I do like Hester," said Fen fondly. "Bess seems nice, though a little…eccentric. She has sponsored a painter who will be painting her portrait with her six dogs." She hesitated. "Do you remember…?" she began, then stopped.

Oswald's ears pricked up. "Remember what?"

"'Tis nothing…"

"Just tell me," he said firmly and patted her on the rump.

"I had my portrait painted once with Bors. On the occasion of my fifteenth birthday."

"Bors was in the portrait?"

"He was just a pup."

"Where does it hang?" he asked. "At Thurrold?"

"No," she said quickly.

She was probably worried he would demand its return, he thought wryly. "At your brother's place?" he guessed.

"Oh—no."

"I should like to see it," he said, trying a different tack. Then he remembered they were still engaged when she was fifteen, and she had started, "Do you remember…" He raised his head off

304

the pillow. "It's at Vawdrey Keep," he guessed, almost kicking himself.

"So I believe," she said awkwardly. "I mean, it was sent there as a gift, so for all I know it is there still." They both fell silent.

"I don't remember seeing it, Fenella," he admitted at last.

"That's not really all that surprising," she said, letting him off the hook. "For you were not around Sitchmarsh much that year, as you were soldiering. And not long after my birthday you were taken hostage at the battle of Adarva." She stared at his shoulder a moment but did not ask the question that was plainly on her lips.

"Where I got my scar," he said in a harsher tone than he had intended.

She paled but held his gaze. "So it was at Adarva." She paused when he did not continue. "You do not wish to discuss it?"

"Not really," he said dismissively, and made a last-ditch attempt to preserve the happy mood that was fast dissipating: "Maybe we should get your portrait painted again," he suggested. "With Bors, of course."

"It's nerve-racking enough selecting a poet," said Fen with a brief smile. "Let alone a portrait painter." She was already retreating, he could feel it, even though she hadn't moved a muscle.

"So, commission Lady Bess's artist," he suggested.

"If you like," she said quietly and tucked her head back on his shoulder.

It took them both a while to go off to sleep, but neither one of them spoke another word.

23

Oswald woke the next morning from a series of disturbing dreams about locks and keys. He lay a moment, frowning over the conviction he had seen a small ornamental key like the one in his final dream. Then he noticed a lock of Fen's hair was tickling his face, and abruptly the vision was gone.

As was his habit, he was far over onto his wife's side of the bed. She was lay on her side and he was curled around her warm, fragrant form. He could tell from her relaxed state that she was still sound asleep. He resisted the urge to press closer to her delicious body, and instead rolled away.

It was a wrench, and he told himself he had no right to feel so hard done by. He had only slept beside her for six nights. Why then, did it feel like the habit of a lifetime? It would not do to become dependent on her presence. After all, he had every intention of sending her down to the country before the month was out.

That had always been his plan, he reminded himself, when something deep inside rebelled at the idea. He had no need of a wife at court, obstructing his work and making demands on his precious time. He had no need of a wife at Vawdrey Keep either, a traitorous voice whispered in his ear. After all, wasn't he going to tear it down? He splashed his face with cold water from the basin.

What was the point in sending her down there to set the old place to rights? He had a set of plans sat in his desk drawer that laid out the estate he wanted to build brick by brick. If Fenella went down there he had no doubt she would rally the dwindling servants to fix the roofs, and plant the gardens, and generally restore law and order to that ramshackle, dilapidated old shell.

But that wasn't even it, he realized with a cold finger running down his spine. No. The problem was that Vawdrey Keep was a full day and a half's ride from the winter court. And from Caer-Lyonnes, the summer palace, it would take four days of travel. He glanced at the sleeping occupant in his bed. And that was not acceptable. He stepped into his braies and chauses and tied the laces at his crotch as he realized he did not want his wife to be out of his reach.

The notion was so outlandish to him that he felt himself break out into a cold sweat. But he had promised her. He had assured her that there would be very little material change to her life. That she would still be neighbor to all her Sitchmarsh friends and her brother. And when he said it, he had meant it. But something had changed. He wasn't sure what.

How the hells was he going to get himself out of this predicament? There was a scuffling at the door, and he glanced at Fen again, before crossing the room to unlock the door. "Quiet, your mistress still sleeps," he told Meldon, taking the pitcher of hot water from him.

"We'll need to get the bath emptied," Meldon grouched.

"That can wait." Oswald closed the door on him, but he could hear sounds of stirring already in the room behind him.

"Good morning," a sleepy voice hailed him softly. Then he heard a rustle and a faint exclamation and smiled. No doubt she had just noticed her shift was missing after their bath together.

"Good morning, wife," he replied and turned to survey her all flushed and tousled behind the sheet she clasped to her breast. He had half a mind to crawl back under the covers with her. She rubbed her eyes. "And what are you about this morning?" He turned back to find a black tunic and continue dressing.

She yawned. "Eden Montmayne invited me to join a ladies' tapestry circle they hold in the lower gallery every sennight."

"It's good you're making friends at court," he said cautiously. "Perhaps you can improve on your own skills."

She made no answer to this, but he could feel her eyes on his back as he continued to dress. "You rose early," she said. "I usually wake before you."

He fastened the buttons and glanced over his shoulder. She looked a little put out. "Did you miss seeing me climb naked from the bed?" he asked. "I thought I'd spare your blushes this morning." When she made no response, he turned to quirk a brow at her.

"I missed waking in your arms," she said with a small smile, completely taking him by surprise.

He blinked. How the hells was he to respond to that? His mind whirled, but she was already finger combing her hair and swinging her legs over the side of the bed. She had slipped on his green robe and was halfway to the door before he pulled himself out of his thoughts. "Where are you going?" he asked.

She stopped. "To call for Trudy." She tipped her head and pointed to her hair. "I went to sleep on it damp and will need some help taming it this morning." It did look rather fluffy, but

Oswald was damned if he could see why their alone time should be interrupted. Something of this must have shown on his face, for she hesitated.

"See to it after I've left," he said. "You will join me for breakfast, I hope." A look of surprise passed over her face, but she acquiesced readily enough and accompanied him into the adjoining room. A messenger arrived as soon as the food was served with a coded message from Bryce that meant one of Oswald's informants had arrived with urgent news. Oswald tutted. "This is unfortunate," he said and stood up from the table.

Fen, who had been leaning on her elbows looking at him, straightened up. "Duty calls?" she asked.

"Yes," he said shortly and reached into his pocket. "I have something here for you to read." He hesitated, still holding the paper between his fingers.

"What is it?" asked Fen in surprise. She held out a hand, but he did not immediately pass it to her.

"I would appreciate it if you would read it, digest it, and then decide what you want to do with it, without discussion with me."

Fen's look of surprise turned to one of consternation. "I don't quite—"

He placed the folded paper in front of her on the table. "It is an account of how Sir Ambrose Thane and Lady Colleen Thane, née Edland, became acquainted," he said quietly. "Read it through at your leisure."

310

She breathed in sharply. "Oh." She stared down at it a moment.

"I'll leave you to peruse its contents," he said, not quite meeting her eye. Then he made his way out of their rooms and through the palace to his office. For some reason he felt uneasy, and not about the possibly disquieting news from one of his best spies. But about his wife. He somehow didn't like leaving her like that.

They had not actually quarreled the previous night, he reminded himself as he strode along the vaulted corridors. But still, things felt off-balance. And he was not sure if he had timed giving that blasted account to her of Thane's treachery very well at all. *But when would be the right time?*

Bryce was hovering outside his study looking worried. "It's McNee, my lord," he said in a quiet voice. "He's ridden the last three days solid to reach you with this news."

Oswald gave him a hard look. "Very well, Bryce," he said, his hand on the door. "Would you—"

"I've already sent for food and drink," his assistant added.

Oswald looked back at him. "On second thought, Bryce, you can join us," he said.

His assistant looked startled but gratified as he hurried after him. McNee was a man of middle age with dark hair and the beginnings of a beard. He looked exhausted, but, on Oswald's entrance, started to rise from his chair.

"Stay where you are, man. You look fit to drop. Now, tell us what has been happening so that I can update the King."

24

Half an hour later, Oswald breezed through the outer chamber and into the King's state bedroom. Wymer was sat in a claw-footed chair before the fireplace, while a manservant held up several different pairs of blue stockings for his perusal.

"I'll wear none of these," said the King testily. "Those royal blue ones itch like the very devil!" He looked around at Oswald's approach. "That you, Vawdrey? Good of you to spare me some time," he added sarcastically. "I've not seen hide nor hair of you in days!"

"Your Highness, it is vital I have some private speech with you," said Oswald without preamble.

"Oh, aye?" said Wymer, looking alarmed. "Not strangled her, have you?" When Oswald looked at him blankly, he added, "That wife of yours."

"No, sire," said Oswald firmly. "Though you put me in mind of another matter I need to speak to you about afterward."

"You can't go back on it now, my boy," Wymer said sadly, shaking his head. "Your goose is well and truly cooked!"

Oswald looked about them. "It's about the last of the Blechmarshes," he said in a murmur.

"Everyone out!" roared the King. The courtiers straggled about the room leaped to their feet. They filtered out apart from Bathilde, his old trusted nanny, who made sure the chamber door was secure. "What's that bitch done now?" he asked, then looked sheepishly across at his old nurse, who clicked her tongue. "Sorry, Nurse," he said absently. She nodded her sheep-like head and returned to folding his smalls.

"I'm afraid three men broke into Mendip Hall," Oswald said, naming the residence where the northern princess was being held under house arrest. "And attempted to wrest her from Lord Mycott's custody."

The King jumped out of his chair. "If you're going to tell me she's broken free..." he started angrily.

"Calm yourself, sire. She is not at large, but safely back under lock and key."

"*Back* under lock and key?" burst out Wymer, turning purple. "You mean she was at liberty? And I knew nothing of it?"

"She was taken only as far as the gatehouse," said Oswald soothingly. "And got no further."

Wymer paced over to the window, his back to Oswald. "Well, there's nothing else for it," he said. "She'll have to be executed now." He turned back confrontationally to Oswald. "Even you must see that, Vawdrey?" he said, his jaw jutting out. Oswald was silent. "My life and the life of my son are in peril, every moment that female still breathes..." he fumed.

"She returned to Mycott herself," said Oswald calmly.

"What?"

"It's true. She convinced the sole remaining plotter to leave her and returned to Mendip House on foot, alone."

314

"He escaped?" demanded the King.

"He was just a boy, according to Mycott. The two older males were both killed in the struggle."

Wymer's face twitched. "They will never stop plotting to topple me and place her on my throne while she's still alive!" he fumed. "Why my own council refuses to see that is beyond me!"

"You will merely make a martyr of her, if you were to behead her," said Oswald resolutely. "Wars are waged in the name of dead martyrs. And need I remind you that just across the sea there are countries who would look askance at the execution of a young, defenseless princess of royal blood…"

"The Blechmarsh bloodline is cursed!" muttered Wymer bitterly.

"She calls you cousin," pressed Oswald doggedly. "Mycott himself says she remonstrated with the attackers and told them to leave her be, as she was under your protection."

"Hah! Likely a ruse for his benefit, the old fool!"

Oswald held his tongue, for the King knew as well as he that Mycott was fiercely loyal to Wymer and nobody's fool.

"So, you expect me to just sit back and do *nothing*, while enemy forces rally under her banner!" complained the King. "This is intolerable!"

"Nay, Your Highness. I agree a change of strategy is needed," said Oswald.

"He agrees!" cried the King, throwing up his hands. "Glory be!" He wandered over to a golden goblet and took a draught of ale. "I suppose," he said, glowering fiercely, "that you've some ideas in mind for this change of strategy?" Oswald opened his mouth, but before he could even reply, the King was exclaiming in disgust. "Of course you do! You've got some nerve, Vawdrey, I'll give you that. Walking in here, bold as brass, telling your sovereign what he can and cannot do!"

Oswald watched him warily as the King paced back and forth. Finally, he swung back around and looked Oswald up and down. "I suppose I will have to be led by you," he said wearily. "Though it pains me to say it. You've not led me astray yet." He huffed and shook his head as he returned to his seat by the fire. "Let's hear it, and it better be good," he warned. "Take a seat with me."

Oswald approached the fire and drew up a chair. "This may sound rash but hear me out."

"Rash? You?" The King looked skeptical.

"I want you to bring her to court."

For a moment Wymer did not react at all. Then his face turned very red. "Bring her to court, he says. The false claimant and would-be usurper for my throne. At my court." He peered at Oswald. "Then what?"

Oswald paused. "Neutralize her threat," he said simply.

The King exhaled noisily. "And how would this be achieved?"

316

"How you take any woman's power," Oswald said wryly. "Marry her off. To a man whose loyalty you would never question."

Wymer's hand flew to his golden beard. "Marry her off, you say," he ruminated, fingering the hairs thoughtfully.

"To a man who has no ambition to rule," reiterated Oswald.

The King coughed. "To some lower-level noble, you mean?" he suggested warily.

"Maybe even to some obscure knight."

Wymer wheezed. "A princess of the blood?" he said in shocked accents.

Oswald refrained from pointing out the King was talking about chopping her head off not mere moments ago and merely nodded.

"This is a radical suggestion indeed," the King agreed. "Have you discussed it with the privy council?"

"No. I wanted your agreement before proceeding any further with it."

The King fidgeted in his seat. "I must think this over," he prevaricated.

"Of course."

"It is not a decision that can be taken rashly."

"Indeed not."

"Let me ruminate on this awhile."

"Yes, Your Majesty."

Wymer considered him out of the corner of his eye. "Too bloody clever for your own good," he murmured. "What was the other matter?" he asked, suddenly remembering.

"Other matter?"

"You wanted to ask me about," said the King, clicking his fingers. "You mentioned it previously."

Oswald took a breath. "I want to get my wife's previous marriage to Thane legally annulled."

"Do you indeed?" grunted Wymer. "Why, in the name of all that's holy?"

Oswald was silent a moment. The King's beetling brows rose. The excuses withered on his tongue. "For my own sanity," he admitted slowly.

The King leaned forward in his chair. "Indeed?" he said. "Now this I have to hear!"

25

Fen made her way down to the lower gallery in a somber mood. She had read the account of her former husband's courtship of his new wife with a strange feeling of detachment. There had been no seal on the paper, and she did not recognize the handwriting. It was not Oswald's; she knew that much.

Had he asked one of his informants to put it together? And why, she wondered dazedly, would he have done that? *I thought you might find it edifying*, he had said. But she found her curiosity these days was more taken up with her current husband than her past one.

On the page she had found a rather dry account of the acquaintanceship of Sir Ambrose with the Edland family, who resided in the county where he had been based during his time in the north.

A list of dates reeled off the numerous occasions he had dined with the Edlands at their home. It looked like once a month had escalated to once a week in the last six months. Was it really so recent an infatuation? She was surprised. Ambrose had never been terribly impulsive.

After reading it, she had sat a moment in quiet contemplation, and then approached the fireplace and thrown it in. She watched as it blackened and curled and then she had gone and dressed. That was that, she thought. And then with relief: *Well, according to Oswald, I was never really married to him anyway.* It was a liberating thought. She didn't have time to hanker after the old days in any case. She had far too much else to be going on with.

Sometimes she questioned if she was ever going to get the hang of life at court. It seemed such a bizarre existence to her. Take the Vawdreys, for instance. Oswald apparently had so much wealth that he could afford to build his own palace. Yet, to all intents and purposes, he lived in three rooms with his brother and one manservant!

The life of a courtier seemed so strange after running a comfortable household in the country. She seemed to have no particular function and could discern no obviously useful role that she fulfilled for her husband. Of course, Oswald had made it plain to her from the outset that he would be eventually sending her down to run his country estate. And once in situ there, she would know exactly what to do.

But this business of his building a palace alarmed her, and he had still said not one word to her about it. Clearly, it was known at court as not only the Schaeffers knew of it, but also Bess Hartleby. Yet still, he had not seen fit to mention it to her. Perhaps, a disagreeable voice whispered in her ear, she had no place at this palatial estate of his dreams. Her steps slowed as she considered this.

After all, what was she but a forgotten detail from his youth? She really had no place at his side, in this illustrious position he had carved out for himself. Would it be so very surprising if they were to inhabit separate residences in the future? No, she realized, it would not. In fact, she thought hollowly, it made perfect sense. Once she was pensioned off to the country, he could set about planning his dazzling future without her.

She felt a pang in the region of her chest and touched a hand to it lightly. Today she was wearing the newest gown to arrive from signor Pezzini, a rose-gold gown with wide gold embroidered bands at the cuff, neckline, and down the front of her dress. It was formfitting with long buttoned cuffs which showed glimpses of the chemise underneath and sweeping skirts.

In truth, she felt as if she were dressed for a banquet rather than a tapestry morning. At least the neckline was up to her collarbone this time and revealed no cleavage. She reached the lower gallery with no mishaps, though on entering she immediately recalled this was the venue where she had glimpsed Ambrose's celebratory wedding feast.

Strangely enough, her second thought was that Oswald's office must be located somewhere hereabouts. It was strange to think that only two weeks had passed since she had stumbled into that room in a mud-stained wool dress with her foolish request for his intercession.

Her memories were a little hazy and had the quality of a half-remembered dream. *Had there really been a secret passage behind a wall-hanging in his study?* she wondered curiously. Or had that particular memory been induced by her fever? Her thoughts were interrupted when she was hailed by Eden Montmayne, who was approaching her with another lady whose looks were so fair that Fen blinked.

"Lady Vawdrey." Eden dropped gracefully into a curtsey. "I am so glad you are joining us this morning. I would like to introduce you to my cousin, Lenora Montmayne."

"The famous beauty," said Fen without thinking. She had to force herself not to stare at that flower-like face. Her skin was like soft petals and her eyes like forget-me-nots. "I can see you are full deserving of your reputation Lady Lenora," she said, curtseying.

Lenora Montmayne gave her a gracious smile. "You are too kind," she demurred politely but clearly knew it was nothing more than her due. She yawned delicately.

"Lenora," Eden said with a slight frown. "This is Fenella, Lady Vawdrey, wife to the Earl Vawdrey."

Lenora's hand dropped and she turned another look on Fenella, her vivid blue eyes blinking. "Oh," she said. "How nice."

"Er, yes," agreed Fenella.

Eden noticed another group of ladies arriving and excused herself to hurry away and greet them. She left Lenora standing next to Fen. "Your cousin is so very industrious, is she not? Does she run very many ladies' gatherings here at court?" she asked Lenora.

Lenora's vague expression dropped for a moment and she regarded Fen with surprise, almost as if she had forgotten her existence. "Oh!" she said. Then appeared to have to make a concerted effort. "Yes. Eden is always occupied with something or another." She shrugged a shoulder and fell back to contemplating nothing, running a silk scarf through her fingers.

They stood a moment in silence, and Fen realized that her companion was not even going to attempt any small talk. "Do— do you—enjoy life at court, Lady Lenora?" she ventured.

Again, Lenora turned toward her almost blankly. "Oh yes," she said, and then relapsed once again into perfect silence. Fen stole a sideways look at her perfect profile. She really was astonishingly beautiful with her golden waving hair, pure brow, and long black lashes. Fen could feel no animosity or hostility from her. She stood beside her happily enough.

Mayhap, people usually drank her beauty in and simply did not require conversation from her? Fen pondered. Still, she could not help but feel a little awkward, just stood there while other small groups of women milled about, talking away. "Do you enjoy tapestry-making?" she asked a little desperately.

Lenora tipped her pretty head to one side as if she'd never even considered it before. "I suppose," she said with another elegant shrug.

"I once embarked on a most ambitious project in my youth," Fen blurted, unable to stand the prolonged silences any longer. "I decided I would make a wall hanging for a gift to my betrothed." She gave an awkward laugh. "The borders were stuffed to the gills with heraldic beasts signifying the joining of our houses. But even worse than that, the central figure was an idealized depiction of him as an angel, complete with wings and a halo made of roses."

Lenora's round blue eyes did not so much as blink. "How nice," she said again, and Fen gave up. Mercifully, it was only a few moments later that Eden returned and swept her away to join a party of ladies who were sat along the cushioned window seats, busily stitching together panels of heavily stitched cloth.

"If I could sit you here, next to Lady Martindale," said Eden, gesturing to a diminutive lady who sat in a window alone except for a large pile of tapestries. "She has a fine, delicate hand and is very productive."

Lady Martindale raised timid eyes to meet Fen's before flinching away and staring back at her needle and thread. "Lady Martindale, permit me to introduce Lady Vawdrey who will be joining us from today," said Eden firmly, though Fen had made no such promise to her knowledge.

"Good morning," whispered Lady Martindale, her pale face flushed as she started to struggle up from her seat. She was so short that her feet did not touch the ground.

"Please do not trouble yourself to stand," said Fen, hurriedly sitting down beside her on the green cushion which covered the stone bench. "I am happy to be able to join you."

"Today we are employed in stitching together pieces we have independently worked to make a larger whole which will eventually extend down the south gallery that runs parallel to the kitchen gardens," explained Eden.

"I see," said Fen. "A worthy endeavor."

"We like to think so," said Eden briskly. "I will leave you with Lady Martindale to demonstrate."

Lady Martindale's face turned an even redder shade as she stared down at her work, and Fen peered over her shoulder to look at the exquisitely worked wildflowers, skillfully entwined and bordering some worthy devotional text.

"How beautiful," she said. "I have produced floral depictions on tapestry before now, but they were not half as finely wrought as yours."

Lady Martindale's color ebbed and flowed at the compliment. Clearly, she was a very introverted lady, thought Fen dolefully. She was starting to understand why Hester Schaeffer avoided these sorts of things like the plague.

"My mother selected the text," said Lady Martindale, glancing almost fearfully down the room as if checking for her parent's presence. "But I was permitted to select the flowers myself."

"I see," said Fen, wondering at Lady Martindale's age. She wore a gown of burgundy and a collar of fine turquoises inlaid in gold. She was not dressed as a very young lady, as the mention of her mother seemed to suggest, although her face was youthful.

Her pale brown hair was worn up under a veil with a gold striped border. If pushed, Fen would guess her age was in her early twenties, but her manner was much younger. "Is your husband one of the King's courtiers?" she asked boldly, realizing nothing more was forthcoming.

Lady Martindale's hazel eyes widened with alarm, and she once more glanced about her as if checking she was unobserved. "No," she muttered, her eyes downcast. "That is—I live here, with Mother." Her voice died away, and she lowered her face over the cloth, her fingers flying over her tiny stitches.

Fen glanced up and found an older woman staring down coldly at her. "Good morning," she said pleasantly and noticed the guilty start Lady Martindale gave.

"Will you introduce us, Mathilde, or just sit there like a tongue-tied ninny?" the older woman asked cuttingly.

Again, Lady Martindale's face flamed. "I—your pardon," she stammered. "Mother, this is Lady Vawdrey. Lady Vawdrey, this is my mother, Lady Doverdale."

Fen rose and bobbed a curtsey before sitting straight back down again.
Lady Doverdale gave a vastly dignified curtsey. "I hope my child has managed some conversation with you, Lady Vawdrey, however scanty. I assure you, she was not raised a mute."

Fen sat up straighter seeing the miserable slump of her companion's shoulders. "Indeed," she said cheerfully. "Lady Martindale and I were just arranging to work a panel together," she lied boldly, guessing the timid Lady Martindale would hardly contradict her.

She could feel her companion's terrified gaze fixed on her face and reached across to pat one of her thin white hands reassuringly. "Her work is superb, and I would dearly love to learn her method for making leaves and petals appear alive."

Something flickered in Lady Doverdale's eyes and for a moment she looked almost pleased. "Is this true, Mathilde?" she asked her daughter sharply.

"Yes, Mother," she murmured, so faintly Fen could hardly hear her.

"Well!" exclaimed her mother. "That is the most interesting thing you have done for a twelve-month!"

Fen kept the smile plastered to her face as Lady Martindale colorlessly repeated, "Yes, Mother."

Lady Doverdale's sharp gaze ran over Fen a moment. "You are not what the Queen led me to expect," she said surprisingly.

Now it was Fen's turn to flush. "Oh dear," she said. "I'm afraid Her Majesty was most disappointed in me."

Lady Doverdale's eyebrows rose. "Hmmm," she said thoughtfully. "But perhaps that was your intent," she suggested with a grim smile. "It has been observed that you are great friends with Lady Schaeffer. Hester Schaeffer has tried to convince everyone who's met her in the last thirty years that she is a vapid creature of little distinction."

Fen bristled at such a description of her friend. "I believe Hester to be a woman of both character *and* distinction," she objected.

Lady Doverdale smiled thinly. "Perhaps you also are not so easily fooled by her façade," she suggested.

Belatedly, Fen remembered that Hester had no desire to wait on the Queen or be considered a senior member of court. "Are you one of Her Majesty's retinue, Lady Doverdale?" she asked, changing the subject.

"Mother is the Queen's Mistress of the Robes," said Lady Martindale timorously. From the surprised look on Lady Doverdale's face, Fen could see she was not used to her daughter joining in any conversation voluntarily.

"Ah, yes, of course, as you were telling me, Mathilde, when we were interrupted," said Fen glibly. She smiled up at Lady Doverdale again, whose eyes narrowed in response. "Will you permit me to help sew this border?" asked Fen, turning back to the younger woman. Lady Martindale swallowed and nodded.

"I shall leave you to it," said Lady Doverdale after a heavy pause.

"It was nice to meet you," said Fen, picking up and threading a needle. They both worked quietly side by side for a while before she felt Mathilde Martindale's hand softly touch her sleeve. She looked up.

"Did you mean it, when you said—?" started her companion.

"Every word," said Fen. "Though I do not have a loom at my disposal here."

"We could work on my loom," said her new friend shyly, before taking a breath and adding with great daring, "Fenella."

"That would be most agreeable," said Fen, feeling suddenly elated that she had found a new friend.

In all, Fen spent a very enjoyable morning sat in the long gallery, feeling the winter sun streaming through the window onto her back. Mathilde Martindale was a sweet little thing, and Fen found she was worth coaxing out of her shell as they whispered over their needlework.

It reminded Fen of simpler days when she had spent time with her female cousins from Thripstone. They had always come to stay with them at Sitchmarsh Hall for the Winter Solstice. She and her new friend made plans to meet the following afternoon in Mathilde's rooms to work on their plans for a shared tapestry, and they parted just outside the long gallery.

Impulsively, instead of returning to the rather bare and unwelcoming Vawdrey rooms, Fen's footsteps turned toward her husband's study. She had a sudden mind to see him again in his natural habitat. She knew not why precisely, save for the fact it was becoming more and more pressing to her that she gained some sort of understanding of this husband of hers.

Whenever she thought she had grasped some comprehension of his character, he slipped away from her, enigmatic as ever. Finding the room turned out easier than she'd anticipated. She recognized the stretch of corridor with its vaulted stone ceilings and suits of armor at once.

When she reached the door, however, she hesitated, suddenly uncertain of herself. What if he was engaged in some business of the realm and sent her away? Even worse, what if there were others in his office with him, important men of state? She realized she could not simply knock and go in.

Glancing around, she wondered where Bryce was usually to be found, when to her consternation, the door suddenly opened. Fen's head whipped round, and she came face-to-face with one of the many medium-sized, bearded men in nondescript suits that so often seemed to flock around her husband. She opened her mouth, but before she could so much as utter a sound, a hand clamped over it and her wrist was seized in a punishing grip, and she was dragged inside.

"Wheeler!" exclaimed a shocked voice, which Fen realized was Bryce.

"This one was listening outside," the man behind her said in clipped tones.

Fen started to argue that she had not heard a thing, but his hand over her mouth prevented it. She was still facing the door and could not see the inhabitants of the room. Fen heard the sound of a chair dragged being back from behind a desk.

"Let her go at once," said her husband's voice, which seemed to be growing nearer. Then she found herself seized in another pair of arms. Familiar ones this time. Then a dryly spoken: "This happens to be my wife."

Profuse apologies spilled from Wheeler's lips, which Oswald seemed to pay little heed to. He turned her round, his hands resting on her upper arms as his eyes scanned hers. "Though I confess I do not know what she is doing here." There was a question in his voice.

"I came to see you," Fen told him indignantly. She felt rather foolish after being so manhandled and tried to brush down her crumpled skirts and straighten her bodice. She put a hand to her hair and hoped her veil wasn't askew. She tried to avoid Oswald's gaze, but thought he probably saw her discomfiture all too clearly. Just when she started to think she was fitting in, she made an idiot of herself again!

He reached out and caught her hand, drawing back her sleeve to examine her wrist. "If you've marked her, I won't be pleased," he said calmly. Again, Wheeler apologized, and Oswald ignored him. "You're dismissed," he said without looking at him, and turned her wrist over. "I will see you next week."

"Yes, my lord." The door shut behind him.

"It's fine," Fen assured him.

Bryce hurried over and peered at Fen's wrist. "I shall fetch a poultice of chicory and nutmeg," he said, tutting. "For 'twill counter any swelling."

"It's not swollen at all," Fen protested, trying to draw her hand back, but her husband held it fast. "Indeed, you are making quite a fuss about nothing." She gave an uneasy laugh.

"Thank you, Bryce," said Oswald with a nod, and his assistant hurried away to fetch the poultice. Oswald drew her hand through his arm and led her toward his desk. "You wanted to speak to me?" he said, drawing out a chair and depositing her into it as thoughtfully as if she were an old, infirm woman. To Fen's disquiet, instead of rounding the desk to take his seat, he propped himself against the desk, so he was right in front of her and looking down at her.

Fen cleared her throat. "'Twas nothing, I just thought I would see if I could remember where your room was…" She trailed off wretchedly. When he said nothing, she peered up at him and found him steadfastly regarding her. "You took off so abruptly this morning," she blurted. "I suppose I wanted to see if you were well, and naught was amiss."

He seemed to consider this a moment. "There's always some crisis," he admitted with a shrug, "that needs my urgent attention."

"Of course," she said, starting to rise out of the chair. "I'll just make myself scarce so you can—"

"No," he interrupted her with a frown. "That's not what I meant. I was trying to explain."

331

Fen sat back down in her seat. "I shouldn't have interrupted you," she said, gazing around the room. Anywhere rather than at her perceptive husband's gaze. Her eyes fixed on the wall hanging on the far wall and she blinked, remembering a secret passageway.

"I did wonder if you'd remember that," said Oswald. His voice sounded rueful.

Fen jumped. Were her thoughts really so transparent? "I—um, well I was half asleep…"

"You were dead on your feet," he corrected her. "I shouldn't have left you."

The words hung in the room, and Fen told herself not to attach more import to them than he'd intended. He meant that night she'd cried herself to sleep after seeing Ambrose remarried. Not the night she'd cried herself to sleep all those years ago when her father had told her their betrothal was at an end. "So there really is a hidden walkway behind it," she said aloud. Even to her own ears, her voice sounded husky with emotion. She needed to pull herself together.

"Would you like to see?" he asked, startling her.

Her eyes flew to his; he looked deadly serious. "Really?" He nodded. "Does it run all the way through the castle?" she asked, rising from her chair.

"The older parts of it."

She felt rather than heard him follow her across the room. He really was very light on his feet. She stopped by the curtain, tracing the faded depiction of the twisted vines. "This is rather dreary," Fen observed. "Maybe Lady Martindale and I should weave you a new one?" she suggested.

"But the last thing I want to do is draw attention to it," he pointed out to her with a twisted smile.

"Maybe a moral exhortation against curiosity?" she joked as she lifted the curtain. The door did not seem to have a handle.

"That could work," he conceded lazily and reached up behind her to press the top corner. The door sprang open.

Fen peeped around it but all she could see was a shadowy passageway. She shivered at the blast of cold air which hit her.

"Shall we go out?" he suggested in a low voice.

Fen craned her head to look over her shoulder at him. "Where to?" she whispered, wide-eyed.

"Aphrany."

"Can we?"

"Why not?"

"But what about—I mean, do you have you the time?"

"I can spare an hour or so for my wife, I hope," he muttered, his hand slipping around her waist and urging her through the door.

"I don't have my outdoor things," she gasped as he pressed her forward into the cold stone passage.

"All will be provided," he said enigmatically as they started down an uneven flagstone floor. "Mind your step."

"What will Bryce think when he returns?" Fen could hear the excitement in her voice.

"I'm always giving him the slip," said Oswald. His voice was very close behind her. It wasn't wide enough to walk side by side. "He won't be too perturbed."

"It doesn't get any narrower, does it?" Fen asked anxiously as she groped along the walls.

"Not the way we're going. Turn left. Then up three steps."

Fen concentrated on feeling the roughly cut stone steps beneath her slippered feet. They were very steep and wound around a column. She wished she'd worn her ankle boots now.

"You're doing well," he told her, and she felt his hand at her middle back, steadying her. "Now head straight ahead."

"Is this a bridge?" Fen asked in alarm. She could feel the floor sway.

"Hold the rope at the side."

Fen made a grab for it and felt Oswald step up behind her. "I'm not sure I like this," she admitted uncertainly.

"I'm right here." She breathed out. He was very calm and confident in the dark shadows. She felt his hand at her waist. "Now walk forward until I say to halt." Fen squeezed her eyes shut and did as she was told. In truth, she could scarcely see any less than when they were open.

"Halt," he said, squeezing her side. "Now feel ahead for a gap in the wall."

Fen reached out her hands and swept the walls until she felt the edges. "Found it."

"Now climb through."

He lifted her from behind as Fen clambered through the hole and breathed out in relief when she found herself on wooden floorboards again. He swiftly followed her through the gap. "We're over the worst bit, the rest ahead is plain sailing," he assured her. "I need you to wait here for a moment while I fetch us cloaks."

"Cloaks? From where?" She tried to keep the anxiety out of her voice.

"Just down to the left, I won't be long."

He touched his hand to her cheek and then he was gone. Fen shivered and rubbed her upper arms. She heard a scuttle that she was very much afraid was a rat. Only by the greatest exertion did she manage not to yelp. She busied herself by feeling for any rents in her dress, for she was sure she'd heard a rip as her gown had snagged on something. Before she'd discovered any, she thought she heard a footfall and froze. It seemed to come from the opposite direction in which Oswald had disappeared.

She shrank back against the wall and held her breath. *There!* She definitely heard another step being taken and then another, but by someone very fleet and light of foot. It was retreating

335

away from her. She craned her ears and fancied she heard a door faintly swing shut.

So intent on it was she that when she heard Oswald's murmured "Fenella" behind her, she jumped in surprise. He shook out a cloak and then passed it around her shoulders. It was a thick woolen one, and although she could not see the color, she immediately felt its benefit. "Give me your hand." She reached out and felt her fingers enveloped by his. "Stay close. I will lead the way now."

"Very well," she whispered back.

He tugged on her hand and she fell in step behind him. Their path seemed to follow a steep incline though there were no steps. After a while the wooden floorboards gave way to loosely packed earth, and Fen could feel small pebbles beneath the thin soles of her shoes. "Stay," he cautioned as he came to a halt.

Fen could see light streaming in from behind the outline of a door. Oswald paused to listen, and after a moment or two, he cautiously opened the door, and they emerged into a small walled garden. He secured the door behind them and looked swiftly about. "All clear." He kept his voice low and drew her hood up so it covered her head. "If we follow the path outside this garden it will take us into the courtyard of the palace kitchens." Fen nodded.

"If any of the guards challenge us, let me do the talking."

Fen gulped. "Yes."

"Don't look so worried," he said, wiping a smudge from her nose with his cuff. "I have the King's permission to roam wherever I choose." She nodded again and he reached for her hand.

The kitchen courtyard was bustling with servants and tradesmen making drop-offs. They slipped through there without raising any comment and from thence down a busy walkway.

"This leads to the palace west gate," Oswald informed her. He was wearing a long black cloak over his fine suit of clothes. Fen glanced down and found hers was a dark green wool.

Fen eyed the palace guards nervously as they approached the tall stone arch, but there were plenty of people walking before and after them, though Fen did not recognize a one. They seemed to be servants rather than nobles. The two of them passed through the gate without comment.

Fen breathed a sigh of relief. "That was somehow quite nerve-racking, husband," she admitted when they had left the soldiers behind them. She had to stop herself from glancing back at them over her shoulder. "When Gil and I arrived, we did not do so from this gate."

"No," Oswald agreed easily. "Doubtless you came in by the north entrance."

They were crossing a wide bridge, now flanked with azure flags bearing the King's rampant lion. It was a crisp, cold December day, and Fen could see her breath puffing out before her as she gazed at the soaring spires, arches, and lurching roofs before them. She squeezed Oswald's hand and he looked down at her. "Cold?" he asked.

She shook her head. "Excited," she corrected him with a smile. "What would you have told the guards if they had stopped us?" she asked curiously.

He seemed to consider his answer a moment. "That I had delivered a missive to someone." He shrugged.

"To Lord Vawdrey?" she asked.

He pulled a face. "Nay, not to me. I have a certain…reputation. Someone whose name bore less sinister association."

Fen swallowed down the words that sprang to her lips. She didn't want to spoil their impromptu trip by asking him unwelcome questions about his role as the King's spymaster. "And what would my role have been?" she asked instead. "Your sister?"

He gave her a sideways look. "They would not have believed that."

"Why not?" He held up their clasped hands and quirked an eyebrow at her. "You could have let go of my hand," she pointed out.

"No, I could not," he said firmly.

Fen blushed, though really, she had no notion why. She bit her lip and stared instead at the tall looming buildings with their timbered fronts and black painted beams. They seemed to grow wider as they reached toward the sky, the jutting upper stories, propped up by pillars and wooden struts. "So, not your sister," she said aloud, gazing up at the overhanging windows. "What then?"

"My doxy probably," said Oswald.

Fen whipped around to look at his straight face. "Doxy?" she repeated, aghast.

His face was entirely serious, but she noticed his eyes were laughing down at her. "My sweetheart then?" he suggested. For some reason, Fen had to fight to catch her breath. It was cold after all. "We're heading toward the main square," Oswald said, taking pity on her tongue-tied state. "It's market day, so there should be plenty to see."

"Oh—I don't have my purse," lamented Fen, finding her tongue once again. "And I wanted to buy a deck of cards for Gil as a Solstice gift."

"I have plenty of coin," said Oswald, sounding unconcerned, "if there is aught you wish to buy."

"But I—" Her words were cut off as they turned a corner and came out into a wide and bustling marketplace in full swing. Fen drew in a breath at the array of stalls, traders, and street hawkers.

"It's just as well you don't have your purse," said Oswald dryly as he tugged her down the first row of stalls. "Or you'd probably soon lose it. Stay close to me. You need to have your wits about you here."

"I often went to market day at Ashby," Fen protested. Even as she said it, she knew the comparison was laughable. Ashby was a small market town, not one-tenth the size of this vast city. Her husband, however, was far too polite to point this out. He

339

simply steered her through the thronging crowds, drawing her sharply to one side when a herd of cattle were driven through or pushing her to the front where he thought she might find a stall that she wanted.

She soon found a deck of Livelihood cards to her liking. They were rather nicer than Sir James Attley's pack, with colored figures depicted on them rather than the black-and-white wood-cut images. "I wonder, should I get a pack for Roland also?" She turned back to ask Oswald, who was stood behind her. "Do your family exchange gifts at Solstice Eve?"

Oswald held up two fingers to the stall owner, who handed over two packets tied up with string. "Not for many a year," he admitted, handing over payment. He tucked the cards into a pocket inside his cloak and took her hand again.

"Will your brother Mason come to court for the Solstice feast?" she asked, raising her voice against the crowd. "Or will you go to Cadwallader?" She was not sure he had even heard her above all the hubbub. He tugged her forward toward another stall which had poles all round displaying colored ribbon and scarves. In spite of the fact she owned so many, Fen found herself exclaiming over a veil decorated with pretty birds all along the edges. "Oh, these are pretty!"

"Embroidered by my own daughter's hand," said the old woman sat perched on an upturned barrel. "Two-penny each."

Fen could have sworn she heard her say two for a penny to the woman before her, but before she had even opened her mouth, Oswald had handed over a coin. "Pick four," he said. "Perhaps you could give one to Linnet." At her surprised look he added, "For Solstice."

340

So, he had heard her after all! She picked one with bluebirds for her sister-in-law who she'd never met, and then one with red-breasted robins for Mathilde Martindale, green finches for Eden Montmayne, and bright kingfishers for Hester Schaeffer. She just hoped they wouldn't think them too provincial, as they were all such fine court ladies.

"Not picking one fer yourself?" asked the old woman shrewdly.

"How did you know I wasn't choosing one for myself?" asked Fen, startled.

The old woman cackled. "Cos you, my fine lady, would be goldcrests." She ran a scarf through her fingers before holding it up for her perusal.

Oswald reached across, presumably with another two pennies, for the scarf was thrust into Fen's hands and she turned around and found herself herded back into the throng. "You do not haggle!" she said loudly. "With the stallholders. You're supposed to negotiate."

"Over a few pennies?" Oswald shrugged, unconcerned. "Who else do you need to buy for? Solstice gifts," he prompted.

"For my—for Orla," she corrected herself, referring to her ex-sister-in-law. "And I would like to get something for Trudy," she said, naming her maid. "Oh, and Meldon, of course," she added. "How about you?"

He thought this over. "I don't generally," he admitted. "Mason's children?"

"Oh yes. You said your godson was a babe in arms. How old are your nieces?"

"Three years. Lily and Margaret are twins."

"Something for them to play with then?" she suggested.

Behind her an altercation had broken out, but she had only half turned her head at the cry of "Stop thief!" when Oswald drew her close to him. "Keep walking straight ahead," he said calmly. "We'll head toward that inn with the sign of the ram's head."

Fenella craned her head above the crowd to make out the inn sign daubed in muted colors. Was it a ram? Her husband's eye was far keener than hers, she realized. Behind them the sounds of jostling and fighting were unmistakable, but Oswald had placed himself firmly between her and the hubbub, so she relaxed and pocketed the scarf. Out of the corner of one eye she noticed a young man sat at a stall with brightly clothed puppets. He sat whistling and sewing a miniature peacock-blue jacket.

"Oh, look!" she said, catching Oswald's sleeve. "How about a puppet for the girls?" He followed her as she forged toward the toy-maker's stall. "Oh, these are pretty," exclaimed Fenella, looking at the brightly painted ceramic faces. "And there are knights!" she said, pointing to the back of the stall where they stood in a row. "Oh, and little wooden horses' heads on sticks!" The young man passed her a knight wordlessly to examine. "Thank you," said Fen, turning it over carefully. "You are very clever." The small knight wore a yellow tunic and brown leather boots. He had a cheerful open countenance and rosy, red-painted cheeks.

"Looks rather like Roland," said Oswald disparagingly. "Same vacuous stare."

Fen ignored this. She was starting to realize that insulting each other was the Vawdrey brothers' way. "I have an idea," she said, turning to him impulsively. "Why don't we buy three? One for each of the children, and they can be named for you, Mason, and Roland!"

Oswald looked rather pained. "Do you have one in a black tunic?" he asked, turning to the young man, who simply shrugged and gestured to the ones on the stall. They only seemed to deal in colorful wares.

"You would be the scarlet tunic," said Fen.

"Scarlet?"

"Like the robe you wear," she explained.

Oswald looked taken aback. "I only wear that in the privacy of my own chambers," he said sternly.

"I think of you as scarlet," said Fen obstinately. "Now, should we get the blue or the green one for Mason?" asked Fen, looking at the row of knights.

Oswald sighed. "You choose," he said, reaching for his purse. The young man hopped up from his stool and reached for the dolls Fen pointed to. The entire transaction took place without him uttering one single word. When he took the payment from Oswald he swiftly bowed, then returned to his sewing.

343

"Do you suppose…?" Fen whispered, but her words were swept up in the crowd, as she was swept forward, clutching the dolls to her breast.

They stopped three stalls down, and Oswald bought a simple cloth bag with a long handle. He took the dolls from her one by one and stuffed them into the bag. Then he extracted the scarves and the decks of cards from his own cloak and added them as well.

"Wait," said Fen, reaching for the scarf she had stowed away, but her inner pocket was empty. "Oh no…"

Oswald held up a hand. "Fear not," he said. "They're all here." He held up the bag before slipping the strap over his neck and shoulder.

"But the last scarf you bought was given into my keeping," explained Fen. "The goldcrest one."

"Yes," Oswald agreed simply. "But when that was extracted from you, half a furlong ago, I took it back."

"Someone took it from me?" gasped Fen, blinking. "But I never…"

Oswald pinched her chin. "I know."

She clutched the front of his doublet and leaned against him a moment. "Do I look like the veriest bumpkin?" she asked bashfully.

"No," he said and dropped a brief kiss against her mouth, surprising her. "And anyway, it's my place to look out for you."

His hands rested at her waist. She could feel them even through her cloak. "And my pleasure," he added softly.

She gazed up at him. Her heart throbbed in her chest, almost alarmingly.

"What is it?" he asked.

"Nothing," she said, ducking her head. "Only, 'tis rather cold, now I come to notice it."

He accepted this without comment, merely taking her hand and interlacing his fingers with hers.

They negotiated their way through the rest of the market without further incident. Fen picked up small rosewood boxes for Orla and Trudy that were cunningly carved with great skill. She would put sweet sachets of dried herbs and flowers inside for them to store with their linens.

She fleetingly thought of buying a gift for Lady Sumner but deduced that lady would not appreciate so humble a gift. On passing a stall covered in woolen hoods, Fen turned to Oswald and reminded him to buy something for his assistant.

He eyed the hoods doubtfully. "Perhaps a book?" he said, picking up a tricolored hood in blue, yellow, and red. "These look rather frivolous. Poor Bryce would not appreciate a long tail or the leaf design edging."

"But Bryce always dresses like a monk," Fen reminded him. "I think a warm, fur-lined hood in black or brown would be most acceptable to him. Or perhaps green," she mused. "Though, certainly no tail."

345

The stallholder, having heard her, popped up with a sage-green hood lined with brown fur and matching buttons to fasten, which he presented to her with a flourish. "Oh, now can you not see him wearing this?" asked Fen, holding it aloft. "This looks the very thing."

Oswald rolled his eyes, though he reached for his purse obligingly. "You shall be the one who gives it to him," he said, handing over the payment.

"Happily," replied Fen, folding the hood. He held the bag out to her, and Fen was just stuffing it in with their purchases when she noticed her husband go very still. She straightened up in alarm to find a small, rather wrinkled man standing blinking at them from a few feet away.

He had two dead rabbits tucked under one arm which were presumably for his supper. Fen glanced at Oswald and then back to the older man expectantly. He cleared his throat. "Mr. Roberts," said the man, addressing her husband with some reluctance.

"Carleton," replied her husband with a nod. "It seems you *do* recognize me outside your establishment after all."

The old man's face creased in what Fen assumed was a smile. "So it would seem, sir. So it would seem." He looked curiously toward Fen but made no comment.

Oswald paused a moment before continuing: "Allow me to introduce my wife. Mrs. Roberts, meet Mr. Carleton."

Fen tried not to react to her new name, but instead extended her hand to shake.

Mr. Carleton also struggled not to look surprised and shook her hand. "Mrs. Roberts," he said, giving her a hard look.

"It's very nice to meet you, Mr. Carleton."

The two men bowed again, and Mr. Carleton disappeared into the throng. Oswald offered his arm, and she took it.

"So…not your doxy then," she joked, glancing up at his profile. He still looked a little stern, and for a moment she thought he was angry.

His expression relaxed almost immediately, and he raised her hand to kiss her knuckles. "Your hand is cold." He frowned.

"Nothing to signify," she hurried to assure him, but he was already glancing around and then tugging her in the direction of the tavern. Fen, who had been enjoying herself, was in no hurry to leave the hustle and bustle of the marketplace. "Which house do the Robertses live in?" she asked, gazing about her.

Oswald cast her a curious look, before falling in with her playful mood. "The biggest one, of course."

Fen laughed appreciatively. "That one?" She pointed to a large timbered monstrosity of a town house, at least four floors high and boasting an impressive courtyard and adjoining stables.

"Naturally." He inclined his head. "Only the very best for the Robertses."

"Mr. Roberts must be a very successful merchant, I think," mused Fen aloud. "Perhaps even a town alderman or a councilor?"

"I like to perform my civic duty," he murmured with a mock modesty that had Fen giggling again.

They had reached the inn by now, and Oswald opened the door for her. Fen gazed around at the low ceiling and dark interior. There were great swathes of ivy pinned and draped across the ceiling beams in honor of the Midwinter festival and tied with bright red ribbons.

A fire burned merrily in the hearth, casting an inviting flicker over the far wall. Oswald headed straight for it, towing her in his wake. He had no sooner helped her out of her cloak and seen her settled on a corner wooden bench than a server approached. Oswald ordered a wassail bowl to share a hot spiced punch and seated himself at the bench opposite her. "Warm enough?" he asked, reaching for her hand.

Fen nodded, feeling the warmth from the blazing fire at her back. "'Tis very cozy in here," she assured him. "And it does one's heart good to see the decorations up for the Midwinter festivities. Back home—" She stopped herself. "Back in Sitchmarsh," she corrected herself quickly, "preparations will be well underway for the Solstice celebrations."

Oswald frowned. "I daresay the palace will catch up in a month or so," he said. "The Yule log will be brought in and the greenery to decorate the halls."

"Yes?" said Fen hopefully. "That will be nice, but I cannot help but think…"

"Think what?" he asked.

Fen shrugged. "Why, that when every other evening is a fancy banquet, the feast of Midwinter will not have the significance that it does for everyday common folk."

Oswald's head turned before Fen had even noticed that a server was approaching them with a steaming pedestal bowl of mulled punch on a salver. The bowl was a lovers' cup made for sharing, with a tall lid, carved in the shape of an acorn. Toasted bread was laid on the platter with which to mop up the last of the punch.

It was set down before them, and Oswald handed over payment and removed the lid before sliding it toward her. "You miss the country," he said. "It is not to be wondered at, since this is the first significant time you have spent away from it."

Fen nodded as she lifted the cup and took a sip of the fragrant hot liquid. It tasted of apples, cinnamon, and nutmeg with a kick of something else. She lowered the bowl and slid it toward Oswald, before commenting. "It is very good. Very warming." She watched him lift it to his own lips and take a drink.

"It's not just that this is a large town," she said, mustering her courage. "I miss—making plans, the responsibility and challenges of running a household." She hesitated. "At the palace, you are a part of the royal household. You have no say in how the halls will be decorated, or what food will be served at your table." She looked across at her husband to see if she had offended, but Oswald's gaze on her was hooded and she could make nothing from his expression. "For a bachelor, it must be highly convenient," she acknowledged.

349

"It is a big change for you," he said simply, lowering the bowl and then pushing it across the surface toward her. "Drink some more."

She waited for him to mention the fact she would be sent to Vawdrey Keep soon enough, but he made no mention of it. Feeling confused, Fen lifted the bowl and took a hearty swig. It packed a punch and Fenella took courage from its potency. "Of course, when I am sent to Vawdrey Keep, I will soon have the running of a household again," she ventured and looked through her lashes at him as she moved the bowl back across in his direction.

His mouth twisted, and for a moment, she thought he would say something, but words were not forthcoming. Instead he took a deep draught and plunked the bowl back on the table. He cleared his throat. "No doubt the Robertses would celebrate the festivities in the old style, despite their town existence." He quirked an eyebrow at her, and Fenella could not help but laugh.

"Of course," she agreed. "Their town house would be wreathed in ivy and mistletoe across every lintel and mantel, and all tied up with ribbons."

"What else?" he asked, pushing the bowl back toward her.

Fen picked up a piece of toasted bread and dipped it into the foamy drink left at the bottom of the bowl. "I think…they would have a piece of the yule log in every hearth," she listed. "Even in the servants' quarters. And on the three nights from Midwinter's Eve, ghost stories would be told to the entire household."

She took a bite of the toast before continuing: "Fruit and candle arrangements would glisten on every table surface." She chewed her bread in heavy thought. "Honey-plum puddings would boil in the kitchen, and any passing wassailers would be bade to come in, drink from the cup, and give their blessings upon the house." She finished a little self-consciously. "How does that sound to Mr. Roberts?" she asked.

"As though Mrs. Roberts indeed likes to celebrate the Midwinter in the grand old style," he said gravely.

"Yes," she agreed, and even to her own ears she sounded a little forlorn. Of course, she was being quite ridiculously over-the-top. Ambrose would never have allowed such extravagances at Thurrold Manor. "I expect Mr. Roberts would have to rein in his wife on the expenses," she joked. "And remind her that his coffers are not bottomless!"

Oswald reached for some of the bread and wiped it around the inside of the bowl before taking a bite. "I think Mr. Roberts is very keen to do whatever keeps Mrs. Roberts happy and by his side," he said quietly.

Fen's eyes widened at his serious tone. "Oh—but I am sure—that is, Mr. Roberts can have no worries about that," she stammered awkwardly. "Forgive me, I was speaking without thought and—"

"You said naught amiss," he said calmly, but Fenella wasn't convinced.

"Indeed, my lord—" she started again.

351

He reached across to put his hand over hers. "I assure you, Fenella." She bit the inside of her mouth and regarded him anxiously. "Tell me about your morning," he said, nudging the platter of bread toward her.

Fenella picked up another piece of toasted bread. "Well, I spent my morning with Mathilde Martindale," she said distractedly. She glanced about to make sure no one was close enough to hear her speak of courtiers. "She is a sweet and pleasant young woman. If a little shy."

"Most people would say extremely shy," said Oswald. "I have scarcely heard her speak above two words in the last three years."

Fen pulled a face. "I think she is a little cowed by the presence of her mother," she admitted, before getting caught up in her subject. "Tell me, where is her husband, Lord Martindale? Is it not extremely unusual that she lives at court when he does not?"

"It is certainly unconventional," Oswald agreed with a small smile. "But you see, timid Lady Martindale is already on her third marriage."

Fenella almost dropped her piece of bread. "What?"

"Yes." He nodded. "And yet, she has never had a single night away from her dear mother's side."

Fen blinked. "H-how does that work?"

Oswald settled his elbows onto the table and steepled his fingers. "Her first two husbands were in their dotage. Her father, Lord Doverdale, was extremely powerful at court. They married her in order to ally themselves with her father. Both of them had children older than the bride, offspring they were feuding with, and did not wish to inherit their fortunes."

Fen drew back aghast. "Their marriages disinherited their own children?"

He nodded. "The two sons of the first marriage contested the will and had some family property revert to them in the end, but the legal wrangle took over five years and was very bitter."

"Oh, poor Mathilde," breathed Fenella. "She would not have liked that at all! And what of the second marriage?"

"It is believed that some private settlement was made on the family to keep it from coming before the King and causing a scandal."

Fen shuddered. "How awful." Oswald merely smiled. "And her third husband?"

"Lord Martindale was somewhat different. They were married by proxy. The rumor is," he said, lowering his voice dramatically, "that they have not even met." Fen gasped. *No wonder poor Mathilde never spoke of her husband!* "Her mother arranged it, the indomitable Lady Doverdale."

"I have met Lady Doverdale," said Fen, wincing. "It is small wonder that her daughter lacks a voice."

"She has a formidable reputation," agreed Oswald.

"And is one of the Queen's foremost ladies-in-waiting, I hear."

"The Queen perhaps considers her an antidote to the pretty faces forced on her by the King," he suggested.

Fen considered this. "That would make sense. After all, I met the most famous court beauty this morning and she had precious little to say for herself. I imagine being surrounded by twelve such ladies would be something of a trial." She caught herself quickly. "Not that I mean to suggest that Lady Lenora is not a very excellent young woman…"

"I know exactly what you mean," said Oswald. "There is no vice to her character, but I sometimes worry that Roland will end up wed to her." He pulled a face. "Imagine being sat opposite her on every feast day."

"She would be very beautiful to look at," pointed out Fen.

"I was thinking more of the conversation flow," he admitted. "Painful."

Fen gave a choked laugh. "It is strange, is it not? For her cousin Eden has so very much character and yet Lenora…"

"Has none," finished Oswald dampeningly.

"Is Roland very enamored of her?" she asked with interest.

Oswald gave her a pained look. "Roland?" he asked ironically. "Enamored of a lady?" He shook his head. "I fear my brother has a very shallow yardstick for measuring the fairer sex."

"Their beauty?" hazarded Fen.

"Exactly."

"Well, it would be better he offered for Lenora than Helen Cecil, if palace gossip is to be relied on," she pondered aloud. "If it is beauty alone that he prizes in women."

Oswald looked surprised. "You have heard that rumor then?"

"Oh yes. Hester Schaeffer told me Helen Cecil is likely to become the King's paramour."

"If she isn't already." Oswald shrugged.

"Poor Queen Armenal," said Fen sadly. Oswald pursed his lips but said nothing, and Fen wondered if he thought her naïve or provincial to expect fidelity from the King. She ran her fingernail over the bumpy grain on the wooden table and tried to think of a less contentious subject of conversation.

She was flushed and happy and didn't want the cozy intimacy of the meal to end. Spending time alone with Oswald Vawdrey was a heady experience. She felt quite giddy. Or could that be the mulled cider? She looked up to find him watching her. "Thank you for making the time today, she said, tucking her hair behind her ear and feeling suddenly shy again. "I know how much the King relies on you."

Actually, she didn't, but that was what she'd heard. Since her, frankly disastrous, meetings with both monarchs she had successfully managed to avoid meeting either of them in the days that had followed. She hoped devoutly that she could continue that way.

Oswald frowned slightly at her words. "You're my wife, and as such I will always have time for you." It seemed to Fenella that he looked a little surprised by the words coming out of his own mouth. She smiled at him warmly, and he reached across to take her hand. "Come, we had better make our way back."

At the reluctance in his voice, Fen felt a warmth spread right through her chest. It must be the punch, she told herself sternly as she rose from the bench and took his arm.

26

It was not until a full two weeks later that Fenella heard any more of a proposed annulment of her marriage to Ambrose Thane. She had been at court for over a month now and was walking back toward the palace after a good long walk through the castle grounds with Hester Schaeffer. They had been to visit Fen's horse, who was looking very content in the stables, which had put Fen's mind at rest.

She had fed her an apple and checked with the groomsmen about her exercise before she and Hester had continued on their way. They walked a good way for it was a cold, crisp morning with a bright blue sky, and it was pleasant to be out of doors. Fen wore her new thick scarlet knitted gloves with their gold rosettes and a rather splendid new cloak of celestial blue wool lined with a matching silk.

They meandered a good deal on their walk, as neither was in a hurry to reach a destination, and Bors was an old dog who liked a sedate pace. Hester's sleeker hound, Juniper, danced around her mistress in circles and covered at least three times as much as the rest of them. They were finally on their way back to the castle when Bors, plodding at her heels for most of the walk, gave a low woof of surprise and then plunged ahead of them.

"Bors!" called Fen, but then she saw him dart into one of the arbors where she could just make out the form of a person in the shadows. Bors pranced about him excitedly.

"Who's that?" asked Hester.

"I haven't the faintest idea," admitted Fen, screwing up her eyes. He was far too short to be Oswald or Roland. "But whoever it is, Bors knows them."

"You there," hailed Hester. "Show yourself, fellow!"

There was a rustle and a cough and then, after a moment's hesitation, Sir Ambrose Thane stepped forward onto the path. Hester's dog bared her teeth and snarled and had to be called off.

"Ambrose!" exclaimed Fen, caught by surprise. He was wearing a striped doublet and yellow hose with very long pointed shoes. He looked most peculiar to her eye, but perhaps 'twas the fashion?

"Indeed?" said Hester curiously. She peered at Ambrose with interest. "Presumably there is a reason he is lurking in the King's shrubbery." She was holding on to Juniper by her collar now.

"I can't think what," replied Fen.

Ambrose drew himself up indignantly. "I was hoping I might be permitted a word with you, Fenella," he said, shooing away Bors, who was still looking to him for a pat on the head.

"Have you greeted Bors yet?" she asked him frostily. "Or is ignoring old acquaintances your new practice?"

Ambrose looked startled by her words. He glanced down at the dog as if he had not even really seen him there. "Is that really Bors?" he asked absently. "I would not have recognized him."

"Come here, Bors," Fen called, patting her leg. Her dog returned to her side, and she stroked his head. "Dear old bear," she murmured. "You have new friends now."

Ambrose took a step toward her, and Juniper set up a cacophony of barks that made her mistress exclaim. "Dear me," said Hester, "Sir Ambrose has a most unfortunate manner with dogs." She unfastened a length of cord from her waist and slipped it through her dog's collar. "I believe I will walk Juniper a little further up the path. But I will remain in view," she assured Fen, straightening up. "At all times." She gave a brief nod to Ambrose Thane and then swept along the path before them.

"I don't know what she meant by that," said Ambrose fretfully. "I hardly think you need a chaperone where I am concerned!"

Fen ignored him, and his gesture toward the arbor he had emerged from. She had no intention of sitting closeted with him in a small space. "I believe I will walk behind Lady Schaeffer," she said. "Whether you choose to walk beside me is your affair, Sir Ambrose."

He looked taken aback by her formality and stood stock-still as she swept past him. After a moment, she heard his footsteps hurry after her when he realized she was not going to halt and wait for him. "Wait," he puffed. "Upon my word, your attitude surprises me, madam!" he complained as he drew level with her and matched her steps.

"*My* attitude?" echoed Fen. "I am not the one who dissolves bonds and rescinds vows on a whim, without even having the courtesy to inform those directly involved." She continued steadily. "If it were not for Orla, I would still be sat at Thurrold

359

awaiting your return." She flickered her gaze to his face. "How did you intend to tell me that I was supplanted, Ambrose? Would you have ridden up to the door with your new bride?"

He huffed. "I am surprised at you, Fenella. You are being far too dramatic."

"And you, sir, are being far too familiar," Fenella told him loftily. She gazed into the distance. "You should address me correctly as Lady Vawdrey."

He spluttered at this. "Outrageous, madam! You have the nerve to pretend that you are the injured party in this affair!"

Fenella noticed that despite his ire, he kept his voice hoarse in an effort that Lady Schaeffer should not hear him. Almost she rolled her eyes. Trust it to Ambrose to twist things around so that he was the one hard done by. She had always known, of course, that he was self-pitying at times. But this was a new low. "You petitioned for divorce without even having the decency to tell me," she pointed out.

His step faltered at this accusation. She had so very rarely ever gone on the attack with him during their marriage that this must be an unwelcome and unexpected turn of events for him indeed. She had always been a gentle and conciliating helpmeet during their marriage.

"Given time, I would of course have approached the matter sensitively," he claimed, tugging on his cloak as if it had become a little tight around his throat. "There was no need whatsoever for you to come to court in such an odiously forward manner! I would probably have written to Gilbert to break the news to you," he hazarded uncertainly.

"Gil? You think my brother would have broken the news to me tactfully?" Fenella gave a mirthless laugh. She didn't believe him anyway, not entirely. "In fact, what you mean is that you would have told him to collect me from Thurrold so you did not have to face me on your return."

Ambrose's face flamed and she saw she had hit on nothing but the truth. "You are determined to think the worst of me," he complained. "Despite the fact that your own actions are far from above reproach."

Fen took a steadying breath. "I was always a faithful wife to you," she said. "And true."

"Aha! But were you, madam? Were you? I wish you would tell me so in writing," he said bitterly.

Fen frowned at him. "I do not think you are in any position to criticize my behavior," she said frankly.

"So, you admit it then?" he demanded. "That you are complicit in Lord Vawdrey's attempts to *ruin* me?"

Fenella's gaze darted to his in surprise. "Ruin you?" she echoed.

"I do not know what else you would call it," he said bitterly.

"I do not believe you," she said simply. "I can see no reason why one so elevated as Lord Vawdrey should trouble himself to sabotage your career."

361

He gasped. "You—" He drew himself up but then noticed she had left him several steps behind her as she continued walking.

He hurried to catch her up. "So, you pretend not to be aware that Lord Vawdrey has approached the King, asking him to formally annul our marriage of eight years?" he asked shrilly.

Fen remembered Oswald's words in the bath and colored faintly. "He did mention something of that nature," she admitted.

"Spite! Sheer spite," Ambrose said indignantly.

"Why should you care?" she asked. "You clearly set no store by our vows in any case."

"Why should I...?" He almost seemed to reel at her words. "I can scarcely believe my ears, you unnatural woman!" he cried. "Perhaps Colleen is right, and you are pouring poison in his ear against me!"

Fenella stopped in her tracks and turned on him. He took a step back at the look on her face. "How dare you, sir," she said, her voice ringing out, "speak to me, thus. Do you imagine me unprotected? If so, then you are gravely mistaken."

Sir Ambrose darted an alarmed glance around them. "Keep your voice down!" he implored. Bors was looking from one to the other of them in confusion. He gave an agitated bark.

"My dear Lady Vawdrey, is all well?" asked Lady Schaeffer from in front of them. She had come to a halt.

Fen hesitated, but Ambrose's agonized expression decided her. "All is well, pray let us continue," she said calmly. They started off again.

Ambrose was breathing hard through his moustache. "You must understand, even an ill-educated woman such as yourself, how an annulment, if it is approved, will set me in some considerable financial difficulty."

Fen's frown cleared. So, it was not a question of hurt pride or honor, she realized, just money. If they were never married, then he was not entitled to the marriage settlement her father had made on her. "Did the Lady Colleen not come to you sufficiently dowered?" she forced herself to ask calmly. She felt a little numb. Even she was shocked that she felt so little pain.

Ambrose's expression struggled with the propriety of such a question. How easily outraged he was, she thought distractedly. Was he always so priggish and judgmental? She had used to think him a kind and decent man. She would use neither word about him now.

"Perhaps you rushed into a decision that has had rather more repercussions than you originally envisaged, Sir Ambrose," she wondered aloud.

"Not at all," he bridled. "As a divorced wife you would not have had any claim on my estate! I would, of course, have given you some small pension and one of the smaller properties to live out your days." He pondered a moment. "Perhaps Morebrook Farm."

363

Fen smiled. "But if we were never legally married then neither Morebrook Farm nor the other properties I brought to you are yours to grant," she pointed out gently.

He bridled. "This is outrageous! I am being robbed of what is rightfully mine, in full view of the King! And what's more, everyone knows it!"

"That must be very lowering for you," she said dampeningly. "Much like a wife who has been abandoned by an ungrateful spouse." He made an explosive exclamation of displeasure. Fenella twitched her skirts, ignoring him.

"I hope you do not rue the day you threw in your lot with that family," he sneered. "Their star may be in the ascendency now, but they are not without their own notoriety."

"I wish you joy of your new in-laws also," she told him briskly. "Tell me, how do you like having a resident mother-in-law, Ambrose?" she asked sweetly.

His face froze. "For all your faults, I did not think listening to gossip was one of them," he said icily.

"Gossip? But I have heard no gossip," she said, opening her eyes very wide. "Is all not harmonious in your new household? What a pity!"

"And whose fault is that?" he asked in an angry undertone. "You have turned my own sister against me! She has been most unwelcoming to Colleen. You have sown discord among my servants and…"

"None of this is true, Ambrose," she cut across his words. "I did not have time to brief the servants before I left, and as for Orla…your sister was not at all welcoming to me in the early days of our marriage either. I believe you told me to 'weather it' at the time."

He struggled a moment with his response. "I find you sadly changed, Fenella," he said at last. "You never used to be such a shrew."

She looked at him critically. "I find you changed also, Ambrose," she acknowledged. "But I think now," she pondered, "that I always saw you in an overgenerous light. After all, I believed myself to be jilted and left on the shelf when you came along. I was grateful when you married me."

She looked at him, and it almost seemed like she saw him through a fresh pair of eyes: the fussy little moustaches; the pompous bearing; the bandy legs. He really should not wear yellow hose, which served only to accentuate the problem. "But I was not in need of rescuing by you, after all," she said. "And your financial woes are no longer my concern." Before he could answer, she called to her friend. "Hester, may I take your arm now?"

Lady Schaeffer halted while Fenella caught her up. She did not look back over her shoulder and she did not take her leave of him. "Bors!" she called, snapping her fingers. Her dog lumbered to her side.

After a few moments, Hester Schaeffer squeezed her arm. "He has gone," she said in a low, conspiratorial voice.

Fenella breathed out a breath she had not even been aware she had been holding. "Thank you for remaining with me."

"Wild dogs could not have dragged me away, let alone my little Juniper," vowed Hester. She stooped and let her dog run free again. She hesitated. "Will you tell your husband?" Fen started guiltily. She had not even considered it. "He will not hear it from me," Hester assured her. "In case you decide it is best not to tell him."

"You are a good friend to me," said Fen. "But I think I would rather be open and honest in my dealings."

"That might be wise," agreed Hester. "Considering that one of his spies may be watching us even now!" She smiled, but Fen could see she was half-serious.

Fen turned her head, but all she could see was a falconer in the distance, training his bird. And two monks stood over by a dovecote. She turned uncertainly back to Lady Schaeffer. "I do not think—" But then she remembered the bland-faced men who had returned Bors to her and shivered.

"Honesty is so often the best policy," said Hester.

27

On returning to their rooms, Fen found Roland polishing his armor at the table. At her appearance he looked rather defensive and cleared his throat. "Didn't realize you'd be back so soon," he said, glancing at the mess he was making.

"It doesn't signify to me," said Fen cheerfully. "These are your rooms, not mine." Bors lumbered over to her brother-in-law and rested his head on Roland's thigh. She noticed that Roland managed to give Bors a satisfying neck rub whilst also sending a look of irritation her way.

"What do you mean, they're not your rooms?" he asked. "You're a Vawdrey now, aren't you?"

Fen picked up some grapes and made her way to the window seat. "Your brother told me from the outset that I shan't be at court overmuch once our marriage is established," she explained carefully. "And anyway, these feel far more like bachelor rooms than a home."

Roland snorted. "So, you want me out?" he asked without heat.

"Of course not!"

He swung round in the chair to look at her. "Even though I treat the place like bachelor chambers?"

"That's not what I meant," said Fen calmly. "And besides, once I am sent back to Sitchmarsh then—"

They both turned their heads as the door swung open. Oswald was stood on the threshold looking quite devastatingly handsome in a black doublet that Fen did not think she had seen before. So busy gazing her fill was she that it took her a few seconds to realize he also looked annoyed.

"Is there some reason you are speaking of Sitchmarsh?" he asked coolly as he strode into the room. "Has news arrived from the Keep?" He made straight for the fireplace and placed both his hands against the mantelpiece, staring down at the fire.

"Nay, brother," answered Roland, shooting a quizzical glance Fen's way. "You are expecting some?"

"Then why are you speaking of it?" Oswald asked, ignoring Roland's question and looking directly at Fenella.

"I—Sitchmarsh has been on my mind of late," she confessed. "I am expecting a letter from Orla and—"

"I should probably tell you now," he said in a bored-sounding voice, "that I have no intention of sending you to Vawdrey Keep in the immediate future. Certainly not before spring or even summer arrives." He turned his whole body to face her, a challenging look on his face. "Do we need to have some discussion around this subject?" He walked over to the table and poured a goblet of wine.

Fen reeled. Twice her lips formed words she did not manage to utter. "I am aware," he continued crisply, "that this flies in the face of what I told you initially some two weeks ago, but frankly I find Vawdrey Keep too far from court to be practical as my country seat."

Fenella sat up, realizing she had sunk down into the cushions when he walked around the table and approached, handing the wine to her. She took it wordlessly, her gaze searching his face. She could make neither head nor tail of what he was telling her! Something about his expression put her on her guard. It reminded her of after they had visited the King and he had been angry with her. "But you—" she croaked. "You said—"

"Yes, I did," he answered shortly. "But I am going back on it."

"M-my brother—"

"Is free to visit you, whenever it pleases you."

"Here?" squeaked Fen. "At court?"

Oswald shrugged. "There are guest apartments we could engage for his use on a temporary basis with very little trouble."

Fen took a distracted sip of wine. "I thought to visit with my friends and neighbors!" she protested faintly.

"You thought wrongly," he contradicted her, his eyes hard and angry despite the fact his words were so flat and calm.

And suddenly Fen knew. She knew that he was aware that she had encountered Ambrose Thane earlier that day. *Oh no.* Her mouth went dry. *But how? The monks? The falconer?* It hardly mattered. Somehow, by hook or by crook, Oswald Vawdrey knew. And he was not happy about it.

She came to her feet and placed the goblet down on the window seat. "I do need to have some speech with you, my lord," she said. Annoyingly, her voice sounded quivery and guilty. She cleared her throat and squared her shoulders.

369

"You will call me husband," he answered tersely. "For that is what I am to you, wife." Fen's feeling of panic mounted.

"Should I leave?" asked Roland uneasily. He looked from one of them to the other. Bors gave a mournful whine and disappeared under Roland's chair. Both Fenella and Oswald ignored him.

"I encountered Sir Ambrose Thane earlier today," she said aloud. "When I was out walking with my friend, Lady Schaeffer."

Oswald stood so still it was almost uncanny. He was like a statue and just as cold. "Is that so?" he asked silkily. "Do continue."

Fen felt inclined to do anything but. The fire still blazed in the grate, yet she felt chilled to the bone by her husband's reaction. Why did he not shout and rail at her? Somehow it felt far worse when he became so distant and icily remote.

"By accident or design?" he barked suddenly, making Fen jump in alarm.

"Accident, I assure you!" she blurted. "At least, on my part it was!"

Oswald's gaze became inscrutable, and he gave a chilly nod of his head. "What happened?"

"I went to visit Rowena in the stables," she started. "That's my horse," she added for Roland's benefit. "On the way back, Hester and I decided to visit the rose garden, and then proceed along the—"

370

"Skip to the part concerning Thane," Oswald interrupted her.

"She's not giving you a sworn statement under oath," Roland pointed out. Oswald turned an icy look on his brother, and Roland lapsed once more into silence.

"Sir Ambrose approached," hurried Fen, anxious to defuse the situation. "Just to tell me how much returning my dowry would inconvenience him." Both brothers appeared to digest this a moment in silence.

"What else?" asked Oswald quietly.

Fen thought a moment. She didn't want to make him angry, but she didn't want to lie to her husband either. "He also held me responsible for turning his sister, Orla, against his new wife," she said with a shrug.

She thought he became a very tiny bit less stiff, but she was not sure if that was just down to her wishful thinking. Finally, she could take it no longer and added, "I told him his opinion was no longer of any import to me." His eyes locked on hers as if measuring the veracity of her words.

"That's one in his eye," said Roland with a short laugh. "What said he to that?"

Fen kept her gaze on Oswald, but he also seemed to be waiting for her response. "He said he found my attitude unnatural," she admitted. "And outrageous."

"Pompous ass," snorted Roland.

371

"But, the most important thing," said Fenella, looking straight at her husband, "was that I found I simply did not care what he thought. And Lady Schaeffer backed me up when I made it clear to Sir Ambrose that you would not appreciate him accosting me."

"I do not appreciate it," said Oswald tautly. "It seems I must have a conversation with Thane to clarify this point."

"Oh, but—is that really necessary?"

Roland caught her eye and gave a quick shake of his head in warning.

"'Tis only," she added hastily, "that I should not like a rumor to start that I am attempting to sabotage his career out of spite." She could see that Oswald's lips had thinned with displeasure. "This place seems a breeding ground for the oddest rumors," she added lamely as a scuffle on the door announced that Meldon had arrived with their supper.

The door opened and both he and Trudy entered bearing trays of roasted meat and vegetables. "Your victuals!" he announced loudly. He had no sooner set down his tray than he started grumbling about Roland's armor strewn about the place.

"Not fit for man nor beast!" he finished roundly as Fen helped Trudy to set hers down and then carried the chest plate and shield across to the far corner of the room. Finally, they were settled around the table and Trudy fetched Fen's wine from the window seat to set it before her as the meat was carved and the cabbage and leeks dished out onto their plates.

"Thank you, Trudy."

"Speaking of rumors," said Roland, possibly in an attempt to help cool the situation. "Only this morning I heard some tale you were now bosom friends with Eden Montmayne." He spoke the last two words in tones of utmost loathing.

"I am friends with the Lady Eden," said Fen defensively as she cut up her meat. "And I know that cannot be wrong, for your brother himself recommended that I cultivated her friendship." She looked across to Oswald for corroboration, but he was still remote and did not meet her gaze. "And Lady Schaeffer holds her in very high esteem."

Roland made a rude noise. "Everyone will think you a social pariah," he said, rolling his eyes. "*Lenora* Montmayne is the one whose company you should be cultivating. She is the reigning beauty. Closely followed by that newcomer, that Cecil female." He piled some more cabbage on his already heaped plate.

"That may be so," conceded Fenella, taking another sip of her wine. "And might account for the men of the court clamoring for their company. But what care I for a pretty face on a woman? No, I thank you. I would much rather have the company of ladies who have conversation." She did not add that Lenora Montmayne had no discernible personality and Helen Cecil seemed thoroughly unpleasant. In her experience, men did not like to hear that their goddesses had feet of clay. She shot a look at Oswald, who, to all intents and purposes, was concentrating solely on his meal, which was not like him.

"Oh, and the likes of Mouse Martindale and Bess Hartleby are good company, are they?" scoffed Roland. "One scared stiff of

373

her own shadow, and the other looks like a side of beef in a dress!"

"She does not! You're being ridiculous, Roland," fired up Fen in defense of her new friends. "Lady Martindale may be a little shy and nervous, but if you take time to draw her out, she is very sweet and sincere. And Lady Hartleby may have high coloring, but she has excellent good health and has many tips on how to keep dogs."

Even to her own ears, the last point sounded a little weak, but she did not know all of Bess's good points yet. "And I think it's a bit rich of you to criticize *my* friend's appearance and character when you consider your own choice of company!"

Roland shot a startled look at Oswald, who turned to Fenella with a frown. "What did I say?" she asked in puzzlement.

"I swear I haven't brought any women back here since you married—" started Roland hotly.

"I meant Sir Edward Bevan and Sir James Attley," interjected Fenella. Oswald visibly relaxed.

"Well, what's wrong with poor old Bev?" asked Roland, recovering quickly.

"Nothing, except his sole topic of conversation is his horse, Bromley." At Roland's bewilderment, she elaborated: "The other night, he spent the entire supper speaking of Bromsley's flanks. Poor Lady Fortescue thought it was a place up north."

A look of amusement flickered over Oswald's face so quickly that Fen half wondered if she had imagined it.

"No one appreciates the art of conversation anymore," lamented Roland with a grin.

"Hah!" responded Fen derisively. She pondered a moment. For some reason, she did not want the table to fall silent.

"I think it is very hard," she said hesitantly, "when one does not fit into a certain mold. For ladies, I mean. They are judged so harshly for falling short of the ideal, where men are allowed to have spindleshanks and pimples or an unnatural thirst for horseflesh and no one bats an eyelid."

"Unnatural?" spluttered Roland, slamming down his cup. "I never heard that particular rumor about old Bevan." Oswald shot him a look and Roland subsided.

"You know full well what I mean, Roland," said Fen seriously. "You are meant to be the King's champion, yet I have never heard a man speak as unchivalrously as you about women."

Roland shrugged carelessly. "I speak as I find," he said.

"You have a cruel tongue."

Roland screwed up his face. "I've never spoken ill of you, except to your face," he said ingenuously.

Fen was surprised. "Truly?"

"Truly. In fact, I've even defended you on occasion."

"Because I'm your sister now?"

He shrugged again. "I speak ill of my brothers all the time," he said casually. "Biggest pair of bastards you'll ever meet. Mason, quite literally."

Fen pursed her lips in disapproval.

Roland leaned forward on his forearms. "I even tried to steal Mason's wife one time," he told her conspiratorially. Fen stared. "Maybe I'll succeed with Oswald's?" he said with a wink and shot a look of challenge at his brother. Oswald leaned back in his chair, his eyes guarded, hiding his expression. Fen felt instinctively that he was waiting for her response to his brother's teasing.

"Nonsense," she said, trying to hide her unease at his words. She could tell that Roland wanted to shock her and was determined not to give him what he wanted. "You have a flair for the dramatic, Roland. Perhaps that is why you're such a draw in the lists."

Oswald's lips twisted into a reluctant smile. "Mayhap we should come along and watch you joust tomorrow, Roland?" he suggested. Fen exhaled in relief.

Roland grunted. "Up to you. I only wear the prettiest lady's token though," he warned. "That's one standard I absolutely will not allow to slip. Even for family."

"Meaning you won't wear mine?" asked Fen with mock dismay. "I believe I'll survive the disappointment."

"Would you like to attend?" Oswald asked her directly.

Fen tipped her head to one side to consider it. "Is there any likelihood of Roland being knocked off his horse and onto his backside?" she asked hopefully.

"A very slim chance," responded Oswald with a small smile.

"That's good enough for me," she responded.

Roland snorted. "If that's what you're hoping for, you *will* be disappointed, sister," he said, flexing his muscular arms. "There's no one entered that will give me the slightest trouble."

"A pity," she sighed. "But I should probably see what all the fuss is about."

"Well, don't bring your army of frights with you" was his parting shot as he rose from the table. "A man likes to see a pretty face through his visor. Not the likes of Eden Montmayne and her sour features."

"Eden Montmayne is an attractive and, moreover, an *accomplished* young woman!" she called after him.

She couldn't really make out Roland's response, but the inflection of his words was derisive.

28

Roland had not left the room for long before Oswald dismissed the servants and suggested they turn in to bed. Fen blew out the candles at the table and followed him into their room.

"Your brother is abominably rude," she told Oswald. She had washed and was unpinning her hair.

"He likes you," he said grudgingly over his shoulder as he poured more water into the basin to wash.

She started loosening her braids. "How can you tell?" She drew a hair comb through her newly freed tresses.

"It's quite obvious if you know him," said Oswald dryly. "Roland's a straightforward creature. With few subtleties."

"He's very different to you," agreed Fenella, thinking this over. "You did not share a mother though."

"No. None of us do."

"Perhaps that's why?"

"Perhaps," he agreed without much conviction.

"And you are not like your father either."

"No," he agreed, lowering his washcloth.

"But perhaps Roland is a little more like the old baron?" she ruminated.

Oswald made no answer to this, simply threw down his cloth and approached their bedroom door. He was dressed only in his chauses, which were low on his hips. He turned the key and Fen fell silent as he started drawing off his boots.

She cleared her throat. "So, I start my sittings with signor Arnotti on the morn, and—"

Oswald stopped in the act of pulling off his second boot and turned to her with a frown. "Who?"

"The painter," Fen said helpfully. "You wanted me to arrange to have my portrait done?"

"Oh yes," he agreed swiftly, then straightened up to start unlacing his crotch. "Remind me, where you are sitting for this painting?" he asked casually. "Somewhere public?"

"Well, Eden had rather a good idea about that," Fen told him. "She suggested one of the window seats in the lower gallery. Perhaps sat next to some stained glass and beneath an arch?"

Her husband was sliding his braies over his hips. "And who accompanies you?" he asked before shucking them down his legs.

Fen sat down in a chair to draw off her shoes and stockings. "Well, all my new friends have been very kind and said they will take turns to sit with me. Apparently, it is very dull work indeed to be sat trying to maintain a pose while the artist takes your likeness."

She pondered this a moment before standing up and tugging at her laces. "I suppose the artist my father commissioned was

379

only third-rate at best. I don't remember sitting for very long at all, but it seems signor Arnotti requires simply hours of your time." She looked up to find Oswald surveying her with a heavy frown. "Are you alright?" she asked uncertainly. "You seem…distracted."

"Fenella," he said heavily. "If Thane approaches you again, I want you to tell me straightaway. Knock on my door. Demand admittance. Barge into my office. I don't care who I'm meeting with, the King, the privy council, it doesn't matter. Am I understood?"

Fen's jaw dropped. "Interrupt you?" she squeaked. "In an important meeting?"

"Precisely."

"Just to tell you Sir Ambrose Thane had approached me?"

"Yes."

"Something of so little import?" she stressed.

"He has no legitimate reason to accost my wife," he said, crossing the room to her, completely naked now, to help her out of her gown.

When she stood in her shift, he tilted her chin up toward him. "If you were to choose not tell me, I would still hear of it, Fenella," he warned. "And if that happens, I will have him thrown in the stocks."

Fen's face flooded with color. *The stocks?* "People will think I bear a grudge and am mean-spirited," she stammered.

"I think it will soon become public knowledge that your husband is unspeakably jealous," he answered, casting her dress onto the chair and placing his hands on either side of her waist. "If it is not already."

"You are not," she protested hotly.

"Never before," he admitted, walking her backward toward the bed. "But I seem to have had a change of heart."

His mentioning his heart had a peculiar effect on Fenella. She felt her own throb almost painfully in her chest, and before she could even think to stop herself, she laid a hand on Oswald's bare chest.

His sharply indrawn breath made her start to pull away, but the next thing she knew, she was swept up and onto the bed and being kissed with an abandon that quite took her breath away. And not just her mouth, but her neck, the sensitive area between her breasts, and then her soft belly. Her thin shift was pushed or pulled out of the way as if it wasn't even there. It was bunched up at her waist now as he breathed heavily against her tummy button.

"Fenella," he said huskily. "Don't be shocked."

"Shocked?" she asked, raising her head from the pillow. A small smile started to curve her lips. Oswald Vawdrey was a passionate and sensual man, but she fancied that she was starting to find his measure.

And then his mouth was there, between her legs. Hot and probing and she *was* shocked. *Very*. So shocked she cried out,

381

but soon the shock turned to something else, and the cries turned into something else, and before long, they lay satiated, a panting tangle of limbs whereby she knew not where he started, and she ended.

"Are you crying, love?" he asked, ducking his head to try to meet her gaze, but she hid her face in his neck. And if she had not been crying then, the use of the word *love* meant she soon was. What was wrong with her?

"No," she lied softly and concentrated on the feel of his fingers as they circled her lower back.

"I did shock you," he said ruefully.

"A little," she admitted cagily. She wanted to ask him if that was something that husbands usually did to wives, but caution held her back, and she did not want the specter of her previous marriage to rise up between them again.

There was a pause and then Oswald spoke. "My father did not pay the ransom," he said softly. "I lied to you."

Startled, Fenella turned her head. "What?"

"After Adarva." His words were so quiet, she could barely hear him. Yet, somehow, she knew he was telling her something precious. Sharing something with her that he had not told to another living soul before.

Her mind raced. She held her breath. "He didn't?" she asked softly. "Then, how did you get free from your captors?"

"By my own resources," he said simply.

Fen digested this. She wanted to ask why the baron did not pay his ransom, but she did not want to hurt his feelings or reopen old wounds. "That was clever of you. But what did your father say when you showed back up?"

He shrugged. "Not much. He seemed to be under the impression I was likely dead. Someone must have seen me cut down and reported it to him. Mayhap he thought the demand for a ransom was a ruse."

Fen lay quiet, wondering how he must have felt. "You never showed him your scar, did you?" She already knew the answer.

"No." She wondered if Oswald Vawdrey had always been so secretive, or if he had grown that way after finding so little in common with his loud, booming father and moody, quarrelsome brothers. He exhaled loudly. "I wish to the gods I had come back to you, Fen. Things would have been different if I had."

She held her breath. What was he saying? Her fifteen-year-old self was giddy at his words. He wished he'd returned to her? His scorned little fiancée? "Different? How?" she asked, almost holding her breath.

"I would have been different," he insisted.

Oswald Vawdrey had been twenty-one years old at the battle of Adarva. He had been her fiancée. But she had been a mere child of fifteen. "No," she said ruefully. "I could not have handled you at fifteen." She ached to touch his scarred shoulder. *How he must have suffered.* She wished she could have nursed him back

383

to health. Would they have grown close? Become soulmates? "Can I touch your scar?" she asked softly.

He lay so silent, she expected him to say no, but instead he disentangled himself from her and rolled obligingly onto his side. Tentatively, she reached out to touch her fingers to his scarred shoulder blade. "I might have lost you," she said as she traced the mass of scar tissue.

"No," he replied simply. "If I had died, I would have died your betrothed."

"It's far better this way," she said in a choked voice.

"Yes. I wish..." His words trailed off.

"What?"
"I wish my father could have seen me settled with you. Apparently, it was the last thing he spoke of. At the end. My marrying and settling down. He would have been pleased." He hesitated. "He would have *approved*. And he never approved of me."

She could hear the conflict in his voice without seeing his facial expression. She wanted to make things better. She racked her brain before a forgotten memory surfaced. "Baron Vawdrey sent me a gold coin every year," she blurted, hardly believing she'd said it out loud.

"What?"

"Every year since our betrothal was ended. On the date of our engagement. It used to make me angry because it made no sense. Especially after…" She stopped, reluctant to mention her marriage to Ambrose.

"My father?" he asked, turning back over to face her.

"There was no note or explanation or anything. Just a scribbled line on the paper. 'In lieu of what was promised.' I never spent them. I tried to send them back to him once, but he would have none of it and they were returned the same day…"

"How?" asked Oswald. "How did they arrive?"

"Every year without fail. With his seal. The same line was written, in the same sprawling hand. I asked my father once, and he said there was nothing to be done with so stubborn a man. He recommended I put them in a chest and think no more of it. He told me to mention it to no one."

Oswald slowly stroked her back. "Is that what you did?" he asked.

"Yes."

"In lieu of what was promised," he repeated softly.

"Yes."

He sighed, and Fen shifted her body in closer to his. "Of course, he might have just felt bad that I was thrown over and was sending me compensation?" she suggested.

"That doesn't really sound like my father." His tone was dry.

385

"The chest is in my old room at my brother's place. It didn't seem right having it at Thurrold. Maybe I could give them to Linnet's daughters," suggested Fen, struck with inspiration. "Toward their dowries? What are their names again?"

"Lily and Margaret." Oswald was running the back of his hand down her side now.

"What did Roland mean," she asked in an abrupt change of subject, "when he said he tried to steal Mason's wife?"

Oswald's hand stilled and rested at the swell of her hip. "He was just being aggravating," he explained. "Roland was engaged to Linnet, our sister-in-law, but it was arranged by our father. Roland refused to go through with it as rumor had it she was a misshapen invalid. Father sent Mason and myself to jilt Linnet on Roland's behalf, but she propositioned Mason to take Roland's place. He took her up on the offer. Then later, when it turned out her relatives had told many lies and suppressed the fact she was holding a dukedom in abeyance, Roland changed his mind and tried to get their marriage annulled."

Fen plucked at the bedsheets. Annulling marriages seemed to be rather a Vawdrey pastime. "And...was she? I mean..."

"No," answered Oswald mildly. "Linnet has red hair and many freckles. But nothing else ailed her."

"And your brother Mason and she are happily married now?" she asked.

"Very."

"Was your brother not angry with Roland?"

"Very," repeated Oswald.

"But they are amicable in their relations now?"

He rolled onto his side to face her fully. "As amicable as most brothers," he answered. "Which is to say, not very. But they are reconciled."

Fen tucked her hand under her cheek and studied his face. "Did you never joust in tournaments?" she asked. She was sure that Oswald was far better looking than any other man at court.

His smile turned a little bleak. "At Roland's age I was enrolled in the King's army," he reminded her. "There was no playing at battle back then."

She nodded. "I see."

"Fenella," he said, rising up on one elbow, his tone suddenly serious. "I think you should devote some effort to becoming one of the Queen's ladies-in-waiting. Now we know you are remaining at court for the foreseeable future, it would cement your standing and give you some guidance in how you are to spend your days at court."

Fen's eyes widened with alarm. "Hester Schaeffer does not think that an enviable station at all!" The idea of applying herself to becoming a sophisticated courtier was a daunting one indeed. She had only managed to get through functions before in the knowledge she would soon be back in the country.

"But you are not Lady Schaeffer," he pointed out.

387

"And Lady Doverdale is one," she said darkly.

"And so is your other friend, Eden Montmayne."

"Yes," she agreed reluctantly. "But Eden is so very accomplished and good at everything. And the Queen was most underwhelmed with me when I met her."

"I could speak to the King."

"Oh no," objected Fenella, lifting her head off the pillow. "I do not wish to be inflicted on Queen Armenal! She would not like that at all!"

"Very well, then I shall wait for you to ingratiate yourself with her," he said calmly.

Fen stared at him to see if he was joking, but to her dismay he seemed entirely in earnest. How he expected her to ingratiate herself with the Queen was beyond her!

"And now we've settled that," said Oswald, shifting over her and seemingly unaware of her inner turmoil. "Let's seal the bargain."

And then, like he had every night since their marriage had been consummated, Oswald Vawdrey made passionate love to her. "Tell me you want me, Fenella," he said tightly.

"I want you," she repeated obediently.

He cocked his head to one side. "Not enough," he said. "Not yet." His thumb started a slow circle against the part of her that quickened the most. "I want you, Fenella. I want all of you. Do you understand?" Her brow puckered. She had no clue. His fingers were distracting. What was he demanding of her? He gave her a slightly pained smile. "You don't and that's my fault," he said in a low, shaking voice. "But I'm going to make it right. Will you let me, Fenella? I need you to let me."

She swallowed, wanting to please him. Wanting to say the right thing. Her hips were moving fitfully against his. He withdrew his fingers from between her legs and rubbed his hard length against her. Why was he teasing her? Why didn't he just—?

"Tell me there's still time," he said urgently, his voice breaking slightly. "Tell me I'm not too late."

"There's still time," she said. *Time for what?* His expression was heartbreaking, and she wanted to comfort him, to reassure him. "You're not too late."

He entered her then on a swift thrust, groaning deeply. "Sweet Fenella," he said, "You deserve better, but I've made you mine anyway."

Sweet Fenella? He'd never spoken to her like this before! With honeyed words. She was just his wife. Unwanted. Abandoned. But he'd just told her he wanted her. All of her! Her head spinning, she moved against him, welcoming his thrusts with soft moans, shifting her hands across the width of his back, caressing him. Of course, she'd never showered affection on him either, she thought, watching his eyes drift shut.

He seemed to like her touch, she marveled. Even when she rubbed it across the forbidden path of his scar. Raising her head, she kissed his neck. She'd never taken the initiative to kiss him

389

either, she thought, flushing. She let her head fall back onto the pillow and looked up at his scorching gaze, catching her breath.

"Fenella," he groaned. "Gods, I want you, wife. Be mine."

"I am," she replied in confusion.

"Tell me." His voice was raw, his thrusts becoming stronger and less controlled. "Tell me."

"I'm yours," she gasped. "All yours."

His gaze darkened. "Yes," he grunted, his hips pounding against hers. "Again."

"I'm yours," she sobbed.

"All mine?" he prompted through gritted teeth.

"All yours. *Oh Oswald. Oh please.*" She shifted desperately against him.

He lowered his mouth to her ear and said in a low, shaking voice, "You're precious to me, Fenella."

Her world tipped on its axis and her control splintered as she sobbed out in rapture, hiding her face in his neck and sinking her fingers into the skin of his back. For a few heartbeats she felt him still stroking deep within her as she clenched and fluttered against him in the grip of passion.

Then he gave a low roar and she felt him throb and then release his seed deep within her. She wrapped her arms and legs around him to hold him close as he gasped and groaned against her, his

390

body shaking as he continued to flex his hips long after he'd stopped spurting, as if he didn't want his body to leave hers.

Her brain rushed madly after a surfeit of pleasure. She was precious? She was just dropping off to sleep when Oswald breathed her name again.

"Yes?" she murmured sleepily.

"They weren't compensation, the gold coins," he said in a curiously calm voice.

She lifted her head from his shoulder. "They weren't?"

"No."

"What were they then?"

"Promise coins." He dropped a kiss on the top of her head. "He was keeping our contract open."

29

As it happened, they did not make it to the tournament to watch Roland joust, as Oswald was called into an emergency privy meeting. He sent a hastily scribbled note to his wife via his assistant, apologizing and promising they would attend the next one.

Of course, he could have told her to attend without him, his conscience pointed out, irritating him. Roland's friends would no doubt have been pleased to escort her and she had made a number of good female friends at court already. But tournaments tended to be a rowdy affair with a public gallery, and the thought of her attending without his escort was somehow unacceptable to him.

He glowered at the thought of her bumping into the likes of Thane and his new bitch of a wife. He'd be damned if he'd see her at their mercy. Of course, he reminded himself, Fenella had said that the sight of Thane no longer distressed her. The thought of that bastard having the nerve to upbraid her on her "unnatural" behavior galled him, but his wife seemed averse to him bringing Thane to account, and these days, he *simply did not wish to displease her*.

After all, he had gone back on every single promise he'd ever made her. As a husband, he wasn't entirely sure he was doing a much better job than that worm, Thane, had. The thought left a bitter taste in his mouth. Nearby someone cleared their throat, and he looked up in surprise to find the chamber had pretty much filled with council members while he had been reflecting on the state of his marriage. He signaled to Bryce, who signaled to the footmen to carry in the large, covered canvas. A murmuring broke out among the ranks as he stood up from his seat.

"My lords," he said. "The King has called this extraordinary meeting today for us to discuss the matter of the Blechmarsh princess." He nodded to Bryce, who whipped off the black covering to reveal the large oil painting depicting the Princess Una sat astride a large black destrier and holding a sword.

"Gads!" remarked Lord Sutton with disgust. "She's an ill-favored wench!"

"Which is the horse and which is the princess?" asked Lord Caterby snidely. "Their nostrils are nigh on the same size!" A burst of laughter greeted Caterby's pronouncement.

Uncomfortably, Oswald chose this moment to remember Fenella's words about men's shortcomings being so much more easily overlooked than women's. Caterby was an ugly bastard himself, but it had never held him back. He cleared his throat. "Gentlemen, let us focus on the issue at hand," he urged.

"Which is?" asked Lord Schaeffer, looking up from shuffling his papers.

Oswald smiled faintly. "Marriage," he said and heard gasps all around him. "His Majesty has been struck with inspiration on how we may negate the threat of the last of the Blechmarsh line."

A ripple of disbelief ran through the occupants of the room. A few of them scoffed at the idea the King had come up with any such plan.

393

"Wymer's plan, you say?" cried Lord Caterby.

"A likely tale," snorted Lord Sutton.

Oswald ignored him. "Candidates, gentlemen, if you please," he said, looking around the room expectantly. "I need not explain, I hope, that they must be lacking in both ambition and an overly impressive lineage. After all." He paused heavily. "A wife is raised or lowered to her husband's status, is she not?"

Lord Sutton rubbed his moustache speculatively. "There is something in what you say, Vawdrey," he agreed cautiously. "If we marry her off to some lowborn knave then she herself becomes…" He looked around expectantly.

"Why, nothing more than the legally wedded wife of a lowborn knave," chortled Sir Reginald de Bomfrey.

Lord Schaeffer looked horrified. "She is a princess of the blood," he said censoriously.

Oswald gave him a hard stare. "Would you rather she shed that blood in order to retain her elevated status?" he asked softly. Lord Schaeffer quickly shook his head and stared down at the tabletop.

"Just how fat a purse is the King offering with her?" asked Lord Caterby frankly. "The poor fool would need some inducement." He looked back toward the canvas and visibly blanched.

The rest of the room turned their gaze on the portrait, and Oswald narrowed his eyes at the oil painting. Did Una Blechmarsh really bear the stamp of her father's features so faithfully? he wondered. Or was that merely a conceit of the

394

artist who had been keen to flatter him? That massive frizz of yellow hair must surely be a wig, he reasoned. And could she really be so stocky and muscular of build? In his experience, women seldom had such barrel-like chests and wide, square faces.

"Why, she looks just like a man," said Sir Reginald derisively, cutting across his ruminations. "Look at the size of her great meaty fists! Legs like great ham bones!" He shuddered. "Good luck to the poor bastard that ends up leg-shackled to her!"

*

All in all, it had been an extremely wearisome day, Oswald reflected as he locked his desk drawer. The handful of names that had been half-heartedly offered up as prospective bridegrooms had all been dismissed by King Wymer as a damned insult.

After four years in office, Oswald recognized the beginning of an uphill struggle when he saw one. This problem was going to rumble on for weeks if not months before he managed to force a solution through. He rubbed his temples distractedly and looked up to find Bryce standing silently in the doorway with a document in hand.

"I'm finished for the day, Bryce," he said rather sharper than he'd intended.

"You'll want to receive this one, my lord," his assistant said mildly.

"Oh?" He somehow doubted it. "What is it?" he asked impatiently as he rounded his desk and outstretched his hand.

395

"Something the King had me draw up," said Bryce, bringing him up short.

"The King?" asked Oswald. Why the hells would Wymer ask *his* assistant to draw him up some papers? Bryce handed the document over, and Oswald saw at once that it bore the heavy wax seal of King Wymer.

As his eyes scanned the document, he nearly swallowed his own tongue. It was the official annulment of Fenella's first marriage to Sir Ambrose Thane. He looked at Bryce, who had tactfully withdrawn his gaze and was looking over his left shoulder. "It's been finalized?" he asked, even though he held the proof in his own hand.

His assistant nodded. "And notification of the fact sent to Sir Ambrose."

Oswald breathed out a ragged breath. "You were right," he conceded. "I needed this after today." He was almost tempted to sit back down, but he was eager to get back to Fenella.

"Congratulations, my lord," said Bryce.

Oswald's gaze snapped back at him, but his assistant looked his usual serious self. "What did the King say?" he asked suspiciously. "When he commissioned you to act on this piece of work?"

Bryce coughed. "His Majesty—ah—expressed the wish that it might restore to you the peace of mind and evenness of temper that you are famous for."

Oswald pulled a face, for he was under no illusion that the King would have phrased it anything like as tactfully. "And your reply?"

Bryce's gaze flickered. "I opined that I thought it would provide some measure toward returning your equanimity," he answered serenely.

"My good Bryce," said Oswald dryly. "You are finally starting to speak like a politician."

Bryce looked modestly gratified. "I believe you are right, my lord. For the King kept addressing me as Price," he said. "And I did not even correct him, my lord. Not once."

Oswald could not help but smile at this. "And how would you feel about changing it officially?" he asked. "For the purposes of advancing your career?"

Bryce appeared to consider this a moment. "Alas," he said, "the only reason my uncle withdrew me from the seminary was because I am the last of our particular branch to bear the name. I fear I could not change it without risking his wrath."

It occurred to Oswald that his assistant would never have imparted such personal information even so recently as a month ago. The very clear boundaries they had once operated under had been blurred of late. And even stranger, he was not quite sure he could regret the fact.

"Lady Vawdrey would be very interested to hear this, Bryce," he admitted.

Bryce made an exclamation and reached into the pouch he wore on his belt. "Which reminds me, these arrived today, my lord. From the Antonys of Aphrany." He handed over two small wooden boxes.

Oswald opened the first and found Fen's modest gold posy ring had arrived. He checked inside and found their initials. For some reason, his hand flew to the small gold padlock on his chain. *Not Forgot.* He had been so sure the locket had been his mother's, but now it struck him as odd that he could not remember. But why else would he wear such a keepsake?

He tucked it back inside his shirt then turned to the second box. Inside it were the two rings he had privately commissioned from Mr. Antony, two thick gold rings with a ruby in the center of each. The rings were decorated with blue enamel. On the smaller ring there were two silver panthers set on either side of the stone, and on the larger ring the ruby was thronged with two silver bears. This way, when they wore them, they would be wearing each other's heraldic beast.

He stared at them a moment before snapping the box shut. He handed the first box back to Bryce. "This needs to go back to Antony's," he said. "And another inscription added to the inside of the band. The date of my marriage to Fenella, fourteen years ago. And the words *Not Forgot.*"

Bryce nodded. "Yes, my lord."

"These are satisfactory," he said, holding up the second box with the matching rings. He glanced back at the annulment papers. "I will read this through at my leisure, but I am confident you have done a thorough job, Bryce. As always."

His assistant blinked and then flushed faintly. "Yes, my lord. Sir Ambrose has twenty-eight days to comply." He hesitated before adding colorlessly. "My research indicates he will most likely find it necessary to withdraw from court and retire from public life."

Oswald considered this a moment before replying quietly. "That would be satisfactory also." Which was the bloody understatement of the century as far as he was concerned!

He made his way back to their rooms with a lighter tread but was not pleased when he could hear loud voices as soon as he turned down the corridor. *What now?* As he got closer to the door, he recognized Meldon's belligerent tones and someone else.

"I tell you, I was given strict orders to bring this here stuff to these quarters," the stranger was insisting.

"His lordship didn't tell me nothing about it!" Meldon ranted. "And I've not got the time to be unpacking all this paraphernalia!"

Oswald swung the door open in some trepidation and found the entryway blocked up with two large chests and an even larger object swathed in hessian sacking. "What is all this?" he asked, stepping over one of the chests. "And where is my wife?"

"Her ladyship ain't returned from a-getting her portrait painted," Meldon told him with a sniff. "She's been at it all day."

"All day?" echoed Oswald. "Her plans were to sit only during the morning."

"Aye, so she was, but when you canceled the tournament plans on her, she decided she may as well devote another five hours to it," said Meldon. "Lady Schaeffer sat with her this morning, and then that Lady Martindale what wouldn't say boo to a goose, she sat with her all afternoon planning out their next tapestry."

"Well, that's what this is!" said the stranger, tipping back his hat to scratch his head. "A portrait from storage at Vawdrey Keep and some old tapestries. Knowles, the steward, he said you sent him word that you wanted 'em, my lord…"

"Ah yes," said Oswald, his frown clearing. "So I did. But I will admit, I did not think Knowles had much hope of finding them." He crossed the room, extracted a sword from a wall rack, and returned to cut the strings swaddling the sacking. He wrestled a moment with the hessian before it fell away to reveal a rather murky portrait of a young lady in a dark green dress, staring out with an expression of the utmost seriousness. Oswald took three steps back to take a more critical look at it.

"Well, that's the mistress, and no mistake," said Meldon. "Though I don't ever remember seeing that picture at the old Keep."

"It was in storage, Knowles said," supplied the stranger helpfully. "Under a pile of old furnishings."

Oswald held up a hand for silence as he continued to peruse the portrait. He could see why Meldon recognized her, but in his opinion, the artist had not possessed either the talent or the quality materials to do Fenella true justice.

The shining amber eyes looked a mere light brown, and her glowing, creamy skin just looked pale and rather flat on the canvas. He had got the heart shape of her face right and the eyebrows, but he had not captured the charm or the wit that made up the whole.

He guessed she looked about fifteen years or thereabouts, and certainly the dog, Bors, who sat on her lap, was a mere pup. He was just about to glance away and ask them to open the trunk when he saw it. The pendant suspended on a chain at the front of her bodice.

His hand flew to the chain he wore tucked into his tunic. The gold padlock shape was most distinctive, and Oswald's throat closed a moment. It had been Fenella's. He had worn her token on his person for more than a decade. Unknowingly. His fingers tightened around the locket.

Meldon cleared his throat. "M'lord?"

Oswald's startled gaze flew to his. "Yes?"

Meldon shifted on his feet uncomfortably. "You looked like you was having a turn."

"I'm fine." Oswald waved a hand and walked rather unsteadily to lean against the table. How could he have forgotten such a thing? He never forgot things! Even the finer details. His head was reeling.

"Shall I open the trunk, m'lord?" asked the newcomer.

Oswald nodded as he poured himself a much-needed glass of wine. His hand, he noticed as he lifted it to his mouth, shook with a faint tremor.

Meldon helped the other man prize open the lid and they dragged out a long rolled-up tapestry. His eyebrows shot up. Clearly Fenella had not been a mere dabbler in the art. This would have been a labor-intensive piece of work that would have taken her many months to complete.

"Careful!" Oswald barked as the man unrolled its considerable width with a kick of his boot.

"Sorry, m'lord," he said hastily, and crouched down to unfurl the rest of it.

Oswald walked closer and blinked at the scene laid out before him. It had not yellowed or faded with age, possibly from being in storage, and the bright array of colors and stitches could clearly be seen. His heart sank. Why the hells had he got the impression she was not proficient in tapestry?

This would have taken her hours and hours of work. He cast back his mind to her telling him that seemingly throwaway story of how she had sent him a betrothal gift. And he had confessed that he had never even seen it. Even worse, he seemed to remember uttering some bloody stupid comment about his father probably letting his dogs sleep on it. He turned cold all over.

Fifteen-year-old Fen would doubtless have expected a word of praise from her betrothed for all the time she had invested in this. He glanced back over his shoulder at the grave-faced girl on the portrait. She would have sat for *fucking hours* waiting for

402

some word of thanks from him! Or at least some acknowledgment of her precious gift. And he hadn't done a damn thing.

He couldn't even trust his memory anymore, since he had clearly forgotten all about the locket she had given him. Had he seen the tapestry and simply shrugged it off as a girlish whim in his callow youth? He walked slowly around the edges, his eyes poring over the large decorative border which depicted thorny vines decorated with roses and intertwined with a procession of bears and panthers up on their hind legs, as if dancing.

The central panel was a large angelic figure with a halo of roses, brandishing a fiery sword and stood under a heavy tree, bursting with fruit. Oswald was not sure of the significance of the central image, but the intertwining of their heraldic beasts showed that this was clearly a celebration of the joining of their houses. A celebration he had somehow missed at the time. Gods. It was so big it nearly covered the whole floor!

He cleared his throat. "I want this hung immediately," he told Meldon.

"At Vawdrey Keep?" asked his servant uncertainly.

"No, here," he clarified, pointing to the bare walls. The gods knew they had little enough by way of decoration.

It was, he realized uncomfortably, a far cry from the fantasy home of Mr. and Mrs. Roberts that Fen had described. "The portrait can be hung over the fireplace," he said. "And—er—Meldon. See about getting some ribbons and greenery installed in here for the Midwinter festival."

403

Meldon bridled indignantly. "The old baron never asked me to do nothing of that nature—" he started belligerently.

"Well, I'm asking you now! Get your goddaughter to do it!" Oswald bit back in irritation. "If that's beyond you!"

He flipped a gold coin at the delivery man, who was standing by gawping at the two of them. "For your troubles," he murmured in dismissal.

"Thank you, m'lord," gasped the man, blinking at the value of the coin and backing out of the room before Oswald could change his mind.

"What did you give him so much for?" grumbled Meldon. "They'll all be expecting the same treatment!"

Oswald ignored him and turned on his heel, making for the bedchamber. In there he found Fenella's maid tidying her mistress's clothes away.

"Ah, Trudy," he said, swiftly masking his irritation. "Perhaps you could help Meldon to hang the tapestry next door?"

"Yes, m'lord," she said, bobbing a curtsey and backing out of the room. He closed the door after her with a frown.

It had never occurred to him that palace quarters left anything to be desired before, but at this precise moment in time, he felt distinctly underwhelmed with them. He paced the room a couple of times and was just debating whether to go in search of Fenella when he heard the outer door slam. Hurrying out into the adjoining room, he was irritated to find it was only his brother returning with yet another silver cup and a battered

404

shield. Roland groaned and dropped down into a chair with a grimace.

"I'm surprised you're not out celebrating," Oswald commented. "First place?"

"What else?" asked Roland arrogantly. He set the decorative cup down before being distracted by Meldon's antics. "What's he doing, stood on that chair?" he asked.

Oswald ignored him, as it was blatantly obvious Meldon was hanging the tapestry. Instead, he poured his brother a cup of wine.

"That picture's not straight," said Roland critically as he took it from him. Trudy darted back to tip it to the right. "That's better," he said grudgingly. "Though the likeness is terrible." He looked at Oswald. "Don't tell me you paid good coin for that."

"That's not the portrait I commissioned," said Oswald irritably. "That's one her father had done years ago."

"He was robbed," said Roland, taking a swig of wine. "I'm sure Bors was far better looking than that as a puppy."

"Any objection to your new cup being placed on the mantel with some flowers in it?" asked Oswald, picking up the large vessel and turning it over in his hands.

"Yes," snapped his brother, snatching it back. "I'm having it melted down on the morrow. And why's everyone trying to make this place habitable? Are we expecting visitors?"

Oswald dropped down heavily into the seat next to him. "Would you say this place is suitable for a newlywed couple to start out married life together?" he asked.

Roland gave him a sideways look. "How the hells should I know?" He scanned Oswald suspiciously. "What ails you?" he asked. "You don't look yourself."

Oswald shrugged. "I scarcely know these days," he admitted. Roland clicked his fingers and whistled. "Bors isn't here," said Oswald. "Presumably he's with his mistress."

Roland shrugged a shoulder irritably. "What do I care where her dog is?" he asked.

Oswald looked at his brother in exasperation. "You're always fawning on it!"

"Me, fawning?" asked Roland indignantly. "At least I don't sit my own wife on my lap in company!"

Oswald bit back his reply as the door opened and his wife walked in, her dog on her heels.

"Good evening," she said, looking rather tired as Bors barged past her to fling himself at Roland's legs. She dropped her cloak on a chair and started pulling off her gloves.

"There he is!" said Roland, patting Bors's barrel-like body like a drum. "My good boy!"

"I'm so sorry we missed your tournament, Roland," said Fenella with a quick smile. "Only—"

She stopped abruptly, staring at the wall hanging. "Wha—?" She dropped a glove on the floor and Bors darted forward to scoop it up in his mouth. "Um…" She raised a hand to her head and stared at it a moment. "Is that what I think it is?" she asked faintly.

Oswald was already out of his chair, steering her toward the window seat. "You look tired," he murmured. "It must have been draughty and cold, sat in the long gallery all day."

The servants tactfully withdrew, Meldon giving the tapestry one last doubtful look. "Just hope it holds!" he murmured under his breath. "Damn thing's plaguey heavy!"

Fenella clutched at Oswald's arm and turned a very dull red. "Why are you hanging that up?" she asked in strangled tones. "It really ought to be relegated to a dark cupboard!"

"Why?" He frowned. "I see naught amiss with it." Fenella stared at him.

"Do you mean the wall hanging or the portrait?" asked Roland with interest. Bors dropped the glove in his lap as an offering.

"Portrait?" repeated Fenella. She glanced up and gave a yelp on catching sight of the painting. "What's *that* doing here?"

"Why would I not display my betrothal gifts?" asked Oswald with annoyance. Fen sat down so fast she looked winded. "How's the new portrait coming along?" Oswald asked her, pouring her a drink.

She took it from him, still eyeing the tapestry with a pained expression. "What? Oh, er… I hardly know," she admitted.

407

"Signor Arnotti does not permit you to look at a work in progress."

She took a hasty sip and then coughed, as it appeared to go down the wrong way. "In any event, Bess is happy with the painting he did of her oldest hound, Padraig. She said he caught his noble expression most admirably."

"That's something at least," said Roland, pointing to her portrait accusingly. "Poor Bors looks like a smudgy blob in that one."

Fen grimaced. "More to the point, *I* look like a smudgy blob in that one."

Roland laughed, and for some inexplicable reason Oswald found himself feeling aggravated. He glared at his brother. "Why are you not out with your degenerate friends celebrating?" he asked ill-naturedly.

Roland shrugged. "Didn't feel like it, as it happens."

"A hollow victory?" asked Fen with interest. "Whose token did you wear?"

Roland shrugged again. "Lenora Montmayne," he said without much enthusiasm.

"Indeed?" said Fen with more interest than Oswald cared for. Fen seemed to catch his impatient gaze on her and gave a start. "Oh, I almost forgot we are dining tonight with the Schaeffers." She glanced down at her burgundy gown. "I'm already in my newest gown for the portrait sitting. I don't need a change of clothing, do I?" She looked appealingly at Oswald.

He let his gaze wander over her. Any excuse to look at her was welcome these days. Perhaps he could put the new portrait side by side with the old when it was finished?

"Husband?"

He refocused on her face. "You don't need to change your dress," he said, swiftly replaying her query in his mind.

"Good." She patted her leg and Bors trotted over to her for some fuss. "Would you believe that Ambrose did not even recognize Bors?" she asked indignantly. "Why, he still looks as noble as he ever did."

"Thane's an idiot," said Roland with disgust. "A man who can't even recognize his own dog doesn't deserve to be recognized as a man."

"Or a husband," said Oswald casually. He withdrew the rolled-up document from his tunic and tossed it toward Fenella.

She caught it clumsily and clasped it to her. "What is it?"

"Annulment papers," he said briefly. Fen's eyes widened, but she said nothing, though Roland gave an exclamation.

"You did it then," said his brother with a low whistle. "I thought it was just a rumor!" He held out his hand, and for some reason Fenella handed it to him. He unfurled it with interest.

"I think I might go and change my veil," said Fen, standing up. "I told Hester that I had one with a gold border and she said she

409

was thinking of getting one." She walked toward the bedroom and Oswald's eyes followed her moodily.

"Does this mean you get Fen's original dowry?" asked Roland, squinting at the script.

"No idea," said Oswald distractedly. "I haven't actually read the fine print yet."

His brother looked surprised. "Why else did you do it then?"

But Oswald was already walking toward their bedroom, after his wife. She was unpinning her veil when he entered the room. She looked over her shoulder at him and smiled. He shut the door and walked over to where she stood before the mirror.

She lifted a different veil. "Do you think this one will look as well?" she asked. "Usually, I let Trudy choose. She has such a good eye—" She broke off, catching sight of his expression. "What is it? What's wrong?"

"I suppose we do have to go to the Schaeffers'?" He scowled.

Fen watched him in the mirror with a slight frown. "We did not make it to the Duchess of Horberry's feast last week," she reminded him.

Oswald found he did not much care. "Should you mind very much if we missed it?" he asked.

Fen placed down a hair pin carefully. "Hester is my closest friend at court," she said. "And I should like to make a good impression on Lord Schaeffer for your sake." She looked wistful.

"For my sake?"

"Hester told me that Lord Schaeffer was your mentor at court in the early days." She tilted her chin up. "If I could just win over one person and not show myself up as some awful countrified embarrassment of a wife…"

"You're hardly that," he interjected swiftly.

"It would be one big step toward becoming a lady-in-waiting," she said, picking up her hair comb. "It is kind of you to say I am not an embarrassment, but I am not an asset to you at court either. And I should like to be. If I can."

She looked so fiercely sincere in this wish that Oswald knew not how to reply. Instead he reached inside his tunic and withdrew the box of rings, opening it and placing it on the surface before her. "Wear this," he said, picking out the smaller ring. She held out her hand and he slid the ring onto her finger.

She gazed down at it a moment. "Vawdrey panthers?" she asked, looking at the decoration on the blue enamel band.

"And Bernard bears," he said, holding up the box with the larger ring still in the box. "Like in your tapestry."

Her startled eyes met his, and she reached for the box and extracted the larger ring, slowly turning it over, before hesitantly holding it out to him. Instead of taking it, he held his hand out toward her.

Catching his meaning, she slid the ring onto his finger, where it fitted snugly. Her hand slid into his, and they stood silently a

411

moment, their hands clasped fast together, and Oswald found himself feeling strangely moved.

The strangest feeling nagged at him that he had experienced something like this once before. But when he tried to force the memory, it instantly disappeared.

30

Fen woke feeling groggy and disoriented. They had passed a pleasant evening with the Schaeffers and she had found herself relaxed and at ease for once at a social engagement. She had possibly had one more goblet of wine than she should have, but she had enjoyed herself and she flattered herself that Lord Schaeffer, who had seemed tense and a little stuffy at the outset, had also warmed to her.

She had gathered from the conversation that there was some delicate negotiation going on at present at court. She tried not to look too inquisitive or ask questions displaying her ignorance. She had, of course, heard of Princess Una and her claim to the throne, but she had no idea that there were still plots being quashed and uprisings being quelled on a monthly basis!

She had heard that the princess was a fierce creature, raised to join her father in battle, but according to Lord Schaeffer she was a poor, weary soul who had been dragged from battlefield to battlefield and longed for nothing more than to lead a peaceable life.

"'Tis said she both looks and acts like a man and rides a horse *astride*," Hester had told her in the hushed voice of one repeating scandal.

"What's that, Hester?" Lord Schaeffer had asked, beetling his brows at her.

"Nothing, Andrew dear," his wife had replied, before winking at Fen.

Fen had been itching to ask Oswald if he'd ever met the princess, but she remembered only too clearly that he had been most displeased when she'd shown an interest in his work, so she had instead suppressed her curiosity.

When they had returned to their rooms, her husband seemed in a strangely reticent mood, though he was physically as affectionate as ever. If anything, he had been *more* so than usual. After a bout of vigorous lovemaking, he had immediately curled up behind her instead of the usual rolling away and then coming back together as they slept.

When she first woke, his head had been pressed into the back of her neck and he was gently stroking her hip. He'd shushed her when she started to ask the hour, and turned her around so she fell back to sleep in his arms.

When she woke again, he was gone, but he had left his scarlet robe for her at the bottom of the bed. The first thing she did after washing was to replace the heavy ring he had given her back on her finger before dressing for another four-hour sitting with signor Arnotti.

It would have been tedious indeed, if were not for Eden Montmayne, who had kindly accompanied her this time. They talked of the Queen, who Eden greatly admired, and Eden's many artistic pursuits: dancing, poetry, tapestry, music—there seemed no end to them. Fen noted how Eden apparently flourished at court with all her talents.

She wanted to ask if she had no admirers or suitors, but something held her back. Perhaps the fact that Eden was an orphan, and her uncle was probably too busy fending off suitors for his beautiful daughter, Lenora, than he was trying to find a suitable match for his niece. At midday, signor Arnotti announced the light was no longer conducive to his aims and picked up his canvas and bag of brushes and left.

"He is very abrupt, is he not?" wondered Fen aloud.

"Oh yes. That is why he has not heretofore made it as a fashionable portrait painter," said Eden. "He lacks the ability to flatter or amuse his patrons."

"I hope he manages to flatter them on canvas," joked Fen weakly.

She had nearly been put off her breakfast by the sight of her pudgy fifteen-year-old self staring out of a frame that morning. She heartily hoped this portrait would be able to replace her old one.

Eden looked a little unsure. "He certainly has a very unique eye. I do not lay claim that his vision will universally please," she said cautiously.

"But Lady Hartleby was very pleased, was she not? With his work?"

"Signor Arnotti has only made the preliminary sketches of her dogs thus far," said Eden with a shrug. "Bess herself has not yet committed to sit for the prerequisite amount of hours he requires for a portrait." Eden gave her a sidelong look. "Which is why he is now working exclusively on your painting."

"Oh dear," said Fen. "She really did only want a painting of her dogs."

Eden smiled. "We shall see who comes out the victor. They both have very strong personalities, do they not?"

"They most certainly do!" agreed Fen fervently. "Still, I should not wish to be embroiled in their quarrel, for I do not have many friends at court, and I had hoped Bess would be one of their number."

"I do not think she is so easily offended," said Eden. "Perhaps you might invite Lady Bess to join you in a walk with your dogs?" she suggested. "I hear you and Lady Schaeffer exercise your hounds most days."

"That is a very excellent notion," Fen agreed, brightening up. To her surprise, a page hurried over with a note for her. She took it from him and hastily retrieved a coin from the purse suspended from her belt. "Thank you." She broke it open. "Why, it's from Mr. Entner!"

"Your playwright," said Eden.

Fen scanned the letter. "He writes that he has finished his play!"

"Ah, that is good news," said Eden with satisfaction.

"He asks if he can deliver a copy of it to me this afternoon." She turned the page over to read the postscript. "I am to send a reply with the deliverer of the note."

She looked up to find the page still hovering nearby. "Yes, that would be agreeable," she told him, and he took off, his green hose flashing. "I am going to walk down and meet him in the main courtyard."

"I will come down with you," said Eden. "For it is on my way."

They linked arms and made their way down together. Mr. Entner bowed very low when he saw both her and Eden, and to Fen's eye, he looked even more nervous than the last time she had seen him. He dropped his hat twice and made very poor eye contact as Eden bade them farewell. He waited until Eden had disappeared from view and then handed over the bundle of closely written papers to Fen.

"*The Tragical History of a Lady Most Foully Betrayed in Three Acts: A Morality Play*," Fen read aloud from the front page. She peered over the top of the manuscript at Mr. Entner. "But what happened to the donkey?" she asked in bewilderment.

He shrugged. "My muse took me in a different direction," he said evasively.

A pucker of apprehension appeared on Fen's brow. "What happened to her?"

"I couldn't get beyond the first few scenes," he replied. "The donkey metaphor seemed labored and—"

"Not the donkey," Fen corrected him testily. "The tragical woman most cruelly betrayed." She held up the manuscript.

Mr. Entner reddened. "Foully betrayed," he corrected her. "I could not do the subject matter justice by summarizing the plot. 'Twere much better if you simply read it yourself."

Fen had a sinking feeling about the whole thing. She clutched the pages so hard her knuckles turned white. "Mr. Entner—" she started.

417

He shot up to his full height. "Rehearsals have already started," he said defensively. "People are saying this is my most seminal piece of work."

"People?" she echoed.

"My wife and brother-in-law then."

Fen looked about them. All around, courtiers and servants were milling. She lowered her voice. "Very well, I shall read it, Mr. Entner, but make no mistake if I find—"

"Your very gracious servant," he said loudly, bowed, and then scurried away as Fen stared after him.

Fen made her way back to their rooms feeling deeply uneasy. Hester Schaeffer was coming over to visit with her in two hours, which she hoped would give her ample time to wade through Mr. Entner's play.

She closed the door behind her, dragged a blanket out of the chest, and bundled herself into the window seat to plough through it. At various points, Meldon appeared to throw some more logs on the fire. Trudy tiptoed in at one point for some direction on what refreshments they were serving to her guest later, but otherwise Fen was left in peace to decipher Mr. Entner's cramped hand, as a grandiose tale of woe and treachery unfolded before her horrified gaze.

"Hester," Fen announced hollowly as soon as her friend arrived. "I have read Mr. Entner's play."

Her friend regarded her thoughtfully. "Oh dear, is it really that bad?" she asked, drawing off her gloves. "It is so difficult to find a playwright of good quality these days."

"It is not the quality that troubles me," blurted Fen. "But rather the subject matter!"

"Indeed?" Hester Schaeffer's eyebrows shot into her hairline. "Pray do tell. No!" she said, throwing up an elegant hand. "On second thought, allow me to guess!" She chose the seat facing away from the window and selected a piece of marchpane that Trudy had set out for them. Fen watched her distractedly. "Patricide!" her friend ventured with her eyes glowing.

"Nay."

"Matricide?"

"'Tis not murder of any kind."

"Oh, not incest *again*," sighed Hester in disapproval. "One gets so tired of it!"

"Suicide!" burst out Fen. "Of a lady most unhappily thrown over by her husband."

Hester leaned back in her seat with a thoughtful expression. "Oh, I *see*," she said. "Clever Mr. Entner."

"Clever?" echoed Fen, wringing her hands. "Everyone will think I put him up to it!"

"And what if they do?" Her friend shrugged. "'Tis considered a vastly elegant way of getting revenge on an enemy. Having a thinly veiled insult acted out to them as a play."

"Is it?"

"Why of course, my sweet Fenella. Why do you suppose Sir Inverdale sponsored that piece of theater last year that set everyone by their ears? *Lady Jarrow's Innocence.*"

"I've never heard of it," admitted Fen dully. She picked up a piece of marchpane and ate it distractedly, barely even registering what it tasted like.

"I forget Thane kept you buried in the country," sighed Hester. "Well, it was naught but a cleverly concealed barb about the checkered history of Lord Heber's third wife. Everyone knew she was the mistress of the Earl of Wallace."

Fen tapped her foot impatiently. She was not one whit interested in any of these awful-sounding people! "But—"

Lady Schaeffer held up a hand again. "No, no, my dear Fenella. You must allow yourself to be led by me in such things. Depend upon it, you are upsetting yourself over naught." Fen chewed on her bottom lip. Could Hester be right? "Why don't I read it?" suggested her friend.

"Oh, would you?" said Fen eagerly. "Now that really would reassure me!"

"Of course," said Hester soothingly. "Now, pray put it completely out of your mind, for I want to tell you what

Andrew said to me as soon as you and Lord Vawdrey left us last night."

Fen, who was in the act of tidying all the papers together into one pile, abruptly stopped. "What did Lord Schaeffer say?"

"He said that *despite* the fact he refused to listen to rumor as a matter of principle, he could see that everything being bandied about regarding your and Lord Vawdrey's marriage was entirely true." Hester sat back in her seat with an expression of utmost satisfaction. "Now what do you say to that, my dear?"

Fen paled and stared down at her hands on her lap. "I don't know what *is* being bandied about," she said with a helpless shrug.

"My dear," admonished Hester. "What about your servants? Have you not been interrogating them?"

"No," admitted Fen. "Trudy did tell me some gossip on her first day, but I didn't think I ought to encourage it."

Hester rolled her eyes. "How else are you supposed to find out what is doing the rounds? Unless you have a gossipy friend or two." Her eyes were roaming around the room with a faint pucker between her brows. "My dear, who is that positively gloomy child?" she asked, staring at Fen's portrait.

Fen puffed out her cheeks in frustration. "Hester, please!"

"A younger sister?" hazarded Hester. "If so, you must bring the poor child to court. She looks as though her life is positively dreary! I must say"—she leaned forward in her seat and gazed about her—"it does look a good deal more colorful in here than the last time I visited you. Is it that rather extraordinary tapestry? Where did you get it?" When Hester looked as if she would get up to examine the tapestry, Fen nearly jumped out of her chair.

"But what is the current gossip about my marriage?" she demanded in exasperation.

Hester smiled triumphantly and settled back in her seat. "Ah—a sensible question! Never fear, I shall tell you." She took a sip of fruit juice. "Why, that you have quite overset your poor husband's orderly bachelor life onto its head! That he no longer knows whether he is coming or going. That his every waking moment is consumed with thoughts of you and wiping your previous marriage from the annals of history."

Fen stared at her friend, aghast. "But—"

"Do not deny it!" she said, holding up her hand. "For even my prosaic spouse now believes it to be nothing more than the truth!"

Fen cast her mind back to the previous evening. "But Oswald did nothing last night to make Lord Schaeffer believe such a thing!" she objected.

"Did he not?" asked Hester archly. "Did he not indeed?"

Fen cast about in her memory, but nothing sprung to mind. Her husband had been his usual attentive self, but she could find no reason for Lord Schaeffer to believe him suddenly infatuated with her.

"Apparently Lord Vawdrey has been similarly distracted during his council duties. It has been much commented on. Andrew said even the King remarked upon it last month. It has been highly diverting for them all. Before now they have all thought him quite the perfect politician. Almost single-minded in carrying out his duties, with no life outside of it whatsoever."

Fen twisted her fingers in her lap, remembering her father's beliefs that ambition had caused Oswald Vawdrey to break his vow to her. But in her experience, he had been nothing but thoughtful and solicitous of her feelings since acknowledging her as his wife.

True, she had managed to displease him on a couple of occasions, but he had climbed down off his high horse swiftly and shown that he was sorry by his actions, rather than his words. She did not like the thought that she was bringing his reputation into any kind of disrepute.

"He is always very conscientious in his duty to the King," she said defensively. "And it seems to me that he takes his duties as head of the Vawdrey family very seriously."

"Oh, everyone knows that," said Hester with a sweep of her hand. "And he has very firm convictions. Otherwise, why would he cross King Wymer about the fate of the Blechmarsh princess? Everyone agrees that he has quite a brilliant mind. It is only that he has always seemed"—her friend broke off with a wince and a shrug of her shoulders—"something of a cold fish."

Fen nearly choked on her marchpane. "That—that does not sound like the husband I know," she answered truthfully. "He is not cold at all, but rather—" She broke off, not wanting to be indiscreet.

423

For how could she explain that her husband's public image concealed a very sensual and passionate man? She could not. Nor could she explain that when Oswald spoke in his most polite, cool voice, he was often masking some fury. "Sometimes," she ventured, "his words tell one story, but…"

"His actions another?" suggested Hester.

"Yes. No. Not exactly," sighed Fen. It was more complicated than that. "He is not the most straightforward man, but…" She halted, realizing she could not explain it adequately. "He is a very good husband," she finished lamely.

"You must not look so serious," Hester implored her. "I want to hear all about this annulment business." She helped herself to another piece of marchpane and settled back into her seat. "Now make sure you tell me everything and leave out not a single detail."

*

Hester stayed some two hours and left promising to read the play as soon as she was able. Fen found she could not settle after she had left, but instead unpacked and reordered all of her trunks with her ever-growing amount of clothing.

She even made a bundle of her Sitchmarsh dresses to give to Trudy. Her maid would be able to alter, or perhaps cut them down for her children, or do whatever she wished with them. She had no excuse for keeping hold of them now she had no firm date that she was going down to the country.

After this, she wrapped up warm in her sky-blue cloak and scarlet gloves and she and Bors went for a walk in the castle grounds. It was a crisp and cold afternoon, and Fen lost track of time as they enjoyed the fresh air.

They had walked all the way to the rose gardens before Fen realized that it was rapidly turning dark, and they would have to think about turning back. They made haste to hurry back toward the castle but did not beat the descending dusk. The exercise had blown the cobwebs from her mind, but she was still in turmoil over the play which loomed over her like a dark cloud on the horizon.

So absorbed was she in her thoughts that she almost fell over the profusion of trunks and boxes piled up outside their rooms. Bors barked as she stumbled and caught hold of the door handle, which swung inward with her still clinging on to it, and scraped her knees on the floorboards.

A hush fell over the room, and she looked up, to her embarrassment finding the reception room full of occupants, all of whom were staring at her. Fen stared back at them, a cold feeling creeping up her spine. Her gaze went from the two small little girls sat on the window seat, to a red-haired lady sat by the fire holding an equally red-haired baby, to a tall, glowering male stood with his back to the fire. Her gaze fixed on him, and she swallowed.

Now this was definitely a Vawdrey. The dark hair, the powerful build, the height all gave it away. If she wasn't mistaken, this was Mason Vawdrey. Which meant, she thought dazedly, that this was her other brother-in-law with his family.

425

"Hello," she croaked, still clinging to the door handle. The sound of footsteps behind her had her turning to look back over her shoulder as Oswald came striding down the corridor toward her, a hard and angry look on his face.

He didn't even blink an eye at finding her on her knees. His hands were under her armpits in an instant, dragging her to her feet. "Where the hells have you been?" he hissed, spinning her round to face him. "I've had Bryce running from room to room, checking on your friends' whereabouts! Lady Schaeffer said she left you here some three hours ago!"

"Oswald, your family—" she began, darting her eyes toward the other people in the room, but he ignored her.

"You didn't tell your maid or Meldon where you were going!" he continued to rage, slashing one hand through the air. "What the hells was I supposed to think when I got back here and found you missing?"

"Missing?" Fen's mouth dropped open. "I just went for a walk with Bors," she said helplessly, and started to glance around for her dog, but Oswald's hand caught her chin and brought her attention forcibly back to him.

"Don't. Do. That. Again," he said ominously.

"Walk my dog?" asked Fen in confusion. His expression turned livid, and she hurriedly tried to explain: "Neither Meldon nor Trudy were here, and I didn't think it was as late as it was when I set out." To her embarrassment, tears had sprung into her eyes, and she tried to blink them back. "The portrait sitting took up such a chunk of my time this morning that I fell behind. I'm sorry—"

426

As if becoming aware of their audience, Oswald released her so abruptly that she almost tottered back, except his hand shot out to catch her again above the elbow. "Let us discuss this later," he said stiffly, and turned her about to face his family. "This is my brother Mason and his family. Linnet, his wife. My nieces, Margaret and Lily, my nephew, Archie."

So, he had been aware of their presence! Fen managed an awkward curtsey as Linnet, hampered by a baby on her lap, nodded her head with a hesitant smile. Mason Vawdrey was frowning at her, his arms crossed, and a severe look on his face. He did not look pleased to meet her.

"Girls, come and greet your new aunt," Linnet directed her daughters, who dropped down off the window seat and approached her, dragging their feet. They only got halfway across the room before they bobbed their curtseys and fled back to their window seat. "I'm afraid they're rather shy until they get to know you," she added.

"It's very nice to meet you, girls," Fenella called after them feebly. She felt in utter disgrace, her face hot and no doubt red as a ripe apple. Looking around the room, she was unsure where to put herself. She could hardly run to their bedroom like a frightened rabbit.

Instead, she unfastened her cloak and draped it over a chair, wishing she could sink through the floorboards. Collapsing into a corner seat, she busied herself unfastening her gloves and trying not to feel conspicuous.

"You must not sit there in a dark corner," Linnet protested, "or you will make me feel like we have driven you away from the

427

hearth. Do draw your chair near to the fire and sit with me. I have been so anxious to meet you."

Fen looked up and saw her sister-in-law had a kindly and earnest look on her face—that, and a good many freckles.

Linnet smiled again invitingly and shifted the baby on her lap. "I declare I can scarcely feel my legs," she groaned. And no wonder, for her baby was a large one, thought Fen, looking at his chubby cheeks. Mason broke off speaking to Oswald and wordlessly reached down to take the baby from his wife. He slung his son over one shoulder and turned back to his brother without pause in the conversation.

Fen stood up and started to lift her chair, only to find it taken out of her hands by her husband, who carried it over to the fireplace and set it down next to Linnet's. He, too, returned to his conversation with Mason, almost seamlessly. Fen noticed, as she arranged her skirts, that they were talking about the state of the roads on the journey down from Cadwallader.

Fen cleared her throat. "I do hope your journey was not too arduous," she said, taking her cue from them. "It must be difficult traveling with small children."

"Oh, not so as you'd notice," said Linnet cheerfully. "We've got our servants Gertie and Nan with us, who positively dote on them. And Cuthbert, Mason's squire, always helps out too."

She looked around distractedly. "Where is that boy? He must have snuck off. Either to the kitchens or the stables, I'll be bound."

Feeling a gaze on her, Fen turned her head to find the infant gazing steadfastly at her from his father's shoulder. He crammed one of his chubby hands into his mouth and drooled on it.

"What a fine boy," said Fen. Despite his shock of red hair, the brooding glower already marked him out as a Vawdrey. "I understand he is my husband's godson."

"Yes, that's right," answered Linnet, sounding pleased. "I do hope my brood won't get under your feet too much over the next couple of weeks."

Fen looked up, finding the two dark-haired little girls had crept in closer to hear their conversation. "Oh, of course not," she said encouragingly. "I hope we shall all become firm friends."

One of the little girls leaned against the arm of Fen's chair. Her hand crept up to place a small silver thimble on it. "For you," she whispered.

"Why, Lily, how thoughtful," said her mother. "A present for your aunt Fenella."

"How kind," said Fen, feeling quite touched. "Is it a Solstice gift?"

The little girl nodded but couldn't quite meet Fen's gaze. It occurred to Fen that Lily had some fellow feeling for a female so clearly in disgrace.

Another little girl appeared at her other elbow and tugged on her sleeve. "Yes?" asked Fen. "You must be Margaret."

"Meg," the other girl confided. She seemed a little bolder than Lily, for her eyes fleetingly did meet with Fen's. She pointed at the portrait above the fire. "Is that your little girl?" she asked.

Fen winced. "Um, actually that's me. When I was younger and first betrothed to your uncle Oswald."

Both girls' gazes were riveted on her now. "How fascinating!" said Linnet, clasping her hands together. "I've always been curious about Oswald's betrothals."

"Well, I'm afraid I only know about his first one," admitted Fen.

"Girls," said Linnet, looking at her daughters. "Aunt Fenella was chosen for your uncle by your grandfather, now what do you think about that?"

Both sets of green eyes widened. "Grandfather!" whispered Lily.

"You knew our grandfather?" asked Meg.

"Yes," agreed Fenella. "He had a big, booming voice and a large bushy beard."

"That was him," sighed Linnet fondly.

The girls, clearly taking this as an endorsement, crowded in closer. "Want to see your ring," said Meg. Fen held up her hand and all three females inspected it.

"Vawdrey panthers," murmured Meg, while Lily settled for running a finger over the ruby.

"How beautiful!" exclaimed Linnet. "And how thoughtful of Oswald." She looked as if she wanted to say more but was mindful of her children's presence. Instead, she settled for: "I do hope we can spend some time getting to know each other this Solstice."

"That would be nice," agreed Fen. Feeling a gaze on her again, she looked up expecting to see baby Archie, but instead found it was her husband looking at her. She smiled, but he turned swiftly away.

Supper was a much noisier affair with the Cadwalladers in residence. Cuthbert, who turned out to be a good-looking blond youth of about fifteen, reappeared, and after helping to carry the dishes through, joined them at the table to eat. Meg and Lily hung off his every word as he explained he had been to see the horses stabled.

Baby Archie was passed between the servants and the family as he reached for food, cutlery, and generally whatever was placed out of his reach. Whenever his will was thwarted, he let out a mind-numbing squawk and his face turned quite puce. "He's very strong-willed," Linnet said in what seemed to be simultaneously an apology and a boast as she tried, in vain, to extricate her hair from his grip.

Roland turned up as the final course was uncovered. "Gods," he groaned. "Did you not think to give us any warning?" He dutifully kissed Linnet's cheek and ruffled the girls' hair.

"Why?" asked Mason. "So you could make yourself scarce?"

431

"Is that you, Cuthbert?" Roland asked, sounding startled. "You've finally found some inches."

Cuthbert grinned and wiped his greasy fingers absently onto his tunic. "I'll be taller than you before next summer," he boasted.

Roland snorted before catching sight of the decimated meal. "Is this all that's left of the goose?" he complained. "Well, I like that!"

Gertie and Trudy were duly dispatched down to the kitchens to fetch more food, and Linnet moved around, ostensibly to make room for Roland. When she made a beeline in her direction, Fen suspected it was a deliberate ploy to have some quiet chat with her. She shuffled her chair across to make room for her sister-in-law.

Oswald at present was caught up in conversation with his two brothers, so they were free to converse. Archie was resettled onto his mother's lap. He was yawning now and blinking his eyes as if sleepy. Linnet filled Fen's goblet and then her own. "Now, while we have the opportunity," she said in a low voice, passing Fen her drink, "I would dearly love to hear how things stand with you and Oswald."

Fen took a hurried sip of the wine and winced. "I'm sure you noticed I am quite in his bad books at the moment but are just too kind to say it."

"Oh, that," said Linnet dismissively, "but that was nothing. He was just annoyed because he was concerned for you. One has to make allowances for husbands sometimes. They get very het up when they fear for your welfare."

Fen's eyes widened. "But I was only…"

"Oh yes, I know," agreed Linnet hurriedly. "But perhaps, when his whole day is taken up with such unpleasantness as a spymaster's are wont to, he could be excused for becoming a little overprotective."

Fen sat back in her seat. She had never considered that Oswald's line of work might have an effect on his behavior. He was talking now with Cuthbert. With a start, she realized Linnet was still speaking as she mopped the dribble from Archie's chin. "And mayhap," she suggested. "Sometimes, when he seems a little tense, you could reach out and just give him a little touch."

Fen, who was in the act of putting down her goblet, nearly missed the table. "A touch?" she repeated in surprised tones.

"The merest gesture," elaborated Linnet. "A fleeting touch, say to the back of his neck, or between his shoulder blades. Just to let him know." She beamed.

"Let him know what?" wondered Fen aloud.

"Why, that you support him, and he may depend on you."

Fen considered this as she mopped up the spilled drops of wine that had sloshed out of the cup. "It's just," she said with a faint frown, "that, well, Oswald is so very important, and I don't want to be thrusting my presence forward. Or trying to distract him," she said painstakingly.

"But you see," said Linnet, "sometimes they *need* to be distracted."

433

"They do?" asked Fen uncertainly as Archie lurched forward on his mother's lap and snatched a piece of buttered bread off the table.

His mother seemed unconcerned. "Oh yes," she carried on. "When they're angry and bellowing or perhaps sinking into a brooding sulk."

Fen's eyes widened. "Oh but—" She broke off.

"Yes?" said Linnet encouragingly.

"Well, Oswald doesn't really do any of those things. He's, well—" Fen watched as Archie squished the bread between his fingers. "Quite reserved in many ways."

Linnet nodded. "That is certainly the impression he gives. And yet—" She jiggled Archie on her knee. "I have certainly heard some interesting tales since your marriage which have made me wonder…" She broke off with a smile.

"Made you wonder?" prompted Fen as Archie reached for a second piece of bread with his other hand.

"Finish with that one first, dearest," advised Linnet. Her son ignored her, and she turned back to Fen. "I wondered if perhaps Oswald is not quite so different from Mason after all."

Fen pondered this in some confusion. Mason Vawdrey seemed like a terrifying ogre to her. Oswald was more like a dark prince under a spell. "What stories did you hear, I wonder?" she asked with misgiving.

434

"Oh well, the one where he dragged Sir Thane down the corridor in nothing but his nightcap until he renounced all claim on you. That one's my favorite."

"His claim on me?" echoed Fen, quite mystified.

"Oh yes, we heard at least four versions of that story, which reached us even at Cadwallader. In my favorite version, Sir Ambrose offers his every family treasure from his coffers in exchange for your return. 'For no jewel,' quoth he, 'could compare to the one I have lost, which was peerless.'"

Fen's mouth dropped open. "But that's not what happened at all!" she protested, shocked.

"Oh, but it's such a good story, don't you agree?" asked Linnet enthusiastically.

Fen stared. "I never even heard it before!" And it gave her a nasty reminder of that wretched play of Mr. Entner's.

"Of course, Oswald is something of a villain in that retelling," admitted Linnet. "But sometimes the villains are so much more intriguing than a dull, worthy hero. Don't you agree?"

Fen had no idea how to respond to this. Luckily Archie chose this moment to hold out both chubby, buttery fists toward her.

"Oh, look at that," crowed Linnet. "He wants to come to his aunt Fenella!"

"Does he really?" asked Fenella. With nervous hands she heaved the boy onto her own lap. He tipped back his head to solemnly look at her. "You're a fine big boy," she told him.

435

Archie let out an ear-splitting screech. "What is it?" Fen gasped.

"Oh naught," his mother replied airily. "He's just testing out his lungs." She looked at her son with maternal pride. "Isn't that right, my dearest?"

Archie dropped a piece of mangled bread on Fen's skirts and then looked up at her to see how she accepted this beneficence.

"Thank you?" Fen ventured. He beamed.

"You're very good with children," said Linnet generously.

"I haven't really had much experience," admitted Fen.

"You can't tell in the least," Linnet assured her.

31

As she undressed, Fen thought furiously about *The Tragical History of a Lady Most Foully Betrayed*. She would have to send word to Hester tomorrow and see how she was faring with her read-through. Something would have to be done about it. After her conversation with Linnet, she had some vague idea that a rewrite could solve all her problems. As it stood, the play was terribly gloomy.

The betrayed lady was a virtuous martyr upon whom misfortune after misfortune was heaped until she died of a broken heart. Her faithless husband abandoned her in the first act. She was forced into a loveless remarriage in the second act, and in the third she expired.

But perhaps, thought Fen, if the play was rewritten, then she would not be viewed afterward by everyone as some kind of forlorn victim? Or perhaps if the second husband could be turned into a villain instead of an uncaring, ambitious sort, then surely people would know that it was not Oswald?

"Fenella?"

Fen looked up startled to see Oswald looking at her in the mirrored glass. Had he asked her something? "Your pardon," she said hurriedly. "I did not catch what you said."

He frowned and lowered his washcloth. "I said I hope the arrival of more Vawdreys does not discomfort you."

"Of course not," she said, laying her dress over the back of the chair. "Linnet and the children are very pleasant company."

"Then why do you look so worried?" he asked bluntly. "Is it my brother, Mason? His bark is worse than his bite, I assure you."

"It's not that at all," Fen assured him. "I was only thinking through some…hypothetical matter."

He rolled his eyes. "Is Eden Montmayne dragging you to philosophical debates now?" He went back to washing his neck. "My advice," he said, "is not to accompany her if you don't care for it. You can say no."

Fen bit her lip and laid her stockings over the arm of the chair. "Would you rather be viewed in history as a villain or a victim of circumstances?" she asked. Then added rashly: "I think I'd rather be a villain."

Maybe that was it, thought Fen, dropping her garters. The foully betrayed woman could be depicted instead as a scheming villainess! Then everyone would know it wasn't her! She stooped for her bright green garters and clutched them to her chest. It was sheer inspiration! She would ask Mr. Entner to rewrite the roles on the morrow!

Oswald straightened up and gave her a quizzical look. "You, a villain?" he repeated, unlacing his tunic.

"Yes," agreed Fen enthusiastically.

Oswald cocked his head to one side as if considering it. "And what villainy would you be guilty of?" he asked.

"P-poisoning?" she suggested uncertainly.

438

Oswald's lips twitched, and she thought for a moment he would laugh.

Fen felt unaccountably annoyed. "I could be a villain if I wanted to," she said, plunking a hand on one hip. She cast about wildly for something other villainous women could perpetrate. His gaze seemed to linger on her, and Fen remembered she was stood only in her thin shift. "I could be a scheming seductress," she said unthinkingly. To her surprise, the humor seemed to drop from Oswald's face.

His eyes traveled over her and seemed to darken. "Prove it," he said in a husky voice and threw down the cloth he was drying himself with. Fen caught her breath. *What?* He crossed the room, and to her disappointment, instead of drawing her into his arms, he brushed right past her and walked toward the bed.

Fen swiveled on her heel to turn and watch as he climbed onto the bed. Unusually, he was still wearing his white linen braies. Fen frowned; her husband *always* slept naked. He settled on his back, his arms folded behind his head.

"Come and seduce me, Fen," he said, and crossed his ankles.

Something about his casual pose irritated her. Did he think she couldn't? "I will," she fired up, then lapsed into a thoughtful silence as she cautiously approached the bed. One glance at his tented braies assured her he was not as indifferent as his pose suggested. "You did lock the door, didn't you?" she asked, momentarily distracted.

He definitely smiled at this. "Yes. Stop stalling for time, madam wife."

"I'm not." She frowned, sitting on the edge of the bed next to him.

Thinking of Linnet's words, she placed her hand on his muscular belly. From his reaction, she guessed it was not the reassuring touch her sister-in-law had spoken of. Oswald's stomach muscles rippled beneath her touch, and he gave a muffled noise of surprise and something else. Her eyes flew to his.

In answer to the question in her gaze, he said, "I thought you would kiss me first." To Fen's surprise, he sounded slightly breathless. He withdrew his hands from behind his head and reached up to grip the headboard. "Don't stop."

Fenella left her hand where it lay, and at his words, she traced the bunched muscle with her fingertips. This time he drew in a sharp breath before letting it out again on a shudder. Fen was enthralled. She had no idea how she was doing it, but it was definitely working.

A notion struck her, and before she could lose her nerve, she stood up from the mattress and drew her shift over her head before dropping it on the floor. The flickering candlelight was hopefully more flattering than the cold light of day, she thought as she turned slowly in a small circle, displaying herself for her husband to view.

Her gaze flew to his for reassurance, and she was almost scorched alive. Oswald Vawdrey's gaze was searing. He hadn't moved an inch, and his eyes were glued to her. Emboldened, she clambered onto the bed, trying to make her movement fluid, then swung a leg over his so she settled across his muscular thighs.

He groaned at this and shifted under her slightly. She knew a moment's panic that she might be too heavy, but before she could voice it, he ground out, "Move higher up, Fen."

"Are you uncomfortable?"

"You could say that."

She glanced down at his burgeoning crotch area and shook her head. "Not yet," she said, remembering his own unhurried explorations of her body. She felt tingly and a little breathless at this point herself. He huffed, and she placed her hands daringly on his inner thighs. His body jerked, and he let out a startled exclamation, half sitting up.

"I need to take these off," he muttered, reaching for the ties on his braies.

"Why did you leave them on?" she asked, intrigued.

"So you could take them off me." He gave a short laugh. "I thought you might run short on seduction ideas."

"I can take them off," she objected. "Let me."

"No," he said emphatically. "There's only so much I can stand." He had them untied, and Fen climbed off him with a sigh as he efficiently shucked them off.

"I was supposed to be seducing you," she reminded him, reaching for the top bedsheet.

"You are," he said thickly and caught her wrist. "Don't disappear under the bedclothes." He pulled her back over him as he fell on his back. Fen settled awkwardly in his lap. His hands were on her backside now, squeezing and fondling her.

"Um," she started uncertainly.

"You're still in charge," he told her. Sadly, thought Fen, now she really had run out of ideas! Absently, her hands fell down to lightly pet the part of him bumping insistently against her soft belly. His hips pressed forward hard, and his eyes closed. Fen could see the muscle in his neck strain.

"Fen," he panted. *Oh*. Now that he *definitely* liked. Tentatively, she closed her fingers around his thick staff and lightly squeezed. His grasp on her behind tightened, and he muttered something she couldn't quite make out. She ran her thumb up and down his turgid length and then dipped below to lightly trace his balls. His eyes flew open, and their gazes met. Fen felt herself melt in what she glimpsed there.

Feeling flushed and reckless, she pressed forward and kissed him lingeringly on the lips. His mouth opened beneath hers, and daringly Fen slid her tongue into his mouth. Their kiss exploded in wet, molten heat.

Fen rubbed her bare breasts against his chest and wound her arms around his neck. His hands slid around from her buttocks to her hips, and he pulled and pushed her against his hard maleness until he was where he wanted to be. Fen wrenched her mouth from his as she confusedly realized she was still on top.

As if aware of her thoughts he murmured, "Trust me, it works this way too."

442

Fen nodded, her eyes wide as he seized her thighs and pulled her down onto him as he thrust up, until he was fully sheathed inside her. Fen whimpered at the sensation of fullness, which felt considerable from this angle.

Tentatively she dropped her knees down onto the mattress on either side of him. "How does this…?"

"Give me a moment," he said tightly. "Don't move yet."

Move? Fen sat still, feeling him throbbing inside of her. Which must mean he *really* liked it, as he never achieved rapture before her. Fen cautiously sat up straight, gazing down at him. A few locks of his dark hair had fallen forward onto his face. He was so handsome, she thought, misty-eyed, even more so than when he was a youth.

Oswald's eyes flicked open and focused on her. "*Gods*," he whispered. "I don't know if I'll last long." He reached up and palmed her heavy breasts, making her shiver. Then he slid one hand down the middle of her belly, dipping between her legs. When he touched the slick, warm folds there, surrounding his hardness, feeling where she took him into her body, Fen shuddered.

His other hand was still at her breast. As one thumb rubbed over and around her nipple, the other found the sensitive pearl between her legs and began to move in the same motion. Pleasure streaking through her body, Fen threw her head back and began to rock forward and back as the feelings intensified and seemed to swirl where she felt him, hard and thick, giving her what she needed. His hand at her breast slid down to grasp her hip, encouraging its fitful movement to take on a more purposeful stroke.

"Move on me, Fen," he urged, his voice gravelly and rough, lacking the usual polish. Anxious to please him and find her own relief, Fen fell forward, planting her palms on the mattress on either side of his shoulders.

She shifted her hips over him, making him grunt and groan even as she bit her lip to stifle her own. She huffed and puffed, grasping the bedsheets as she rose and fell over him. "Wait," she gasped at last when she felt like her arms were too wobbly to support her anymore and she couldn't keep up the pace. "I'm—"

"Too good at this," he groaned, releasing the headboard and rolling her over onto her back. Fen arched her back and wrapped her legs around his hips as she felt the beginning of her own release. To her surprise, he only drove into her twice when with a muffled roar he pressed her into the mattress and spilled his seed inside her. Fen tightened her clasp on him, and they lay in a tangle for a few heartbeats, breathing heavily.

When he lifted his head from her shoulder, he looked a little shaken. "I think you've proved your point. You're a very effective seductress."

"I was, wasn't I?" marveled Fen. Oswald kissed her again, lingeringly before stretching out and curling around her, his hand on her stomach. Fen fell asleep without even once thinking about the wretched play.

32

The next morning, Fen woke groggily to find Oswald had already left. She crawled out of bed and started to wash with the half-full jug of tepid water still left on the side. She had a slight feeling of dread already when she thought about Mr. Entner and his play. Trudy poked her head through the door just as she was finishing her ablutions.

"Oh, milady, I wasn't sure as you'd be rising yet."

"Not to worry, Trudy," Fen assured her, drying the back of her neck. "Could you please put me out some clothes for the day? You're much better at picking them than I."

Trudy beamed and hurried into the room. "You're sure you don't want more hot water?" she asked as she started pulling out stockings and a clean shift.

"No, thank you. Are any of the rest of the family at breakfast yet?" asked Fen nervously.

"They're all sleeping in after their journey yesterday."

"Excellent," murmured Fen. With a bit of luck, she could slip away for her sitting with signor Arnotti without any awkward exchanges first. She hurriedly pulled on the gown of emerald green with gold flowers embroidered down the sleeves and sat fastening her front lacing as Trudy brushed and dressed her hair. "This is a lovely dress. I must tell my husband to stop buying any more. I must have a dozen at least."

"Don't you have to wear your plum-colored dress for the painting?" puzzled Trudy as she pinned the veil to her coif at the back of her head.

"Oh, not today. He said he'd finished his preliminary sketches of my figure. Next, he will be studying my face. He's concentrating on the way the light falls and such," said Fen vaguely, having no idea how painters worked.

"Good thing we've put your hair out of the way then," murmured Trudy smugly as Fen donned her enamel ruby ring and her pearls.

"You think of everything, Trudy."

"You've had two letters come this morning, milady. I put them on the table for you to have when you break your fast."

"Two letters?" asked Fen in surprise as she rose from her chair. While it was true, she was expecting a letter from Orla, she had no notion who the other could be from. She made her way into the adjoining room and only just bit back an exclamation at the sight of who loomed there, wolfing down a large platter of salted fish and white bread.
"Oh! Good morning, my lord," she faltered as she pulled out a chair opposite her brother-in-law Mason Vawdrey, Duke of Cadwallader. He was a rather imposing sight to have to confront at this time of the morning.

His eyebrow rose at her formal greeting. "You'd better call me Mason," he said abruptly. It was clear he took no pleasure in the thought.

"Thank you, I will. And I hope you will call me Fenella," she said cheerfully. "I thought for a moment you were Roland. You must be something of the same height." She looked around distractedly for Bors.

"He's not here," said Mason.

"Who?"

"Roland."

"I'm looking for my dog," Fenella explained. "Though in truth, they are usually to be found together. Roland seems determined to purloin Bors's affections. I'm convinced he lets him sleep with him, though he denies it every time and claims he sneaks into his chamber in the night."

Mason looked at her and Fenella pressed her lips together. Was she talking too much? She knew some gentlemen did not wish to be prattled at so early in the morning. But she was nervous and couldn't seem to stem the tide.

"Roland has stolen your dog?" Mason repeated blankly. He looked at her sternly, as if convinced she was making it up.

"To all intents and purposes," Fenella agreed and reached for a piece of bread.

He considered this a moment, then dismissed it with a shrug and recommended chewing.
Fen turned over both her letters and was surprised to find that one was from Gil. Her brother was not known for the frequency of his correspondence. Indeed, she had received only one

447

dashed-off note from him since he had returned to Sitchmarsh nearly two months ago.

She broke his open before Orla's and frowned down at her brother's scrawled hand with a sigh. It seemed even worse than usual, she thought distractedly, taking a mouthful of salted cod. And no wonder, for on scanning the first two lines it seemed her brother had written it in something of a temper. She blinked at his vehemence.

He was being "pursued by a harridan" who turned his house upside down, he complained, "and blighted his life." Fen's eyebrows rose. She by no means admired her brother's taste in women, but she doubted that the current fancy, a buxom widow, would have shown her hand before she had her feet firmly under the table.

Fen had always thought Sarah Yondy to be a rather unpleasant woman who hid her sharp edges behind a cooing tongue. She wondered what could have happened for Sarah to have dropped the coy façade she usually employed around men. Unfortunately, the next paragraph was a mess of inkblots and crossing-outs.

Though she stared and held the page to her nose and then away from her face, the full length of her arm, she could make nothing of it. She turned it over in defeat and found her brother seemed to expect her to do something about it! *I beg you will call her off her quarry, your own poor brother, whom she has backed into a corner and looks to wolf down in one bite.*

Fen lowered the page in consternation. Whatever could Gil expect *her* to do about Sarah Yondy? She hadn't spoken to the woman in at least three years and they had never been friends!

Gil had finished with a flourish and signed himself off "your beleaguered brother." Well, she thought it was *beleaguered*, though it could have just as easily been *badgered* or *bludgeoned*.

"Do you have a problem with your eyes?" asked Mason, whose presence she had completely forgotten.

Fen looked up hastily. "No, no. 'Tis just my brother's penmanship is so very bad. I can make neither head nor tail of it."

Mason was still regarding her suspiciously. Rather like he thought someone had traded his brother a broken-down old nag, thought Fen indignantly. "I can see perfectly well, I assure you."

He snorted and gestured toward the sprawling tapestry taking up most of the walls. "If that's true, then why did you give Oswald a pair of wings?" he asked.

Fenella drew in a deep breath, feeling her face redden. "Because I was fifteen and full of fancies," she admitted, still avoiding looking at it. Maybe she could hang a shield over it or something? Roland was always leaving pieces of armor around the place. She poured a cup of water and drank it down, only too aware that her brother-in-law was still watching her narrowly.

"He's the finest man I know," said Mason Vawdrey abruptly. "If you've any sense you'll realize your good fortune fast and make sure you don't let him down."

Let him down? Fen felt her face drain of color as she watched her brother-in-law throw down his napkin and rise from the table. He gave a sharp nod in her direction and strode from the room. Fen sat a moment in complete silence, her appetite suddenly quite lost. She pushed her plate away and covered her face with her hands.

That wretched play had been hanging over her as soon as she awoke this morning, like a grisly specter. She needed to *do* something! In some haste she went to fetch her writing things. She stuffed Orla's letter into the purse which hung from her belt. She would read it later when sitting for her portrait.

Dipping her pen into the ink, she wrote a short note to Hester asking if she had read the play yet and if she could meet with her that day to offer her any advice, explaining she would not be free before two o'clock. She was just folding the missive when the door squeaked and Mason's squire, young Cuthbert, sauntered in dressed in a yellow tunic which matched his golden hair.

"Morning, Lady Vawdrey," he greeted her agreeably.

"Good morning. You've missed your master, I'm afraid."

"I've seen him," said Cuthbert. "He wants me to make myself useful about here today." A faint cloud passed over his face, as if he would much rather be further afield. "What's that?" he asked, perking up. "A letter? I could deliver it."

He looked so hopeful, Fen found herself passing it to him. "Do you know where the Schaeffers have quarters in the palace?"

"No, but I can soon find out," said Cuthbert.

"Well, that is for Lady Hester Schaeffer."

Cuthbert disappeared out the door before she could even fetch him a penny. As he went out, Meldon came in, grumbling and carrying a tray with more bread and butter. "Young villain," Meldon muttered without any heat. "He eats more herrings of a morning than any Vawdrey about the place!"

Mindful of Oswald's concern the previous day, she thought she'd better tell all the servants this time. "Meldon, I am going to the lower gallery to sit for my portrait this morning. I won't be back until midday."

"Again?" he asked waspishly. "How many paintings you having done anyway?"

Fenella ignored this. "Do you know where Bors is? I thought to take him with me."

"He's still abed," sniffed Meldon. "Want me to fetch him from Master Roland's chamber?"

Fenella demurred. Hopefully signor Arnotti had finished painting Bors already. She heard the clock strike nine and hurried to fetch her cloak. Mathilde Martindale had promised to sit with her that morning and was doubtless already waiting for her.

The morning passed swiftly enough. Signor Arnotti seemed a lot less excitable this time and only tutted and exclaimed at her a few times. He was resigned to the fact she would want to stretch her legs on the hour and was not vociferous in his complaints. Mathilde had been waiting for her when she arrived

451

with a plump, elderly woman who sat and dozed nearby leaving them to talk.

"She's my old nurse and my mother's before me," Mathilde had whispered by way of explanation. "She's a dear old thing really, blind as a bat and quite deaf."

"An ideal chaperone then," joked Fen, and Mathilde had giggled.

To her surprise, Fen found herself explaining her current woes to her new friend. "You see, I'm most concerned that my husband will not be at all pleased when he finds us the implied subject of the piece. But Lady Schaeffer seemed to think I was making a fuss about nothing. I wonder, what is your opinion on the matter, Mathilde? You are far more seasoned as a courtier than I."

Mathilde bit her lip. "Mother won't allow me to watch any plays at all," she said sadly. "But I should dearly love to see one with you as the heroine, Fenella."

"But that's just it, it's nothing like me!" objected Fen. "This heroine is a piteous, miserable creature. A mere puppet in the hands of others."

Mathilde looked stricken by this, and remembering her friend's peculiar circumstances, Fenella hurried to clarify. "She is married first to one man who callously abandons her and then another who is interested only in power and neglects her until she expires of a broken heart."

Mathilde's eyes opened wide. "Oh, but—forgive me, but that is really nothing like you, Fenella," she said softly. "I—I do not

452

like to repeat gossip, but surely you are aware of what everyone is saying." She lowered her voice over the last few words and glanced over at the artist, who was employed mixing paints.

"Not really," admitted Fen. "Even though I currently reside here at the palace, I am not mixing in royal circles and have only a small acquaintance."

"Only the favorites have private audience with the King and Queen," agreed Mathilde. "And you have not been here long. I am sure that once people get to know you—"

"Oh, but I am not overly concerned at currying favor," admitted Fen. "I am happy to have a close circle of intimates and consider myself fortunate in the few friends I have." She pressed Mathilde's hand and her friend blushed. "I know, of course, that there was some talk when I appeared at the palace," Fen admitted. "And Hester did tell me there was gossip afoot on the subject, but she was surprisingly reticent about its nature. I know after Oswald returned my pearls to me—"

"Oh yes—now that was a wonderful story," whispered Mathilde. "What a pity that Mr. Entner did not include that in his play!"

Fen winced. "I want the story to resemble my circumstances less, not more!"

"True," said Mathilde. "Though you must admit it would be a much better story than the one he concocted, which sounds rather maudlin."

"It's utterly dismal," agreed Fen. "But my worry is that it will be scandalous and estrange my husband from me." To her dismay, she felt her eyes well up with tears.

"Oh, Fenella," her friend murmured sympathetically, squeezing her hand. "Perhaps—well, perhaps you should speak to him of it."

"To Mr. Entner?"

"No, I meant Lord Vawdrey."

Fen blinked. Well, he did keep telling her to come to him with her worries. But he had so much more to concern himself with at present. "Perhaps," she agreed. "But he is rather occupied of late with delicate matters of state…"

"The Blechmarsh princess," murmured Mathilde, instantly comprehending.

"Quite." Not that she knew anything about it really. "And I do so wish I could be more of a—a helpmeet to him. Do you understand? I—I feel so helpless and useless here at court. I'm not really sure of my function." She wiped her eyes and took a couple of deep breaths to pull herself together. "I hate to think of myself being an actual hindrance and—and bringing disgrace on him."

"Oh, I'm sure you could never do that!" objected Mathilde, who looked, if anything, completely out of her depth. It occurred to Fen that she could not have picked anyone less suited to advising her on such a matter as poor Mathilde, who was thrice married, yet never a wife. Her friend leaned over and patted her hand. "Depend upon it, no one here at court will believe these characters depict you and Lord Vawdrey. They sound really nothing like you."

Fen felt a flicker of hope in her bosom. *Could that be true?* After all, it would have been much more accurate if the heroine had shown herself completely inept in wifely virtues than some kind of saintly victim. "Thank you, Mathilde."

Her friend accompanied her back to their rooms, which were full of half-dressed children when they returned. Little Archie was screaming and wailing while the Cadwalladers' maids tried to unpack trunks and find missing clothes.

"Oh dear," said Linnet, who had on a very fine ice-blue dress but had loose hair and only one stocking on. "I do apologize." Her gaze fell on Mathilde Martindale and widened with surprise. "Why, Lady Martindale! I had no idea you were a friend of Fenella's."

Mathilde's reply was quite drowned out by another lusty wail from young Archie.

"I can't do nothin' with him this morning, milady," said her maid, Nan, tearfully. "He just won't be consoled and Gertie's a-dressing of the girls. I need to do your hair too…"

"Oh dear, if only I did not have an audience with the Queen today," tutted Linnet. She turned back to Fenella. "I don't suppose…" she started hopefully.

"Let me see if I can find Trudy," said Fen in alarm, rushing toward the bedroom. She opened the door and scanned the room, but her maid was nowhere to be found. By the time she'd checked out in the corridor and then returned, the noise had abruptly stopped. Had he fallen asleep?

To her surprise she found all quiet in the communal area. Mathilde stood to the far end of the room next to the window, rocking the baby in her arms. She was so diminutive of stature and Archie was such a bouncer that it was surprising she could get her arms round him, thought Fen.

She watched the wondering expression on Mathilde's softened face. She glanced up, as if feeling Fenella's gaze on her, and beamed. Fen blinked. Mathilde Martindale looked positively radiant, despite her tearstained cheeks.

"You've been crying," said Fen in dismay. "I'm so sorry, let me have him if it's causing you distress…"

Mathilde shook her head vehemently. "No," she whispered hoarsely. "They're happy tears." She gazed down at the baby's slumbering face with an expression of adoration. "I never knew—" She broke off distractedly as they drifted toward the window seat together.

"He certainly seems very peaceable now," commented Fen as they sat down together.

"He's perfect," breathed Mathilde rapturously.

"Where is everyone?"

"The Duchess of Cadwallader has taken her daughters to meet the Queen."

"The servants must have made themselves scarce," said Fen dryly. She darted a shrewd look at her friend as they sat side by side. "Have you never thought about having a baby, Mathilde?" she asked cautiously.

Mathilde shook her head, her cheeks reddening. "Never," she whispered.

"Did neither of your previous husbands want children?"

"Oh no," her friend replied, looking shocked. "They were *quite old.* And besides, they did not like the children they already had. Which is why they wanted to marry me," she added sadly. Archie's face scrunched up and he gave a whimper. "Do not fret, dearest one," murmured Mathilde. "For your mother will be returning ere long."

Archie's little stiffening body relaxed, and his chubby chin wobbled as he settled back against Mathilde's bosom. She shot a look of triumph at Fen.

"You're a natural," Fen whispered, and Mathilde turned quite pink with pleasure.

"He does seem to like me, does he not?"

"I should say," agreed Fen. "The entire time I was holding him last night, his head kept swiveling round to look at me with positive outrage!"

Mathilde giggled and lowered her face to kiss the slumbering baby's brow. His eyes flickered open to look at her, then drifted back down again.

"You see," said Fen. "He is quite content to be held by you."

Mathilde gave a happy sigh. "I wish…" she began, but then closed her mouth again, without voicing her wish.

"Why don't you?" asked Fen curiously.

"You forget, I have never even met Lord Martindale," Mathilde pointed out stiltedly. "We were married by proxy. And he—that is—I have heard…" She broke off agitatedly.

"But you *are* married," pointed out Fen, frowning in puzzlement. "Why should you not have a baby if you want one?"

Mathilde shook her head. "No, it is quite impossible," she said. Just then the door latch sounded, making her friend start almost guiltily.

It was Linnet's maid Gertie, looking deeply apologetic. "I'm so sorry!" she began, then did a double take, seeing her young master asleep. Her hands flew to cover her mouth. "How ever did you manage it?" she whispered, dropping her hands and tiptoeing across the floor. "He was in a rare taking when we left."

Fen and Mathilde exchanged glances. "It was Mathilde," admitted Fen. "It seems babies adore her."

"He's such a good baby though," said Mathilde warmly.

Gertie looked surprised by this pronouncement. "That's what the mistress always says!" she said doubtfully. "But hardly anyone ever agrees with her!"

It was a good hour later that Meldon announced that Lady Schaeffer had arrived. Fen looked up from where she was crouched on the floor rolling walnuts to Archie. He squealed, picked them up, and mouthed them before dropping them again and waiting patiently for the next one.

Hester grimaced. "I'm not overly fond of children," she announced, casting a dubious eye over Archie.

"Oh, since his nap he's been quite congenial," Fen assured her, clambering to her knees. Mathilde picked up a walnut and commenced rolling duties.

"Where's his nurse?" asked Hester disapprovingly as she sat in a chair.

"We've been keeping him tolerably amused while the servants unpack the Cadwalladers' things," explained Fen.

"And he's been a sweetheart," piped up Mathilde.

"It has actually been quite fun," Fen admitted.

"Don't go clucky on me now," said Hester darkly.

"Pardon?"

"Broody."

"Oh." Fen colored up. "There would hardly be any point." To her dismay, the regret in her voice was only too apparent. At both her friends' enquiring gazes, she added, "I have been married for years and never caught after all."

Hester cleared her throat. "Forgive me, dear," she said tactfully. "But was not Thane absent from the country for a good deal of your marriage?"

Fen opened her mouth, then closed it again. "Well, yes," she admitted.

"Whereas your current husband hardly seems to let you out of his sight, now does he?" Hester said sotto voce.

Fenella looked back at Archie, who held up his arms to Mathilde in an unspoken demand. Her friend delightedly complied. A baby of her own? She tamped down the brief flicker of hope she felt ruthlessly. It would not do to cherish false hopes which probably wouldn't come to fruition.

Mathilde kissed Archie's chubby cheek and rocked him in her arms. If she wasn't careful, Fen knew she'd be wearing the same expression of gentle yearning on her face. She gave herself a brief shake. This was not what she wished to discuss after all! "Have you had a chance to read Mr. Entner's play, Hester?" she asked, after clearing her throat.

Hester was peeling a grape and popped it in her mouth before answering. "The first act," she said, nodding her head. "I am a lamentably slow reader and Andrew kept talking last night when I was trying to start the second."

"And what do you think?" asked Fen anxiously.

"A little slow to start," said Hester, tipping her head to one side. "And one does rather want to wring Lady Mawby's neck at

460

times. Your pardon," she said, glancing at Fen. "But she is rather verbose."

"Lady Mawby is the character based on me," Fen explained to Mathilde.

"How nice," said Mathilde, who was gazing worshipfully at Archie.

Fen tsked. "It is *not* nice," she said firmly. "Lady Mawby is a ninny who runs around wringing her hands and soliloquizing when she should be… Oh I don't know."

"Riding up to court and demanding an earl's hand in marriage," suggested Hester slyly.

Fen huffed. "That is not quite how it happened, Hester. Despite what court gossip says!"

"Oh, but I love that story," said Mathilde. "You are like a fearless heroine from a ballad."

"Heroines from ballads are never fierce," Hester corrected her dampeningly. "They always expire of broken hearts. Which I suspect Lady Mawby will by the end of act three, am I right?"

Fen nodded dismally. "But not before she has spoken a great many more lines and been forced to marry the cold and unfeeling Lord Orlando."

"Now I'm looking forward to that part," said Hester, holding up a finger. "I expect sparks to fly."

"You will be disappointed in that hope," said Fen. "Lord Orlando is a complete cold fish." *And absolutely nothing like Oswald.*

"That's a shame," tutted Hester.

"All he cares about is his honor and advancement at court."

"And Lady Mawby fades away?" suggested Hester, helping herself to another grape.

"Entirely."

"Oh dear. What a pity."

"What do you think I should do?" asked Fen helplessly. "Can I insist on a rewrite?"

"Oh indisputably, if you are his patron."

"But what would you have him change?" asked Mathilde. "The ending? Have them live happily ever after?"

"No, you couldn't do that," said Hester dismissively. "It is clearly a tragedy. There are conventions and rules at play."

"Could I ask Mr. Entner to make Lady Mawby a widow instead of a divorcée?" suggested Fen.

"Oh, he won't want to do that," said Hester, sounding shocked. "After all, this is his trump card. *This* is what he is counting on to give the play its frisson of scandal. The fact is he is trading on your history for inspiration."

462

Fen rubbed her temples distractedly. "What if I asked him to change the character of Lord Orlando?"

"Make him less of a damp squib?" said Hester sympathetically.

Fen brooded on this. "What if I asked for him to be made the hero?"

"Forgive me, but do you think that Lord Vawdrey would be happy to be the main subject of such a play?" asked Hester gently.

Fen realized she had a point. "Or the villain of the piece then. Then no one could think it was Oswald."

Hester and Mathilde both looked dismayed by this idea. "Oh no!" they both exclaimed.

"What if people thought you were saying that Lord Vawdrey truly is a villain?" said Mathilde, hefting Archie over her shoulder.

"There is that," admitted Fen weakly. "What if Lady Mawby were made into a villainess instead?"

Both ladies seemed to be struck speechless for a moment. "There are already enough rumors circling about you," said Hester dryly. "Without you adding more fuel to the fire."

"I'm afraid I agree," said Mathilde quietly.

Hester Schaeffer shot a surprised look at her.

Fen groaned. "What can I do then?"

"Simply ride it out," suggested Hester. "It will be a three-day sensation at court, nothing more."

"Maybe no one will go to see it," suggested Mathilde.

"A lot of these folk and morality plays sink without a trace," agreed Hester. "They spring up in the marketplace one day and are gone the next."

Fen sat back in her seat with a troubled look on her face. "I hope you are right," she murmured. "I really do."

*

Hester and Mathilde had left by the time Linnet returned with her daughters. Mathilde had wanted to stay longer, but Lady Doverdale had sent her old nurse along to collect her. Archie had received many kisses before she'd left. He'd cried a few tears on the departure of his favorite, but Fen had eventually managed to distract him with the help of Nan, who had now finished with the unpacking. They took turns, pointing to things out of the window to him, singing to him, and walking him around the room.

"We're back," sang out Linnet as she sailed into the room an hour or so later. Cuthbert came in behind her, carrying Lily and Meg, one on each arm.

"What pretty dresses," cried Fen, for both little girls were in their very best dresses of daffodil yellow. Meg smiled, but Lily hid her face in Cuthbert's shoulder.

"They're tired," said Linnet, coming up to Fen and peeking at her son's face. "Thank you so much for taking care of Archie. Has he been asleep long?"

"Not long. Nan has just popped down to the kitchens to fetch some supper for the girls," explained Fen. "She and Gertie have finished unpacking."

"That's a relief," said Linnet. "Girls, let's find Gertie and get you changed out of your finery for supper."

When she had finished setting out the children's meal, Nan took Archie back and Fen was able to slip away to her room. She wrote a short note to Mr. Entner, requesting a meeting with him about his intentions to stage his play. Realizing she did not have the direction of his lodgings, she addressed it to Eden Montmayne in the hopes she could forward it for her. Then she sat in a chair by the fire to read Orla's letter.

After breaking it open, she realized there had been some delay with its delivery as it was dated over two weeks ago. Bors strolled in and flopped down at her feet. The logs crackled, and she settled in for a catch-up with all things Sitchmarsh. Little had she known, eight weeks ago when she'd rashly left for Aphrany, that she would be so long gone from her home county.

She hoped Orla's letter would mention her friends and acquaintances rather than her own grievances as the last one had. In this, she was not to be disappointed. Orla wrote that Ambrose and his new bride had gone on a visit home to Thurrold Manor and it had *not* gone well.

Orla dismissed Colleen as a vapid little fool and wrote that her mother, Lady Edland, was overbearing, arrogant, and meant to rule the roost. *As you can imagine, my dear Fenella, this did not endear her to myself or our servants.* Fenella remembered Ambrose's words in the shrubbery that day when he berated her about turning his sister against his new wife. This must have been what he was writing about, she realized. Their reception on this visit home.

You must not imagine that I am the only person to draw this conclusion, Orla continued, *for our friends and neighbors have been much perturbed by your usurpation. Indeed, the only person in the neighborhood who has welcomed them with open arms is that bold-faced hussy Sarah Yondy! You may imagine my reaction when Ambrose informed me they were to dine at her house last Thursday week!*

I left him in no doubt of my disapproval, of that you may be sure! And great was Ambrose's perturbation when it dawned on him that the invitations he issued far and wide for folk to meet his upstart "wife" (not that she deserves the title!) were being shunned by the respectable folk of Sitchmarsh.

And would you believe, my dear sister, that he then turned to me in the expectation that I should try to sway public opinion in his favor? I need hardly tell you the reply I made! In a show of solidarity, I have ridden out to Sitchmarsh Hall three times in the last week to commiserate with your brother, Gilbert.

I am sorry to say that the first time I arrived I found him with a very sore head from carousing. I gave him a very stern lecture on the evils of overindulgence, you may be sure! Such was his malady that he received my strictures most meekly and promised he would not overimbibe again before Solstice Eve. I have ridden out twice since then to test his resolve and ensure he has kept his promise.

Fen lowered the page as it suddenly dawned on her that "the harridan" Gil had been complaining was plaguing the life out of him could in fact be Orla! She gave a snort of laughter, and, extricating her foot from her slipper, stroked Bors's back with her stockinged foot. Bors flipped over onto his back to give her access to his stomach. Nothing loath, Fen wriggled her stockinged toes along his stomach and Bors let his tongue loll out of his mouth as he panted in approval.

A knock on the door startled Fen, and Bors gave a short bark, rolling onto his stomach to preserve his dignity. A blond head peered around the door, and she realized it was Cuthbert. "Any notes you want delivering?" he asked hopefully.

Fen realized he probably wanted to make himself scarce for a while. "I do have one for Lady Eden Montmayne as it happens," she said, pointing toward the small table.

Cuthbert wandered over and picked it up. "This isn't the right one," he said. "This is addressed to Mr. Entner."

"I know," Fen explained. "But I want it to be delivered to Lady Eden for her to forward on for me. I don't know Mr. Entner's address. I did write a covering note to Eden, it should be there."

Cuthbert scanned the second page. "This is it," he agreed, and refolded them with Eden's note on the outside. "Anything else?"

"Allow me to give you some coin this time," said Fen, rising from her chair.

"Not necessary." Cuthbert shrugged. "I'm on a retainer and you're family, so…" He let his words trail off though he still hovered by the door instead of leaving.

"Have you been Mason's squire for long?" asked Fen politely.

Cuthbert nodded. "A year last Michaelmas. I was Lady Linnet's page before that."

"It must be a position of great responsibility," she said gravely.

Cuthbert gave another shrug. "My master doesn't enter the lists," he said with a trace of bitterness.

"I fear my husband is the same," said Fen sympathetically. "I think it's because they were soldiers. Could you not ask to support Master Roland for a while at court? That way you would get to experience the tournaments."

Cuthbert's eyes widened. "Support Master Roland?" he repeated. "Do you think I could?"

"I don't see why not," said Fen. "The family are clearly very fond of you. I can't imagine they would deny you the experience. And Roland has no page or squire of his own that I can discern."

Cuthbert nodded slowly and seemed to look upon her with a dawning new respect. He started toward the door before turning back impulsively. "Did you really show up at court with your wedding papers to show to Lord Vawdrey?" he asked.

Fen considered this. She guessed he had been hearing all the palace gossip. Of course, technically, this was nothing but the truth. "I did," she said, inclining her head. "But shall I tell you a secret, Cuthbert, for your ears only?"

He cocked his head. "Yes?"

"When I did it, I thought to coerce Lord Vawdrey to act as my champion. I did not dream he would turn around and lay claim to me for a wife."

Cuthbert seemed to consider this. "They do say as he's a dark horse," he said at last. "My granny's a witch," he added with great insouciance. "I got the sight too. Want me to read your palm?" He said it so obligingly that Fen found herself holding out her hand. The boy drew up a chair beside her. She could not imagine a more unlikely witch if she tried, with his golden curls and pink-and-white complexion. "You been sleeping under an oak tree," he said, startling her greatly. "Sleeping and waiting for a half-dead man." Fen gave an involuntary exclamation and tried to draw back, but his grip was surprisingly strong.

"You didn't ought to do that," he said sternly. "It's bad fortune, sleeping under trees. Everyone knows that. So's waiting for the dead. Lucky for you, he didn't die all the way." He traced a line on her palm. "Only part of him was killed. A part what you can give back to him, if you've got the courage."

Fen stared at him, feeling oddly deprived of breath. She knew it was pointless telling him that she'd never slept under a tree in her life. That wasn't how it worked. He was looking at her expectantly. "Thank you," she said.

"You gotta give me something now," he said with a small sigh.

She knew that also and fetched him the silver pilgrim's token out of her drawer.

He took it and turned it over. "A coin would do."

"I want you to have this." She didn't really know why.

He untied a leather thong from around his neck and threaded the token onto it alongside several other trinkets. Then he slipped it back into his shirt. She thought of the padlock pendant and shivered. "Who's the man?" he asked curiously.

She knew at once what he meant. "Oswald Vawdrey."

"When did he half die?"

She didn't even hesitate. "The battle of Adarva. He was certainly grievously injured." She thought of his mangled shoulder blade. "He probably almost died."

Cuthbert nodded thoughtfully. "I never heard him speak of that tale."

"No one has," said Fen. "Except me." They sat a moment in companionable silence, the logs crackling in the hearth. Bors whined and the spell was broken. "I promised to walk him with my friend Bess at five o'clock," said Fen, listening to the bell clang in the courtyard.

Cuthbert jumped out of his chair. "I'll go and deliver your note, milady."

"Thank you, Cuthbert."

She couldn't quite shake off the strange mood that had descended on her until she emerged into the vestibule that separated the outer and the inner courtyard and felt a blast of icy cold air.

Drawing her cloak around her, she heard Bess's booming voice before she could spot her friend. Three prancing hounds preceded her, sleek and rippling with muscle. Bors eyed them with tolerance as they gamboled around him.

"Hah, there you are," Bess hailed her heartily as she sailed around the corner in a large orange cloak. "I've only brought the bitches with me this evening. Didn't think your old boy would appreciate the young bucks nipping at his heels, eh?" She jostled Fen in the side good-naturedly.

"That is a kindness I'm sure he appreciates."

"Looking a little peaky, if you don't mind me saying so, Lady Fen," Bess commented as they crossed the first courtyard. "You been sat being painted all day long?" She sucked in her cheeks. "Not wise to be sat still so long. All your black bile will sink to the bottom of your spleen and make you melancholic." Her brown curls bounced as she made this pronouncement, and her velvet feathered cap almost slipped off her head.

Fen's eyes widened. "Oh, I shouldn't want that. But I only sat for signor Arnotti this morning."

"Ah, I'm glad to hear it," said Bess. "Though I understand your portrait is coming along very nicely now, and signor Arnotti spends a good deal of time on it in his studio."

Fen was surprised. She did not find the artist very forthcoming about his progress. "That is heartening to hear," she said. "I understand you remain unpersuaded with regards to having your own portrait done."

"He told you that, did he?" asked Bess, not sounding very pleased and turning even ruddier in color.

"Oh no," Fen hastened to explain. "'Twas Eden who told me, not signor Arnotti."

"Humph," said Bess, looking somewhat mollified. "Got a finger in every pie that girl."

"She's certainly very busy about court."

"Some would say too much so," snapped Bess. Then she seemed to remember herself. "Ho, Clementine!" she bellowed, and her white hound came bounding back. "Not too far ahead of the pack, you hussy!" Clementine dove off again to catch up with Bors and the others.

Fen watched her friend covertly. Whilst Bess was usually an eccentric character, she seemed a little more on edge today, she thought. "And how is Padraig?" she asked after Bess's oldest and most beloved dog. "I understand his likeness on the canvas was most masterfully done."

Bess inclined her head. "With a profile as noble as Padraig's you could scarcely fail to produce a work of startling beauty," she boasted. "I daresay," she added with a short laugh, "that even a second-rate artist could do a passable job with such a fine subject."

"I daresay," agreed Fen.

"Not that I'm saying he is second-rate," added Bess self-consciously. "Far from it. From what I have seen in his studios his work is very fine."

"You have been to his studio?" asked Fen with interest.

Bess pulled up short. "And why shouldn't I?" she asked.

Fen gazed at her in amazement. "No reason at all. I was merely making conversation."

Bess grunted. "You may depend on it that busybody Miss Eden Montmayne has been there prodding and poking among the canvases!" She jutted out her chin aggressively and Fen almost wished she had not arranged to meet her.

"She does a lot of work espousing artists for patrons," she said mildly.

"Hah!" was all Bess answered. "Perhaps she'd do better to apply her energies to other purposes, such as finding a husband."

"Well, if she had," said Fen a little sharply, "then you or I would not be having our paintings done."

This seemed to bring Bess up short. "Quite right," she said a little gruffly after a pause. "Wasn't thinking straight." It wasn't like her, thought Fen, wondering what had got into her friend. She could be a little fiery, but she was usually good-natured with it. "Benedict tells me your portrait is nearly completed now," said Bess.

Fen pondered this a moment. "Who is Benedict?" she asked at last, defeated.

Bess coughed. "Why, signor Arnotti, to be sure." Her ruddy complexion deepened.

"Oh I see," said Fen, surprised they were on first name terms. Bess was an heiress and noblewoman, despite her eccentricities.

"To be frank, it looked finished to me when I saw it two days ago," Bess continued. "But Ben—I mean signor Arnotti," she corrected herself hastily, "is something of a perfectionist."

"Have you seen my portrait?" asked Fen in surprise.

Bess nodded. "Oh yes."

"But I thought he didn't permit anyone to look at his pictures unless they were fully finished?" exclaimed Fen.

Bess fiddled with her glove in a very un-Bess-like fashion. She looked almost coy. "Oh yes," she agreed vaguely. "But that mostly applies to his subjects."

"I see," said Fen. "Perhaps I should ask to see your portrait?" she added rather tartly.

"Now don't be cross," begged Bess. "It doesn't suit you. And besides, I never did sit for one. You can see the one of Padraig, if you like," she added generously, seeing Fen wasn't quite appeased. "He did him very lifelike."

"Well, I just hope he has done Bors justice," said Fen. "Or my brother-in-law will be sure to take issue with it."

"Bors?" repeated Bess with a frown, eyeing Fen's dog. "Is he supposed to be in it?"

"Don't tell me he's missed him out!" said Fen. "Oh, that really is too much! I was quite specific!"

"Well, I'm no artist," said Bess. "But wouldn't he look a bit well...odd in that composition?"

"I don't see what's odd about it," retorted Fen. "He sat quite happily at my feet for hours in the long gallery. Signor Arnotti certainly had ample opportunity to capture his likeness, and so I will tell him if he has forgotten to include him!"

"Well, I'm sure you know what you're about," said Bess with a shrug. "Benedict said patrons are usually dissatisfied about something or other. Tell me," she said, turning impulsively and seizing Fen's gloved hand. "What do you think of him?"

"Well," started Fen weakly, for she was taken aback by Bess's earnest expression. "I can't really form an opinion until I've seen an example of his work. Lady Eden said he was most accomplished and—"

"Not as an artist," entreated Bess. "As a man!"

Fen blinked. In the few strained exchanges she had had with signor Arnotti she had gained the impression of an unpredictable and impatient man with beetling brows and a mop of hair that stood on end on his head from where he tugged it

475

distractedly as he worked. She had a feeling this impression would not go down well with Bess.

"No," said Bess, holding up one finger. "Do not water it down, but speak plain, I beg you."

"Well…" started Fen helplessly, "I've barely had much speech with him. And when we did it was mostly just me asking for permission to move or take a break. Or him demanding that I sit still or turn my head or stop turning my head."

To her surprise Bess looked rather gratified by this. "He does not pay you any out of the way compliments?" she asked hesitantly.

Fen blinked again. She could imagine nothing less likely from the grouchy painter. "Definitely not!"

"Such as how you are the first sensible woman he has met in this country, or how much he likes your forthright manner of speech?"

"No. He has never paid me a compliment of any kind," answered Fen truthfully.

Bess sighed. "Thank you," she said with a gratified expression on her face that quite threw Fen. She could barely get any more than two words strung together after that from her usually garrulous friend and their return journey to the castle was mostly undertaken in silence.

After parting ways Fen made her way back to their corridor, deeply worried. Surely her friend was not in danger of forming some unsuitable kind of attachment? She had no idea of Bess's family setup. Had she no brother or kinsmen to guard her from fortune hunters? After all, a wealthy woman with connections like Bess must have someone looking out for her.

Though truth be told, it was hard to think of signor Arnotti as a seducer of noblewomen. Surely fortune hunters took pains to make themselves a lot more agreeable than the rather uncouth artist? The compliments Bess had mentioned were hardly fulsome. Perhaps she was overthinking things. Mayhap Bess had just been enjoying a little male company in a harmless sort of way?

33

It was perhaps not surprising that Fen was distracted at supper. Oswald did not appear until the table was laid, and he only had chance to kiss her cheek briefly before they were all seated and the food dished up.

The meal was game pie, stewed leeks, and onions, which none of the children, including Cuthbert, seemed to like. Meg pushed hers around her bowl until the gravy dripped over the side, and Lily shed a tear when her father told her sternly to eat it. Fen noticed with interest that he undermined this almost immediately by setting her on his lap and sending Gertie down to the kitchen to fetch bread and cheese for them instead.

"The girls are tired," said Linnet apologetically. "They've had a long day today." Little Archie was being tended to by Nan over by the fire and was contented with his lot for once.

"How did it go with the Queen?" asked Fen.

"Oh, she was very gracious with them," said Linnet, lowering her voice. "Only, it is a little tedious for small children to sit still for so long." Fen nodded; she could well believe it. "Queen Armenal did ask me several questions pertaining to you, Fenella," her sister-in-law told her complacently.

Fen nearly dropped her spoon. "She did?" She darted a look over at her husband, but he was listening intently to something Mason was telling him.

"You have not spent much time in her company it seems?" said Linnet, looking puzzled. "I had thought—what with Oswald's position at court…" She broke off awkwardly.

"Oswald does want me to try to ingratiate myself with the Queen," admitted Fen. "Alas, I have not managed to impress her overmuch so far."

Linnet seemed to relax a little at her words. "But you would like to," she said with visible relief. "That is the important thing."

Fen nodded. "At first, I did not expect to spend much time at court," she confessed. "My husband told me that I would find little change in my day-to-day life."

Linnet looked startled at this. "I do not quite follow?"

"As I would be going back to Sitchmarsh," she explained. "Where I'm from, and where Vawdrey Keep is situated."

"Oh, I see," said Linnet, still not looking convinced. "I have never journeyed there, but from things Mason has said, I understand it is in some considerable state of disrepair."

"Yes," agreed Fen. "And Oswald now seems to have some reservations about its suitability for his seat in the country."

"I have heard him say that he meant to pull it to the ground and rebuild," murmured Linnet, glancing at the three brothers. "But I have never repeated that, as I do not know how everyone would react to so radical a course of action."

"He has never discussed such plans with me," said Fen truthfully. Her eyes rested a moment on her husband, who appeared to be listening to a question from one of his nieces.

"Perhaps it was just a passing thought," suggested Linnet.

479

"Perhaps," muttered Fen, dropping her gaze as he looked up to find her watching him.

"I was impressed," said Linnet in a sudden change of subject, "to see how much you have drawn the little Martindale out of her shell. I have never seen her look so animated. Or speak so much."

Fen nodded, but before she could make a reply, a trencher of bread and cheese clattered down on the table before them. The children cheered, and plates were hastily shoved away as the loaf was torn into.

"More pie for me," said Roland, happily scraping the contents from the abandoned plates onto his own.

The girls were yawning long before a cake covered in a layer of nuts was brought in for the after-dinner course. Linnet disappeared briefly while they were put to bed, but by the time Fenella had cut slices for the adults she had reappeared. The two of them retired to the window seat together to eat theirs whilst the Vawdrey males remained around the table.

"Let us leave them to it," suggested Linnet, "whilst we have a cozy chat."

Fen plumped a cushion and leaned back. In truth, she had not much appetite for the cake, but she was keen to elicit some advice from Linnet, as to moving in royal circles. She soon found that it was not about court that Linnet wished to converse, but surprisingly, about their father-in-law and the promises he had wrung from her on his death bed.

"I have been so worried," confessed Linnet. "For when someone is on their death bed, you do not feel you have the right to deny them what they ask of you, however unreasonable. And poor Father was so very insistent about Oswald, though he was rambling at one point and I found it quite hard to follow. It seemed he considered him to be quite promised to someone, but when I asked Mason, he said Father had promised Oswald in marriage to dozens of girls over the years, so I was quite stumped."

Something stung Fenella into speaking. "He meant his first betrothal. That is the one Baron Vawdrey thought was still valid. The one agreed with my father, Sir Jeoffrey Bernard."

Linnet's eyes widened, and she sat bolt upright. "Yes!" she said. "Bernard! That was the name he spoke of! I had forgotten it until now. Wait! Do not tell me that you are 'the little Bernard girl' of whom he spoke?"

Fen nodded. "Though it is a long time since anyone addressed me as such."

Linnet leaped out of her chair. "But this is wonderful!" she exclaimed, her face aglow. "It means everything Father wanted has come to pass. Well, almost everything," she amended, "except Roland." She clapped her hands to her face. "And it all happened by itself! Oh, how thankful I am!"

She surged forward and clasped Fen's upper arms. "Welcome, sister." She kissed Fen on both cheeks.

"Thank you," stammered Fen.

"I do hope you will not hold it against me that I tried to play the matchmaker for Oswald," said Linnet in sudden dismay. "Indeed, I was never proficient in the role, and Oswald told me himself that he and my friend Enid Jauncey were not remotely suited!"

"Of course not," Fen hurried to assure her, ignoring a pang. *Enid who?*

"If I had known that he was already married, I never would have dreamed of such a thing!"

"Oh, I'm sure."

"But what a stroke of good fortune that your marriage turned out to be legally valid," Linnet rattled on. "That must have been why Father was so fixated on Oswald's marital standing. He must have wanted things set to rights."

Fen was starting to feel awkward. In an effort to distract Linnet, Fen asked, "But what was it that Baron Vawdrey wished you to do about Roland?"

Linnet's face fell. "Oh *that*. Well"—she looked around furtively—"well, Father said 'Whatever you do, Linnet, do not allow that rascal Roland to marry some fool girl with more hair than sense. I won't have him saddling my poppets with a litter of idiot cousins.' Though how he expected me to prevent it, I do not know!"

She looked aggrieved. "And Mason won't even enter into any discussion about it, for he says it's all a piece of nonsense and I should put it from my mind."

Fen pulled a sympathetic face, though to be honest, she thought brusque Mason had a valid point. Trying to get Roland to do anything would be an uphill battle. Trying to *prevent* him from doing something would probably be even harder.

Fen retired not long after. It had been a long day and she felt surprisingly exhausted. However, once she had climbed under the covers, sleep eluded her. Worry crept into her mind—that confounded play, Bess's strange behavior. She rolled first onto one side and then the other but found she could not settle.

She was lying flat on her back with the sheet over her face when she heard the door open and close again. Lying quietly, she listened to her husband undress and wash. She was just considering folding down the blanket to speak when she felt the covers draw back and the mattress dip.

Oswald reached for her in the dark and drew her against his warm body. With a sigh, Fen rolled into him and felt herself relax against his solid form. His hand rested at her waist in a light clasp. Even the sound of his breathing was comforting. Fen felt her eyes drift shut as sleep washed over her. Just before all was dark, she fancied she felt his lips brush her brow, and smiled.

34

Again, when she awoke her husband had already left for the day. Trudy was laying out her clothes for the morning. "I hope I didn't wake you, milady."

"Not at all. I have sadly overslept the hour," Fen said, flinging back the bedcovers. "What o'clock is it?"

She was supposed to sit for another four hours that morning, she remembered joylessly and cursed the day she had ever agreed to have a portrait painted. Whoever would have thought it would be so onerously time-consuming? Surely it would be soon finished now. Even Bess thought so, and she seemed something of an expert these days.

"The clock has not long struck nine," Trudy replied, crossing the room to fling open a trunk.

Fen hurried to the washstand. "Did you see Lord Vawdrey before he left?" She had barely spoken to him yesterday, she thought with a pang. It made her uneasy, or mayhap that was just her guilty conscience?

"No, milady. Uncle said he left at the crack of dawn."

"So early?" Fen turned to look over her shoulder as her maid laid out green stockings and red garters for her. It seemed that her husband had hardly been around the last two days.

"Everyone's talking about that business with the northern princess, milady," said Trudy by way of explanation and looked around excitedly. "They say the King do wish he'd married her now, instead of the western Queen."

Fen almost dropped her sponge. "Surely not," she said in a startled voice.

"That's what they do say," said Trudy. "After all, she's not given him any heirs, have she, Queen Armenal? Not like good Queen Eleanor." She sighed. Fen digested this as she ran a dry cloth over her neck and shoulders. "Do come over by the fire, milady. You're a mass of gooseflesh. I can brush your hair in the warm."

Fen drifted over to the fireplace, and Trudy attacked her tangles industriously. "I wonder why the King does not have his heir at court," she said aloud. "Is it due to poor health? I had heard the young prince's constitution is considered delicate like his mother, the old Queen's."

Trudy hesitated. "They do say Queen Armenal is not very maternal," she said, her mouth thinning with disapproval.

Fen wondered. It seemed a little hard to blame it on the Queen. "Lady Linnet did say that the Queen was very good with her daughters yesterday."

"Oh yes, I daresay," said Trudy. Her lips pressed firmly together.
Fen did not want to entertain the idea that Oswald might be involved in drawing up plans to rid the King of his current wife. After all, he had told her to ingratiate herself with Armenal, had he not? Would he have done that if divorce was imminent? And surely it was not so easy for a King to divest himself of a Queen as it was to grant a divorce from a nonroyal such as herself?

"Begging your pardon, milady," said Trudy, who was now swiftly braiding her locks and arranging them. "I did not mean to say aught to offend you."

"Oh, you didn't," Fen assured her. She remembered Hester's advice. "Indeed, I am very grateful when you bring me what word is circulating the court. I should be aware of it," she added with a smile. Trudy looked gratified. "Tell me," said Fen. "Have your family any plans for the Solstice feast?"

Trudy launched into an account of her various offsprings' plans to return to the homestead for Solstice Eve as all three were now apprenticed out. "Indeed, you must have Solstice Eve as well as the day itself for a holiday," Fen told her firmly.

"Oh no, milady! Whatever would Uncle say?"

"I am quite determined," said Fen. "You must have your family celebration together."

"Oh, milady!" Trudy touched her apron to the corners of her eyes.

"Yes," said Fen. "And I have left a small token of my thanks in a purse in the top drawer for you. The yellow one." Trudy's eyes widened. Before she could protest, Fen added, "'Tis for gifts for your children, and I won't hear any more about it."

Her maid was profuse in her thanks, and Fen thought she would have to write to Orla and send her the scarf she had bought her before long as there was now only a week remaining until the Midwinter festival.

She ate a hurried breakfast with only Bors and Cuthbert in attendance before hurrying off to meet up with Eden, who had promised to sit with her that morning. Poor Bors could barely keep up with her.

To her surprise, it was not Eden who stood waiting for her at the foot of the steps, but instead one of the Queen's ladies-in-waiting, whose name quite eluded Fen. "Good morning," she said warily at her approach. Bors gave a low woof.

"Good morn, Lady Vawdrey." The blonde curtseyed neatly. She had a very fancy head veil on that was frilled and pleated. Fen thought it looked rather fussy and overdone. Bors, she ignored completely.

"Is Lady Eden unable to join me this morning?" Fen asked. She hoped this wasn't a replacement, as she suspected she would not be easy company.

"The Queen has sent Eden on some other errand," the other explained with a delicate yawn.

"Oh, I see," said Fen, glad her friend wasn't ill at least. "Thank you for bringing the message."

The other lady gave a high laugh. "I do not run about the palace delivering messages for the likes of Eden Montmayne, I assure you," she said shrilly.

Fen eyed her. "You have some other errand?" she asked pointedly.

The lady inclined her head. "Her Majesty awaits you in the Lower Gallery," she said grandly.

"What?" Fen nearly tripped on her own hem. "Queen Armenal?"

"Well, it's not the King," said the other with a giggle. "You're hardly the sort to tickle his fancy."

Fen ignored this impertinence and hurried along to the Lower Gallery where she knew signor Arnotti would be set up with his paints and easel. Bors followed on her heels, and after turning the last corner, Fen saw the Queen's tall figure dressed in a flowing gown of burnt orange.

She appeared to be in animated conversation with the surly artist and Fen's heart sank. To her surprise, as she neared them, she noticed the Queen was on the other side of the easel, looking at the work in progress.

"Good morning, Fenella," the Queen hailed her, looking from the canvas to her and then back again. "Remarkable," she murmured. "Quite remarkable. Your vision is such that it quite lifts the subject matter from the mundane to the divine. And yet, it is a true reflection," she added thoughtfully.

"Good morning, Your Highness," she murmured. "Good morning, signor," she said, looking at the artist, who wasn't bristling for once with hostility. Instead he was looking at the Queen with interest.

"I should like to paint you," he said abruptly.

The Queen laughed delightedly. "But I am not so sure I would care for the experience," she said. "You are a good deal too honest to be a royal artist."

488

Fen shot a look at the artist, but instead of looking chagrined, he was thoughtfully pulling on his moustache.

"There is truth in what you say," he conceded, and dismissing her royal presence from his thoughts, he snatched up his brush and glared at Fen. "You—sit!"

Fen cast a look of despair at him before settling herself on the familiar window seat. "Don't forget Bors," she said sternly as her dog settled at her feet with a huff.

The Queen was making her way around the other side of the canvas now to join her. "Wherever did you find such a creature?" she asked, looking intrigued. To Fen's dismay, she was arranging her skirts to sit down at the window next to hers.

"Eden," she said simply by way of explanation and the Queen nodded.

"Of course," she said. "I might have known."

It was on the tip of Fen's tongue to ask how she had earned a personal royal visit, but she did not quite dare to voice it. "I am very honored to have you join me this morning, Your Majesty," she said instead.

"Yes," conceded the Queen serenely. "It is not usually my practice to single out individuals in such a way." Fen blinked and waited for her to continue, but the Queen was looking around her with interest. "I do not usually venture down here," she said. "Is it not rather draughty?"

"It can be," Fen agreed. "I believe there are plans afoot to hang tapestries along the walls once they are completed."

"Indeed?" The Queen sounded only mildly interested.

"Yes. Eden is in charge of that endeavor also."

"Such a very intrepid young woman," said the Queen with a sigh. "I believe she puts us all to shame."

"I am doing a panel with Mathilde Martindale," Fen carried on. "We are planning roses intertwined with lilies and a border with cowslips."

"I am sure that my good Lady Doverdale will insist on adding some improving text to this feast of flowers," she said with only a trace of gentle cynicism.

"She will find that difficult, not being consulted," said Fen outrageously. As soon as she'd said it, she felt her face flood with color. Why had she said that?

To her relief the Queen burst out laughing. "And there it is," said the Queen triumphantly. "The spark that I did not detect. I knew I must have overlooked something, or you would not have so captivated one such as Lord Vawdrey. But perhaps you were deliberately pretending to be so dull when I met you that time?"

Fen struggled to make a reply to so rude a question. "I—er, no. Not intentionally, Your Highness. I was very overset at the time. Being thrown over by my first—I mean, by Sir Ambrose Thane."

The Queen nodded. "Ah yes, I had perhaps overlooked the effects of abandonment on your temperament." Fen tried not to bristle, but it was hard. She looked sidelong at the Queen and wondered if she was being deliberately offensive. But she did not think she was. "Of course, you could not have loved so inconsequential a man," she said casually. "But one does get used to the status quo, I suppose."

Again, Fen struggled with her reply. "At the time, I thought I was fond of him," she said awkwardly. "Of Thurrold Manor, my home of those years, I was very attached."

The Queen nodded. "Yes, naturally," she said with more sympathy. "I still miss the home of my youth," she sighed. "But I doubt I will ever visit it again. The truce between my brother Wilhelm and Wymer has been transitory at best."

Fen suddenly thought of Trudy's words that morning. If Wymer ever divorced Queen Armenal, would she be permitted to return to the Western Isles? It was possible King Wilhelm of the Western Isles would declare war at such an insult. She bit her lip.

Were these the kinds of things that Oswald had always to contend with? she wondered faintly. How hard it must be! It dawned on her that Queen Armenal was looking at her again with frank interest.

"I have always found the Vawdreys to be a family most interesting," she said. "Mason, the middle son, was very much in the mold of his father. And the youngest son too, Sir Roland, I would say is very much of the same impression. But," she said, tapping her chin thoughtfully, "Lord Vawdrey, he is how you say—a different kettle of fish?"

491

"Yes, I should say he is," agreed Fen. He was superior in every way, to her mind.

"This is what dismayed the old baron," said the Queen, nodding to herself. "Mark my words. He would want his heir to be the chip off the old block."

Fen brooded on this. "He's tall and dark," she objected. "Like his brothers."

Armenal pursed her lips thoughtfully. "That he is, both. And yet, I believe it was not so much the physical resemblance I meant as much as the temperament. Sir Mason and Sir Roland, they are forceful and brusque. A thought enters their heads and they give voice to it. Loudly and with conviction."

Fen had not known either brother for long, but she could already see this was nothing but the truth. "But why should the old baron not want Oswald for his heir?" she asked, returning to their discussion. "He's clever, everyone says so! And handsome…" Her words trailed off. In her view, he was by far the handsomest, though all the maidens swooned over Roland.

"Yes, he is all those things," agreed the Queen. "But stubborn old men like to see their own reflections in their children. Oswald is something of a changeling, is he not? Cut from a different cloth. He is quiet, thoughtful. Baron Vawdrey did not know what this eldest son of his was thinking. And at times"— she held up a finger—"he had the very real suspicion that this son and heir was *far* cleverer than he was. This made him uneasy. He liked to think that he alone knew best."

Fen thought of that Solstice feast so long ago, when the baron had addressed all the hall and called his nineteen-year-old son "a fine young peacock" to the amusement of his guests. Had his father always tried to put him down in public? Her chest ached. "He should have been proud his son was smarter than he," she muttered.

"Perhaps deep down he was," replied the Queen. "But the baron was not the sort of man who liked to parade such emotions. Emotions, in his book, they were for the women. I understand he mellowed a great deal in later life," she added.

This seemed true enough from all that Linnet had told her. Fen brightened, remembering that Oswald himself had told her the baron would approve of her restored place at his side. She remembered, too, the gold coins he had sent her and what Oswald had said about them standing under a sacred oak.

"It is so interesting, is it not," said the Queen in a change of subject, "how sometimes the unlikeliest matches seem to work out a good deal more successfully than ones you would anticipate?"

Fen thought about this. "I can think of no examples," she admitted after a moment. Back home in Sitchmarsh, imprudent marriages most often ended in unhappy lives.

"Well, take your own husband," suggested the Queen. "Lord Oswald Vawdrey."

Fen's heart missed a beat. "Yes?" she croaked.

"Until now, I would have imagined him ideally matched with some cool-headed, composed type. Such as Lady Anne Sumner."

493

Fen's heart plunged down to her slippered feet. "Really?"

"Rather a bloodless beauty, nothing really ruffles her. Have you met?"

"Yes," agreed Fen without enthusiasm. "I understand she is already married," she said rather pointedly.

The Queen's smile widened. "So she is," she agreed.

"And—if you'll permit me to say so, Your Majesty," said Fen, feeling a blush rise up her neck, "I don't think they would suit one another. Not at all."

Queen Armenal looked slyly amused. "I am sure you are in the right of it," she said gravely. "I am merely telling you of the impression I gained, erroneously it now seems." Fen nodded, but still felt put out. "I was never convinced that Helen Cecil would have suited him," continued the Queen. "That was just a foolish notion of Wymer's."

"Helen Cecil?" repeated Fen blankly. She had met her too and not particularly liked her. "But isn't she—?" She broke off her words in sudden embarrassment. "Oh, Your Majesty—" she stammered. "I—I meant—"

"You're right, of course," said the Queen with supreme indifference. "She is the King's latest mistress." She shrugged. "He has these peccadilloes, but they never last particularly long. She is quite witless after all, and I daresay he thought she would be restful company."

Fen thought of Helen Cecil's lovely but haughty face. "I do not think she would be remotely restful to be around," she answered without thinking.

The Queen laughed. "You are in the right of it," she agreed. "In fact, she is rather stupid, but thinks herself to be the sophisticated lady. If he had the taste to take a woman of character, then I would worry. But he would never have the wit to take up with a woman such as yourself."

Fen sat in astonishment at the Queen's casual tone and the fact she thought her a *woman of character*. "But don't you—" She started tentatively. "Doesn't it ever—?" Fen hurriedly broke off her words. She had almost forgotten herself.

"Ask me," commanded the Queen. "For I can tell you were about to say something interesting."

"Don't you mind—about the King, I mean," asked Fenella awkwardly, "taking mistresses?"

The Queen settled back comfortably on her cushion. "I would only mind if he chose someone cleverer than me," she admitted frankly. "You see? I take you as my confessor. I am quite honest with you."

Looking at the Queen's lively face and sly eyes, Fen doubted the King would ever find such a lady. "I am not built for love," continued the Queen matter-of-factly. "It is best to know these things about oneself from the outset. I like to observe the dance and pull on the strings to make the puppets perform their steps. Do you understand?"

Fen wasn't sure that she did. It wasn't the nicest image. And she had seen the Queen dance with grace and beauty in the banqueting hall. But she knew dimly that was not what Armenal meant.

"And I am always very careful to be oh so kind and polite to Bathilde," continued the Queen with a mirthless smile. "She is the only woman to inspire devotion of the unwavering in the King's bosom. You have met Bathilde?"

"Bathilde?" Foggily Fen's memory churned, recalling the King's bedchamber. *Wait!* "Was she the elderly lady—?"

"With the face of the sheep? Yes," said Armenal, snapping her fingers. "She is the only woman to really hold his heart. The nursemaid. You see, at one time, she slapped his fingers and wiped the tears. Little Wymer, the budding despot, he respects this alone and will love her until the day he dies." The Queen sat back in her seat with a satisfied nod.

"Is it really true she still puts him to bed every night?" asked Fen in disbelief.

"No, of course not," said Armenal dismissively. "But she *is* the only one is permitted to wake him every morning. You may be sure I buy her the biggest present every Midwinter and on her birthday in June. That way, if he should ever take it in his head to mutter the bad things about me in his private chambers…" She trailed off her words.

"Bathilde would scold him?" suggested Fen.

"She would give him the look most severe! That is all it takes. You think these flibbertigibbets, they have the sense to buy the present for the old nursemaid?" Fen shook her head. "Not at all," said the Queen. "They would scorn to look upon her. All they respect is youth and beauty. They think this is the only path to power. They are all just fools." Fen nodded, impressed.

"You see that one up there?" she said, nodding to the top of the corridor where every so often her lady-in-waiting drifted into view. "She was one such, very briefly."

Fen sucked in a breath. "But why do you have her for a lady-in-waiting?"

The Queen arched a sardonic eyebrow at her. "Not by choice, I can assure you, but eventually I will prune these cankered roses out of my retinue. Of that you can be assured. Even now, I have, how would you say, an inner circle? My trusted ladies. They occupy the better positions. I would not expect them to trot after me and to wait in cold corridors while I chat," she added contemptuously, "like the watchdog."

"Would Lady Doverdale be considered one of your inner circle?" suggested Fenella.

"Yes, and your sister-in-law, the Duchess of Cadwallader," agreed the Queen.

"I see," said Fen.

"Which brings me to my next point," said Queen Armenal easily. "How would you like to attend an afternoon of entertainments tomorrow in the Yellow Chamber? It will be presided over by myself, and our mutual friend Lady Eden will be leading the dance."

Fen gulped. It did not escape her notice that she was being given a royal invitation to the event. Perhaps she had somehow won the Queen over, despite her awkwardness and the fact she had nearly put her foot in it at least twice! "It would not involve my actually dancing, would it?" she asked nervously. Sadly, Fenella knew herself to possess two left feet.

The Queen shook her head. "It is only those poor unmarried creatures who are required to dance for the entertainment of others," she said sagely.

"Then I would be delighted," she said, for she had not made plans other than another wretched sitting for signor Arnotti in the morning. It would be good to catch up with Eden also, for she could find out if her letter had been successfully forwarded to the playwright.

"Good," said the Queen, rising up from her seat. "I shall look for you there, Lady Vawdrey."
Fenella hastily stood and sank into a deep curtsey. Bors sat up on his haunches and yawned. The Queen smiled at them both and drifted back up the corridor. She watched her for a moment until signor Arnotti cleared his throat quite violently. "Your pardon," said Fen with dignity and returned to her seat.

35

"Is it true that the King wanted you to marry Helen Cecil?" Fen asked her husband at supper. Everyone had seemed to be in the midst of their own conversations until she spoke, but now suddenly all eyes were on them.

Oswald put his knife down carefully and looked her straight in the eye. "Where did you hear that?" he asked.

Fen didn't see any point in beating around the bush. "From Queen Armenal," she answered.

He paused a moment. "The King never asked me at any time to marry Lady Helen Cecil." He said it with an air of finality, but Fen could immediately see the weakness of the answer.

"But did he want you to?" she persisted.

Oswald frowned. "I'm not a mind reader, Fenella," he said. "And I can assure you, I have never had any private conversation, or even met with Helen Cecil in public, to my knowledge. I wouldn't even recognize her if I did."

That was rather more reassuring, and she relaxed back against the back of her seat. "Politician's answer if I ever I heard one," scoffed Roland. "What you should have asked him was, 'To your knowledge did the King ever want you to marry Helen Cecil?'" Oswald directed a look that silenced him, and the rest of the table.

Mason cleared his throat. "I hear the Mayburys will be returning to court ere long," he began, and Linnet backed him up by exclaiming an interest in this piece of news.

Fen leaned forward in her seat so there was less space between herself and her husband. "Did you, um, ever think that Lady Sumner might make you a very good sort of wife?" she asked in a rush. Once again, the rest of the table went into a profound silence, and all the heads turned their way. Fen turned scarlet.

"Need I remind you that Lady Sumner is a married woman?" said Oswald cuttingly. "And has been for several years now."

Fen clutched her goblet hard between her fingers. "But her husband is ever so old," she pointed out with determination.

"I have no interest in the marital status of Lady Sumner," he answered her after a couple of heartbeats. "Was it also the Queen who put this into your head?"

Fen gazed at the bottom of her cup. "She may have mentioned something," she mumbled distractedly.

"Since when have you been one of Armenal's cronies?" asked Roland.

Fen was half inclined to ignore his rude question, but when she looked up everyone was looking at her curiously. "She came and sat with me awhile today while I was being painted for my portrait."

"Did she, indeed?" asked Oswald grimly. "With the express intent of sowing discord into my marriage, or some other aim?"

"Oh, I am sure the Queen did not—" began Linnet anxiously, but Mason reached across and placed a hand over hers. She pressed her lips together and lapsed into silence.

"She didn't tell me her intent," said Fen mutinously.

Oswald threw down his napkin and dragged his chair back from the table. To Fen's surprise he reached across and grabbed her wrist, pulling her up and out of her chair. "Excuse us," he said shortly. "We will be retiring early." He strode toward their room, towing Fen in his wake. She cast a look back over her shoulder to see the rest of the family's eyes trained on them with varying expressions of surprise or interest.

"My lord—" she started to protest as the door slammed behind them, only to find herself pressed up against it.

"What are you doing?" he asked conversationally.

Fen had no idea why she was panting, although her husband's lower body was pressed into her own in a somewhat suggestive manner. He probably didn't intend it to be, she told herself, trying to think calming thoughts. One of his legs was pressed between hers in a way that was quite depriving her of all breath.

"I was just—"

"No," he said.

"No?" Despite his controlled manner of speaking, it occurred to Fen that he was not calm. Not at all. There was a small tic in his jaw that she had not noticed before.

"If you want to ask me—" He broke off his words and stared fixedly past her ear a moment, before taking a deep breath. "There are some things that should be said between a man and a wife," he said tersely. "Without an audience."

"What things?" asked Fen, realizing that despite his dominant stance, her husband was definitely on his back foot. She relaxed against the door, but he immediately crowded further into her. Fen took a deep breath.

Again, he seemed to struggle for words. "If I can tolerate Thane's existence on the face of this earth, then I don't think you have any reason to feel ill used," he said, narrowing his eyes.

Fen considered this. "I suppose that's fair," she said. "Though after you jilted me, you had several other betrotheds, or so I heard. And now I find there were other women as well." Her voice rose on the last four words.

"Other women?" There was a definite edge to his voice now. Fen had no idea why she was pushing this, but she was feeling reckless. Like pulling a lion's tail, *or perhaps it should be a panther's*, she thought, thinking of the Vawdrey crest. "There have been no other women," he said in a softly menacing voice. "Are you trying to deliberately provoke me?"

"Enid Jauncey!" Fen flung at him.

His expression flickered a moment. "A neighbor and friend of my sister-in-law," he said. "What has she to do with me?"

Fen found she was breathing hard now. "How should I know? I've heard precious little of your exploits over the years."

"Exploits?"

"And why did Lady Sumner lend me her clothing when I first arrived?" asked Fen, her color mounting. She hadn't even realized that still rankled. "Did you buy them for her?" she asked wildly. "Is she your—?"

"Don't you say it," warned Oswald softly.

"Mistress!" yelled Fen defiantly.

Both of them were breathing hard now. Oswald stepped back so fast that Fen startled to topple forward, then she found herself yanked over toward the bed, his hands gripping her waist and hauling her without effort.

Her feet left the floor and she was flung unceremoniously down onto the mattress, face first. As she struggled to sit up, he was on her, shoving her flat and tugging at the lacings that ran down the back of her dress.

Fen squirmed and wriggled, but it made no difference. The bodice of her dress went slack, but to her surprise, he didn't drag it off her. Instead his weight briefly left her, and she felt her skirts being flung up, exposing her legs and backside. "What are you doing?" she squeaked.

"Can't you tell?" he asked, settling behind her. "We've done it this way before. Like the beasts. Remember? I'm going to mount you from behind." Fen gasped, stiff as a plank, but it made no difference as his warm hand slid around to her tummy and then dipped lower to cup her between her legs. He was lying on top of her now, pinning her in place. "Open your legs wider." She felt his voice vibrate deep in her stomach and turned bright red.

503

"I can't, you're squashing me flat!" she lied, mortified at the view he must be getting of her fleshy backside. He hadn't even removed her stockings! She had lost one shoe in the tussle in the doorway, but she fancied the other hung off her foot. She kicked her leg and heard the shoe fall to the floor with a dull thud.

"No matter," said Oswald calmly. He shifted over her, so he was straddling her waist, but facing her feet.

She stiffened at the outrage. "What are you doing?"

"Just enjoying the view," he said lightly and ran his hands over the twin globes of her buttocks. He leaned down and brushed a kiss first on one and then the other.

Fen gasped. "Y-you're the wrong way around!"

He laughed softly. "You sound so outraged, Fenella. But if you feel so strongly about me not having a mistress, then there is a certain price that has to be paid."

"What price?" huffed Fen, feeling his hand rest on her behind and then lightly trace down the crack until his questing fingers slid right into her secret female place that ached and tingled and was already embarrassingly wet.

"Oh!" Fen dropped her face onto the mattress and bit her lip as she tried not to react to the wicked fingers which probed and stroked and slid, until she found herself opening her legs of her own accord to give him better access. Her cheeks burned, as she found herself acting the wanton.

"It doesn't seem you'll mind overmuch," he said lightly, teasing.

Fen felt her forehead break out in a light sweat as she started to move desperately against the slide of his fingers. She whimpered.

"There?"

She nodded her head desperately, forgetting he wasn't looking in the direction of her face. "Please!" she burst out.

He redoubled his efforts and Fen felt an explosion behind her eyeballs. She shouted hoarsely, and he shoved his fingers deep inside her, his thumb still rotating lightly against the little bead that was so sensitive. As the euphoria subsided, he flexed his fingers, prolonging her tremors and drawing them out until she was nothing more than a shimmering, melted puddle of bliss.

Fen's eyes drifted shut, and she was barely aware of the fact she was being rolled onto her back. She groaned and felt him resettle over her, but she kept her eyes resolutely shut. Mayhap, he would take pity on her and realize her legs were too weak to hold her up right now if he wanted to do it like the beasts of the field. She needed a breather at least. Then she felt his hair brush her thighs, and her eyes sprang open at the precise moment she felt his warm breath against her most intimate place. "Husband!"

He glanced up as he rearranged her limbs, so that her knees were over his shoulders. "You've a price to pay, remember?"

Fen gazed at him. "A price?"

"For my not employing a mistress," he answered.

Fen huffed out a breath as her mind reeled. Her position was most indecent. Somehow her green stockings and red garters intact made it even worse. She could only imagine the picture she must present to his eyes. She looked back at him uncertainly, but his rapt gaze was between her open legs.

"Gods, you're so—" he said thickly, and then lowered his mouth to her. Fen sucked in a shocked breath. He had done this to her before, of course. But she hadn't been fully dressed. And she hadn't had her legs flung over his shoulders. And she hadn't known what to expect. This time felt very different as she clutched the bedsheets and writhed like a snake against the mattress.

He took a lot longer over it this time. Almost an indecent amount of time. With embarrassing speed, he brought her to the brink of the cliff again and again, only to avoid the crisis and then try a different approach which grew and grew until she was back on the precipice again.

In this position, there was no escape from that tormenting mouth which seemed to have learned her every weak spot and secret delight. She shivered. She shuddered. She started to rock herself against his mouth. She was so close. So, so close. When he lifted his head and wiped his mouth with the back of his hand, Fen stared up at him in speechless indignation! Before she could complain at such treatment, however, she noticed the molten heat in his eyes.

"Up!" he said, his voice gravelly. "I need to be inside you. Now." He was unhooking her legs and rolling her back onto her stomach. He deftly unfastened his crotch and Fen's eye was drawn to his angry-looking manhood which sprang forth.

It stood pointing almost straight up and looked more swollen than ever. He didn't bother to remove his long black chauses or undo his tunic. "Up on your knees," he urged her, his hands at her waist.

Fen scrambled to her knees, but her skirts were getting in the way in the front. "Wait," she panted. "My dress..."

But he was past waiting. As she fumbled, trying to drag the caught-up material from under her knees, he was lining their bodies up behind her. She felt the swollen head of his man-root at her needy entrance and whimpered. The next thing she knew, he had driven its full length into her and was so deep her eyes watered. "*Oh, my lord!*" she shrieked, and he stilled.

"Fen? Are you—?"

She lowered her head and wailed as her shuddering body was engulfed in wave after wave of sensation.

He groaned, "That feels so good. You're going to make me reach it too soon." Then he slammed into her again and again, his hard hips pummeling against her soft, cushiony body.

Fen's arms gave out partway through and she turned her face to the side so her cheek rested against the mattress as he hammered his way right through her own rapture and loudly achieved his own.

He lay a moment, covering her back as he recovered his breath. Then he peeled himself off her with a reluctant sigh and turned her over. "Let's get this off you," he murmured.

Fen's eyes fluttered open. It was a good job he'd loosened her gown at the start, she thought. Or she wouldn't have been able to catch her breath once he'd started with her. She looked down in dismay at several rents at the front of her dress from where the front of her skirt had torn away from the bodice. *Whatever will Trudy think?*

"I'll buy you a new one," said Oswald, seeing the direction of her gaze.

"I'm sure it can be mended," she said as he lifted her gown up and over her head.

He dropped it over the side of the bed, straightened her shift, and then palmed her cheek, looking into her eyes. "Was I too rough?"

Fen felt her color flood back again. "No," she said.

"You're sure?"

"Quite sure," she said, turning from him self-consciously to pull back the covers.

"Fen." She looked up. "You know those things I said about paying prices and mistresses was all just bullshit, don't you?"

She hesitated. "Previously, you did say you'd lived a celibate life for many years," she said, looking to him for confirmation.

He nodded. "That's right, I did."

Fen thought this over as she slipped under the covers. She had been a fool to overreact the way she did about Lady Anne. She was ashamed of herself. That lady had done nothing but act kindly toward her, even if she wasn't very friendly.

Oswald was refastening his crotch, and to her surprise, apart from some hectic color in his face, looked otherwise completely unscathed from the encounter.

"Are you not joining me in bed?" she blurted, watching him straighten himself.

"I certainly am," he said with a faint smile. "But I'll go and see about some hot water first. I don't want you to be uncomfortable."

Fen pressed her thighs together and acknowledged that a wash would be good. She hugged her knees as he went out the door and shut it behind him, her feelings in a tumult. She had never thought herself a particularly jealous woman before.

If she wasn't careful, she'd give him a disgust of her, she thought anxiously. Men hated jealous women, or so everyone said. She was just experiencing a severe dip in her emotions when the door reopened and Oswald himself came in carrying a jug of hot water.

"Come on," he said. "Let's have you."

Fen slipped from the bed and joined him as he poured some into a bowl for her and handed her some sweet-smelling soap leaves.

She quickly worked up a lather and gave herself a thorough wash under her shift.

Oswald made no comment about her modesty, just handed her a drying cloth, and when she had finished, stripped down and washed himself. Fen got back into bed, and he joined her mere moments later, sliding right across into her space and taking her in his arms.

Her husband settled against her back, kissing her shoulder and holding her close. A comfortable silence stretched, when to her surprise, he suddenly broke it. "Lady Anne Sumner is in my employ," he said quietly. "She's a spy for the Crown. I never felt anything for her. Any time we spent together was just business. Since you and I have been reunited, Bryce has made sure she receives any orders from him. He's made it clear it offends his sense of propriety for me to be in a room alone with her."

Fen considered this for a moment. "I do like Bryce," she sighed. "It was foolish of me to bring Lady Anne Sumner up like that," she said, hanging her head. "I'm sorry. I hope I didn't show you up too badly in front of your family. I will apologize to them all on the morn."

"You'll do no such thing," he told her firmly. "It's really not necessary. You should have seen the way Mason carried on when he first wed Linnet. He was always flying up into the boughs about something or other."

Fen thought about this a moment. He was kind to make excuses for her, but she had been out of order. "It shouldn't have bothered me," she said. "But it did. The Queen said that she thought Lady Sumner would be the sort of person who would be ideally matched with you." She paused while Oswald made an irritated noise. "But she meant no mischief by it."

"Oh, didn't she?" he said grimly.

Fen carried on in a rush. "I know I shouldn't care about your association with Lady Anne, now I know she's protecting the realm. But I can't help but be glad that Bryce is a stickler for propriety," she admitted wretchedly.

He lay very still a moment. "Say that again, Fen."

"I never thought of myself as a petty, jealous wife before," she said in a small voice. "But it appears that's what I am."

To her surprise, her husband loomed over her a moment, before rolling her on her back and taking her under him. "I don't mind you being jealous, Fenella," he said, taking her mouth in a deep, drugging kiss. He pulled back. "You can be jealous all you want. It only seems fair. After all, I won't be able to rest until I've run that bastard Thane clear out of Aphrany."

Fen opened her mouth to respond to his astonishing news, only to find her lips taken again in a strangely tender, yet erotic kiss. His tongue danced against hers, and daringly, she responded in kind. He made a strangled noise into her mouth, then his hands were running up her thighs, bunching up her shift.

"I'm going to get you all dirty again," he warned.

Fen huffed out a breath as she felt his manhood, hard and heavy against her stomach. "So…no mistresses?" she said, biting her lip as he hooked her knee and drew it up.

511

"None," he said simply. "I only want you. Wrap your leg around my waist."

Fen breathed out a breath she hadn't known she'd been holding. *I only want you.* It was strange to think her jealousy had so inflamed him, but it seemed that was indeed the case. This time their coming together was slow and thorough. Fen ran her hands up and down his back and sides, and if he wasn't kissing her lips, it was her throat, or her breasts.

"You're so beautiful, Fenella," he told her, his mouth against her ear. "And you're all mine."

Afterward, as they lay entangled and depleted, Fen drifted off into a dream about a small wooden bridge she could not cross because a man had hold of her hand and would not let go. She frowned in her sleep until she recognized the ring on his finger bore her family crest of the Bernard bear, and then she relaxed. For some reason, she could not raise her eyes to his face, but she was content to let him lead her away from the bridge, toward an oak tree that stood on a hill.

36

"Fenella." Fen's eyes opened, even though the word was spoken quietly. Oswald was dressed and stood by the side of the bed. "Come and break your fast with me," he said, and held out his hand imperiously.

Fen rose at once and he enfolded her in his peacock-blue robe and led her into the adjoining shared room.

Meldon was stumping round, setting down plates of food from a tray. "Shall I fetch more?" he asked, squinting at them and then the contents of the table.

"I'm sure that's ample," said Fen, who wasn't really hungry. She yawned.

"I should have left you in bed," said Oswald ruefully. "It's only that I'm going to be very busy over the next few days." He hesitated. "With this whole Blechmarsh princess matter coming to a head."

"Oh," said Fen, sitting down beside him. She wanted to press him for more details but did not quite like to.

"I'll be rising early and returning late."

Fen's face fell. "Oh, that's a shame."

"It feels like I never get to spend any time alone with you these days," he added with a faint frown.

Fen smiled and propped her chin up with her hand. "I'm glad you woke me."

"Good." He leaned over and kissed her on the lips.

Meldon cleared his throat disapprovingly as he set down a jug of water and a jug of ale. "What are you about today?" Oswald asked her, ignoring his manservant.

"Mathilde Martindale said she would accompany me this morning as I sit for signor Arnotti. We have to finish our tapestry design and I thought I would teach her how to play that card game Livelihood." Oswald nodded, tucking into some toasted bread. "It's exceedingly dull sitting on that window seat," admitted Fen. "If my friends hadn't rallied around, I don't know what I would have done."

Oswald took a sip of water. "Hopefully the result will be worth it," he said.

Fen spared a glance for her adolescent portrait and heartily seconded that wish. "If it is even half-decent, at least we can consign that other portrait to a dark cupboard," she said hopefully.

Oswald frowned. "I'm rather fond of that other portrait," he said and reached inside his tunic to touch something. Fen remembered his chain and wondered if it was a talisman. "There's no rule that I can't have two portraits of my wife, that I'm aware," he said lightly.

"What about you?" asked Fen. "Are there any boyhood portraits of you at Vawdrey Keep?"

Oswald grimaced. "Good gods, no. My father was not remotely sentimental. At least, not until old age," he amended.

514

Fen felt disappointed. "Perhaps we could have a portrait commissioned of you from signor Arnotti?" Seeing from his expression that he was not keen on the idea, she added quickly: "A matching portrait?"

"A matched pair of paintings might have merit," he conceded.

"To hang side by side?" suggested Fen.

He smiled at this. "You're getting rather good at maneuvering me, wife," he said, narrowing his eyes.

"Do you think so?" asked Fen wistfully.

He laughed. "Oh, I think so."

Fen smiled. "I don't know if it's possible to entirely domesticate a panther," she joked.

He reached across the table and laced their fingers together. "You seem to be managing just fine."

Really, she chose the stupidest moments to come over shy, Fen thought a full hour later as she reflected on her husband for the hundredth time that day. She unpacked the Livelihood cards, a book of poetry, and the preliminary sketches she and Mathilde had put together for their tapestry panel.

Mathilde had met her in the West Vestibule, and they had taken up the spot by the window where signor Arnotti was hopefully now adding the finishing touches to his latest work. The artist didn't look any calmer to Fen's eye but still wore that habitual

515

half scowl she was now so accustomed to as he skulked behind the canvas.

Really, she had no notion how Bess could discern anything pleasing about the man's company! Clearly, poor Bess had never spent time in the company of a truly charming man, such as her own husband. Fen explained to signor Arnotti that she had not been able to bring Bors this morning as he was out with her brother-in-law, but the artist just grunted at this and shrugged so she returned to her friend.

"I thought it might be diverting after we've finished our tapestry plan layout to have a game of cards," she told Mathilde, after they had enquired politely after the other.

Mathilde, whose mind was clearly elsewhere, gave a small start. "Cards?" she repeated blankly.

Suddenly it occurred to Fen that, with her friend's extremely sheltered upbringing she might not be permitted to play. "Oh! Of course, if you would rather not—"

"No, no, I would love to," Mathilde hastened to assure her. "And Nurse is not collecting me until one o'clock, so no one need know."

Fen bit her lip. "I would not wish to put you in any moral quandary—" she started.

Mathilde reached across and touched her hand. "It won't." She smiled at her, but to Fen's mind she did look like she had something on her mind. "Fenella," she started hesitantly. *Here it comes*, thought Fenella. But to her surprise her friend was drawing something out of her alms purse. "I hope you will accept this small token as a Solstice gift. It is only a trifle and I promise you, it is mine to bestow."

"Oh!" said Fen, looking down at the small carved trinket box. "Why, it's beautiful, Mathilde! And I have bought something for you also, but I thought to give it to you on Solstice Eve."

Mathilde flushed slightly. "I think I might—that is, Mother often takes us into the country for the Midwinter festival."

"Then I must give you mine this morning when we return to the living quarters," Fen told her. "Do you think your nurse will permit you to call at my chambers for it?"

"Oh, I'm sure of it," said Mathilde. "And perhaps I might have another hold of Lady Linnet's baby."

Fen laughed. "He would be very pleased to see you again, I'm sure. You are quite the favorite." She opened and closed her trinket box, then clasped it to her chest. "How thoughtful you are. I love it."

Mathilde flushed. "I think we must endeavor to complete this design today," she said, looking down at their design for the flower panel. "Or it will not be completed at all." Fen looked at her in surprise. "I mean," Mathilde corrected herself hastily. "In time for the new year."

"Oh, I see," said Fen. "Yes, we do need to get a move on, or ours will not be done in time to join the others." They bent their heads over the paper until signor Arnotti signaled his displeasure and Fen had to sit up straighter and peer down her nose to see it. "What say you to some marigolds, entwined with

517

the cowslips?" suggested Fen, as Mathilde added finer detail to their preliminary sketches.

"I think that would look very pretty," her friend agreed. "I did show you my technique, did I not, for building up the petals?" She looked slightly anxious as she peered up at Fen. "You see, I have made a note in the border when to use that particular stitch?"

"Yes," Fen assured her. "You did." To her surprise, she noticed Mathilde was making meticulous notes with directions for every stitch to use. Maybe her friend always did her designs this way? It was certainly very thorough. "I thought we could entwine our initials at the bottom corner," suggested Fen. "Or maybe use a floral device to suggest our names, using the language of flowers."

A funny look passed over Mathilde's face. "I think that's a lovely idea," she said in a muffled voice. "But perhaps we could decide that later."

"Yes, whatever you think is best," said Fen, but it did seem a bit odd not to note that down when she was being so precise about everything else.

"Stop screwing up the face!" barked signor Arnotti, emerging purple-faced from behind his canvas. "This is not to be borne!"

Fen gave him an irritated look. "I would have thought you'd have finished my face by now, signor!"

"It is the light diffusion on your face that occupies me," he spat out. "Not your features."

Fen sighed and tried to relax her facial muscles. "Are you going to watch the dancing in the Yellow Chamber this afternoon?" Fen asked. "I believe Eden is dancing and the Queen will be in attendance."

"Oh!" said Mathilde. "No, for I have a small, troubling cough today." She coughed delicately on cue. "And will not be able to stand around and watch the performance this afternoon. My mother will be there," she added as an afterthought.

Fen did not receive this news with any enthusiasm. "That's a shame," she said. "About your cough," she added, quickly hoping her friend did not perceive an insult to her mother. "I doubt very much Hester will be going, as she avoids such gatherings like the plague." She sighed. "It is hard when you are faced with a roomful of strangers."

"I have heard that Lady Bess Hartleby is going," Mathilde told her, which perked Fen up. At least she would have someone friendly to stand with, even if Bess had been acting quite oddly lately. "Her uncle, Sir Reginald Hartleby, is lately engaged to one of the Queen's ladies, Lady Constance Pryor."

Signor Arnotti's head emerged once again, and Fen braced herself for a criticism, but he said nothing, merely regarded them thoughtfully and then retreated. It was on the tip of Fen's tongue to mention Bess's odd behavior the previous day to Mathilde, but she could not really do that with signor Arnotti himself within earshot, so she suppressed the impulse.

"Well, that is fortunate for me, at any event," she said and left it at that. She watched Mathilde's design filling out the border with approval. "The other idea I had was that we could have a central text after all," she said. "But not an improving one," she

519

said hastily. "Something around the bonds of female friendship I thought might be nice."

Mathilde's head bowed over the design a moment, and when she looked up her eyes were moist with tears. "I think that would be lovely," she said softly. "Though that subject is not much celebrated in classical literature."

"Because it is all written by men," said Fenella briskly. "We can compose our own tenet, if needs must."

"Yes," agreed Mathilde and left a blank rectangular shape in the middle of the paper. "That can be added in." She hesitated. "In that case, I think our design is as good as completed," she said, straightening up.

Fen clapped her hands. "Excellent. Most excellent. And now, poetry, do you think?" she asked lifting a red leather-bound book out of her bag. "Or cards?"

"Cards, I think," said Mathilde, tapping her chin. "We can read the poetry after, and then we won't have to worry about Nurse arriving."

"Good idea." Fen spent the next ten minutes explaining the game of Livelihood to her friend in great detail. Mathilde's eyes glazed over, and Fen had a feeling she would not be adept at the game, but to her surprise, as soon as they started laying down cards, she found that Mathilde was quite the protégée.

Fen watched in amazement as her friend's pile of cards grew and her own diminished. "You really are extremely good at this," she marveled.

Mathilde glanced down at her pile of cards and flushed. "Oh—beginner's luck, I'm sure," she said uncomfortably.

"It's remarkable," said Fen. "I had thought that I was quite good, but—" She sat in surprise as her friend trumped her cleric's card with that of the topless female.

"Whore," said Mathilde absently. Fen gasped. Mathilde looked from Fenella to the card and back again. "Is that not what it's called?" she asked in confusion.

"Roland told me it was a nursing mother!"

Mathilde blushed to the roots of her hair. "I do apologize," she stammered. "I must not have been attending to what you said!"

Fen remembered how Roland's friends had told her not to play it with any other ladies. She looked shrewdly at "Mouse" Martindale. "Have I been very naïve?" she asked slowly.

Mathilde fidgeted unhappily on her low seat. "I—have a confession to make," she said, hanging her head. "I have played this game before."

"Who on earth with?" asked Fen in astonishment.

Mathilde went an even darker shade of red. "The palace pages," she admitted. "They're very dear little boys. And I've been so terribly lonely over the years..." To Fen's horror, her friend burst into tears. "Please don't tell my mother," she begged, groping for her kerchief.

"Of course I won't!" responded Fen hotly, patting her on the shoulder. "You've done nothing wrong to find allies where you

521

can." She wasn't sure how sweet the pages were though, teaching the sheltered Mathilde most unsuitable words!

Mathilde mopped her eyes and sat back. "I give them sweets and mend their hose, and they teach me their games, or tell me their woes. They are most horribly neglected, you know, and left to their own devices after being sent by their families to court."

Mathilde looked so sincere that Fen's heart went out to her. Was this another outlet for her thwarted maternal instinct? She wouldn't be surprised. "Before you came to court"—Mathilde hiccupped—"they were my only friends."

"I see," said Fen. "Of course. Please don't distress yourself." She glanced over at the easel, but it did not seem that signor Arnotti was remotely interested in their conversation, so she relaxed.

By degrees, Mathilde was comforted, and they abandoned the cards for the poetry book and sat side by side in companionable silence. Mathilde's old nurse arrived promptly as the clock struck one and made much exclamation about Mathilde's red-rimmed eyes and nose.

"It's my cough, Nurse," Mathilde explained. "Indeed, my throat is rather sore too."

"Oh dear, oh dear," her nurse fretted. "We must get you back to bed immediately." She steadfastly refused to allow her charge to come by the Vawdrey rooms to collect her Solstice gift. "We must get you to bed at once, my lady," the older woman fussed. Mathilde looked regretful but subsided under her nurse's insistence.

"It is of no matter," Fen assured her, though she had not seen Mathilde cough once, except the decorous small cough she had given to illustrate her point. "I can send your gift along presently with Cuthbert."

"I had hoped to see Baby Archie one more time," said Mathilde wistfully.

"Oh no, milady," exclaimed her nurse in shocked tones. "Not when you're so poorly! That wouldn't do at all!"

Fen embraced her friend, despite Nurse's disapproval. "Will I see you on the morrow?"

"In three days hence," said Mathilde. "I should be recovered enough for us to start our tapestry together. Shall we meet in the usual place—the long gallery? At the usual time?"

"That would be lovely."

Mathilde squeezed Fen's hands tightly. "Don't forget," she said cryptically.

"Forget?"

"To think of a text about female friendship," said Mathilde with a tight smile. But strangely, Fenella did not think that was what she *had* meant. She paused, but Mathilde had already let go of her hands.

"Until Friday," Fen called after her as she was whisked away by her tutting nurse. Mouse looked at her over her shoulder and gave her a wobbly smile. Fen had no idea why she felt so unsettled by the whole encounter, but there was no mistaking the fact she was rattled.

She returned to change for the dance performance and don a little jewelry as befitted a royal function. Trudy helped fasten her diamond girdle around her hips, and she changed her head veil for one of the very finest gauzy ones she owned.

"Thank you, Trudy," she said, delving into a drawer to find the veil she had bought for Mathilde in the marketplace, decorated with finely stitched red-breasted robins around the edges. When she found it, she carefully folded it and tied a ribbon about it before hurrying out to find Cuthbert.

"Would you be so kind as to deliver this to Lady Martindale?" Cuthbert accepted it curiously. "It's her Solstice gift," she explained. "You probably won't be admitted as she has come down with a cold, but if you could give it to her nurse, I would be very grateful. She resides in Lady Doverdale's suite of rooms."

He nodded, and Fen noticed he did not seem half as chatty today. "Is all well with you, Cuthbert?" she asked hesitantly.

He shrugged. "Roland doesn't want a squire," he said moodily. "Apparently he's never had one. He refuses to."

"Oh, that's really too bad!" exclaimed Fen. "I wonder why not?"

"He wouldn't let me read his palm, so I don't know," said Cuthbert with a scowl.

"He really ought to step up and take some responsibility at his age," said Fen. "How about if I speak to my husband?"

"Will he make him?" asked Cuthbert with sudden enthusiasm.

"Well, he is the head of the family," Fen reminded him. "Though I fancy he will be subtler in his methods. He usually gets what he wants. And if I ask him for something, he generally lets me have it."

"But…" Cuthbert hesitated. "Aren't you in disgrace?" he asked simply.

Fen started. "What? Oh…" She remembered being dragged from the dinner table the night before and blushed. "N-no," she said with embarrassment. "That is all quite forgotten now!"

Cuthbert nodded sagely. "That's what my Lord Cadwallader said."

"What's that?" asked Fen, wondering what on earth Mason could have to say about the state of her marriage.

"When we was sat round eating salted herrings this morning, your maid brought out your dress and it was all ripped," said Cuthbert. "And my lord said, 'There's hope for their marriage yet.'"

Fen stared at Cuthbert in mingled horror and annoyance. "Yes, well," she said weakly as words failed her.

"But you'll ask Lord Vawdrey?" Cuthbert fastened his blue eyes on her hopefully.

"Yes, I will," she assured him. "By the way, Cuthbert," she asked on impulse just before he disappeared out of the door. "In a game of Livelihood, what trumps a cleric?"

"A priest, do ye mean?" he replied, scratching his head. She nodded, guessing he must play a regional version. "A strumpet," he supplied promptly, and shut the door behind him.

Aha! She had thought as much!

37

Fen hurried down to the Yellow Chamber, and had a stroke of good luck when she saw her friend Bess making her way unhurriedly down the corridor. "Bess!" she called. "Wait for me!" She hurried up to her and they exchanged greetings. "I understand you are going to this dance performance with the Queen now?"

"Yes," admitted Bess glumly. "Though not by choice, I assure you!" She glowered. "Uncles are the very devil, don't you know. I've got a new hawk to train and nigh on a dozen more useful things to do than gawk at a load of nubile females."

"Yes, I had heard that your uncle is lately betrothed to one of the Queen's ladies."

"Old fool!" said Bess. "You'd think he'd have something better to do at his time of life than take a wife half his age!"

Fen blinked. "You are close to your uncle?"

"He's my legal guardian, if that's what you mean," she said bitterly. "And if he marries that model of decorum, Lady Constance, then I will likely be taken into their household and forced to spin and weave and do all manner of women's occupations." She spat the last two words as if they were obscenities.

"Oh, well, perhaps this afternoon's entertainment will take your mind off it?" Fen suggested and earned a scathing glance in reply.

"Not bloody likely," Bess grumbled.

The hall was rather full when they arrived, and to Fen's surprise, both the King and Queen were seated upon the dais. She had thought only the Queen would be in attendance. Bess towed her through the crowds until they found a less populated area next to a large pillar.

"Looks like a quiet spot," said Bess as the two of them stood unobtrusively to one side. "Don't want to get hemmed in so we can't escape if it becomes too damned tedious," she said, looking about.

Fenella winced, hoping no one could hear her outspoken friend. One look at the tall, rather fancy-looking ambassador from the Western Isles made her worried he was smirking at them. She couldn't quite remember his name, but she knew they had been introduced.

"Do you know any other of the dancers?" asked Fen hurriedly as the ladies filed into the room in a single line and took up their positions in a square formation. To her eye, there looked to be about sixteen of them in number. Eden was stood front and center, and at twenty-two, was probably the oldest in the bunch.

Bess puffed out her cheeks. "Not likely. Looks like they're hanging out for well-connected husbands," she said with disinterest. "That one there with the meek downcast eyes and the white hands is the one that's caught my uncle's eye."

Fen looked at Bess's prospective aunt and thought she looked rather younger than Bess. She didn't voice this opinion. Thank goodness she was already married, she thought as the musicians struck up and the ladies started to weave complicated steps as they moved in and out, touching hands before spinning away.

She would never have been able to keep up with such intricate patterns. Eden was easily the most fleet of foot and elegant of form as she glided across the floor, her black hair sleek and shining, her pale neck long and delicate. Her slim body bent and swayed in time to the music, and it was obvious the other dancers were looking to her to keep time and follow her lead.

But as the crowds around them began to discreetly whisper, Fen noticed that the name on most people's lips was that of the prettiest girl in the group, Lady Helen Cecil. From the faux-demure look on her face, it looked like she was well aware of the stir she was causing and was rather enjoying it.

"Who's that one?" asked Bess. "Smug-faced one, with the big eyes."

Fen cleared her throat. "I believe that's Lady Helen Cecil," she murmured as discreetly as possible.

"Eh? Isn't that the King's latest trollop?" asked Bess with interest.

Fen made a strangled noise in her throat, which, to her dismay, quickly turned into a coughing fit. The tall gentleman to her left stepped up to her and presented her with a handkerchief, which she took with thanks and dabbed her watering eyes.

"Countess Vawdrey," he greeted her with a bow, and hearing his low, drawling voice, she remembered his name at once.

"Viscount Bardulf," she said with a curtsey, and offered him back his handkerchief. He waved a hand for her to keep it and turned back to watching the dance.

Fen turned back too and found she did recognize one other of the young ladies, Lady Helen's older sister, Jane Cecil. Jane performed the steps competently enough, though she had neither Eden's grace and suppleness or the voluptuous lure of her sister. In short, the eye was not drawn to her as it was the other two. Bess nudged Fen in the side and nodded her head toward the royal couple.

Queen Armenal was watching the dancers with every apparent pleasure, a smile about her lips, and King Wymer was tapping the arm of his seat in time to the music. "Wonder if she knows," whispered Bess hoarsely, presumably referring to the Queen. Fen shot an uneasy glance at Viscount Bardulf. Had not Oswald said something about him being a countryman of the Queen's? His narrowed eyes were fixed on the formation of the dance, and he gave no indication of having heard them.

"Eden's easily the best," said Bess, nodding toward Eden. "Shame she's so uppity."

"Uppity?" whispered Fen. "She's always been most agreeable to me."

"Oh, me too," agreed Bess, tugging at her wimple. "But people do say she's a bit aloof and rather prim and prudish."

Fen thought suddenly of Roland. What was it he'd said of Eden? Knowing Roland, it was probably something shallow about her looks. But to Fenella's mind, Eden looked lithe and slender as a faery dancer.

Suddenly, the ladies all turned in a circle, and the dance was ended. Everyone clapped politely and the ladies dropped into low curtseys, the last strain of the music dying away. The King cleared his throat, but before he could speak, Armenal cut clean across him with her loud, carrying voice.

"A most commendable performance. I congratulate you, my dear Eden, on your masterly execution. You had by far the lightest and most graceful step, as always, but I fancy I see another close on your heels." Her gaze traveled over the party of young women. "Lady Jane Cecil," she said benevolently, and Fen watched the ripple of surprise her words created. The Queen paused, nodding at the reaction. "You see," she said, holding up a finger and taking the murmurs for agreement. "I am not the only one to admire such dainty steps."

Lady Jane turned quite pink with pleasure. "Your Majesty," she said breathlessly and sank down into another low curtsey. At her side, Fen noticed Lady Helen's smile looked a little fixed at the fulsome praise her sister was receiving.

"Come before me, young woman," said the Queen, beckoning to Jane. To everyone's amazement, the Queen removed the brooch from her own bodice, which had an opal in it as large as a pigeon's egg, and pinned it to the trembling Jane's dress. "Accept this trifle as a small tribute to your talent," said the Queen benevolently.

"Your Highness, I am overcome," said Jane, who really did seem to be on the brink of grateful tears. The Queen held out her hand, and Jane clasped it as reverently as if it were a holy relic.

"It is no more than you deserve," said the Queen, and Jane seemed to almost float back down the steps to rejoin the other dancers, her expression dazed, but deliriously happy.

"Most commendable, my dear," muttered the King, whose thunder had clearly been stolen by his consort's antics.

"You are too modest, husband," Armenal told him. "In this I am led by you, as in all things."
The King looked bewildered. "Did you not yourself recommend that I considered Sir Phillip's niece for one of my attendants?" she said with a gentle smile. "And you were quite right, for she is clearly the most superior young lady of the current crop by far."

The King sat like a stunned bullfrog, his mouth opening and closing. "Quite, quite," he agreed in a strangled voice. Though it must have been obvious to everyone that it was his paramour, Lady Helen, who he was trying to secure the position for.

When Fen looked back at the group of young ladies, Lady Helen was finding it hard to mask her chagrin at being so overlooked in her sister's favor. Clearly, she was not used to being eclipsed.

Viscount Bardulf gave a gentle laugh. "And there's the killing blow," he murmured. "Bravo." He melted away into the crowd, and when he reappeared, he was at the Queen's side.

Eden materialized at their side. "Did you enjoy the demonstration?" she asked.

"It was very instructive," said Fen, thinking of the royal couple's relationship. "Your dancing was sublime, my dear."

Eden waved this off modestly. "The result of many days of practice."

"The Queen seemed to think that Lady Jane Cecil was practically as good as you," said Bess rudely.

Fen opened her mouth to disagree, but Eden responded instead, with great dignity. "She certainly gave great encouragement to Lady Jane."

Fen wondered what on earth was going on with Bess, as she seemed to have taken an unaccountable dislike to Eden. She frowned at her and then turned back to Eden. "To my mind, there was simply no comparison to be made," she said truthfully. "I wonder," she said in a low aside. "Did you receive that note I sent care of yourself for that playwright fellow?"

"Oh yes, I meant to speak to you about that," said Eden. "I forwarded it to the address I had listed for Mr. Entner, but alas, it was returned this very morning. He has left those lodgings for cheaper ones. Unfortunately, his old landlord did not have a forwarding address."

"Oh dear," said Fen, her face falling. "So, he has not received my message."

"I'm afraid not," said Eden. "But never fear, I am sure he will be in touch soon with details of when the play is to be performed."

"That's what I'm worried about," mumbled Fen, but the other two were already turning and executing low curtseys. To Fen's horror, King Wymer had descended and was making his way through the crowd toward them. Fen watched his approach with alarm. Surely he would not acknowledge her, she thought as he seemed to make a beeline for her. Not when she knew how much he disliked her!

To her dismay, King Wymer came right up to her and glanced over her, his lips pressed together with disapproval. She dropped into a curtsey, and he gave her a brief nod. "I bet your husband paid a pretty penny for that girdle belt," he grunted. "Poor devil."

Fen flushed and looked down at the glittering diamonds on her belt. "As you say, Your Majesty," she agreed miserably. The King rocked backward and forward on the balls of his feet a few times. Fen glanced around, hoping someone else might come along to alleviate the awkwardness. *No such luck.*

Indeed, both Bess and Eden had faded tactfully away at his arrival. Pressure mounted with every second for her to speak and break the silence. "The—erm—weather is very fine today, sire. Is it not?"

Wymer shot her a look of disgust. "Gads, woman, if you've nothing worth saying, you'd best hold your tongue!"

Fen blinked, then turned to face forward again. "As you wish, sire," she said sadly. King Wymer was clearly no more reconciled to her existence than he was two months ago. She had no idea why he had singled her out for his attention, and she devoutly wished he had not!

She shifted uncomfortably, noticing how many people were shooting looks of envy and curiosity toward her. Doubtless they had not overheard his brusque words and thought they were passing the time of day. Pressing her own lips together firmly, she clasped her hands in front of her and did her best to shut down her feelings of discomfort.

After a few moments, Wymer surprised her by clearing his throat. "You might want to take it a little easier on him," he said gruffly. "He's not used to feminine ploys."

Fen blinked at him in astonishment. "Ploys?" she repeated faintly.

"Aye, ploys!" said Wymer, nodding his head. "You're all the same, never happy unless you've got us dancing to your tune!" Fen cast about in bewilderment but could think of no reply to that, unless to point out that her lute was back in Sitchmarsh. She knew instinctively that would not go down well. "You've got him all twisted up and back to front since you ensnared him in your machinations, woman!" he continued sternly. Fen bit the side of her mouth and eyed the King nervously. "Cat got your tongue?" he barked.

"I'm afraid I've nothing to say that will please you," she admitted.

"Humph! Like that, is it?" The King tsked and gave a quick shake of his head. "Poor bugger," he muttered under his breath and took his leave of her without even a backward glance.

Fen gazed after him, utterly mystified by both his words and his actions. She almost wondered if they spoke an entirely different language!
She gave a start when Eden's voice spoke in her ear. "The King does you great honor by having a private conversation with you," she said with satisfaction.

535

Fen struggled with a reply. "I'm afraid," she said, selecting her words carefully, "that His Majesty is not pleased by my marriage to Lord Vawdrey."

"Nonsense," said Eden with a frown. "It is very much remarked upon how he singles you out. And I am sure," she added complacently, "that he means the highest respect to your husband by doing so."

"Perhaps," conceded Fen weakly. After all, he did seem most concerned that she was a troublesome wife to Oswald. She sighed and vowed to ask her husband for advice on how to handle Wymer's dislike at some later point. "My husband seems to think that King Wymer will suddenly one day realize he does not detest me after all. Sadly, I think he is somewhat optimistic."

Eden played with her handkerchief. "On the whole I think Lord Vawdrey may be right. His Majesty has shown great favoritism in paying you attention today."

Fen spluttered. "You would not say so if you had heard the topic of our conversation."

On this though, Eden refused to believe her.

38

Oswald found his wife extremely quiet that evening as she prepared for bed. On the one hand, he appreciated the quiet, as he was exhausted after a long day maneuvering ministers into doing what he wanted. On the other hand, he felt immediately uneasy and wanted to know what was on her mind.

She barely spoke a word as she undressed and braided her hair in a single rope. He watched her covertly in the mirrored glass as he stood shaving over the washing basin. She climbed into the bed and lay there a moment with her hands clasped over her stomach. "Is there any especial reason why your brother Roland won't take his own personal squire?" she asked, surprising him.

How the hells should I know? was what sprang tetchily to his lips, but he tamped that response down and instead grunted, "No, not that I'm aware."

"Poor Cuthbert wants most dreadfully to attend the tournaments and jousts and so forth," she said confidingly. "I suggested he squired for Roland for a time here at court, but when he asked him, your brother turned him down. Rather ignominiously as I understand it."

"Sounds like Roland," said Oswald sourly. He had no idea why his wife thought their bedchamber was the place to ask him questions about his own brother. He didn't appreciate it. *Not one bit.*

She lapsed into silence for a moment. "I went to an audience with the King and Queen today," she said, surprising him again. "It was funny but…" Her words trailed off, a faint frown on her face.

Oswald half turned to look over his shoulder at her. "Our exalted rulers," he said dryly. "What about them?"

"Do you think they actually like each other?" asked Fen, looking confused.

"I don't think 'like' comes into it," he answered with a shrug. "Their marriage was arranged to align the houses of Lisle and Argent."

Fen considered this. "Yes," she said after a moment or two. "But, that's not really all that different to most marriages at court." She sounded a little sad.

Oswald frowned and swung back round to look at her. "They didn't meet until Armenal was fetched from her ship at the port and transported to the cathedral," he said dryly. "Whereas we met several times, over a three-year period." He watched her turn pink. He just knew she had been comparing them. He turned back to the mirror, but his attention was still mostly on her as he dragged the straight razor down his jaw.

"It's almost like…" She bit her bottom lip. "Like, they're opponents…"

"In the midst of some kind of battle," he finished for her.

Fen sat up in the bed. "Yes," she said, looking impressed. "That's exactly what it's like."

He turned back around to face her, wiping his face down with a cloth. "That's because they are."

"But I don't think the King's fully aware of the fact," she said. "Or, if he is, then he doesn't realize that the Queen's much better at it than he is."

Oswald smiled grimly and he threw down his cloth. "That is something you might not want to repeat outside of these four walls."

"I wouldn't say it to anyone else," she said guiltily and lay back down flat on her back. Oswald breathed out and started unbuttoning his cuffs. "They say the King loved his first wife, Queen Eleanor. Do you suppose that is true?"

Oswald shot a look at her, but she was staring resolutely at the ceiling. "I wouldn't know," he said carefully, after a heavy pause. "She had already died by the time I became a permanent fixture at court."

If Wymer *had* loved his first Queen, thought Oswald, he had certainly not been faithful to her. He knew of at least two royal bastards from that era that were common knowledge. He decided not to share this with Fen.

"People are saying that the King may divorce Queen Armenal, and instead marry the Princess Una," she rambled on.

Oswald drew in a breath. "Are they?" It was frankly news to him. He pulled a face as he shrugged off his tunic. He doubted the King would appreciate such a rumor. "You should not set much store by gossip," he said. "There is not often much substance to it."

Fen appeared to digest this a moment. "Queen Armenal said the only woman the King has ever really loved is his old nurse, Bathilde," said Fen.

Oswald paused in the act of pulling off his boots. "She said that?" In his experience the Queen was rarely so frank.

"Well..." Fen plucked at the bedsheets. "Not in so many words, but...pretty much."

He stripped down the last of his clothes and swiftly blew out the candles as he rolled into bed. "Is something bothering you?" he asked as he arranged himself around her. Oswald was dog-tired from his efforts to rush through the agreements about the princess coming to court. He was facing a lot of opposition, not least from the King. Even so, he could tell Fenella was troubled.

She sighed softly. "Not really. Are you tired?"
His libidinous body perked up, despite his mental fatigue. She was as delightfully soft and cushiony as ever. "It depends," he grunted. Gods, that was churlish. Sometimes he shocked even himself! "What do you need?" He hoped it was something simple, like his cock.

"You're not going to arrange a royal divorce, are you?" she asked in a small voice.

"No," he answered. "Put that from your mind."

She breathed out. "I'm glad."

For some reason that touched him on the raw. "I fail to see why you should feel sensitive around the subject," he said. "I told you, you've never even been divorced." Fen lay still, no doubt

540

stunned by his lack of sensitivity. "Is that it?" he asked. "Or is there more?" He was being sarcastic, but clearly his wife took it as an invitation to ramble on at him about a bunch of random things before he was to be permitted to sleep.

"How can I make the King look favorably on me?" she asked suddenly, completely blindsiding him.

"Why the hells would you want to do that?" he asked in a harsher tone than he'd intended.

Fen turned to look at him over her shoulder in surprise. "I thought that was what you wanted," she said in confusion. "You said—"

"No, it bloody well isn't!" he interrupted her rudely. "You should be worrying more about pleasing me than the King!"

Fen stared at him. "Well, I—" she started, but got no further, as he finished irritably with:

"Now perhaps you'll lie still and let me get some sleep." His tone was cold and angry. Fen's expression froze, and she quickly turned her face away and lowered her head to the pillow, trying to hold herself stiffly away from him. Oswald let her, rolling onto his back away from her. He heard her take a shuddering breath and then nothing.

Oswald lay in the dark. He was bone weary, but sleep didn't come. He lay listening to his wife's hitched breathing, until it evened out and she drifted off to a blameless sleep, while he lay feeling ashamed of being such a prick.

He knew what he had to do before he could sleep. He reached out and seized her waist, pulling her firmly back into his hard body, tucking her in tight against him. He had no sooner curled around her warm body than his eyelids drifted down, heavy with sleep.

The next morning, he did not wake her but rose swiftly and proceeded to the council chambers for an early gathering. His morning was as difficult as he'd anticipated. The other lords were appalled that he was rushing things through so fast. He started off calm and collected in the face of their many objections, but it was not without a price. The tic in his jaw was pronounced before he'd been in there for more than a few moments. Any modicum of calm was merely a mask.

"What about the added expense to the royal household, eh?" blustered Lord Lowan. "Are the King's coffers expected to pay the expenses for her own court to join his?"

"Her *court* at present consists of one blind old servant," said Oswald blandly once the furor that greeted Lord Lowan's words had died down. "Who has been with her since birth." That rather damped down the outrage of his fellow privy members but did not stamp it out altogether.

"What about the will of the people?" demanded a red-faced Sir Barret Covington-Bart. "They will not stand for another Blechmarsh hovering so close to the throne, depend upon it! There will be a public uproar of epic proportion!" He looked around at the sea of faces barking "Hear, hear" and "Quite right!"

Oswald waited for the hubbub to die down. "Do you think so?" he asked mildly. "That is not what my men on the ground are

542

reporting." A hush fell over the room at the allusion to his spy network. He paused for effect. "It seems the populace at large view the idea of the Blechmarsh princess as a figure of sympathy and even, dare I say, romance?" He let his eyes travel over the room as the council fidgeted and fumed in their seats.

"And do you not see the danger in that, sirrah?" burst out Lord Caterby. "Allowing such a person to capture the imagination of the unwashed masses? We could have an uprising on our hands! A rebellion! You seem to forget we have seen our country torn asunder by war—"

"Some of us," Oswald interrupted him coolly, "have seen those battlefields at rather closer quarters than others."

The inference was clearly felt by all present as they shuffled their feet and cleared their throats. Not one of them had ever served in His Majesty's army as he had.

"None of us disputes that you have an informed opinion, Vawdrey," said Lord Schaeffer hastily. "However, you are not the only one qualified to sway the King's opinion on these matters and—"

"Whoever has an alternative solution to the problem has had the past month to approach the King," said Oswald in a loud, stern voice. "His Highness has informed me that he has heard none, save the chopping block!" You could have heard a pin drop. "The King has accepted the idea that marriage to a commoner is the only effective way to neutralize the Blechmarsh threat to his throne and that, gentlemen, is the solution we will be actively pursuing."

He ignored the low mutters and groans. "I would have preferred her safely married before we received her here, but none of us have managed to put forward a candidate the King will endorse." He held aloft a piece of paper with the King's seal displayed on it. "I have here, proof of King Wymer's authorization. The Blechmarsh princess has already begun her journey to a point of rendezvous where she will be received by the King and then escorted back to the Winter Palace."

Shock and consternation greeted his words. "Already begun her journey?" cried out Lord Lowan in horror.

"Quiet!" bellowed Oswald. He waited with furious eyes for the tumult to hush. "Is there any here who would gainsay the will of the King?" he roared. "If so, approach me now!"

A deathly silence met his words. He let his gaze travel slowly and coldly over the length and breadth of the room. "I thought not," he said nastily. "The meeting is now concluded. We will reconvene at two o'clock to decide who will accompany the King and act as escort." He marched across the room, and it wasn't until he'd shut the door behind him that he heard the murmur of conversation started up again.

Oswald had thought the afternoon session would be easier. He thought wrong. He noticed the strange undercurrent in the room as soon as he entered and called the council to order. A sort of nervous energy emanated from his peers. He ran through the plans for the handover of Princess Una from her "protector" Lord Mycott, who until recently had been openly acknowledged as her jailor. The whole thing was an exercise in ceremonial pomp.

For the last nineteen months, the princess had been living under house arrest in relative penury. However, now she was to come to court and accept the sovereignty of her "royal cousin" King Wymer, she was to be treated to a formal reception and escort.

The King and his escort of twenty-five nobles and full guard would meet Lord Mycott on an open field where Princess Una would be expected to show her reverence and sign more documents renouncing all claim to the throne. Then she would be accompanied back to Aphrany with all due honors and accompanying ostentation. The other lords accepted these directions meekly, yet Oswald scanned them with a keen eye. Something was amiss, though he could not quite put his finger on what it was.

Biding his time, he collected the list of nominations for the King's company. But although names were duly put forward, there was a lot of whispering and murmuring behind hands. His gaze fell on Lord Sutton, who had the air of someone with an upper hand. This was surprising given how the situation had been taken out of his hands.

Oswald waited, at several salient points throughout the afternoon, for someone to challenge him on some point or other. Nothing was forthcoming. Despite this, the atmosphere seemed to get, if anything, steadily worse. He saw Lord Lowan jostle Lord Caterby in the ribs at one point, but when he turned in their direction, they resolutely avoided meeting his gaze.

It was not until the meeting had been formally closed that Lord Sutton made his move.
"At least in this arena, you still command the power and respect that is your due, Vawdrey," he said airily. "If not the domestic sphere."

545

The room gave a loud and collective guffaw. Oswald returned Sutton's gaze until the others' dropped away and the members started to rise from their seats and talk among themselves.

He could feel their hurried gazes cut to him as they started to drift out of the room. Oswald watched them filter out with an enigmatic expression, though his brain was ticking away all the while. 'Twas plain his colleagues all thought he had lost his grip on his personal life, though why he was not sure. Yet. Looking up he saw an unhappy-looking Bryce hovering by the door, his eyes mournful. *Ah.*

Oswald beckoned to his assistant, and he shuffled forward, practically wringing his hands. "You have something to tell me, Bryce," said Oswald.

"Yes, my lord," said his servant unhappily. He reached into his robe and withdrew a piece of parchment proclaiming: Performing live in the marketplace today: "The Tragical History of a Lady Most Foully Betrayed in Three Acts: A Morality Play" written by J. E. Entner playwright by appointment to the Countess Vawdrey.

Oswald stared at it a moment without comment. "This play is being performed daily in the marketplace?" he asked, surprised to hear his voice sound so steady.

"Yes, my lord."

"When did it start its run?"

"The day before yesterday, my lord."

"You have seen it?"

"Not I, although I thought it prudent to send Jeffries along to view it this afternoon and check there was no question of slander."

"And?" Oswald's tone was sharp.

Bryce shrugged. "The—erm—the central character is divorced in the first act by a neglectful husband of several years. She remarries in the second act." Bryce coughed discreetly. "The character of the second husband..."

"Yes?"

"Is—er—clearly based on yourself," said Bryce unhappily. "He wears black robes only and is rather a sinister individual of ambition and influence."

"Sinister?" Oswald eyed him, and Bryce turned pink.

"I meant no insult by that, my lord," he said hastily. "Only that the play makes use of your—um—reputation."

"I see." Oswald's lips drew into a grim line. "The playwright claims his play is endorsed by my wife?" he asked icily.

Bryce hung his head. "He does, my lord. Though," he added quickly, "he may be lying about that."

Oswald pondered this and looked back at the flyer with its smudgy representation of the Vawdrey crest. His expression turned grim. "Well, I shall soon find out," he said.

Bryce cleared his throat. "You should be aware, my lord," he said hesitantly, "that the play seems to have garnered quite a lot of attention already in a relatively short space of time. Jeffries spotted several members of court in the audience this afternoon."

"Is that so?" Instead of accompanying his assistant back to his study, he passed his sheaf of lists to Bryce. "Have these put on my desk," he said. "I will work on them tonight."

"Yes, my lord," said Bryce, stealing a concerned look at him. "Shall I make a start on the plans?"

Oswald considered a moment. "Yes," he agreed. "The King wants entertainment and tents for the field meet. He wants an overnight encampment to celebrate the Blechmarsh capitulation." He spoke with heavy sarcasm, for the truth was the Blechmarsh cause had been defeated four years ago during the war. This was just ceremonial play-acting and what's more, everyone knew it. "I will be back within the hour."

By the time Oswald had reached their rooms, he'd worked himself into a fine temper. Still clutching the flyer, he found his wife sat cozily in the window seat with his two nieces and her dog, looking through an illustrated book of days. She smiled up at him as he entered the room, though he saw her expression quickly change as her eyes roamed over his face.

"Is everything well?" she asked in alarm, jumping up from her seat. She turned back to Margaret and Lily. "Carry on without me, girls," she urged, drawing apart from them. They happily rearranged themselves, crowding against Bors, wrapping their arms around his barrel-like body and resting their cheeks against his neck as they flipped the page.

Oswald strode toward the fireplace and waited for Fen to join him there. When she did, he turned on her accusingly, though he said not a word.

"What is it?" she faltered.

He found he did not trust himself to speak for the moment, and wordlessly, he handed her the flyer.

Fen's hand flew to her mouth. "*Oh no!*" she uttered faintly and turned quite pale. His eyes narrowed as he watched an expression of horrified guilt flit over her face. "Has he—is it…?" She caught her breath. "Is it being performed now?"

He nodded. "Oh yes, Fenella. It is being performed as we speak, in the marketplace below. Probably several performances a day."

Her hand shot out to grip the mantel, and he noticed her knuckles turn quite white. "How did you find out?" she asked faintly.

He paused, tasting the bitter taste of betrayal in his mouth. "It seems several of our acquaintance have already seen it," he said stonily, and had to look away from her face. "Do I take it that you were fully aware of the turn the story has taken?"

"You mean that Mr. Entner dropped the allegorical donkey?" asked Fen in a strained voice. She nodded unhappily.

"I suppose," said Oswald in a detached tone that didn't quite hide his anger, "that it didn't occur to you that I would want to be informed that your friend, the playwright, had decided to cash in on the notoriety of your reputation?" he asked coldly.

Fen flinched at the idea that she had a reputation. "I—he..." She trailed off miserably. She made a visible effort to pull herself together. "I did fear that you would not be pleased," she said stiltedly. "But I find it hard to gauge things at court. I did not know if I was overreacting."

He tipped his head to one side. "Overreacting?" he repeated quietly. "By completely ignoring its production and allowing your husband to become a figure of ridicule and scorn among his peers?"

Fen's cheeks flushed with color at the edge to his words. "I thought no one would attend it," she admitted wretchedly and hung her head. "I hoped it would sink without a trace."

"Did you?" Oswald's lips twisted, but it was more of a grimace than a smile. "Well, it was a vain hope, Fenella. As I understand these things, more and more courtiers will be slipping away daily to watch the debacle and throw their pennies Mr. Entner's way. They will then spend their evenings whispering about it behind our backs."

"No," Fen whispered, the blood draining from her face.

"Before we know it, no doubt it will have reached the ear of the King. After that, Mr. Entner can drag his show around the shires. Perhaps it will reach all your friends in Sitchmarsh before the spring?"

Fen looked sick to her stomach, but he couldn't find it in him to take pity on her. "But perhaps you enjoy being at the center of

550

so much sordid rumor?" he speculated. "I must admit, for my part, I dislike being a vulgar display but each to their own."

Fen's gaze was so wounded, he abruptly changed his tack. "Let us look on the bright side," he said bitterly. "Mr. Entner's fifteen children will be fed." He realized how demoralized she must feel when she did not correct him as to the correct number of the playwright's offspring. He knew she would know it.

"What can we do?" she uttered miserably.

"Do?" repeated Oswald. "I'm afraid there is only one course of action open to us, under such circumstances."

Fen looked up anxiously. "N-not gaol!" she stammered. "He has a family to support!"

Oswald gave a bitter laugh. "Gaol?" he repeated. "Good gods, no. That really would confirm me in the role of cold-hearted villain. No, there can be no question of repercussions for the enterprising Mr. Entner," he said wearily. Suddenly he felt tired of the whole thing. *Heartsick of it.*

"What then?"

"Why, what else? We must send word to the marketplace and invite Mr. Entner to bring his players up to the castle to perform for us all in the Great Hall. Before a royal audience, no less." His words were cold, devoid of emotion. As though oddly detached from the situation, he watched Fen stiffen.

Her jaw dropped. "Invite them to the castle?" she faltered incredulously. "Invite the King to see it?"

"All of our acquaintance at large," agreed Oswald. "We will fill the Great Hall. We must attend and smile and applaud throughout as if we are excessively diverted by such a work of fiction."

"B-but that will be seen as an endorsement! Wouldn't it?"

"I repeat, we must seem excessively diverted by this *work of fiction*," he said forcefully.

Fen gazed at him. "I don't know if I can do that," she admitted.

"You can, and you will," he told her grimly. "You will invite Mason and Linnet, and yes, even Roland and his friends, and we will attend en masse." Fen made an involuntary noise of dissent, but he ignored it. "And you will wear your brightest jewels, and your widest smile, and we will let everyone see that you are nothing like the ridiculous character from this melodrama."

Fen swallowed. "What if Mr. Entner refuses to bring it to the palace?" she asked in a small voice.

He gave her a withering look. "I'm not even going to dignify that with an answer." Her face crumpled and he had to look away. "I will send word to the marketplace inviting their company tomorrow night for our entertainment. You will employ your time this evening and tomorrow writing invitations to watch your play. The first you will send to the King and Queen."

Her head came up at this. "*My play?*" she repeated blankly.

"Your name endorses it," he said in a clipped voice.

"But I thought it was a play about a donkey!" she said with a flash of spirit.

He looked back at her. "Are you trying to tell me that you haven't read it?" he asked softly, narrowing his gaze.

Her gaze skittered away from his. "No, but—"

"Then you have endorsed it," he said angrily. "At least have the decency to own it!" At his loudly spoken words, Bors barked behind him, letting him know he didn't appreciate him speaking to his mistress that way. Oswald ignored him.

Fen's lips trembled; she bowed her head. "Yes, my lord," she said.

He nodded, grim-faced. "I will have a general notice put up," he said, "inviting anyone at the palace who wishes to attend to do so."

Fen swallowed and nodded again. He turned from her in disgust and exited the room. As he closed the door behind him, he heard his nieces' little feet thump to the ground and then run across the floorboards toward her. Clearly, they thought he was a villain too.

39

Oswald did not return to their chambers that evening. Instead he worked steadily through the itinerary for the royal reception of Princess Una. Fifty tents, he specified, for the attendant nobles and for the entertainers. They would need a goodly amount of soldiers too as the King was so determined to attend himself, fully decked out in armor.

Pages, pig roasts, royal guards, scribes, and squires. There would be no women present, for the illusion was one of a triumphant war party. The princess would be attended by her aged servant and Lady Mycott and her daughters, which would follow protocol for decency's sake.

Bryce remained attendant and made copious notes, disappearing at various intervals to send out messengers with requests. He sent the invite to Mr. Entner and his troupe of players and canceled the musicians that had already been booked to perform the following evening in the Great Hall.

Bryce meticulously wrote out a general notice about *The Tragical History of a Lady Most Foully Betrayed in Three Acts: A Morality Play* being performed at the special request of the Earl and Countess Vawdrey, with all courtiers welcome to attend. A company of soldiers was dispatched to meet with the Mycott party with express instructions for where they would rendezvous with a map, pinpointing the exact point that they would meet the royal party in two days' time.

He also dictated the notice to be given to the nobles who would be accompanying the King. It was well past midnight by the time the preparations had all been made. Despite his words to the contrary, Oswald found his steps returning to his personal chambers after all. That angered him too.

He had no reason to go back on his word. He could easily find a vacant apartment with very little trouble, but instead, he wanted to go and take a look at his sleeping wife and check—what? That the treacherous bitch hadn't run off to Sitchmarsh and left him?

He shook his head. It beggared belief that he should be reduced to this. *Him?* It was a bitter realization. He wouldn't stay. He would collect some clothes and leave her there, sleeping in his bed. *Where she belonged.* The faithless, traitorous wife it seemed he could not do without.

When he reached their rooms, he found Mason up, clearly awaiting him. They eyed each other warily, and Oswald crossed the room to open his bedroom door and look inside. The huddle in the bed did not move, and he could see Fen's dark hair spread across the pillow. He shut the door and returned to the communal room where his brother was pouring him a glass of apple wine.

Oswald walked to the table and wordlessly picked up the handwritten invitation on the top of a large pile. It was addressed to Lord and Lady Schaeffer inviting them to watch tomorrow night's entertainment in the Great Hall. Oswald read it without comment and dropped it back on top. He threw himself down into a chair opposite his brother and accepted the goblet that was passed to him.

"You've been busy," Mason said, taking a swig of his own drink. "All the plans in place for Friday?" he asked, referring to the collection of the princess.

555

Oswald gave a short nod. "As good as. You will accompany the King, of course."

Mason grunted his assent. As one of Wymer's most senior generals he could hardly get out of it. "Lot of fuss and nonsense," he added. "But I suppose you had to appease the King somehow, as you were so determined to spare her neck."

Oswald took an absent sip of his drink before replacing it carefully on the tabletop. He was an infrequent drinker, preferring to keep a clear head. He certainly could not afford to lose his wits over the next few days.

"What's this business about us all going to watch a play on the morrow?" Mason asked, nodding toward the pile of invites that Fenella must have laboriously written out all evening.

"Seems pretty self-explanatory to me," Oswald responded mirthlessly.

"Presenting a united family front?" asked Mason, a pucker between his brows. Oswald shrugged a shoulder. "Seems a damned funny time for theatricals," growled Mason. "When you've got all this other business afoot."

Oswald gazed back at him stonily. "It is the Midwinter festival after all," he said.

Mason's eyebrows shot up. "You're going to try and pass this off as part of the Solstice festivities?" he asked.

"I am," said Oswald smoothly.

Mason shook his head. "You can fob off everyone else, but don't try it with me." Oswald said nothing. His brother narrowed his gaze at him and took another draught of apple wine. "What did she do?" he asked abruptly.

"I'm not about to discuss this with you," said Oswald. "Or anyone."

Mason nodded slowly at this. "What's between a man and his wife is private," he agreed, and almost in spite of himself, Oswald felt himself relax infinitesimally. "But if you need a brotherly opinion…" He shrugged. "You know where I am."

"I do," agreed Oswald. He took another sip of wine and made a sudden decision. "I'm sending her down to Vawdrey Keep," he said in a hard voice. "After the Solstice." Mason looked surprised, but held his tongue. "I'll do better here without her distracting me," said Oswald calmly. "I'm in the midst of difficult negotiations at present."

Mason shot him a strange look. "You're always in the midst of difficult negotiations," he said dryly. "If you send her away for that reason, you may as well give up on ever recalling her back."

"I never planned on keeping a wife at court," said Oswald coolly. "That was always the plan in the long run. I told her this from the outset. Fenella is a country-bred girl. Court life does not agree with her."

Mason gave a spluttering laugh. "So, your plan is to stick her in Vawdrey Keep and leave her there?"

Oswald inclined his head. "As you say."

"It won't work like that," said Mason knowingly. "You'll be thinking about her the whole time. Worrying she's been bitten by a dog or fallen down a flight of steps."

Oswald shot a curious look at him. "That's absurd. Do you really worry like that when you're apart from your Linnet?"

"I make damn sure I'm not apart from her for long," said Mason mildly. "And yes, she's on my mind constantly."

Oswald shifted in his chair. Mason's candor over such matters surprised him. "Fenella's very capable," he said. "She's not been sheltered like Linnet. The countryside is her natural habitat. It's here that she's a fish out of water."

"That may be so," admitted Mason. "But it's not just the worry. You'll want to hear her voice. Know what she's been up to. Remind her that she's yours."

"Again, that's you, Mason. You're the possessive one, not me."

Mason gave a snort. "Really?" He regarded Oswald beneath his dark brows. "You watch her like a hawk, you know."

Oswald smiled thinly. "That's because I can't trust her," he said, ignoring the clamoring of his own conscience at such a statement. "Her being here is a constant inconvenience I don't need. Once she's gone, I'll be able to concentrate on my work."

"We'll see, brother, we will see," replied Mason aggravatingly. "For the cleverest man I've ever met, you've got the strangest idea of how marriage works."

"Few marriages are like your own, Mason," pointed out Oswald.

"You mean loving?" asked his brother directly, surprising him. Oswald found himself at a complete loss for words. "You could have that with her," said Mason slowly. "I don't understand why you wouldn't want that for yourself."

Oswald opened his mouth then closed it again. "We're made differently," he said. "Our natures. Yours and mine."

"I'm starting to suspect not that differently." Oswald could not have been more surprised if Mason had broken into song. Since they had been small boys all anyone had ever done was point out their differences. Their father more than anyone. His brother regarded him impassively. "I suppose you know what you're about," he said doubtfully. "I know you're a damn sight cleverer than me."

Oswald wondered about that briefly. Then he nodded. "I've just come to collect a few things," he said briefly. "I'm not sleeping here tonight."

His brother gave him a hard stare. "Whatever she did, I hope she deserves this treatment," he said quietly. "Because if not…"

A floorboard nearby creaked and Oswald shot a glance toward his bedroom, but all seemed as it should be. He rose from his seat without allowing his brother to finish his statement. "I'll see you on the morrow," he said dismissively and headed to his bedchamber. Mason made no response, and Oswald eased his way through the door into the shadowy room.

For a moment, he thought Fenella lay rather too still. Her position had altered from earlier, and her face was turned into the pillow, so he could not make out her sleeping expression. He moved stealthily around the room, collecting what he needed, and then let himself out. Mason's cup lay abandoned next to his in the room next door. His brother had already gone to join Linnet.

40

Dawn broke and Oswald resigned himself to the fact he would not get a wink more sleep. It seemed almost as though he had tossed and turned for the last four hours straight. He had only been married a little over three months, he told himself savagely as he threw back the covers. It made no earthly sense that he would feel unable to sleep in a bed without her! And yet, for some reason, he had continued to reach for her in the night, his instinct not falling in line with his stony reasoning.

He passed a long, drawn-out day meeting with various dignitaries to arrange Friday's events. He delegated what he could, but due to the sensitive nature of the situation, he had to make sure he kept a close eye on proceedings. By lunchtime he had sent several of his agents ahead to check out the lay of the land and to ensure all was as it should be at Mendip Hall, where the princess was under lock and key.

He had men, of course, in the area already who were sending regular updates, but it was better to be safe than sorry. After all, the King would be in attendance. He did not return to the Vawdrey chambers until well after six o'clock to wash and dress for the evening's entertainment in the Great Hall.

Fenella was already in the bedroom, sat in a very formal gown of dark green with gold embroidery at the sleeves. She wore her rubies and emeralds at her throat and her diamond girdle at her hips. Trudy was dressing her hair in a high arrangement of loops and braids. They both fell silent as he entered the room, though Fenella greeted him in a subdued voice.

He answered in kind, and neither of them met the other's gaze. As soon as Trudy had pinned her veil in place, Fenella stood up and walked into the adjoining room. Her maid followed her, leaving him to finish washing and dressing on his own.

He took his time. After all, there was precious little for them to say to each other. He meant to avoid spending time with his wife as much as possible until after the Midwinter festival when he could send her safely on her way. After all, he had to wean himself off her company at some point and these three days would be ample opportunity to achieve that bachelor state of mind he had held for so long. Or so he told himself.

By the time he'd donned his doublet and followed his wife out, he found Mason, Roland, Linnet, and Fenella all waiting for him. At his appearance, Linnet slipped an arm through Fen's and whisked her out of the door into the corridor and he fell in step behind them, with his brothers on either side of him.

"I hate theatricals," murmured Roland mutinously. "Damned if I can see why I should have to sit through this one."

"Well, take heart," said Oswald. "There's an unflattering portrayal of me in the second and third acts, so you'll derive pleasure from that if nothing else."

Roland perked up. "The devil you say?"

"Have you read it?" asked Mason.

"No."

Mason grimaced. "Lady Schaeffer returned it this morning, so I attempted to wade through it, but…"

"Hester Schaeffer?" broke in Oswald, startled.

562

"Yes."

"What the hells was she doing with it?"

Mason's eyebrows rose. "By all accounts, Fenella wanted her opinion as she is no judge of plays."

Oswald frowned at him as his brain scrambled over this nugget of information.

"What?" asked his brother.

Oswald shook his head. "It is of no matter," he said, staring at the figure of his wife as Linnet chattered brightly and Fen nodded her head. She looked pale but resolute.

As they turned the corner to approach the Great Hall, Oswald stepped up level to the ladies and took Fen's arm. "We had better go in together," he muttered. Fen made no verbal response, just rested her hand on his arm without comment. Linnet fell back to take Mason's side, and Roland yawned loudly.

When they entered the hall, Fen gasped, and Oswald realized it was the Midwinter decorations that had caught her eye. They must have gone up that very day for every corner was now decked with great swathes of ivy, mistletoe, and laurel. Candles flickered from among the boughs and bowls of glistening fruit.

Fen's head spun round as she took in the Solstice finery and Oswald found himself glad that she was distracted by it, for at their entrance everyone had turned to look at them and the murmuring swelled very loud indeed.

Oswald scanned the room and found, to his surprise, both the King and Queen in attendance on the dais. He bowed in their direction and Fen curtseyed as he led her toward their usual places at the top table. She looked flushed, her lips parted as her gaze fell on the central table arrangements, which were great bowls of steaming cider punch with ladles decorated with ribbons.

He remembered a happier time—their visit to the inn in Aphrany when they had drunk such a drink from a lovers' cup. Fenella really loved the Solstice festivities, he remembered, but there was a shadow across her face now that hadn't been there on that first occasion. He had to fight the urge to take her hand or try to comfort her.

It was a bizarre reaction to her perfidy and one that annoyed him. Instead he focused on who else was in attendance in the packed throng. Everyone, it seemed. The walls were lined with pages who had decided to attend, whether their masters required them or not. He recognized Cuthbert's golden head from a gaggle of teenage squires who were huddled in one corner, heckling the servers who brought out more bowls of punch and silver goblets. He counted pretty much every member of the privy council at the top three tables.

"Will you take a drink?" Roland was doing the honors, and sloshing the punch into the cups, passing them round their table. He thought Fenella would decline, but she nodded at the last minute and cupped the steaming brew in her hands. She bestowed a tremulous smile on Roland, which made Oswald's vision flicker.

Mason nudged him. "Relax," he muttered. "She's doing a better job of masking her feelings than you are!"

Oswald reined himself in but was under no illusion that he was doing himself credit. His sister-in-law was eyeing him with concern, but she turned away and clapped with the others when a paean was struck up at the front of the hall and a silence swept over the room. Everyone craned their necks to see the players who were entering.

Oswald's eye was drawn to a diminutive figure who wrung her hands and cast herself on her knees before a short actor wearing violently yellow hose. Laughter rippled through the room at the visual reference to Sir Ambrose Thane, who had worn some very similar during his recent sojourn at court.

The actor playing him directed a knowing look around the audience and puffed out his chest, strutting around making very pompous boasts about his successes abroad and with women. His "wife," clearly a smooth-faced male, rocked and cringed on his knees to hear such cruel words from "her" spouse. Oswald's eyes darted to Fenella, but she looked as stunned as he.

"You didn't tell me it was funny," said Roland accusingly. "I thought it was going to be one of those dull morality plays!" He poured himself another goblet of punch and settled back to enjoy the performance. The longer the scene continued, the more the audience laughed.

The oafish husband bragged and swaggered. His lady wife cringed and swooned at her misfortune. Everyone laughed heartily, and Oswald allowed his attention to wander from the players to the other people stood around at the front of the hall.

His gaze fell on a harassed-looking man of middle age who was watching proceedings with a bewildered air. He kept consulting the manuscript in his hands, nodding and then gazing at the chortling audience in astonishment. *Mr. Entner*, thought Oswald. It must be him. He glanced at Fenella to confirm this, but her own gaze was riveted to the stage in a sort of fascinated horror.

The actors froze at the end of the act, and the hall erupted into applause. The servers had barely had a chance to replenish all the punch bowls before the music started up at the front, warning everyone the second act was about to start.

This one started dynamically, with a tall, striking actor walking on, dressed entirely in black and looking rather ominous. This was greeted rapturously by the audience, who were torn between gaping at Oswald's reaction and watching the play unfold before them. Such was the volume of noise from people's murmurings that Oswald couldn't actually hear the plan that the cold-hearted villain was outlining to the audience. He frowned.

Suddenly another character entered—a portly looking fellow who was carrying a long list and looking rather tormented. He seemed to be pleading with the sinister male—a Lord Orlando Mawby—not to pursue some disastrous stratagem, but the other would not listen to him.

Roland gave a loud crack of laughter. "It's you and Bryce!"

Oswald's head swiveled around to look at the lower table where his assistant usually sat with other scribes. Bryce's eyes stood out on stalks. He watched as a couple of his fellows slapped Bryce on the back, his assistant turning rather pink. Oswald turned back to find that his doppelganger was reeling off a dastardly list of reasons why he should marry the virtuous Lady Vyella.

Primarily, it seemed by marriage he would gain some sort of smoke screen, behind which to hide his nefarious activities. Meanwhile the unfortunate lady was prostrate with grief at her abandonment.

Oswald reached across and poured himself a cup of punch, which he had initially declined. He found himself relaxing, despite himself. Fenella studiously avoided his gaze. Her color was high, and she had a fixed smile on her lips that looked rather painful to maintain.

"Who wrote this tripe?" Mason growled in his ear.

"Don't think you'll have heard of him," he replied dryly and reached across the table impulsively for Fenella's hands. She stared a moment before placing her hands in his. They felt like ice, and Oswald frowned before interlacing their fingers. He squeezed lightly, and she shot a look of agonized confusion his way, which made him feel an utter heel.

He leaned forward. "When did you consult Lady Schaeffer about the play?" he asked in a murmur. She craned forward to catch his words.

"The day I received it," she replied. "I read it of course, but…somehow I did not realize it was a comedy. I was quite concerned, so I asked Hester for her opinion…" Her words died away as another fresh burst of laughter had her turning toward the front of the hall.

The heroine was being propped up by Bryce's character while a leering Lord Mawby looked her over and rubbed his hands together in wicked intent. Fenella gasped. "Somehow, when you read the lines, you don't imagine the way the actor will deliver them…" she added distractedly.

Oswald leaned in again. "Look at Entner," he said, nodding toward the front of the room. Fenella's gaze focused on the figure in the wings. "I don't think he realized it was a comedy either," he added.

Fen's eyes went wide and she looked back at Oswald in confusion. "I don't think I quite understand…" She trailed off hopelessly.

"Everyone seems to be enjoying it in any event," he said with a shrug.

Fenella's pained gaze fixed on him. "I'm so sorry," she whispered.

"Don't, Fen," he warned her. "We're entertained, remember. Enjoying the spectacle." She nodded and, swallowing, returned her gaze to the front of the hall.

Oswald glanced over at the royal dais. The King was leaning forward, his gaze fixed on the players in fierce concentration. The Queen, by contrast, was looking directly at him, a half smile playing about her lips. He had the uncomfortable suspicion she knew exactly what was going on. He would have taken another swig of cider punch, but his hands were still interlaced with his wife's, so instead he resigned himself to watching the rest of the wretched play.

By the time the unfortunate Lady Mawby had expired in a heap, a victim of cruel circumstance, the punch had been freely flowing for over an hour and the crowd was in a rollicking and somewhat boisterous frame of mind.

"Damned odd end, for a comedy," said Roland, and it seemed he was not alone in this thought as a few loud boos were heard from the rowdier element of the audience. Oswald watched a shower of apple cores scatter across the actors and a cry of "For shame!" go up. He looked across at Mr. Entner, who, obviously no stranger to a hostile crowd, had placed his manuscript above his head and was urging the actors to take their bows.

In an abrupt change of mood, a loud cheer went up when the actors who played Sir Andrew Vane and Lord Orlando Mawby made their bows. Lady Mawby hastily clambered to his feet and made his bow, clutching his false hair braid, which seemed to have become detached from his head during the death scene.

Then it was the turn of Price, the put-upon servant of Lord Mawby, who received very loud applause from Bryce's table. The actors then beckoned to Mr. Entner, who came on and made a largely inaudible speech, although Oswald thought he could make out a hurried thanks to his patroness.

He glanced at Fenella, who had clearly not heard a word of it and was wearing her fixed smile again. With a sigh, he held out his hand to her and drew her to feet. Everyone clapped for Fenella, who looked extremely bewildered and clung to his hand as if it was a matter of life or death. "Take a curtsey," he murmured to her, and she did, earning even more thunderous applause.

"It seems it was quite a success!" she quavered, looking shaken before sinking thankfully back onto the bench.

"Except for the rotten ending," put in Roland. "That really let it down."

"Yes, Entner may find he has to rewrite that ending before he tours the provinces," said Oswald thoughtfully.

"It was the resourcefulness of the actors that made it a success," said Linnet. "If it had not been for their delivery, the lines they spoke were really rather dull."

"I'm just glad it's over," said Mason. "How soon can we leave?"

Oswald was looking round. People were starting to file out of the Great Hall, but no one seemed to be in a particular hurry. "It will probably take a while. Did you wish to have some particular speech with Mr. Entner?" he asked Fenella, who blanched.

"No," she said hollowly.

"Not even to forbid him from touring with it?" Mason frowned.

"I rather think that horse is now bolted," said Oswald. "Banning it would only see it gain more infamy. And who would regulate such a ban? No," he said, shaking his head. "It is far better to just brazen it out."

"The King's leaving," said Mason in an aside. "That should get everyone moving."

Indeed, there did seem to be something of an exodus in the King's wake, and it was not long before they were able to follow suit. Fenella took his arm when he offered it, and they made their way out of the hall, with many people slapping him on the back or congratulating them on the evening's entertainment.

Fen's smile was definitely forced by this point, though she was clearly giving it her best attempt. When they reached their rooms, she hovered a moment by their door. It was plain she wanted to say something but knew not how or what. "Husband—" she started, but he cut her off.

"Go to bed, Fenella."

She swallowed. "Aye, husband," she said quietly and shut the door behind her.

"Early start on the morrow for you two," said Linnet, looking at her husband and Oswald. "You'll be leaving at first light for the encampment, is that not so?"

"Aye," Mason agreed.

"Roland's coming too, in his official position as King's champion," said Oswald.
Roland had not accompanied them back to their rooms but stayed out drinking with his friends.

"No doubt he'll return soon," said Linnet, ever the optimist.

Mason grunted. "Young fool," he said. "It's on him if he spends the ride sick as a dog."

571

"We'll retire, I think?" said Linnet, looking to her husband.

"I'll join you in a minute, love," said Mason, his gaze fixed on Oswald. Linnet bade them a good evening and slipped away to their bedchamber.

"You sleeping elsewhere again?" Mason asked him abruptly.

Oswald eyebrows rose. "No," he replied shortly. Though to be honest, he had not been sure until that moment.

"Good," said his brother and turned on his heel to follow his wife.

When he entered his bedchamber, the candles on Fen's side had all been snuffed out and she lay quiet and still, facing the wall. Oswald undressed and washed and then joined her under the covers, blowing out his candles.

He lay on his back for a moment, staring at the ceiling, and then in a swift motion, he rolled onto his side and dragged her body against his. They both lay silent in the dark room. After a while he felt her relax into sleep, and only then could he join her in oblivion.

41

Fen woke before it was light and lay a moment in confusion before realizing what had woken her. Oswald had left their bed and was moving quietly around the room. She glanced toward the window and could see it was still dark outside. But of course, he was journeying north to collect the Princess Una today.

She lay still as he silently packed his things for the overnight sojourn. She had gathered the King's party would be journeying all day and would reach their destination early evening time where they would set up camp and spend the night. It would be tomorrow morning that Princess Una would join them, and they would then journey back.

It seemed an odd exercise to Fenella, but she understood that King Wymer was fond of symbolic gestures and needed to play the victor, despite the fact he was capitulating in having the Blechmarsh princess under his roof. She closed her eyes as she recalled the nightmare that was the previous evening.

Against all odds, her husband had returned to their bed, but there had been no words of reconciliation or forgiveness. And other words, awful, hurtful words she had overheard him utter, still echoed in her mind, giving her pain. True, he had not intended for her to hear them, but perhaps that just made them more honest.

That's because I can't trust her… Her being here is a constant inconvenience I don't need.

Those words had struck a blow she didn't know if she could recover from. She was inconvenient, not necessary. Worse, she was unwanted. The thought crushed the breath out of her chest and made her pulse race with fear. What would become of her this time? How many times could she be rejected?

She remembered the mockery of the play the previous evening and just felt devastated. There had been no compassion for the ridiculous figure of the Lady Mawby. She had been a figure of derision, not pity. It was hard not to take it personally.

No one at court would be remotely surprised, thought Fen, when her husband sent her down to his country estate and she was never heard from again. That must have been what they were all anticipating from the outset. Even she, naïve country wife, had expected it.

She could have coped with it then, she thought bleakly. Before Oswald Vawdrey had made her fall in love with him all over again, and then just as easily withdrawn his affections. Would he wipe her from his memory as effectively this time as he seemed to do the first? she wondered.

A tear trickled from under one eyelid, but she dared not wipe it away lest he saw the movement and realized she was awake. She couldn't speak to him yet. Not while her emotions were raw and exposed. She needed time to pull herself together, to prepare herself for his rejection after the Solstice was over.

She heard the trunk shut and her husband straighten up. It seemed for a moment that she felt his gaze sweep over her, and then the door shut quietly behind him and he was gone. Fen rolled onto her stomach and hid her face in her pillow. She knew that sleep would not come now, while her senses felt lacerated. But if she lay very still, maybe she could hold herself together in one piece and not fall completely apart.

It was three hours later that Fen set out to meet Mathilde Martindale to start on their tapestry. Despite the fact she knew they would never complete it now, she thought it best to see as much of the good friends she had made before she left forever. There had been a light snowfall in the night, and it was chilly walking along the flagstone corridors.

Fen walked along the Lower Gallery wondering where her friend had got to and pulled her woolen shawl tighter about her. Bors shuffled along at her heels as her escort. She was just wishing she had brought her gloves when a page darted out from the shadows holding a folded paper. He stopped before her expectantly.

"Please, milady, are you the Countess of Vawdrey?"

"I am," said Fen, in surprise. And not just at possessing such a grand title. "Did Lady Martindale send you?"

He looked around furtively. "Yes," he whispered and, to her immense surprise, winked at her.
Bors barged past her to take a look at the newcomer, and the boy backed off nervously. "You're quite safe," Fen assured him. "He's very friendly." He patted Bors's head as Fen reached into her alms purse to fetch him a coin for his troubles. "I take it Mathilde is not coming to meet me," she said as she handed it over.

He pressed his lips firmly together and nodded his head, slipping the coin into his tunic. "Though, begging your pardon, she'd rather you didn't say a word until she writes to you that she's safely reached her destination."

575

Even more bewildered, Fen watched the boy leave and sat down on a cold window seat to open the folded note.

My dearest friend, Mathilde had written in her angelic round handwriting. *Though we have been friends for only a relatively short period of time, our acquaintanceship is one I will always treasure, come what may. You were a refreshing breath of air, and I a stagnating pond, dank and stale.*

Never has my own inertia been more apparent to me than when contrasted with you, bright and fearless Fenella. You have opened mine eyes and dazzled me with the possibilities of a life fully lived. With your example before me, I mean to seize hold, and run with my own lot in the world.

I hope you will not be ashamed of me when my flight comes to light. I hope that in your heart, you will still call me friend. With the greatest love and affection. Mathilde.

Fen read the letter through thrice in stupefaction. Then she burst into tears. Bors jumped up, his two front paws on the bench to check on her. She wrapped her arms around his neck and sat a moment, her heart thudding. Her friend had gone, she knew not where, and she dared not raise the alarm for fear of compromising her.

What had the page said? Mathilde did not want her to speak a word until she had reached whence she was fleeing? Then she would not. Wild horses could not drag it from her. She only wished that her involvement would not drag Oswald into further scandal, for Lady Doverdale was a powerful woman at court. She was sure to be furious that her daughter had escaped the sphere of her influence.

With a feeling of impending doom, Fen crept her way back through the palace, avoiding the more popular walkways and keeping to the shadows. Her mind was racing as she picked over her last meeting with Mathilde three days ago. Had there been clues then that something of this nature might happen?

She remembered Mathilde's strange manner, the way she had been so determined to lay out every last detail for their tapestry panel with full instruction. Now she realized why. Because Mathilde had known she would not be around to complete it with Fenella. Then there had been the way she had said "Do not forget" when they had parted.

Fen covered her mouth with her hand. *Do not forget me*, she had meant. Then there had been that distracted air that Mathilde had worn the whole morning. Because she had been planning on flight. But how on earth had she managed to do it? wondered Fen. She knew of no full-grown lady who was watched as closely as Mathilde.

Indeed, her nurse dogged her every move as if she were still a child. It beggared belief that she could have fled and avoided detection. When Fen reached the Vawdrey quarters, she was not surprised to find a servant and a guard awaiting her. Her heart dropped to her ankle boots.

Linnet was stood conversing with them and turned to look at her with a pale, concerned face. "Fenella, something terrible has happened."

Fen swallowed. "What?" she asked as Bors padded past her and flopped down in front of the fireplace.

"I'm afraid that Lady Martindale has disappeared. The Queen has sent for you. If you will only wait for me to dress, then I will accompany you of course..."

"There is no need," she told her sister-in-law hurriedly. "I have no information, so I won't be overlong. Pray do not concern yourself on my behalf. I am most happy to accompany these gentlemen to see the Queen."

Linnet looked for a moment as though she would argue, but then seemed to reconsider. "Perhaps, if you have no knowledge..." she said uncertainly.

"I won't be long," Fen assured her and looked to the attendants.

"This way, my lady," said the servant, and she followed him along the corridor. To her surprise, they did not lead her toward the solar, but instead to the Queen's private apartments. Of course, she recalled dimly. The King was away, and the Queen would no doubt take the opportunity to do things her own way.

The Queen's suite of rooms was much more welcoming than the King's, thought Fenella, remembering the rather oppressively grand rooms the King occupied. These were much lighter, with green curtains, decorative tapestry hangings, and a merry fire burning in the opulent stone fireplace. The Queen clearly liked pretty things and surrounded herself with them.

Fen was ushered into a sitting area, and, seeing Lady Doverdale glowering by the window, steeled herself for an ordeal. To her surprise, she saw the other lady in attendance was Lady Jane Cecil, who was sat on a low stool by the fire, ostensibly reading from a book of sermons.

"Ah, Fenella," the Queen said by way of greeting. "Come and take a seat here with me. We find ourselves in something of a predicament this morning. You have no doubt heard?" She gestured to a seat opposite her, and Fen sat in it, glancing to the right where Lady Doverdale stood, an ominous dark cloud over her brow.

"When I returned to my rooms just now, Linnet told me that Mathilde is temporarily missing." She squared her shoulders. "Tell me, has she been found?" It would not be from her that they would discover that her friend had fled the palace.

The Queen's eyes glinted with something that could have been amusement. "Nay, she has not," she said solemnly.

"Do you mean to imply that you know nothing of my child's disappearance?" demanded Lady Doverdale. "I might add that I find that very hard to believe." She took two impulsive steps toward Fen. "You are the only new influence that has made itself known within her small circle of acquaintance. I had hoped it would improve her," she said bitterly. "But now I discover the folly of such thoughts. You, madam, are becoming infamous among these corridors, your name synonymous with every—"

"That is enough, I think, my dear Berengaria," the Queen interrupted her gently but firmly.
Lady Doverdale took two deep, heaving breaths and returned to the window. The hand that covered her mouth trembled.

It was curious, thought Fen. Two days ago, she would have been a stammering mess at such accusations. Lady Doverdale's harsh words would have reduced her to a gibbering wreck. But

579

such were the nature of the events in her life lately that this simply paled in comparison.

She eyed Lady Doverdale impassively and then turned back to the Queen. "I can only repeat that I know nothing of Lady Martindale's disappearance," she said coolly and marveled at her own self-possession. Truth to tell, she felt numb to her very soul.

Her calm had been pricked by very real fears for her friend's well-being, but otherwise, Lady Doverdale's suffering left her untouched. She did not believe it originated from an impulse to protect, but rather to assert ruthless control over her daughter. Fen folded her hands in her lap and waited.

"I see," said the Queen pleasantly. "And might I ask, when did you last see the Lady Martindale?"

Fen cast her mind back. "Some three days ago," she said. "Mathilde sat with me while I had a portrait sitting. We arranged to meet again this morn. But when I turned up at the allotted meeting place…"

The Queen spread her hands. "Alas, no Mathilde," she finished for her. Fenella nodded. "But you did expect to see her there, no?"

"Oh yes," said Fenella. "We were to start on our tapestry this morning."

"And she sent no word?" asked the Queen.

Fen hesitated, but only for a second. "No, none," she said brazenly. If she admitted to that, they would no doubt ask to see the note.

The Queen's gaze flickered over her face, and she smiled. "You two are very good friends, are you not?"

Fen cleared her throat before answering a muted, "Yes, very."

"If you truly are a friend to my Mathilde," broke in Lady Doverdale harshly, "then you would tell me exactly what you know about her current whereabouts."

Fen did not look at Lady Doverdale this time. "I'm afraid I can tell you nothing," said Fen firmly.

"Cannot or will not?" asked Lady Doverdale, seizing only on the part that interested her.

"In this instance, they are one and the same, I assure you," said Fen quietly.

"Why do you not return to your rooms, Berengaria?" suggested the Queen. "It may be that your staff have some new information for you. Or have uncovered some clue as to her direction?"

Lady Doverdale made a muffled exclamation and threw up her hands. "Pray to the gods you are right!" she said in a voice of long suffering and strode from the room without any other word of farewell.

A silence fell upon them for a moment before the Queen made a thoughtful noise and tapped her chin. "I do not think you have

581

told to us everything that you know, Fenella," she said. "Which is unkind of you, as I very much wish to share everything that I know with you!"

Fen blinked at her. "You mean—?"

The Queen nodded. "I have every fascinating detail of how it was discovered that the little Mouse had up and left us."

Fen gave a start. So the Queen already knew that she had left of her own accord? She took a deep breath. "I can tell you nothing else, Your Majesty. Except that she has not been coerced and that wherever she is, it is of her own free will."

The Queen smiled at this. "Aha!" she said triumphantly. "She did send word to you. But of course she did!"

"Only that she had left, Your Highness," said Fen, coloring up. "Nothing of her plans or her intent."

The Queen nodded gravely. "This she probably did to protect you from such an interview as her mother just subjected you to." The Queen looked thoughtful. "On the whole, I am inclined to believe you are in the right of it," she said, drifting over to the window and looking out over the wintry landscape.

"And that Lady Martindale has not fallen prey to some wicked plot. That, extraordinary as it may seem, the scheme was of her own devising." A smile curved her lips. "Have you heard yet how she concealed her escape?"

The Queen flicked a hand at Lady Jane, who hastily uncovered a platter of sweetmeats and delicate treats. It dimly occurred to

582

Fen that she had progressed to the figure of guest now, rather than potential witness or coconspirator.

"No, I have heard no detail," she croaked, licking her dry lips. Jane hurried around with a goblet of wine for her and Fen took a long draught. It was sweet and rich and deceptively light. It was not until she felt her head swim slightly that she remembered she had not broken her fast.

To her surprise, Jane did not automatically refill her cup but instead silently offered her water instead. Fen nodded quickly. It would not do to grow loose-lipped around the sharp-eyed Queen, though truth be told, she knew precious little. Jane topped up her goblet and fetched a tray of delicacies. Unfortunately, Fen could not face any of them.

Queen Armenal resettled herself comfortably in her cushioned, tasseled seat. "Very well. Despite the fact you have been so stingy with your knowledge, I am more generous and will share with you! The little Martindale announced she felt unwell on Monday evening and would retire early to bed with a putrid sore throat," said the Queen, continuing with her story.

Jane hurried forward and helped arrange her voluminous skirts as Fen recalled Mathilde's feeble claims that she had a cough. "Her nurse put her to bed with a honeyed posset." The Queen paused as Jane topped up her drink and then backed away to stand unobtrusively in the background.

"Do not neglect your own cup," Queen Armenal told her new favorite graciously. She turned to Fen. "You do not object that Jane remains with us?" She did not wait for her reply, but instead carried on. "I find her entirely useful to me."

"Of course not," Fen murmured.

Jane blushed in gratification and poured herself a drink of half water, half wine before settling on a seat in the corner.

"The next morning," continued the Queen, selecting a snack from the tray, "the nurse found her charge huddled under the bedclothes in a sorry state and streaming with cold. Her mouth she covered at all times with the handkerchief. She sneezed, she coughed, she had a shawl wrapped around her aching head, you comprehend?"

The Queen nodded. "I think that is a clever touch, no? She asked only to be left in peace. The poor nurse, she did not wish to catch the affliction. She left the water, had the servants build up the fire, and left the lady to sleep it off." Fen nodded, taking a sip of her water.

"At intervals, most regular, the nurse, she peeks past the door, but Lady Martindale she is still bundled up and shivering. Her voice is scratchy. She asks most pathetically to be left quite alone. And so, it continues." Queen Armenal held up two fingers. "For two whole days."

Fen placed down her goblet. "Poor Mathilde, it must have been a very heavy cold, I think."

"Your sympathy, it is not shared by her mother. But no! Lady Doverdale, she has no sympathy for the invalid. On the third morning, when the nurse reports to her that the Lady Mathilde is no better, she marches to her daughter's bedchamber and demands she rise from her sickbed."

The Queen looked from Fen to Jane in expectation. "But what does she encounter?" The Queen held up a finger. "I will tell you. Refusal. *Point blank refusal.* The invalid, she hunkers down further in the bedclothes. She protests, oh so imploringly, that she has caught a deadly chill. That she will expire clean away if she emerges from her bed. Lady Doverdale, she is furious to meet such resistance from her heretofore meek child. It is unheard of! She stamps her foot and demands the obedience! The poor nurse, she is clutching the curtains, crying," said Armenal dramatically.

"She is sure the little Martindale is in deadly peril for her health. When suddenly, the mother, she scents the rat." She paused and took a sip of wine, enjoying the moment. Fen glanced across at Jane Cecil, who looked as mystified as she.

Queen Armenal waved a hand before continuing excitedly. "Suddenly, she pounces! The Doverdale, she drags the huddled figure from the bed, when what does she find...?" She sat back triumphantly, taking in Fen's astonishment.

"I hardly know," stammered Fen.

"An imposter," the Queen enunciated precisely. Fen and Jane both gasped. "An imposter who wears her daughter's shift and her daughter's shawl and lies in her daughter's bed, making the cough-cough and covering his face with the bedsheets!"

"An imposter?" breathed Jane.

"*His* face?" repeated Fen shrilly.

The Queen smirked. "Quite. For it was a youth, a mere boy. In short, one of the palace pages. As Lady Doverdale, she drags

585

him from the bed, her daughter's long hair, it falls from under the bed cap and scatters all over the floor."

Fen's mouth fell open. "Her hair?" she uttered faintly. It was starting to sound like some sort of awful nightmare.

The Queens eyes gleamed with amusement. "She—cut—it—off!" she said, punctuating each word with a stab of her finger in the air. "She cut it off and donned the page's suit three nights previously and ran away from court."

Fen collapsed back in her seat, aghast. "I can hardly believe it!" she uttered in a stifled voice. But something about it rang true. *The pages.* The pages that Mathilde had said were her only friends before Fenella arrived.

"Nor I," said the Queen with a trace of regret. "And to think, all this time, I thought the Lady Martindale to be a little bore, with nary a word to say for herself." She clicked her tongue.

"But where has she gone?" demanded Fen. "Has she left no word?" The Queen gazed at her so pointedly that she felt herself turn red. "I mean, did she leave no word for her mother?" she forced herself to say.

The Queen narrowed her eyes, but conceded, "She did leave a very short note for her mother, telling her not to worry and saying she would send word at some later point."

"But—but—" Fen stuttered helplessly. She could hardly bear to think of Mathilde careering around the countryside with a shorn head and dressed in boy's clothes! What on earth would become of her! "What is to be done?" She looked around wildly. "What is Lady Doverdale doing to recover her?"

The Queen was giving her a rather hard stare. "Do not alarm yourself, my dear Fenella," she said slyly. "For did you not say yourself that she had left of her own will and not been coerced?" She turned back to the tray of refreshments and picked out a small stuffed pastry.

That brought Fenella up short. She thought of her own letter. That was true. But whatever had her friend been thinking of? "Wherever she has gone," she said slowly, "she had a destination in mind." The Queen smirked.

"Is her father still alive?" asked Jane.

"No," replied Fen absently. "He died several years ago."

"Some friend of his?" Jane hazarded. "An uncle or a godparent...?"

The Queen sent a look her way, and she lapsed into silence. "What say you, Fenella?" she asked instead.

Fen frowned, thinking furiously of her letter. What was it Mathilde had said? Something about seizing her lot in life and running with it? Her lot in life? Dimly, she thought of Mathilde stood holding baby Archie with tears streaking down her face.

Mathilde was a married woman, not a child. A married woman who had been wed by proxy. She sat forward in her seat, her face tight as she tried to marshal her thoughts. Suddenly, she knew without a shadow of a doubt where her friend had gone. She had gone to her husband, the shadowy Lord Martindale.

587

She gulped and hastily looked up to find the others keenly watching her. "I—I hardly know," she lied. Though in truth, it was barely a lie, for she had not the first notion where Lord Martindale was to be found, any clue as to his character, or the reception Mathilde would find there.

The Queen sat back in her seat with a satisfied smile curving her lips. She sighed happily. "And I was wrong about you too," she said. "Tell to me, Fenella, how would you like to be one of my ladies-in-waiting?"

42

Fen spent the afternoon with Linnet and the children to distract her from her woes, though she did not fool herself that she'd made good company. Luckily, the girls weren't at all shy around her now and were determined to show her all their treasures. This meant she could sit with them and exclaim over their books and hair combs and trinkets without much more being expected of her.

Linnet was kind and did not press her for any more information about Mathilde's disappearance, for which Fen was profoundly grateful. When she'd dragged herself to bed after supper, she'd thought herself exhausted. But as soon as she'd pulled the covers up to her chin, she was prey once more to her clamoring fears. What would become of her? What would become of her friend Mathilde?

She'd received a letter from Orla before supper, which she'd tucked into her purse unopened. She debated now whether to go and fetch it, as it was hard to imagine sleep would ever come, but she didn't want to wake her sister-in-law's family. She had been completely stunned by the Queen's proposition to elevate her to the ranks of her attendants.

She had fallen from grace with her husband at practically the same time her stock had significantly risen with the Queen. How ironic that she would have been delighted by such a triumph a few weeks previously. The problem was the person she would have wanted to please would have been her husband. And he no longer cared for her presence at court.

She glanced down to the fireplace where Bors now dozed. He'd been most put out by Roland's disappearance but had finally consented to join his mistress in her bedchamber. He raised his head from his paws now to look at her.

"All is well, my boy," she told him softly, and he lowered his head again, happy to take her at her word. If only she could allay her own fears as easily. She rolled onto her other side and stared at the gray light coming through the window. It was late, so she thought it meant more snow. Her thoughts turned to the King's party. Would they be warm enough in their tents overnight?

She wondered if Oswald was lying awake thinking of her. Her heart broke a little more to think that if he was, then it would only be hard, unforgiving thoughts. Probably regretting the day she'd come back into his life, wreaking havoc on his reputation.

She sighed, thinking of the fact that she was now tied up in yet *another* scandal. One he remained in blissful ignorance of, but that would not continue. Lady Doverdale viewed her with frank suspicion. She was sure to be implicated when it all came to light, no matter how hard Mathilde had tried to keep her out of it.

Perhaps it was just as well she was being bundled off to Sitchmarsh. The King was sure to be outraged by such goings-on. She dozed off again at some point around dawn and woke around the hour of nine. She could already hear the Cadwalladers moving around in the other rooms and made haste to join them around the table. Cuthbert made a noise when she appeared, his mouth full of herring. He reached into his tunic and produced a note for her.

"Thank you," she said, flipping it over and recognizing the handwriting as Eden Montmayne's. "Good morning," she greeted Meg and Lily, who were sat in their shifts having their hair brushed by Nan.

"Morning, Aunt Fenella," they caroled.

"The mistress is just feeding master Archie," Nan told her grimly through a mouthful of hair pins.

"I see, thank you, Nan." Her own hair was still loose as Trudy had not yet appeared. She wore her rose-pink gown with the gold cuffs and seated herself at the table to finally read Orla's letter. Meldon plunked some toasted bread in front of her and she turned to smile at his crabby face.

"There's this too," he said, handing her a bowl of spiced red wine to dip the toast in. "I noticed as you don't like fish of a morning."

Fen nearly dropped her toast in astonishment. "That's very kind of you, Meldon." He nodded and disappeared with his stomping gait.

"You're his favorite," said Cuthbert.

"Really?" asked Fen skeptically. "I don't think I'm anyone's favorite."

"Everyone says so," answered Cuthbert serenely.

"Well, maybe it's because I employed his goddaughter," suggested Fen. Cuthbert shrugged. "Did I see you throwing apples at the players the other night?" Fen asked him.

"No," he answered, looking untroubled.

591

"It looked very like you."

"It was apple cores," he corrected her. "What did your friend want?" he asked, nodding at her unopened note.

Fen exclaimed; she'd forgotten all about it. She broke it open and scanned the note written in Eden's elegant fine hand. "Eden writes that she has my finished portrait in her rooms. That's funny," she said, lowering the note. "I would have thought signor Arnotti would have wanted the remaining balance before he relinquished it."

"He's done a runner," said Cuthbert, taking a large bite of bread.

"Pardon?"
"In the night." He chewed his bread and leaned against his hand. "With some heiress. Everyone's talking about it below stairs."

Fen gaped at him. "Wh-when?"

"Last night," said Cuthbert. "He's cleared out."

"What heiress?" she asked faintly, almost dreading the answer.

"That half-batty one," said Cuthbert. "With all the dogs."

Fen moaned, placing her head in her hands. "No, it can't be!" But somehow, something clicked into place. Bess's oddly resentful attitude toward Eden. It must have been mere jealousy. Remembering her own feelings about Lady Anne Sumner, Fen even felt a sympathetic pang.

"What is this? What has happened?" asked Linnet, drifting over to the table with Archie in her arms. "Fenella, is all well?"

Fen shook her head. "Cuthbert, tell your mistress."

Cuthbert took a piece of toasted bread from his mouth and reached across the table to dip it into Fen's mulled wine bowl. "That heiress who's a bit peculiar," he said, taking a bite of soggy bread. "She's up and run off with that artist fellow."

Linnet looked back at Fen. "Which heiress?"

"I think," said Fen, looking at her between her fingers, "he means Lady Bess Hartleby."

"That's her!" said Cuthbert, clicking his fingers. "She's taken all six of her dogs with her too," he said. "And her two hawks and four horses. Her uncle's *seething*."

"Is that the uncle who means to marry Lady Constance?" asked Linnet with interest.

"And the artist—is it signor Arnotti?" asked Fen, wanting to be doubly sure.

"Yes, that's him. The one with the eyebrows."

"This is terrible," said Fen. "Now I have a second friend who has run away from court!"

Linnet returned her horrified gaze. "I hadn't thought of that," she whispered, aghast. "But I don't see how you can be held to blame."

593

"Lady Doverdale seemed to feel differently," Fen pointed out. Then another thought occurred to her. "Is not Bess's uncle on the privy council?"

Linnet gave a hesitant nod. "I believe he is…"
"So, he is sure to bring it up with Oswald," said Fen in a small voice. "And be most put out."

Linnet bit her lip before urging her, "You must not take on so." She shifted Archie to her hip. "It would be most unfair of him to blame you. And unreasonable. After all, you had no prior notion of such a thing happening. Did you?" There was a questioning note in the last two words.

"No," said Fen, shaking her head emphatically. "I mean, I thought that Bess was acting a little oddly, but I never dreamt…"

"Better make sure Lady Eden Montmayne don't lose her head and run off with a lute player," said Cuthbert. "Or you'll really be for it."

Fen looked at him with horror, and he tipped her a wink. "You are not funny, Cuthbert," she said, rallying herself.

"Really, I don't think that at all likely," said Linnet earnestly. "Eden is not at all the sort of person to ever do such a thing."

Cuthbert spluttered with laughter. "I only said it in jest," he said, rolling his eyes. "Everyone knows she's got a stick up—" He broke off his words hastily. "Everyone knows she's stiff-necked, that one."

Even though he was only joking, Fen found herself reaching for Eden's note and scanning it anxiously for anything amiss with her single remaining friend. The only odd thing she could see was that Eden made no mention of the elopement, but perhaps she did not want to spread gossip.

After all, Eden was very proper. "I must go and see her presently," she said distractedly. The door opened and Trudy came bustling in. "Ah, Trudy. Could you be so kind as to dress my hair?" she asked, rising up from the table.

"Of course, milady."

"Aren't you going to eat your sop in wine?" asked Cuthbert. He'd already emptied half the bowl.

"You finish it," she told him. "But make sure that Meldon thinks I had it."

"Understood," he said with a cheeky grin.

As Trudy arranged her hair, Fen hastily scanned through Orla's latest letter. She had to read it through twice before she could get the gist of it, the tidings were so astonishing. Her former sister-in-law wrote to tell her that they would soon be sisters-in-law once more!

Orla had decided that Fen's brother, Gil, was quite incapable of managing without a wife any longer. The most logical thing to do, she had decided, was to simply marry him herself. This way, her partisanship for Fen would not be a problem like it was at Thurrold.

It seemed Orla still found the Lady Colleen quite unbearable to be around and Ambrose's new mother-in-law, even worse. She described herself as a permanent "houseguest" at Sitchmarsh Hall, where she had set about at once making things more respectable.

Ambrose had disowned her for what he deemed shameful and unmaidenlike behavior in his sister. It seemed Gil was quite resigned to the fact that he was to marry Orla on Solstice Eve. Fen gasped as her brain reeled, processing the news. She could hardly take in more news at this point. The last time she had seen Gil he had described Orla as "a foolish old maid," but it seemed she had brought him to heel since then!

She was trying to picture them together when Trudy patted her on the shoulder and told her that she was ready. Thanking her maid, Fenella jumped up and made her way to the Montmayne rooms, where she was enthusiastically received by Eden.

"Just wait until you see it," said her friend, leading her into the sitting area. There was a large canvas covered with a sheet in the corner. Eden steepled her hands. "Are you ready?" she asked, almost quivering with anticipation.

To be honest, Fen could not care less at this point about how the actual portrait turned out. She wanted to ask Eden if it was certain that signor Arnotti had eloped with Bess. Still, she took in Eden's excitement and replied. "Oh…er, yes."

Eden unveiled the canvas and looked expectantly at her. Fen gasped and fell back as she took in the rosy beauty on the canvas with her voluptuous curves, bright eyes, and lustrous skin. It was mostly the amount of skin on view that appalled her. Automatically her hand flew to her front to check her lacings were fastened. She stole a sideways look at Eden Montmayne, who was gazing at it in awe.

"Isn't it beautiful?" Eden announced proudly. "A masterpiece."

Fen opened and closed her mouth again without a single word occurring to her. She turned back to the rich oils of the painting and winced at the parted pink lips and the hectic color in her cheeks.

She looked like she was panting! Like she had been running around a field and then flung herself down haphazardly onto the nearest surface! She couldn't fathom how signor Arnotti could have transformed the nice solid window seat she had been sat on into this overstuffed monstrosity.

She had a horrible feeling it wasn't a chair at all. "What am I lolling on?" she asked stiffly. If Eden said it was the end of a bed, she was going to scream.

"It's a cloud," Eden explained. "Goddesses sit on clouds."

"Goddesses?" she repeated and felt absurd relief stealing over her. "So, this is not my portrait then?" She stole another look at it. It didn't really look like her after all, she tried to convince herself.

"Of course it is you," said Eden with a small frown. "But you have to allow for the artistic license. This is how signor Arnotti saw you."

"But where's my dress?" Fen asked. "My plum-colored velvet? I don't even own a...a..." She didn't even know what to call

597

the thing that was swirled around her. It looked like a wisp of sky-blue silk. "Blanket this color," she finished with dignity.

"You absolutely must get something in this color immediately," said Eden earnestly. "It really draws attention to your beautiful fair skin."

Fen stared at her friend a moment and wondered if her wits were disordered. She closed her eyes, trying to think calm thoughts.

"Is something wrong, Fenella?" asked Eden as if only just noticing her agitation. "Do you need to sit down?"

"What is my husband going to say?" asked Fen in a low, anguished voice.

Eden blinked, looking surprised. "Lord Vawdrey? I am sure he will appreciate the superior quality of signor Arnotti's work."

Fen looked at her out of the corner of her eye. The younger woman looked entirely sincere. Perhaps she was wrong? Everyone said that Eden Montmayne had exceptional taste and an exemplary reputation. "Y-you think he will be pleased with it?" she asked, biting on her thumbnail distractedly.

"Of course." Eden nodded reassuringly. "He will recognize the unmistakable talent of the artist and how he has brought out the luminous quality of his subject."

Fen took a deep breath and turned back to the canvas. She ventured another look at it but couldn't manage it without a wince. She was aghast by her bare shoulders and arms. The glimpses of her bare legs through the transparent drapings.

"Perhaps you're right," she quavered. "I'm afraid I am just too ill educated to appreciate such things." After all, she simply wasn't sophisticated. She was the biggest bumpkin in all of Aphrany.

"Oh you mustn't say so," protested Eden. "After all, you put your faith in him when no one else did."

"I was really only led by you," Fenella said raspily. "I—I must write to signor Arnotti to thank him for all of his hard work. Indeed, he has not yet received full payment for the painting."

A slight frown crossed Eden's face. "It's highly irregular but it seems he has up and left us already, and without a forwarding address. We can only hope that he will contact us in due course."

"Well, now that it's all over, I will certainly have a lot more time on my hands," said Fen weakly. "I—er—the canvas is so big I hardly know where to put it." She really tried to keep the dismay out of her voice but had a horrible feeling she had failed miserably. "Perhaps I could have it sent to my brother's until the rebuild has happened at Vawdrey Keep…"

"Oh, but first you must allow it to be exhibited here in the palace!" Eden interrupted her, looking shocked. "This is signor Arnotti's masterpiece. Indeed, I am very surprised that he did not wait to see how it was received."

Fenella looked at Eden. "Display it?" she echoed blankly.

"But of course!"

Fen took a deep breath. "I'm afraid I would have to ask Lord Vawdrey," said Fenella in a firm voice. "My own inclination is that it would not be at all proper but…I know I am sadly provincial in my ways."

Eden broke out in a relieved smile. "Oh, of course! That will be fine. I am convinced that Lord Vawdrey will think the painting most exceptional and deserving of an audience."

Fen avoided looking at the canvas again by averting her eyes from all that pale fair skin. Did she really have so much of it? And couldn't signor Arnotti have made her look a little more svelte? Her palms felt damp from the sweat she had broken out into. She just wanted to get out of the room and never see that painting again, as long as she lived.

The problem with Eden reassuring her was that for all her polish, she simply was not a married woman. After the disaster that was Mr. Entner's play, she would not allow herself to be fooled again. She had already brought utter disgrace onto her husband. There was surely only so much of it that he could stand.

"Well, then," said Eden, looking a little deflated. "Shall I have the portrait delivered to your rooms then, for Lord Vawdrey to view it first?"

Eden was definitely disappointed with her reaction, thought Fen guiltily. "Yes, if you would I'd be most grateful," she said. "Why is it that you have the portrait, may I ask?"

Eden's black eyebrows snapped together. "Oh," she said as if being reminded of something unpleasant. "I don't mean to shock you, Fenella," she said gravely. "But I'm afraid there has been a most unfortunate development. Signor Arnotti has taken a most imprudent step which is sure to impact on his livelihood." She pursed her lips disapprovingly and Fen waited.

"Which was?" she prompted when Eden seemed loath to go into details.

"I'm sorry, but there's no nice way of putting it. It seems he has eloped with Lady Elizabeth Hartleby." Fen shut her eyes a moment. So it was true. "I apologize," said Eden. "I know you are a friend of Bess's but it's apparently quite true."

Fen sat down heavily in the nearest chair, as the certainty of the latest scandal overwhelmed her. Quite suddenly, her only course of action lay open before her in a blinding flash of light. She would take herself off to Sitchmarsh before her husband was forced to send her. There could be no doubt of it now, she thought numbly.

After all, had he not already vowed to send her away after the first disgrace? And since then, there had been another three scandals he did not even know about! Two friends eloping and this scandal of a portrait...

There was no other option. She would preempt the disgrace. Gods be blessed for Orla, her ex and soon-to-be sister-in-law, for she had given her the perfect excuse. She would salvage her pride and let it be known she was leaving court for her brother's impending nuptials.

"Forgive me, Eden," she said impulsively. "But you see, I'm rather in a hurry. My brother has written to me that he means to be wed on the morrow."

"On Solstice Eve?" asked Eden in surprise.

"Yes, my family are all very fond of the Solstice celebrations," said Fen brightly. "I must needs set off within the hour to ensure I reach Sitchmarsh Hall in time."

"Oh, but surely—?" Eden started, her face falling. "You will wait for the King's party to return?"

"Alas, I would that I could," said Fen, springing out of her seat. "I'm just glad I got to come and say my farewell to you in person."

"You will return to court after the wedding, of course," urged Eden, clearly perturbed by Fen's news.

"Oh yes," said Fen glibly. "When my husband recalls me." *Which he won't*, thought Fen as a sop to her conscience for lying.

Eden kissed her cheek and wished her a happy Solstice, and Fen remembered she had a present for her. She would have to send Cuthbert along with it presently. For now, she needed to pack her trunks. It wouldn't take long, she thought as she made her way back. She would only take a few gowns. She would not need the court finery or the jewelry after all. She picked up her pace, dashing a hand across her eyes whenever tears threatened to fall.

There was no alternative. She simply could not face seeing Oswald retreat from her to that glacial politeness that simply *froze* her. This portrait was the final nail in the coffin of her marriage. There was absolutely no way that he would countenance keeping so disastrous a wife at court.

602

He would try to be kind, but his disappointment would be evident, and her heart would simply break. She was useless, quite useless at this courtly way of life. Every way she turned, she ran into a dreadful scandal. Fen barreled through the door to their rooms with a muffled sob.

"Why, milady," said Trudy in dismay, looking up from where she was folding linens. "Whatever's happened?"

Fen gulped. "Nothing of import, Trudy," she lied in a wobbly voice. "I know it is unexpected, but I—er—need to pack some things together for a journey into the country."

"When?" asked Trudy, sounding shocked.

"Now, Trudy, in all haste. You see, my brother is to be married tomorrow, in Sitchmarsh where I'm from. He has written asking me to attend," she improvised.

"But, milady," protested Trudy. "He surely would not expect you to go careering off into the countryside without your husband's leave!"

Fen cleared her throat. "Oh, my husband will not mind," she said airily. "We discussed the possibility before he left." The lies were coming thick and fast now. "I do not need to pack overmuch, no jewelry or fine headdresses. Just the essentials." Though in truth, all her gowns were fancy these days, so she was talking nonsense.

She drifted through to the bedroom, feeling quite numb. She stared in the mirror as she unpinned her gauzy veil, but left the velvet roll her hair was caught up in. Her face was rather pale, but you would never guess that her life was collapsing down around her.

The door closed, and Trudy joined her, pulling out drawers and unfastening trunks as they went about their business. She turned to her maid as they were tightening the strap on her chest. "Trudy, I wonder if you could send word down to the stables to have my horse made ready?"

As her maid hurried away, Fen stared at the trunk, and then at Bors, who was sat watching her. Even though she was not taking much, she would not leave her dog behind, however attached to Roland he might be! But the sad fact was that Bors's days of running alongside her horse were long gone.

She would need some type of conveyance for him to sit in alongside her trunk. She was just pondering this when Meldon appeared in the doorway.

"I'll take ye," he said.

"Pardon?" Fen turned in surprise.

"I said I'll take ye to Sitchmarsh. I made that journey many a time. We can take a wagon."

"Oh, but...Meldon," said Fen, taken aback. "I don't think Oswald would be happy for me to take you away with me. After all..."

"That's where you're wrong," he said, sticking out his chin. "I see my duty before me, and it's to take you to Sitchmarsh. Who's to show you around the old place if it's not me?" He puffed out his skinny chest.

"Well, you see," said Fen weakly. "I was thinking of going to my brother's place first as—"

"Now that is something the master would not like," said Meldon with a thunderous frown.

Fen was surprised by his addressing Oswald as "the master." To her knowledge it was the first time he'd done it. Usually he called him "Master Oswald" as he called Roland "Master Roland." As she understood it, he reserved "the master" exclusively for when he was speaking of the old baron.

"He wouldn't?"

"Stands to reason he'd expect you under his own roof!" said Meldon with a vigorous nod.

"I see," said Fen. "Well…" After all, what difference did it make? Their estates were neighboring. And this way, if Meldon drove the wagon, Bors could sit beside him while she rode her horse alongside them. "If you really do not mind accompanying me, Meldon?"

"It's no more than my duty," he reiterated, and stomped back out. "I'll get a wagon and send a man for your trunk."

"Thank you, Meldon," she called after him.

Hurried explanations to Linnet followed. Her sister-in-law was bewildered and dismayed by her departure. Fenella wrapped the children's Solstice gifts and Bryce's lined hood and left them on the bed for Oswald to bestow them.

She gave her presents for Hester and Eden to Cuthbert to deliver. On impulse, she gave Cuthbert the deck of cards she had bought for Gil. After all, he was to have a wife now, and that was Solstice gift enough. Then, pulling on her thickest cloak and drawing on her gloves, she kissed them all farewell and left the castle.

43

Oswald whipped back the tent flap and strode into the tent he was sharing with his brothers. "We'll be here at least another hour," he said grimly. "I've left Schaeffer to finish up the formalities. Wymer's suffering from last night's excesses. We won't be packing up in a hurry."
Mason scowled back at him, sharing his mood.

"Can't we start off ahead of them?" asked Roland irritably.

"Now, how would that look?" asked Oswald. "The King's champion, lead general, and chief adviser all ride off, and leave him trailing behind undefended."

"He's got a hundred soldiers," Roland pointed out, perhaps not unreasonably.

"You know how the King feels about protocol," Oswald responded tersely.

"What's up with you anyway?" Roland asked him. "You've been jumpy since yesterday. Usually, you're calm as hell about these things." Both his brothers turned to look at him keenly.

"What?" said Oswald. "You don't want to get back before more snow falls? Princess Una has signed all the papers and is ready to leave. It's a good four-hour ride back to the palace, and I can see no call for further delay."

"I'm going to see if I can find out any more," muttered Roland, flinging out of the tent.

"And that's the only reason?" asked Mason.

Oswald's jaw clenched. "What other reason would there be?"

Mason gave him a level look. "Because you're not feeling happy with the way you left things with your wife," he suggested. "Be honest. For once."

"Trust me," said Oswald. "You don't want to know how I honestly feel right now." He closed his eyes.

Mason gave a short, uneasy laugh. "It can't be that bad, surely?"

The worst thing was, when Oswald closed his eyes, he kept seeing her face from when he tore into her about that ridiculous play. She looked traumatized, and for some godsdamn reason, that bothered him too.

He was the wronged party here! But that did not seem to matter to his conscience, which was tearing him to shreds. Oswald massaged his temples. "I've already decided to send her down to Vawdrey Keep," he said in a tired voice. "There's nothing more to be said."

"Oh really?" asked Mason scathingly.

"That was the original plan. I leave her at the Keep, while I carried on at court."

"That was your plan?" his brother asked. "Then what changed?"

Oswald ignored him. "I'll resolve things with her on my return," he said firmly.

Mason snorted. "If she's still there when we get back."

Oswald looked up in surprise. "Where else would she be?"

"You rejected her," pointed out Mason. "Publicly humiliated her—and mind, you're not the first husband to have done that to her. And made it widely known that you don't give a damn about her. Would it be outside the realm of expectations that she might take herself off? There was property in her dowry, I assume? People she could go to—her brother."

Oswald stared at him. "I did not reject her," he said forcefully. "I merely told *you* that I planned to send her to Vawdrey Keep on my return."

Mason shook his head. "And you think she would have been unaware of this decision?"

"I never said one word to her about it," insisted Oswald.

"She'd know," said Mason. "If we could all tell you'd gone cold on her, then you can bet your life she would have."

Gone cold on her? "I never said I didn't give a damn."

Mason rolled his eyes. "You may as well have."

"Fenella's more straightforward than most women," he said obstinately. "She doesn't misunderstand every little gesture or remark."

"You mean she's used to being treated like shit," said Mason.

Oswald stopped in his tracks. "What?"

"That's what you said, wasn't it? By Thane and her brother."

Oswald narrowed his eyes at his brother. "What are you doing?" he asked softly.

"I'm pointing out the blatantly obvious."

"And what is that exactly?" asked Oswald in a dangerous voice.

"You need to treat your wife better."

Oswald exhaled noisily. "Mason, you'd better watch your step. You know nothing about my wife."

"I know she was humiliated and on the verge of tears watching that bloody play you made her sit through."

"And how would you know that?" asked Oswald sharply.

"Because unlike you, I was actually looking at her."

Oswald stared at him. "She wanted to cry?" he asked tightly.

Mason nodded. "And then you left her alone in your bed and spent the night elsewhere. If actions speak louder than words, then you dealt her a hefty blow."

Oswald sat down heavily. *Shit.* The play had been so ludicrous that watching it performed had actually robbed it of its sting for him. Could it be that the experience had been different for Fenella? He felt suddenly cold in the pit of his stomach.

Mason drew out a chair opposite him and sat down. "Linnet once cried because I told her I didn't want to hear her every thought," he confided.

"Really? Why did you do that?" asked Oswald warily.

"Because I was a stupid son of a bitch."

Oswald considered this a moment. "Mason, Linnet never stops chattering at you."

"I changed my mind," said Mason smugly.

Oswald thought about this. Mason had the happiest marriage of anyone he knew. "I may not have been the most considerate husband," he admitted. "But that doesn't mean—" He broke off his words.

Mason looked at him hard. "You resent her because you were tricked into marriage," he suggested.

Oswald gave a short laugh. "Hardly." There was a heavy pause. He met his brother's gaze. "It was the other way around," he said softly. "I trapped her."

Mason's eyebrows shot up. "That's not what everyone thinks."

Oswald shrugged. "People think what I want them to think. It's always been that way."

Mason sat back in his seat, stretching out his long legs. "Roland always said that about you."

Oswald smiled mirthlessly. "Roland's not my greatest admirer."

"Nor mine," snorted Mason. "He misses Father. He's jealous of our closeness."

Oswald shot a look of surprise at Mason. "Roland?"

"Aye. He feels left out."

Oswald digested this in silence.

"Why did you trap her?" asked Mason curiously.

"It was convenient at the time," answered Oswald, sounding tired. It seemed like such a long time ago.

"But not anymore?" *Convenient?* To have a wife who plagued his every waking thought? Oswald gave a short shake of his head. "Why haven't you just sent her down to Vawdrey Keep before?" asked Mason with interest.

"Because I don't want her out of my sight." His voice was harsh. He didn't moderate his tone.

"Yet, you just told me…"

"I was lying through my teeth," Oswald gritted out. "I lie all the time. Didn't Roland tell you that?"

Mason shrugged. "You don't lie about important things. Just"— he waved a hand—"court politics and the like."

"I lie about *everything*," said Oswald bitterly. Mason remained silent a moment. "Maybe if Father had just let me marry her when I was twenty-one," carried on Oswald. "I would have turned out differently."

Mason frowned. "How so?" Oswald shook his head. "Whatever it is, it's not insurmountable," said Mason slowly. Oswald looked up at him sharply but said nothing. "You remember when you said that to me?" asked Mason. "Your scraggy bastard brother, who didn't know how to hold a sword, and had to beg for a place in the practice hall."

"You never begged for anything in your life." Oswald smiled fleetingly.

"Only because you would never stand for it. I knew who it was who looked out for me," said Mason. "Not Father. You." Oswald said nothing. "If anyone ever called you a liar, I would strike him down where he stood," said Mason. His voice had an undercurrent of emotion which made his brother wince.

Oswald opened his mouth, then closed it again. "Alright, maybe not everything," he conceded grudgingly. "But a good deal."

"All men lie," insisted Mason. "They just don't all torture themselves about it afterward."

Oswald closed his eyes briefly. "You just told me I was a shit husband, Mason."

His brother gave a grim smile. "Aye, so I did. Maybe I didn't realize it would send you into a pit of despair." He shrugged. "All men are shit husbands at first. Even me."

Oswald smiled reluctantly. "I remember."

613

"Humph," grunted Mason. "You derived great amusement from my struggles, as I recall."

Oswald's smile twisted. "You were pretty bad at it."

"Careful," Mason cautioned him.

"This marriage. It didn't start…as it should," admitted Oswald.

"Well, no," agreed Mason, scratching his chin. "You jilted her. She worshipped the ground you walked on and you barely noticed her."

"Not that," said Oswald irritably. "I mean, that wasn't right either, but that wasn't my choice." Godsdamn it, he hadn't even considered that first wrong he'd done her! "I meant, by trapping her this time around."

"Is she holding it against you?" asked Mason.

There was a heavy pause before Oswald answered. "She doesn't know."

His brother's eyebrows rose at that. "You might want to keep it that way," recommended Mason.

"Would you really keep Linnet in the dark?" Oswald asked.

Mason gave a laugh. "I'd do all manner of unscrupulous things to keep my wife by my side. Never doubt it." Oswald found he didn't.

The tent flap opened again, and Roland came in, stamping his feet. "It's bitter out there," he complained. "Whose idea was this wretched campout?" He shot an accusatory look at Oswald.

"Mine," Oswald admitted. "I can't seem to stop making bad decisions lately."

"Are you talking about your marriage?" asked Roland, flinging himself into a chair. "Because if you are, I think that's a damned insult to Fenella. If you ask me," he said, fixing his brother with a stern eye, "marrying her was one of your better ones!"

"I agree," said Oswald, surprised that Roland even had an opinion on his marriage.

"I suppose you're cutting up rough, because everyone knows you're flesh and blood now instead of a damn monk," snorted Roland.

Oswald shrugged. "Is that what everyone is saying?" he asked without much concern.

Roland nodded. "Oh aye, Bevan said playing cards with you was the first time you seemed vaguely human and not like a calculating statue!"

"Well, I appreciate your candor as always," said Oswald dryly.

"See," said Roland, pointing a finger at him. "You're doing it again. Retreating behind a mask. Never saying what you really feel."

615

"You want to know what I really feel?" asked Oswald. "I doubt it."

"Try us," said Mason, suddenly wading back into the conversation.

Oswald was silent a moment. Well, what the hell. He may as well. "I feel like there's something corrosive inside my chest," he said slowly, touching his fingers to his heart. "It's going to eat its way out. You don't have the first idea."

"I do know," said Mason simply.

"Indigestion?" hazarded Roland, looking completely lost.

Mason rolled his eyes. "Jealousy. And you're right, it will leave a gaping hole in your chest if you don't do something about it."

Oswald eyed him with annoyance. "I must have missed the part where Linnet was married to another man before you," he said sarcastically.

"I thought you said her previous marriage wasn't legal?" retorted Mason innocently.

"Which, when you think about it," said Roland, frowning, "puts my sister-in-law in a damn awkward position. Living with him for those years as she did."

Oswald glared at them both. "You're both making me feel worse," he said darkly.

"What are you going to do about it?" asked Mason. "Linnet's worried. *I'm* worried. Even Roland's worried."

"And how are we supposed to have the first idea if you won't ever have any plain, honest speech with us?" asked Roland belligerently. "You never tell me anything!"

"For god's sake, Roland," Oswald said bitterly.

"How about I start then," said Roland. "When I was fifteen, I was your squire at Adarva and I saw you cut down in the field and was so traumatized I could not speak of it for three months. By the time I confessed to Father that I thought you were dead, he'd received the demand for your ransom and told me I was not only weak in the head, but a coward for not fighting my way through to your side to check if you were still alive." Mason and Oswald both stared at him.

"You saw him cut down?" repeated Mason incredulously. "Why did you not tell me?"

Roland swallowed. "I thought he was dead," he repeated. "He took an axe in his back."

"An axe?" repeated Mason.

Both his brothers turned to face him, and Oswald exhaled. "I didn't know you'd witnessed anything."

"When I tried to speak to you of it afterward, you dismissed me and said you'd only suffered a scratch," insisted Roland.

"I know," said Oswald in a tired voice.

"You think I don't know the difference between a scratch and a killing blow?" Roland's voice shook.

617

"I'm sorry," said Oswald. "I didn't realize."

"The groomsmen used to tell me stories of the undead who return to avenge those who have wronged them. For years I thought you were a wraith come back to get me for leaving you there." Roland scowled. "Did you know I wet the bed for a six month?"

"Is that why you won't take Cuthbert for a squire?" asked Mason suddenly.

Roland looked startled but then looked away. "Probably," he muttered.

"Did Fen tell you I have scars?" asked Oswald, getting his breath back. "You should know women are prone to exaggerate these things."

"She never mentioned scars," said Roland heavily. "She's very loyal, not that you've ever noticed." The brothers sat in silence a moment.

"Very well," said Oswald, sitting up straighter. "Ask what you will. I'll answer you to the best of my ability."

"I want to see the scar on your back," said Mason.

"What?" This pulled Oswald up short.

"I don't believe your wife is prone to exaggeration," said Mason deliberately. "I think your wounds must have been grievous after Adarva, and for some godsforsaken reason, you refused to let our father or anyone else know of it."

Oswald let out a short, bitter laugh. "What the hells does that matter now?" he demanded.

"It would be a start at least," retorted Mason. "A step in the right direction." He looked toward Roland. "What say you?"

Their younger brother shrugged. "Better late than never."

Oswald appeared to struggle inwardly a moment. Then, with an exclamation, he started unlacing his tunic. "Very well, if it will make you happy," he muttered. After a few tense moments, he shucked it over his head and turned his back to face them.

There was a deafening silence and then someone let out a hiss. "Holy shit," said Roland hoarsely. "A sword never wrought that damage... I was right, wasn't I? It was an axe."

"Battle-axe," agreed Oswald. "You were right."

"You nearly died then," said Mason flatly. "And you never saw fit to *tell* any of us."

"What would have been the point?" Oswald threw over his shoulder. "Have you had your fill?" he asked, reaching for his tunic.

"You could have died," persisted Mason. "It's a miracle you didn't."

Oswald sighed, pulled on his tunic, and dropped back into his chair. "I wouldn't be the first soldier to die in battle."

"But I wouldn't have known," said his brother angrily. "Everything you've done for me. You only joined the army to keep a watch over me."

Roland looked surprised by this. "Did he? I thought he did it to please Father."

Mason shot an exasperated look at Roland. "When did he ever do anything to please the old man?" he asked. "Oh aye, he said nay and yay where he was supposed to, but Father knew deep down Oswald never gave a damn about following in his footsteps. That's why he used to get so frustrated with him. That and the fact he was ten times cleverer than the rest of us."

He turned back to Oswald and pointed a finger at him. "You let me, and Father, think you were four months languishing as a hostage, when actually, you must have been hovering at death's door the whole time," he said accusingly.

"I'm a very fast healer," said Oswald. "My recovery almost alarmed the surgeon. I was up and about by the end of the second month."

"You're doing it again," said Mason heavily. "Twisting the facts to suit your own purpose. Playing down the truth."

Oswald rubbed the side of his face tiredly. "It's second nature to me now, Mason," he said quietly. "Half the time I don't even know I'm doing it."

"You mean lying?" asked Roland with a frown.

"Manipulating the truth," Oswald corrected him. Mason snorted but sat back in his chair.

"But right now, you're being open and aboveboard?" Roland persisted, narrowing his eyes.

"Yes, damn it."

"Right," said Roland. "Then I want to know how Sir Arnold Pryke died."

Oswald eyed him with surprise. "Why are you asking me that? It hardly matters after all this time."

"I've a notion it was you that killed him."

"What?" thundered Mason, sitting forward in his seat again. Oswald sat silent. "Is it true?" demanded Mason.

Oswald closed his eyes briefly. The question hung heavy in the air. "Of course it's true," he said simply. "It seemed expedient. I really couldn't waste any more time playing the prisoner. The situation had become quite untenable."

Mason looked winded. "An assassin killed Pryke," he insisted. "He was found with his throat cut." Oswald shrugged. "What does that mean?" demanded Mason.

"Oswald did it," said Roland. He turned to Oswald, looking triumphant. "I'm right, aren't I?"
Oswald didn't answer him. He looked toward Mason with an odd expression on his face. "When you think about it, it sort of makes sense," said Roland, nodding his head. "I mean, look at the company he keeps. All those agents always slithering about, passing him notes and such like. Then he's hand in glove with that Bardulf character. Bev told me he was an assassin."

621

"Hardly hand in glove!" cut in Oswald, looking annoyed.

"That's the bit you argue with?" asked Mason incredulously. He couldn't seem to stop staring at his older brother. He snatched up his cup of ale and drained it before slamming it down. "All this time, I thought you had no taste for killing."

"I don't have a taste for it," said Oswald. "I haven't killed anyone in five years. If I have my way, I'll not kill again in my lifetime."

"You're supposed to be the nice one among us," said Roland, shaking his head. "With your courtly manners and polite talk. What was it the Queen said about you? The wolf who hides among the palace sheep."

"He is the nice one," said Mason stubbornly.

"Am I?" asked Oswald harshly.

"You were the only one who ever gave a fuck about me, growing up," said Mason. "Nothing you've just told us changes how I feel about you. You're my brother, always were, always will be."

Oswald flinched. "You still want me for Archie's godfather?" he asked quietly.

"Don't be a fool," growled Mason. "Of course I bloody do!"

"You're not getting out of that just by being a stone-cold killer," muttered Roland. "In fact, that probably helps qualify you for the job."

"Let's hear some more about these bad decisions you've been making of late," said Mason, leaning forward and pouring them all a cup of ale.

"I've bought a town house," said Oswald. "In Aphrany. A huge black and white timbered monstrosity. The kind a very rich merchant lives in."

"Why in god's name?" asked Mason.

"Because Fenella once said she likes them," said Oswald. "In a purely throwaway conversation. But for some reason, every word she speaks is seared on my brain."

Roland cleared his throat. "Bit impulsive for you, isn't it?"

"A bit?" echoed Oswald. "I forced the King to sign annulment papers to an eight-year marriage simply because I feel sick to my stomach at the idea of her ever belonging to another man. And the worst of it is that the annulment is the least drastic course of action that occurred to me. For the last three months, in my head, I have been drawing up legal papers to sue Thane for the *eight years* he spent at my wife's side, masquerading in *my* rightful place. In her life, in her heart, and *in her bed.*"

He heard his voice shake with anger and realized his brothers must too. Taking a deep breath, he continued more evenly. "Each time I mentally draft the petition, I request a more severe punishment befitting of his crime."

"What kind of punishment?" asked Mason with interest, sitting back in his seat.

Oswald blew out a shaky breath. "In the latest version, it was beheading."

Roland burst out in a coughing fit, while Mason rested his arms on the table. "What about your wife? Any punishments for her?"

Oswald shrugged an irritable shoulder. "Several," he snapped.

"Such as?"

Oswald eyed his brother with annoyance. "The usual, I suppose."

"Beating her?" asked Roland, looking alarmed. Mason and Oswald exclaimed at the same time.

"He'd never harm a hair on her head," snorted Mason. "Fool."

"What's the usual punishment for a wife then?" asked Roland, looking confused.

"Usually it's just chaining her to my headboard for a few weeks," continued Oswald, "Naked."

"Well, she wouldn't like that at all," objected Roland. "It's plaguey cold in our rooms at this time of year!"

Mason cleared his throat, covering his mouth with his hand. Oswald eyed him distrustfully. "Are you laughing at me?" he asked him, narrowing his eyes.

"Wouldn't dream of it," said Mason in a suspiciously uneven voice before he took a large swig of ale. When he lowered his cup, he surveyed his brother with satisfaction. "You've made such a bloody mess of this. It nearly makes up for you being such a smug, knowing bastard when I was first wed."

Oswald took a deep breath. "Well, I'm glad you can take some comfort in my suffering."

"Why did you buy her another house though?" puzzled Roland. "When you've already got Vawdrey Keep."

"Too far from court. From me," said Oswald briefly. He looked at his youngest brother a moment. "I've a mind to give you Vawdrey Keep anyway."

"Me?" spluttered Roland.

"Why not?"

"You can't give it to me. It's your birthright."

"Yes, I can. I can do what I like. Anyway, I'm going to build my own country estate at some point."

"No, you're not," said Mason shrewdly. "You're going to live in that timbered monstrosity in Aphrany. Because your wife likes it. And you're going to run the kingdom on Wymer's behalf for the next fifty years."

Oswald smiled in spite of himself. "She doesn't like living in three rooms," he said by way of explanation. "And I don't like her being far from me."

"Are you serious?" asked Roland incredulously. "I think you've run mad. An earl can't live in a damn merchant's house!"

"Says who?" Mason challenged him.

"Besides, Father would want you to have Vawdrey Keep," said Oswald, looking at his youngest brother. "You're the only one of us that's fond of the place. I'm giving it to you."

Roland spluttered again. "Love's unhinged you," he said, and then stared when Oswald turned a dull shade of red. "What?"

"He hasn't come to terms with it quite yet," said Mason. "He hasn't said the word in his head, let alone to his wife."

"Are you sure he's the clever one?" asked Roland. "Because I'm telling you now, I'm starting to have my doubts."

44

It was a good six hours later that a lone rider arrived at The Bell and Basket on the Cauldwell Road. After handing his steed to the stable hands to rub down and feed, he strode through the snow toward the inn and hammered on the bolted door. The burly landlord took an involuntary step back when he saw the expression on the man's face.

"We've no private chambers free, my lord," he said, noting the stranger's clothing, which was expensive for all he was clad in conservative black. Oswald looked at him, and he fell back, hastily opening the door to admit him. Almost as soon as he was through the door, he spied his errant servant sat before the fire with the remains of a bowl of stew before him, supping a cup of ale. He was across the room before Meldon had even had a chance to place his drink back on the table top.

"Took yer time," wheezed Meldon. "Thought I'd have to skulk down here all night waiting for you."

Oswald eyed him grimly. "What the devil do you mean by encouraging your mistress on this mad scheme?" he demanded. "And leaving me a damned impudent message to meet you here?" The landlord faded away, rubbing his hands on his apron. "And where the hells is she?"

"I'll take ye up presently," said Meldon. "She's got that big black dog of hers and her own private chamber. She's settled in for the night."

"Well, she can get unsettled," snapped Oswald, seeing red. "I'm taking her straight back to Aphrany tonight."

"Nay, ye won't do that," said Meldon, shaking his head. "Not in her condition."

"What do you mean by that?" he asked. "Something ails her?"

"Not her," said Meldon. "She's a very sensible lass until she's pushed past all bearing."

Oswald fought back the impulse to cuff his impudent servant round the head. "What do you mean by 'her condition'?" he asked, mustering reserves of patience he did not know he possessed.

"Well…" said Meldon, sucking in his cheeks. "The sort of condition any wife gets in when she's a husband always clamoring after her." He eyed Oswald sagely. "Happen you'm more like your father than I ever realized."

"Kindly explain," Oswald said in a clipped voice.

"And you're supposed to be so sharp," sighed Meldon. "It's like this, Trudy, my goddaughter told me that Lady Vawdrey has never had recourse to use any rags since she's been serving her, and that's nigh on three months now."

"Rags?"

"For her woman's time," stressed Meldon.

Oswald, who had been shrugging off his cloak, froze. "*What?*" He stared at Meldon for a few heartbeats. "Impossible. She would have told me."

"Happen the lass's head's been in such a spin, she ain't never thought about it," sniffed Meldon.

"And why is Trudy speaking to you about this, and not her mistress?"

"Well, she didn't want to speak out of turn. But when the mistress she gets this notion to set off for the country without your say-so, well...Trudy thought she'd better let me know. 'Uncle Walter,' says she, 'you cannot let my mistress go haring off like this, not when she's likely expecting.'" Meldon nodded. "So, I left that message for you and drove her here. Luckily the snow gave me an excuse to stop for the night. So here I sit."

Oswald stood very still for a moment. Then his hand shot out to grip Meldon's bony shoulder. "You'll never abandon us, will you, Meldon?" he asked quietly.

"Ain't goin' nowhere," said Meldon. "In fact, I got a fancy to grow old in that big town house o' yours. Town living's easier on old bones than country living. And if I'm in Aphrany, I can see Trudy's young'uns grow up, as well as yours." He took another sip of ale.

"I will accept no less," vowed Oswald, dropping his hand. "Where will you sleep now, if we overnight in this place?" he asked, glancing around.

"There's a shared chamber upstairs I can bunk in, or I can doze down here by the fire," said Meldon, looking unconcerned. "I'll take you up to her, shall I? Then I can bring the dog down with me."

Oswald followed behind as Meldon led him up the rickety stairs and along a corridor leading to a door, which he knocked on. "Milady," he called. "It's me, Meldon."

There was a silence on the other side of the door, and then Oswald heard bolts drawing back.

"What is it?" asked Fenella, peering round. Bors saw him and gave a small bark of welcome. "Oh," said his wife, looking stunned at the very sight of him. "My lord, I did not…that is—"

Oswald turned to Meldon. "Thank you, Meldon," he said, seizing Bors and steering his wagging body toward the manservant.

"I have him, my lord," said Meldon. "Come here, you daft brute."

Oswald stepped into the bedchamber, shut the door behind him, and bolted it. Then he turned to his wife warily. Fen had retreated back across the room and was stood by the fireplace. She had a woolen shawl wrapped around her shift and looked rather stricken. He discarded his cloak onto a chair by the door and then paused. "You are well?" he asked gruffly. She looked pale, but still beautiful. And still his.

She gave a start. "Yes. What are you *doing* here?" she asked faintly.

"I could ask you the same thing," he said, stripping off his gauntlets.

"I—well—I'm going home," she said rather defiantly, and lifted her chin.

"Home?"

"To Sitchmarsh."

"That's not your home, Fenella. Not anymore." That seemed to rather take the wind from out of her sails. He discarded his gloves too and looked at her. "I want talk to you." She nodded, wrapping her arms around her body. "I can't do that while your teeth are chattering," he said, nodding toward the bed. "Get back under the covers."

She shook her head. "No, I want to be standing when you—" She broke off, biting her lip.

"When I what?"

"When you tell me," she said softly.

Oswald frowned at her, then turned and snagged a chair, dragging it over to the fireplace. "How about we both sit?" he suggested.

Fen seemed to sag. "Very well," she said, reaching for another chair, but he had already set one down for her. She sat down and he noticed how dull her eyes were, and red-rimmed. And puffy. She'd been crying. His brother had not been wrong.

"It seems I've given you a false impression somewhere along the line," he said carefully. Fen stiffened. He saw her fingers convulse in her lap. She still wore her rings, he noticed. She'd left the other jewelry laid out on their bed. Seeing his rings still on her fingers calmed him a little. Godsdamn it, Mason was right. He was a possessive bastard after all.

631

"I understand," said Fen in a listless voice. "I understand perfectly. No one could blame you."

"I don't think you do understand, Fen," he answered truthfully. "If you did, you wouldn't be sat here in an inn on the road to Sitchmarsh. You'd be back in our bed, where you damn well belong." He broke off as his voice rose and took a steadying breath. "Your pardon, I didn't mean to raise my voice at you again."

Fen sat up a little straighter. "Where I belong?" she echoed. "But—I thought…"

"Did you? Did you really?" His tone was harsher than he'd intended, but for some reason he was finding it hard to regulate it. His eyes pored over her. "I don't think you thought this through *at all*! Otherwise you wouldn't be putting your husband to the trouble of a two-hour ride to come and find you, after he'd already spent four hours in the saddle this day."

Fen eyes flickered. "But I didn't think you would come to get me," she said simply. "In fact"—she took a deep breath—"I thought you would be relieved to find me gone."

Oswald felt winded. "How? How could you think that, Fen?" he demanded. Her eyes filled with tears. "I told you," he insisted, "that you were precious to me, Fenella."

Fen caught her breath. "Yes, you did," she agreed in a choked voice. "But then you said I was nothing but an inconvenience."

That halted his indignation. *Shit.* "You heard that?" He shook his head. "I was just letting off steam, Fenella. I didn't mean a word of it."

"You said I was an untrustworthy wife," she said in a wobbly voice. "And that—"

"Please, Fen—don't," he said unevenly. "That wasn't intended for your ears. And even as I uttered those foolish words, I knew in my heart they were nothing but a falsehood."

She swallowed and dragged a hand across her eyes. "No, you were right," she said huskily. "And what's more, you don't even know the half of it."

"I was not right; I was not even close," he said firmly. "My darling Fen—"

"No, please don't!" She flung out an arm in appeal. "Please don't be kind. It is better to be honest. We *can't* carry on as we have been. With me taking misstep after misstep and causing a disgrace to your name—"

He was up and out of his chair. "Darling Fen," he said in concern, kneeling down beside her. "Please stop crying. You're upsetting yourself over nothing."

"No, I'm not," she sobbed. "And when you know what else has happened since you've been gone, you're going to—"

"I'm going to take you back home with me anyway," said Oswald firmly. "And just to be clear, your home is wherever the hells I happen to be. No, that's enough," he said, catching hold

633

of her hands. "You need to know there's nothing you can possibly have done that is going to make me not want you."

She shook her head violently. "You don't know—"

Suddenly, he yanked her into his arms and held her there, her head tucked under his chin, her breast to his chest, his hands supporting her weight against him. "Please believe me," he said. "I know I don't deserve your trust after the way I've behaved, but it's true."

"The way you've behaved?" echoed Fen, sounding mystified. "But you've done nothing wrong."

"If only that were true," murmured Oswald. "Then we wouldn't be having this conversation right now." He cautiously bent his head and looked into her face. "Are you calmer now?"

She hiccupped, then her face crumpled. "Will you let me apologize now?" she whispered.

"You're not the one who owes the apology," he said gruffly. "That would be me." Fen stared. "I was a bloody *godsdamn* fool to blame you for that play debacle," he said in a voice husky with regret. "I wish I could take back those things I said to you." He swallowed. "And those ridiculous things I said about you to my brother. And get back that night I spent apart from you, which was nothing but a futile waste of time."

He closed his eyes a moment. "All I could think about for the last two days was how I'd acted toward you… Mason didn't believe a word of what I said, I might add. He and Roland both think you're the best decision I ever made and that I've been treating you shockingly."

"Oswald—"

"Let me say it, Fen," he insisted, and she lapsed into silence. "I'm a reserved, private man, who doesn't like to wear his emotions for all to see. Or to be the subject of idle rumors." Fen tensed up and at this, and he tightened his hold on her until she subsided against him. "When I thought your actions had led to gossip and conjecture, I *totally* overreacted. But I've learned my lesson," he said emphatically. "I don't care if you have a dozen plays written about our marriage."

He took firm hold of her upper arms. "I'm never—ever—letting you go. Do you understand? Your face is so puffy I can barely see your eyes, but I still think you're the prettiest woman I've ever beheld, and I have no intention of relinquishing you while there's breath in my body."

Fen's eyes closed and she seemed to be waging some kind of inner battle with herself. "Some even worse things have happened in the last two days," she said at last.

Oswald looked down at her. "I don't care," he said succinctly, and took her lips in a deep and heartfelt kiss.

As soon as he released her, her worried face bobbed before him. "But just let me explain—"

"No," said Oswald, scooping her into his arms and coming to his feet.

"I—but I need to tell you—"

He walked to the bed and deposited her on the sagging mattress. "Gods, this bed," he complained. "I'll have to go easy on you for once, or we'll end up on the floorboards."

Fen's white face turned pink. "Husband—"

He whipped his tunic over his head. "You have as long as it takes for me to get undressed to explain."

Fen clambered to her knees. "Well," she said, assuming a pained expression. "Mathilde Martindale has run away from court, dressed as a boy," she gabbled. Oswald unlaced his crotch and shucked down his braies. "Her mother suspects I'm culpable, although I really and truly had no notion of her plans."

When he gave no discernible reaction, she continued rapidly. "And Bess Hartleby has eloped with the artist who painted my portrait. Her uncle is on the privy council with you, although I do not know his name. He is sure to be very angered by it though," she added. "And to tell you that it is somehow my fault, though I don't quite know how."

Oswald slid out of his chauses and pounced on her. "How many's that?"

"Um."

"Good," he said, dragging her shift up and over her head.

"That's only two scandals," she said breathlessly as he tossed her shift over the side of the bed.

He lifted an eyelid. "What's the third, Fenella?" he asked so softly that her mind went blank.

"I can't quite remember—" Her breath hitched. "Give me a moment—"

"Too late." He rolled her under him, and they became a tangle of limbs, mouths, longing, and need. Fen cried out way too soon, but he was relentless, despite his words about going easy on her.

As he drove into her, his face above hers, his gaze intent and filled with something that made her chest clench, Fen wrapped her arms and legs around him and sobbed as she was shaken by release again, and felt him reach it within her, and groan deeply against her neck. He rolled them onto their sides and held her close as their heartbeats calmed and their breath returned.

"Stay like this," he said gruffly when Fen went to unhook her uppermost leg from his hip. Then he kissed her tenderly, his hand sliding up and over her hip to her waist and then back down again in a comforting caress.

Fen drew back her face to look at him. Tentatively, she raised a hand to his face and ran it through the lock of hair that had fallen across his brow and stroked her fingers over his cheek. She drew in a shaky breath. "How do you feel about scandalous portraits of your wife?" she asked nervously. "Now that we've established you don't care about unsanctioned elopements."

Oswald gazed back at her. "Scandalous portraits?" he repeated. "I take them entirely in my stride. Once they're firmly in my possession, of course." At the return of the husband she knew and loved, Fen gave a sob and craned instinctively closer to him. "Fenella, *don't!*" he said in a tender voice. "I don't want to ever make you cry again, my darling. Mason told me you were

637

on the brink of tears watching that ridiculous play. I hate myself for not noticing how much it upset you." He stroked his thumbs down her cheeks. "It was so far from truth that I could not take it seriously. I never dreamed that you would be so hurt by it."

Fen closed her eyes a moment and reopened them. "It's just that it played on my worst fears," she explained. "Being— unwanted—and—" She found her chin tipped up again by insistent fingertips.

"Never, never that," he said in a shaken voice. "Never think that." Fen stared at his expression, and found her darkest fears slipping away. It was a few moments before either of them spoke, and when he did, it was in a thoughtful, reflective manner. "I think, on some level," Oswald said, "I knew you were mine when you sailed into my office that day with your brother on your heels. I was certainly determined not to let you out of it until it was settled your place was with me."

Fen gazed at him. "I couldn't tell. I couldn't read you at all then," she admitted. "I thought you were angry."

"Angry?" He sounded startled. "Why?"

Fen cast her mind back. "I sat down and looked up at you, and you were glaring at me."

Oswald's frown cleared. "That was because your fool brother made you fetch your own chair."

Fen opened her mouth to defend Gil. "He is a bit of a fool," she found herself admitting instead. "It's a good job he's marrying a woman of character."

"Is he?"

She didn't get the chance to answer as he leaned forward and kissed her lingeringly on the lips again before pulling back and rolling out of the bed.

"Husband, wait!" blurted Fen, struggling to sit up.

"I'm not going anywhere," he answered, turning to show the jug of water he'd gone to fetch from the table.

"Oh." Feeling rather foolish, Fen pulled the sheets up around her to try to preserve her modesty, even though he was walking round entirely naked.

Oswald was draining his cup. "Fen," he started. "You need to understand that leaving me is never acceptable. No matter what the misunderstanding, or even if I act like an ass."

"Well, you see—" she said.

"I'm never going to be a reasonable husband," he carried on as if she hadn't even spoken. "When I said that to you, I was lying. I can't even tell you I wasn't aware that I was lying because I knew full well that I was lying through my teeth and I didn't care. I would have said anything to make you mine again. And I didn't even realize that I loved you then."

Fen stared. "What?" she said faintly.

"It's true. I didn't even spend an instant in your company that day you walked into my office prattling on about another *fucking* man without realizing that you were all mine. I didn't remember our betrothal for whatever reason." He waved a hand.

"You were a child and so was I, to all intents and purposes. I refuse to feel guilty about that."

He pressed his thumb and finger against his eyes. "I'm tired of pretending to have reason when it comes to you. Because I don't. Not one scrap. I'm not going to pretend anymore, so you're going to have to get used to it."

Prattling about another man? Fen's brain reeled to find out that was truly how Oswald viewed things. She'd been divorced by her husband of eight years and he viewed it as unnecessary chatter about another male! She gave a slightly hysterical laugh. He ignored it. "Um, Oswald…"

"I've bought us a town house in Aphrany," he carried on steadily. "And we'll have to buy another place, close to the summer court, where we can live when the King is at Caer Lyonnes. It seems, unlike the majority of the rest of the royal court, I cannot bear to be apart from my wife."

"A town house?" she gasped after a stunned moment. "Like the Robertses?"

"You want to live in your own household, so that's what we will do."

She stared. "Is it really so simple?" she asked.

He shrugged. "Yes." His gaze was wandering down from her face to where the sheet was slipping down.

She realized she was going to have to at least try before things turned physical again. "Husband," she started resolutely. That brought his eyes snapping straight back to hers. "I may have only been fifteen," she said with dignity, "but I did love you. It broke my heart when our betrothal was ended, and that's probably why I didn't love Ambrose like I should have," she hurried her words, anticipating his reaction. "But our marriage has now healed me." She placed a hand against her heart. "So, I find I can now love you with my whole heart…"

"What are you saying now?" he interrupted her sharply.

"It doesn't matter if you don't believe me," she carried on firmly. "I can prove it over the next fifty years or so of marriage and one day you will…" She bit off her words as Oswald plunked down the water jug and walked back to the bed.

"What did you say?"

She took a deep breath. "I said that I didn't love Ambrose and that I only ever loved you."

He pursed his lips. "You should be very careful bandying around words like that."

"No more than you," she answered pertly. "And now you can see that embarrassing tapestry on a daily basis, so you must have known it already."

"What's embarrassing about it?"

Fen's head snapped up to look at him. "Did you not recognize yourself?" she asked. "You are the one with the pink roses all round your head."

He looked confused. "That's me? I thought that was an angel," he admitted.

She huffed. "That's how I saw you at the time," she admitted, color creeping into her cheeks.

A slow smile lit up Oswald's face. "Angelic?" he asked.

"Yes."

"That's sweet." He placed his palms on the mattress and lowered his head so their brows were touching.

"It was very foolish," she said, avoiding his gaze.

"I'm not angelic, Fen." His voice was low and regretful.

"I know that now!"

"But you still love me?" he asked lightly.

"Yes!"

"You never loved…" He paused. "Anyone else?"

"I never loved Ambrose, no. And he could probably tell, poor man."

She felt him relax a little against her. It really was remarkable; she marveled that he could hold so much animosity toward Ambrose when she felt practically nothing for him these days. She wrapped her arms around his shoulders. "I really am going to try to be a better courtier, to match you," she assured him.

"I forbid you to even try."

"Why?"

He shrugged again. "I want you to direct all your efforts into other channels."

"A better wife then?" she hazarded. "Less jealous and more understanding?"

He frowned. "Is that what you want from me? You're not getting it."

Fen gasped and then laughed. "No, that wasn't what I meant…"

"You can be as jealous as you want. Not that I give you any cause."

She just about forbore from pointing out that she didn't give him any cause either. "What do you want me to direct my effort at then?" she asked in puzzlement.

"Loving me," he said simply.

"Oh." Fen found tears were pricking her eyes. "But that takes no effort at all."

He eased onto the bed beside her. "So, now we've finally got all that out in the open," he said, rolling into her. "Is there anything else we need to discuss, before I ravish you to within an inch of your life?"

Fen started to relax but then remembered the portrait. She stiffened. "Um. We probably should discuss the painting signor Arnotti did of me," she said with a catch in her voice.

643

Oswald frowned. "Are you depicted nude?" he asked calmly.

"No," acknowledged Fen, before adding conscientiously, "but he did not paint me wearing what I posed in."

His eyes narrowed. "What are you painted wearing?"

"Some kind of diaphanous fabric," said Fen uneasily. "You can see my legs. And…things."

"Things?"

"Well, not see them, but they're sort of…hinted at," said Fen painstakingly. "Eden explained that signor Arnotti portrayed me as a goddess." She winced. "Reclining on a cloud."

Oswald sighed, propping himself up on the pillows. "And where is this portrait now?"

"I'm not really sure," Fen admitted. "Eden has it, but she said she would send it along to our rooms. She thought it should be exhibited, but I said not without your permission. I was so upset after viewing it that I sort of rushed off in a blind panic and… That's when I started packing my things." Her voice wobbled. "I thought you would never forgive me."

"Oh, Fen." Oswald's voice was contrite as he cupped her face. "Foolish Fen. I never had any intention of sending you down to the country. Even when I was saying it, I never meant it. Not in my heart. Even when I was furious with you, I had every intention of keeping you firmly attached to my side."

"What about…after that awful play?" she asked in a small voice.

Oswald's lips twitched. "The only part that bothered me about that ridiculous play was the idea that you still weren't over Thane." He dropped a kiss on her nose and then settled back against the pillows.

"Mason told me you had given the manuscript to Hester Schaeffer, and then I realized you had tried to mitigate things. That calmed me down considerably. By the time we went to bed that night, I was already over it."

She rolled into his side and he ran a comforting hand down her back. "I'm sorry I kept overreacting," he said ruefully. "It's the strangest thing, I've always considered myself the most even-tempered Vawdrey in existence. Then you came along and shattered my equanimity to a thousand pieces."

Fen hid her face in his side. "That's what the King said," she admitted in a muffled voice. "He said I shouldn't practice my womanly arts on you."

Oswald gave a choked laugh, and Fen peered up at him. "You don't need to tell me that. The King is all too aware that I have completely lost my mind over you."

"Are you laughing because you don't think I have any female tricks?" asked Fen, giving him a light pinch to his side.

His smile broadened. "Never. I know only too well that you are full of tricks, wife. You have enough to keep me occupied for the next sixty years at least. However, having recently come to terms with my possessive side, I am almost certain that I will want this portrait for my own private viewing pleasure and no one else's. I hope that doesn't disappoint you."

645

"Not at all," Fen hastened to assure him, and laid her head against his bare chest. Then she remembered something and lifted a troubled gaze to his. "There was just one other thing I think we should talk about…" she said.

Oswald tucked his hands behind his head, looking unconcerned. "And what is that, wife?"

Fen took a deep breath. "Your plans to build yourself a palace."

Oswald's brows snapped together. "A palace?" he repeated blankly.

She nodded. "Several people have mentioned it to me, yet you yourself never have. I wondered why."

He seemed to ponder this a moment. "It was more of a country estate than a palace," he corrected her. "Only since we've been married, I haven't given it much thought. I haven't dragged out the plans in months. And I used to pore over them well into the early hours of the morning. Almost obsessively."

"Why did you stop?" Fen asked.

He frowned. "I think," he said slowly, "that at the time, it was the only thing I had in my life that I derived any relaxation or pleasure from. If I had a trying day, I'd get out the plans and add in a moat or another turret. I was planning for some unspecified time in the future when I'd have time for diversion or recreation." Fen opened her mouth and then closed it again. "I suppose this isn't really going to make any sense to you."

Fen grasped her courage and admitted: "I feared that perhaps you didn't want to share it with me," she said in a small voice. He was quiet a moment and Fen steeled herself to hear the worst. After all, he was a very private man, and she had rather forced herself into his life.

"Have you been worrying about this?" asked Oswald incredulously. To her surprise, his tone was more accusatory than anything.

Fen closed her eyes and swallowed. "Well—you'd be perfectly entitled to have—"

"How many times, Fenella Vawdrey," he demanded, "have I told you that if something is bothering you, you are to come directly to me?"

"Yes, but—"

"No," he said firmly. "I would *not* be entitled to plan a future that did not include my wife in it."

Fen looked at his expression and could see he was deadly serious. Despite the fact he was looking rather grim, her mood swooped up and lifted a few notches. "So, your palace?" she said. "Why are you no longer planning for it?"

Oswald hitched a shoulder impatiently. "Well, I don't plan to retire for a few years yet anyway, and frankly I don't feel the need to build a legacy of that kind anymore—"

"No, you misunderstand me," Fen interrupted him painstakingly. "I mean, why do you no longer want to spend your leisure time drawing up your plans?"

647

Oswald crooked an eyebrow at her. "Seriously?" he asked. "I have better things to do with my evenings these days."

Fen continued to look at him expectantly. Then the penny dropped. "You mean me?"

He gave a choked laugh. "I hope I would not be so blunt."

Fen rested her head back against his shoulder with a sigh. "You make me very happy too," she said softly. His arms came down to wrap around her and hold her tight and they lay quietly a moment. Then she asked, "What kind of legacy *do* you want now?"

His hand slid down to rest on her stomach. "Has it occurred to you that in the three months we've been married, you've not had your woman's time once?" Oswald asked.

Fen stared at him. "I'm always very regular," she blurted in surprise. "But you're right, I haven't…" Her eyes widened. "Do you suppose—?"

"I do," said Oswald softly, his hand still resting on her belly. "I think you might be carrying my legacy." Fen laid her hand on top of his and their eyes met. Then his hands shifted to her hips and he urged her up his body. "I want you on top this time."

"What about the mattress?" asked Fen as she shifted over him. It was sagging in an alarming fashion.

"Go slow," her husband recommended with a grin.

45

"How did you know I would be here?" she asked him after she'd collapsed on top of him some twenty minutes later.

"Meldon."

"How?"

"He left a message for me, with Trudy."

"That sly fox," said Fen indignantly. Then she seemed to reconsider. "I suppose really, he's my guardian angel."

Oswald snorted. "Meldon's even less angelic than I am. Don't you dare turn him into a haloed tapestry." Fen gurgled with laughter. "Old scoundrel still thinks I'm wet behind the ears," complained Oswald.

"Actually," said Fen, raising her head, "he referred to you as 'the master' today. It was the first time I've ever heard him call you that."

"Well, today was the first time I learned he has a first name," said Oswald. "It's Walter. Walter Meldon. I still haven't recovered from the shock."

"He doesn't really look like a Walter," Fen agreed.

"I'm exhausted." Oswald yawned. "You've worn me out. Emotionally and physically." Fen smiled against his chest. "There is just one thing *I* ought to say," said Oswald reluctantly. "I lied earlier. When I said I didn't feel guilty about jilting you over our betrothal. I do. I think we should renew our wedding vows at the earliest opportunity."

Fen raised her head again to frown at him. "But you only forgot with your head," she said with a sigh. "Here," she said, placing a hand over his chest, "you never forgot. That's why you wore my locket all those years." She pulled the chain around his neck until the locket lay in her palm.

A look of regret crossed Oswald's face. He seemed to struggle with this a moment. "I didn't remember you gave me the locket," he admitted. "At one point, I even thought it must have been my mother."

Fen tipped her head to one side. "That just means, on some level, you knew it was given to you by someone who loved you," she said softly. "I still have the key you know," she said, struggling to rise up from the bed. His arms tightened around her and he gave a low rumble from his chest. "I only wanted to fetch it." She laughed. "To show you."

"No, stay like this," he objected with a growl. She subsided against him with a sigh.
"Fen," he said awkwardly after a moment. "I want you to know that I did not forget because it was inconsequential to me." He paused heavily before continuing. "After my injuries at Adarva, there was a chapter in my life that was lost to me. To my infinite regret, this is part of it."

Fen was silent a moment before sliding a hand down his shoulder blade to touch his scarring. "It's a very small price to pay for your safe return," she said lightly, "and it isn't truly lost now that you've returned to me."

"When did you give me the locket?" he asked after a moment.

"Before you left to go soldiering. You came to bid me farewell at my father's house. We went for a walk in the grounds and you were very kind to me."

"How was I kind?" asked Oswald with a faint frown.

"You humored a young fifteen-year-old girl and accepted her locket as a good luck token. You held my hands." She threaded her fingers through his. "We were stood under the oak tree," she reminisced, "when your father came to fetch you."

"We were stood under an oak?" asked Oswald. "Holding hands?"

"Yes." Fen was puzzled by his tone.

He gave a short laugh. "No wonder he kept sending you those gold coins."

"Why?" she asked.

"To his ancestors that would have been as valid as a marriage ceremony."

"Oh," said Fen. *"Oh!"*

"What?"

"I've just realized what he meant," she marveled. *"You've been sleeping under an oak tree...* He meant that tree...that I'd been waiting for you to return, all these years." She raised her head to look at him, her eyes filling with tears.

651

Oswald tipped his head. "Is that a line from the play?" he asked in confusion. "I don't remember…"

"It's nothing, just something young Cuthbert said."

"Cuthbert accused you of sleeping under oak trees?"

Fen laughed softly. "It does almost feel like a dream," she said softly. "You know, I've always been confused about our actual wedding. I remember we received a blessing at the betrothal ceremony at Vawdrey Keep, but if that constituted our marriage ceremony…"

"It did," said Oswald tightly.

"Then I was really not aware of the fact," said Fen firmly.

"You were too young at the time," he said. "But I do think it would be a good notion for us to repeat the vows in a holy place."

"Perhaps we could revisit the oak on my brother's grounds when we are next down in Sitchmarsh?" she suggested.

"That is an excellent suggestion. But we should visit the chapel at the palace too, perhaps with just family in attendance. We could send for your brother," he added as an afterthought.

"We should really go and visit with him," said Fen, perking up. "In light of his news."

"His news? Tell me." He looked distracted, his hand stroking over her hip.

"But I did already," said Fen. "He's getting married tomorrow on Solstice Eve."

"He is? I thought that was just a ruse for you to run away from me."

Fen blushed. "Not entirely. It seems Orla and Gil have been spending a lot of time together."

"Mmm?" he repeated. "Gil. Your brother and Orla?"

"Yes. It seems Orla will be my sister-in-law once again. What say you to that?"

Oswald frowned. "What?"

"She has decided she will marry Gil. And bring him up to scratch."

"What do you think of it?" he asked, stalling for time.

"Oh, I think it is the very best notion. She is five years older than Gil and will not stand for any of his nonsense. And she has always wanted to run her own house, so she will soon put an end to his drinking and carrying on."

"So, we will still have family links to Thane?" asked Oswald, not sounding best pleased.

"Oh, but when she marries Gil, she will become a Bernard," said Fen smugly. "And she and Ambrose are completely estranged as she took an unaccountable disliking to Lady

653

Colleen. I think it is the very best notion, for I do not like Sarah Yondy and…"

Oswald rolled her onto her back. "Presently you may tell me why you do not like Sarah Yondy," he assured her. "And I will be very interested and supportive and say all the right things."

She laughed up at him. "Presently?" she repeated. "But not right now?"

"No," he said, lowering his head to hers. "Not right now."

Much later, as Fen was drifting off to sleep in her husband's arms, he murmured, "Why was she dressed as a boy?"

Fen started to raise her head to explain, but he tucked it back into his neck. "Tell me later."

Epilogue

The Royal Banqueting Hall, the Palace at Aphrany

Fen stared down at the many-handled wassail bowl and grasped it gingerly. There were so many spouts she just knew she would get drenched with the mulled punch as soon as she tipped it to her mouth.

Her husband reached around her and plugged some of the spouts with his fingers and thumbs. Fen admired their matching posy rings with *Not Forgot* inscribed inside the bands. "Try it now," he murmured against her ear.

"Boo!" yelled King Wymer, slapping the tabletop. "Cheating! The Vawdreys are cheating!"

"Ah-ah," the Lord of Misrule upbraided him, striking the back of his hand with a staff entwined with holly.

Wymer yelped and sank back into his chair. "Damn that fellow," he muttered with a scowl, rubbing his hand.

Queen Armenal laughed. "You must abide by the rules of the feast, my dear," she reminded him. Next to the Queen sat Princess Una with her extraordinary frizzy wig. Her dark eyebrows were raised, giving her a perplexed look. She gazed around her as if at a roomful of crazy people.

Fen tipped the bowl and swallowed a mouthful of the spicy brew. By some miracle, her gown remained unsoaked.

The Schaeffers sat opposite led the applause. "Bravo!" yelled Hester Schaeffer. "You did it!"

655

"My newest lady-in-waiting has passed the test," said the Queen with satisfaction. Fen passed the bowl to her left, and Roland took it from her with a wink.

"The King's champion must kiss the girl who finds the silver token!" cried the fool, who was relishing his role presiding over the celebrations. He turned a cartwheel and then danced back up to the other end of the table. A burst of laughter greeted him as the boisterous knights toasted his health.

Fen's eyes widened. "But I saw who found the token," she whispered to Oswald.

"And who was that?" he murmured, his arm slipping about her waist.

"'Twas Eden Montmayne!" Oswald's hand at her side drew her closer, propelling her to scoot across on the bench and sit on his lap. "My lord!" she said in scandalized tones. "What will His Majesty say?"

"His Majesty, the Lord of Misrule will entirely approve," replied Oswald, unabashed. And he was probably right, for the King's fool was capering up and down in a mad dance as Wymer sat sulking.

"Roland will never kiss Eden," said Fen a little sadly.

"Ah, but tonight is given over to misrule," Oswald reminded her. "And everything is turned upside down."

Fen glanced down the table, but Eden was clearly not going to own up to having found the silver coin in her honey cake. Even as Fen looked, Eden slipped it under a napkin.

"My cousin found the silver token!" cried Lenora Montmayne with uncustomary exuberance. A whole roomful of heads turned in her direction. "See!" She pointed, flipping over Eden's napkin.

Everyone bellowed and cheered, drumming their knives and goblets against the table. Even in the flickering candlelight Fen could see Eden turn pale.

"Roland…" Fen started, but her brother-in-law was already out of his chair and swaggering toward Eden.

"I claim my prize," he said loudly, and the knights all hooted and drummed their feet against the flagstones.

"Oh dear," said Fen.

Eden was sat ramrod straight in her seat and glassy-eyed. Fen turned back to her husband. "I do hope Roland doesn't—"

"He'll be fine," he said.

"It's not him I'm worried about—" she started, but Oswald caught her chin and kissed her soundly. She barely heard the hooting and clapping in the background, and when her husband released her, she snuggled into his side and glanced up again to check no one was watching them.

She needn't have worried, for all eyes were still fixed on Roland and Eden, who were both stood up from the table,

657

staring at each other. "What happened?" asked Fen in surprise, for Roland had a strange, stunned look on his face. Eden straightened her headdress and sank back into her seat, her face aflame.

"I don't know," admitted Oswald as his brother made his way back to his seat looking a little unsteady on his feet. "But I rather think his kissing the Lady Eden had some unexpected consequences."

"Such as?" asked Fen.

"He found he liked it," said Oswald shrewdly.

Fen drew in a breath. "But—"

"Ah-ah, wife," objected Oswald, holding up a finger. "Don't get distracted with court intrigue. Remember, we are returning to our town house this evening. It's Solstice Eve. Yule logs burn in every grate. You have a full staff to train and a kitchen to supervise in the decoration of the honey cakes."

Fen sighed happily. "Linnet said she, Mason, Cuthbert, and the children will join us all day tomorrow. The girls were vastly pleased with their knight puppets," said Fen. "And Bryce absolutely loved his fur-lined hood. He said he will join us also, and Roland and his two friends."

"I like my present too," said Oswald, referring to Fen's portrait. "But that doesn't mean anyone else is seeing it." It hung now in their new bedroom, above the fireplace.

Poor Eden had been very put out when Fen had explained Oswald had forbidden its exhibition. Her husband had also had her tapestry betrothal gift packed up for the new house, and her childhood portrait.

Fen was greatly touched by how much he now prized the gifts from her girlhood. And she absolutely loved her new house on the town square in the middle of bustling Aphrany. Meldon and Trudy were already comfortably installed there hanging greenery and ribbons from every beam. "I shall write to Orla and Gil tonight, inviting them for a visit with us in the new year."

"A good plan, but you won't be writing letters tonight," responded Oswald.

"I won't?"

"No, for I've other plans for you tonight, wife," he said, rubbing a hand steadily up and down her back.

"I've been thinking," Fen whispered in Oswald's ear. "I believe we should give Roland a puppy for a Solstice gift."

Oswald drew his head back and looked at her askance. "A puppy? We don't want to overload him with responsibilities. He's only just agreed to take on Cuthbert as his squire."

"He'll miss Bors too much now though," pointed out Fen, frowning.

"Sweeting, we agreed we'll stay in the palace at least once a month," Oswald pointed out, squeezing her hip. "He'll still see Bors."

"True, but…"

"Also," said Oswald, "I've now gifted him with our ancestral home, which many would consider gift enough. My father's pack of dogs is still installed there. A more yapping, ill-behaved throng of hounds I've never seen. Believe me, he'll have more than enough dogs to contend with."

Fen considered this. "Oh. Very well."

"And I must say, wife, if you're going to sit on my lap and whisper in my ear, I'd rather it wasn't about Roland!"

Fen wound her arms around his neck and smiled. "I love you, Oswald Vawdrey," she murmured, and kissed his jaw.

"That's better," he conceded.

"I'm going to make our home the happiest in all Aphrany."

He squeezed her tight. "My love," he whispered. "You already have."

THE END

If you enjoyed this book, please consider leaving me a rating on Goodreads, Amazon, Bookbub or wherever else you leave your reviews. I would be very grateful.

You can find my website at: www.alicecoldbreath.com where you can sign up for my monthly newsletter and find out what I am up to.

Also, please do check out some of my other stories! Many thanks, Alice.

If you want to read more about the Vawdrey brothers, then the next book in the series is Roland's story:

An Ill-Made Match

He may be the King's champion, but if handsome is as handsome does, then Roland Vawdrey is the ugliest knight in the kingdom. According to him, there's only one way to measure a maiden's worth and that's her face.

Eden Montmayne is one of the most accomplished ladies in the land. She plays, sings, and dances to perfection, but all Roland sees is a prim, uptight paragon of virtue with only passable looks.

Find out how this unlikeliest of pairings fare when thrown together in unexpected matrimony!

More tales from the Kingdom of Karadok by Alice Coldbreath:

Wed by Proxy

Thrice wedded, but never bedded, Mathilde Martindale has long lived in the shadow of her indomitable mother, and meekly done as she was told. Until one day, she decides to become mistress of her own destiny and leave the royal court to find her own path.

Married by proxy, Lord Martindale has never even met his bride of three years. Wed only to unlock his friend's inheritance, he bitterly resents the mercenary wife who cares only for wealth and prestige.

And then he meets her.